Death Goes Dutch

NEW
BIGOT
TRUMP FOUNDATION
lie to 1st LADY
grades

Other Books by Albert A. Bell, Jr

Daughter of Lazarus

All Roads Lead to Murder

Kill Her Again

Young-adult Mystery

The Case of the Lonely Grave

Non-Fiction:
Exploring the New Testament World:
An Illustrated Guide to
the World of Jesus and the First Christians

Resources in Ancient Philosophy

Death Goes Dutch

by

Albert A. Bell, Jr

Ingalls Publishing Group, Inc.
Boone, North Carolina

CLAYSTONE BOOKS are published by Ingalls Publishing Group, Inc., 197 New Market Center , #135, Boone, NC 28607

Visit our website at: www.highcountrypublishers.com

Cover design by James Geary
Text design by schuyler kaufman

Library of Congress Cataloging-in-Publication Data

Bell, Albert A., Jr. 1945-
    Death goes dutch/ Albert A. Bell, Jr.
        p.cm
    ISBN - 13: 978- 1-932158-65-6 (trade pbk : allk. paper)
    ISBN - 10: 1-932158-65-0 (trade pbk : allk. paper)
    1. Women detectives--Michigan--Fiction. 2. Rich people--Crimes against--Fiction. 3. Korean Americans--Fiction. 4. Dutch Americans --Fiction. 5. Adoptees--Fiction. 6. Michigan--Fiction. I. Title.
    PS3552.E485D43 2006
    813'.54--dc22
                                        2005021631

First printing, March 2006

In memory of my Aunt Beck,
who did so much for my parents
and meant so much to me and my family

Author's Note

I have one regret about this book, and that is that my aunt, Rebecca Willard, did not live to see it published. Beck was a third parent to me, helping my mother (her sister) and father during their final illnesses and being a source of great comfort to me. She was an avid reader, of mysteries in particular but of books in general. When she read my first novel, *Daughter of Lazarus,* she called me that afternoon with comments and questions. When I had finished a draft of this book I thought about showing it to her but decided to wait a bit longer until she could see it as a published book. Unfortunately, she died quite unexpectedly, literally overnight in her sleep. At age eighty, she was healthy and active and seemed likely to live for many more years. Her loss has been keenly felt in my extended family.

Because I had decided to dedicate the book to Beck, and because we are part of a large and close family, I decided to have a little fun. Many of the characters in the book bear the first names of my aunts, uncles, cousins, and their children. I have not tried to match names with characters and I have not used the names to defame anyone, just to provide members of my family with a bit of an inside joke.

All persons in this novel are fictitious. Any resemblance to persons living or dead is purely coincidental. Most of the places mentioned in and around Grand Rapids are real. Dykstra Furniture Company is fictitious and is not meant to be an allusion to any of the furniture companies in the area. Grand Rapids General Hospital is also a product of my imagination. There are several fine hospitals in Grand Rapids, and I did not want to appear to be casting aspersions on any of them.

A number of people have assisted in various ways in the course of the writing of this book.

I received helpful information from people at the Grand Rapids Police Department, the Kent County Courthouse, and the Kent County Jail.

I don't claim that everything I say about those places in the novel is accurate to the letter. This is a work of fiction and sometimes real life has to be adapted to fit the demands of the story, but they helped me be sure that nothing is grossly inaccurate.

I'd like to thank the members of my writers' group at the Urban Institute for Contemporary Arts in Grand Rapids for their insightful comments and for their patience as I worked through the story.

Bob and Barbara Ingalls, of Ingalls Publishing Group, Inc., High Country Publishers, and now, Claystone Books, and their staff, deserve much credit for their committment to quality publishing.

Debra Sietsema, of Hope College's Nursing Department, saved me from a number of factual errors.

Social worker Bonnie Baker provided much helpful information about how adoption reunions are handled.

Thanks to Paul and Jan van Faasen and to Melissa Huisman for reading the manuscript; also to Richard and Phyllis Vandervelde, who not only read and made suggestions on this manuscript, but have also offered encouraging comments on other books of mine.

I, of course, am solely responsible for any infelicities that remain.

—Albert A. Bell, Jr.

Death Goes Dutch

Chapter 1

How do I tell a client that his mother is dead?

That question had been gnawing at me all morning. Josh was due in my office in five minutes and I still didn't have the answer.

My phone rang. When I answered it the receptionist said, "Ms. DeGraaf, Mr. Adams is here to see you."

I grimaced. "Give me two minutes, Joan."

Josh always showed up on time. I like punctual clients as much as anybody, but today I wouldn't have minded if he'd been late.

I straightened a few papers on my desk and thought about the 'staging' of this interview. My desk faces the wall, with a chair beside it for clients. My framed degrees and social work license hang over the desk. In one corner, where my office opens into a large bay window, I have a sofa, chair and coffee table. That might make a more comfortable setting for what promised to be a painful conversation. In the three years I'd been doing social work at this agency—specializing in helping adoptees find their biological parents—this would be the first time I'd had to tell a client a birth parent was dead. I had never felt so conflicted about a case.

Or about a client.

I've always had a good instinct about people and situations. I'm a Korean-American adoptee myself. I joke that the 'inscrutable Asian' part of me senses things. Whatever it is, it kept me from getting in a car when I was seventeen with a bunch of kids who were having too good a time. Three of them died in an accident a few minutes later. Psychologists say that abandoned kids, like me, have a survival instinct, an ability to know when they can trust somebody or when a situation is safe.

And yet I kept getting mixed signals on Josh.

My conflict with him was summed up by his eyes and his goatee. He has eyes like two pieces of chocolate, the dark kind with anti-oxidants that are good for your heart. But just below those luscious eyes is that damn goatee. I've never known a man whose looks were improved by one of those things.

From our first interview I had wanted to like Josh—not in a romantic sense—but I always felt there was something more I needed to know about him. His answers to my questions didn't seem evasive; yet, when I went over my notes later, I found myself somehow ... dissatisfied.

For instance, in our last session I had asked him what he would say to his biological mother or father when they were reunited. His immediate response was, "I hope you're rich." Then he passed it off as a joke. I had to remind myself that he had been a theater major in college and now did freelance advertising and graphics work. Pretence and a glib tongue were the mainstays of his life. How could I know when to take him seriously?

There was a knock on my partly open door and Josh stuck his head in. "Are you ready for me, Sarah?"

"Yes. Please come in, Josh. It's nice to see you."

That wasn't an idle comment. Josh stood a little over six feet and had thick brown hair to go with those dark eyes.

I slapped myself mentally. I couldn't be interested in a relationship right now. I still hadn't gotten over Cal leaving me three months ago. I wasn't ready to get involved with another man. Certainly not with a client. And not with any man who wore a goatee.

"Let's sit over here." I motioned toward the sofa and chair and picked up his file off my desk.

Josh took the sofa, as clients always do. He was wearing an off-white cable knit sweater and brown corduroy slacks that made his eyes appear even a shade darker. He rubbed his hands several times on the upper part of his legs. During several interviews I had come to recognize that as a nervous gesture of his, what psychologists and poker players call a 'tell'.

I sat in the chair across from him, with the file folder in my lap. It contained copies of the documents he'd given me—his amended birth certificate, correspondence from the agency to his adoptive parents—and all the information I had unearthed in the last two weeks.

What I didn't have, though, was his original file from thirty years ago. Nobody in my agency could find it. That worried me. State law requires us to retain all of our paper files relating to adoption cases, and they have to be stored in a secure area. We comply with those regulations, even though we've computerized everything, but Josh's file was nowhere to be found. I'd had to work from documents he discovered in his adoptive parents' safe deposit box after their deaths. With my caseload as heavy as it was, I had taken that shortcut. I didn't have time to turn the place upside down looking for one file.

Josh smiled hopefully. "You said on the phone you had some news for me?"

"Yes, I do."

"Not good, huh?" His smile faded.

"Well, some good, some bad."

He leaned back, as if bracing himself for the blow he could see coming and knew he couldn't avoid, the way I do when the dentist comes at me with that needle full of novocaine. "I can take whatever you've got to say. There isn't a possibility I haven't imagined."

I opened the file and studied the first page. Not because I needed to, but because it delayed the inevitable moment when I would have to inflict some pain on him. A lot of pain, actually, and there was no way to deaden it.

"Josh, I don't know any gentle way to tell you this ... Your mother ... died about five years ago."

He closed his eyes and rested his head on his hand, propped on the arm of the sofa. "Okay, that possibility I *hadn't* imagined. Who was she? What happened?" he asked quietly.

"Her name was Margaret Dykstra."

"Margaret Dykstra? The head of Dykstra Furniture Company?"

"Yes. Did you know her?" Something about his reaction struck me as odd, as though he was feeling a really strong emotion and struggling to suppress it. But, as so often in my dealings with him, I couldn't get a clear read.

"I knew *of* her from what I saw in the paper and on TV. She was always giving stuff to charities or getting an award for something."

"That's her. She was quite well-known in west Michigan, not just in Grand Rapids."

"How did she die?"

"She was working late in her office one night when she apparently fell and hit her head on the corner of her desk. Here's the information sheet I promised you. And this is a copy of the article about her death that appeared in the paper. There's a picture of her with that."

Josh read the first page without any reaction. When he turned to the newspaper article his eyes opened wider. Then he shook his head slightly.

"Is something wrong?" I asked.

"No. For a second there I thought maybe I had seen her before, but it must have just been on the news." He looked at the picture a moment longer.

I was torn between two of the agency's operational guidelines: Don't leave a client upset at the end of an interview, and, Don't get personally involved with clients. In my current emotional state I had no intention of getting involved with Josh or any other client, so what I was about to suggest seemed safe enough.

"There's a sandwich shop near here," I said, hoping this sounded like a business proposition, not just a proposition. "Would you like to get some lunch and talk some more?"

"I don't want to impose on you."

"You won't. I was planning to eat there. Let me get my coat." The lunch I'd brought from home could stay in the refrigerator in the staff lounge until tomorrow.

Chapter 2

It was a typical mid-March day in west Michigan: overcast, cool and windy. An occasional ray of sunlight broke through the clouds, teasing us with the reminder that the sun was there but we wouldn't see much of it for several more weeks yet.

"This is crazy," Josh said, turning up the collar of his coat. "We're still worrying about windchill factors when people in other parts of the country are suffering from hay fever."

I found myself walking close to him without intending to. His lean, muscular body made a good windbreak, I rationalized to myself. "I think spring is scheduled for the last week in May this year," I said, unable to suppress a shiver. Since I hadn't planned to go out of the building during the day, I had worn a lightweight coat.

A frigid blast met us as we turned the corner and lost the protection of the buildings. The shock staggered me. I sensed Josh was going to put a gentlemanly arm around me. I regained my balance by hiking my bag back up on my shoulder and leaning away from him. He did that funny thing men do with their arm when a woman they intended to put it around pulls away. Like I would really believe he meant to just stretch it and pat his hair at that very moment.

He stood three inches taller than me. (I get my 5'8" height and my green eyes from my American father and my 34-A chest from my Korean mother.) From his file I knew he was twenty-nine, a year younger than I am. He'd lived in Grand Rapids only six months. Why anyone so good-looking and so easy to be around was still unmarried, I didn't know. As much as I pry into people's lives every day, I don't ask that question because I don't like people asking me.

Our route took us past Calder Plaza, a Grand Rapids landmark. It's named for Alexander Calder, whose monumental steel sculpture "La Grand Vitesse" stands in the center of it. It's a huge piece, painted a color known as Calder Red. People consider it either a masterpiece or an eyesore. I think it looks like a praying mantis on steroids. I wondered what someone with an arts background, like Josh, thought of it.

"Are you a fan or a detractor?" I asked, gesturing at the forty-two-ton "stabile." Its title is French for 'the great swiftness'—Grand Rapids.

"I'm warming up to it," he said. "It has a fluidity of shape that appeals to me. I'm not keen on the color."

Non-committal, like most of his answers to my questions.

Stepping into DeJong's Sandwich Shop is like stepping back into a small town in the 1950s. At least that's what I imagine it feels like, since I never was in a small town in the 1950s. They offer thick sandwiches on homemade bread and a relaxing view of the Grand River, which flows through the center of town, from north to south.

We beat the noon crowd by a few minutes, were seated quickly, in a booth with worn vinyl seats, and given menus.

"Hannah vill be vit you in a minute," the hostess/owner told us with a trace of the Dutch accent that was once so common in the area. She was a thickset woman, in her sixties.

Our waitress was clearly the teenaged granddaughter of the owner, but she defied the wholesome Dutch image by dying her hair blue on top and yellow around the sides.

After we placed our orders, Josh looked around the restaurant. "I've often sat in places like this, looking at women old enough to be my mother, and I'd wonder, Do I look like her? Could it be her?"

I reached across the table to lay my hand on his. "I know how you feel. And, given how interconnected so many families are around here, anybody in this restaurant could be a relative of yours."

"But you're Korean. You can't really know how I feel."

"All adoptees share that feeling, Josh. I've told you about that trip to Korea that I made with my adoptive parents. Any woman I passed on the street could have been my mother."

"At least nobody has told you your mother is dead."

"Josh, I know this is a bitter disappointment to you. If there's anything I can do to soften the blow ..."

"Are you *sure* you got the right woman? You didn't have much to work with. You couldn't even find my file." He was just stating a fact, but it felt like an accusation.

I removed my hand and sat back. I could feel the ice curtain descending, my automatic reaction when anyone criticizes my work.

I was especially sensitive about it this time, since I had not been able to find that file. "Are you suggesting I've been slipshod?"

His eyes widened. "No, please—don't take it that way. I meant, around here Dykstras are as common as Smiths. Anybody could make a mistake ... Why don't I just say I'm sorry and shut up?"

"Apology accepted," I snapped. "Let me assure you that I made a thorough investigation. I've done this a lot of times. I'm confident about the information I got. It listed your mother's parents and her address at the time you were born. Your grandmother still lives in the same house, one of the biggest houses in Heritage Hill."

Josh whistled softly. "The historic district."

"Yes. I drove by the house on my way home from work one day. It's enormous. A lot of the houses that size have been converted into apartments or funeral homes."

Our waitress, Hannah with the variegated plumage, brought our sandwiches and an order of onion rings for Josh. We ate a couple of bites before we resumed our conversation.

"How did my grandmother—boy, that's going to take some getting used to—how did she react when you called?" Josh asked as he dipped an onion ring in a puddle of ketchup on one end of his plate.

"She was hesitant at first, but then she seemed relieved that the family secret was out and she could talk about it. She verified everything I had dug up. You have an uncle, who now runs the family furniture business. He and his wife have two children."

"Instant family. Would they be willing to meet me?"

I pondered before replying. "Your uncle hasn't returned my call yet. Your grandmother seems eager for a meeting. Usually we recommend that you exchange letters or a phone call before you meet. But your grandmother says she doesn't have time to waste. She wants to meet you as soon as possible."

"I'm game. Let's do it."

"Don't get your hopes up, Josh. These reunions don't always work out well. They put a lot of stress on the adoptee and on the birth family. I've seen a few turn really ugly."

"It's very important to me to try. I've lost my adoptive parents. I have no one."

"I'll do my best to set up something."

"Thanks. Now, is there anything else you can tell me about what happened to my mother?"

I shook my head. "It's all in that newspaper account. The janitor found her lying on the floor beside her desk."

"Did the police look into it?"

"I checked with someone I know on the force"—what an odd way to talk about the man I lived with for a year—"and he says they found no sign of forced entry or a struggle. And no evidence of an injury or a wound, except for a cut on her temple. They think that happened when she hit the corner of her desk as she fell. Her father died of a heart attack in his early fifties, so it may have been hereditary. Or maybe the stress of the job got to her."

"The autopsy didn't establish cause of death?"

"The family refused to allow an autopsy."

Josh screwed up his mouth as if his lunch didn't agree with him. "This may be off the wall, but doesn't that strike you as a bit odd?"

"What do you mean?"

"The president of a major company dies unexpectedly in her office, and the family doesn't want an autopsy?"

"Some people are uncomfortable with the idea of a loved one being cut open, especially if there's no real information to be gained."

"Or if there's some information they don't want people to get."

"What are you talking about?" I lowered my voice because my instincts had raised similar questions, but I didn't want to discuss it in such a public place.

"Nothing, probably," Josh said, leaning across the table. "But she was my mother. If I'd been part of the family five years ago, I would have demanded to know exactly what happened to her. And I'd still like to know."

"Josh, I think you're way out of line here. The Dykstras are one of the most prominent families in Grand Rapids. They've donated millions of dollars to various charities. I know it's a shock and a disappointment to find out who your mother is and to learn at the same time that she's dead, but I don't see any reason to start questioning the family's good name. *Your* good name now, I might add."

"Yeah, I guess you're right." He sat back up and picked up another onion ring. "I won't say any more about it."

I hoped he would keep his word. His comments had put my instinct on alert. What kind of person—what kind of trouble—was I introducing into this family?

Chapter 3

When I called her that afternoon, Mrs. Dykstra was thrilled at the prospect of meeting her grandson. "Why don't you come to the house tomorrow? Would two-thirty suit you?"

"It might be better," I suggested, "if we met in some neutral place, a restaurant or a park." That was the agency's strong recommendation, though not a requirement, for these initial meetings.

"I don't get around very well any more, I'm afraid. Because of my Parkinson's I've stopped driving, and I can't always depend on my family to haul me anywhere. I'd rather you came to the house."

"All right. We'll plan on it." Even as I agreed I decided I would accompany Josh. The case worker usually doesn't participate in the reunion interview, but I didn't want to place an elderly woman in the position of opening her door to a man she'd never met, a man I had known for only a few weeks and couldn't vouch for.

"I'm so thrilled you've found us," Mrs. Dykstra said. "I want to be sure I understand how this came about so I can tell my son and his wife. I'm seventy-four, you know. I don't always get things straight. You say there's a central file of adoptees? That's where you found Peggy's name?"

"Yes, ma'am. It's called the Central Adoption Registry. It's a place, maintained by the state, where birth parents can file a consent form allowing their names to be released if a child who was given up for adoption wants to know the identity of his/her birth mother/father."

"I didn't know Peggy had done that."

"She's the only one who could have. You can't put a consent form there for anyone but yourself."

"I thought adoption information was confidential. How can people check this registry?"

"People can't. Only courts and certified agencies are allowed to access the Registry."

"I see. Well, thank God for it. I've regretted for years my husband made Peggy give up her baby. Tell me, what does he look like?"

I described Josh as best I could. "I've seen a few pictures of your daughter in old newspaper articles. I don't think, Josh bears a strong resemblance to her. Maybe it's hard to see because of his goatee."

"If Peggy hadn't pulled a few hairs out of her chin each day, she would have had one of those. Maybe he looks more like his father."

"That could be." Like an attorney introducing a topic while questioning a witness, I saw an opening to ask about something I'd hesitated to broach this early. "Do you know anything about the father?"

She paused so long that I was afraid we had lost the connection. Her voice went soft when she finally said, "That's a painful subject."

My first thought was incest or some equally unpleasant possibility. "If you'd rather not go into it, that's fine, but Josh will want to know eventually."

"Yes, I realize that. And he has a right to know, of course. But I can't tell him anything. All Peggy ever said was that it was a boy she met in Saugatuck. We have a cottage over there. She said his name was David. She never would tell us his last name."

I could imagine any family would be unhappy to learn that their daughter was sleeping with a boy and had gotten pregnant. A socially prominent family might have an even stronger reaction. "How did you and her father respond to that?"

"Oh, Cornelius—my husband—flew into a rage." The terror of that moment must have surged up from wherever it had lain, festering for thirty years. I could barely hear her when she found the courage to speak again. "I had to pull him off of her. And he called her ... the most awful names." She was starting to cry. "His own daughter. His own beautiful, precious daughter."

A picture of this family was already starting to emerge in my mind: wealthy, religiously and socially conservative, a tyrannical father, a daughter who couldn't or wouldn't conform to his expectations. All the elements for an explosion were lying around, just waiting for a match to fall on them.

"I'm sorry to dredge up what's so painful for you, Mrs. Dykstra."

"It's not your fault, dear. I've had nightmares about that scene for thirty years." She blew her nose. "It's a relief to talk about it."

"I hope meeting your grandson tomorrow will help erase some of those unpleasant memories."

"I'm so excited I could make a 'Depends' joke."

I chuckled. Even in the two short conversations I'd had with Mrs. Dykstra, I had seen glimpses of an earthy humor. She seemed to defy the mold of the stodgy Dutch matron, the sort of women I had grown up among, the sort my mother was on her way to becoming. "I hope this reunion goes well, but I must caution you, on the basis of my experience, that people are sometimes disappointed."

That actually happened more often than I would have expected. Being reunited with a child you gave up years before can be bittersweet. You think you've put the past behind you, but it's always there, its feet peeking out under a curtain. Then, one day, a stranger yanks the curtain back and there it stands. You can't ignore it any longer.

"I'm sure everything will go fine," Mrs. Dykstra said. "And I probably won't sleep a wink tonight."

* * * *

Since introducing Josh to his grandmother would be my last official act in this case, I decided to spend the afternoon writing up my final report. That process would also allow me to review my notes and get things in order for Friday afternoon. As the person in my agency who oversees adoptee reunions I handle about fifteen of these cases a year, in addition to my other work at the agency. The state requires a training course and certification for anyone doing this job. Sometimes it gets tedious, tracking down people from addresses that are twenty years out of date. There have been times when I've felt like a detective. Cal even gave me some tips and the names and phone numbers of some people who could help when I ran up against a wall. Josh's case had, fortunately, turned out to be one of my simpler ones. That would be reflected in my short report:

ADAMS, JOSHUA LAWRENCE

Personal data:
DOB: September 24
Age: 29
Education: College graduate
SSN: 555-00-1212
Address: 1601 Sedgefield Dr., Apt. 6A, GR
Phone number: 555-1934
First contact: Phone call, February 8, 1:45pm
JLA asked about finding biological parents. I outlined steps required.

21

JLA made appointment to come to office on February 12.
First office visit: February 12, 9:30.

JLA arrived on time. Appears well-groomed, well-spoken, college-educated. Grew up in Battle Creek. Attended college in GR. Reports he is a freelance graphics artist. Recently moved to GR from Battle Creek because most of his clients are in this area. Adoptive parents, Matthew and Allison Adams, died in an explosion of a gas heater at their summer cottage two years ago. He did not know he was adopted until he was twelve, when a cousin teased him about it at a family reunion. He asked his parents; they told him it was true.

We discussed his feelings about being adopted. Like most adoptees who have the truth hidden from them, JLA went through a difficult period after he found out and says he still finds it hard to trust authority figures. Reports problems with discipline in high school. Was involved in various kinds of protest groups in college. After the deaths of his adoptive parents he found documents relating to his adoption in their safe deposit box—his amended birth certificate and correspondence from our agency. Since our agency was the one that placed him, he came to us seeking help.

Procedures and Results

Began the search process by having him fill out a "Request by Adult Adoptee for Identifying Information (FIA 1925)." With that form in hand, I filed a "Central Adoption Registry Clearance Request (FIA 1921)." The Registry replied within the required two weeks.

JLA's request yielded a name, Margaret Dykstra, and an address and phone number in GR. Initial inquiry was made by phone, Mar. 3. Margaret Dykstra's mother confirmed Margaret had given birth to a son with same DOB as JLA and had given him up for adoption. Unfortunately, Margaret Dykstra died five years ago. Copies of newspaper articles about her death and a copy of her death certificate are attached. She never married and never had any other children. She has a brother, who is married with two children. Grandfather, Cornelius Dykstra, is also deceased. Biological father's name unknown to grandmother.

It must be noted with concern that JLA's original file has not been located in agency files, in spite of a diligent search.

Chapter 4

Josh met me at the office on Friday and we drove to the Dykstras' house in my car. I wanted to be able to control how long we stayed and to make sure he left the house if Mrs. Dykstra said she wanted him to. On the way there I told him what little I had learned about his father.

"Not much to go on, is it?" he said. "David from Saugatuck."

"It's about par for the course. Over ninety percent of the adoption reunions I handle are with the mother. The fathers, unfortunately, just aren't in the picture very often. Many times they don't even know they fathered a child."

"Did your father know about you?"

I took my eyes off the road for a second. "Let's keep this focused on you."

"Sorry, didn't mean to make it personal, likc it is for me."

It was more personal for me than I could ever explain to Josh. He, and people like him, stood a good chance of finding their biological parents if they chose to look. Even as adoptees, they fit in perfectly with everybody around them. From the first glance people knew I didn't belong. Koreans and Americans both treated me as an oddity—the tall woman with the green almond-shaped eyes, the Asian-brown skin, and the Dutch name. The only clue I had to my identity was a note my mother pinned to the inside of my sweater when she left me at a church in Pusan:

Please take care Sun Ah. Her father American soldier.

"So there's no way you could find him?" Josh asked.

It took me a moment to process that he meant *his* father. "Not with the information I have—a very common first name. We don't even know if he lived in Saugatuck. Maybe his family had a cottage there, like the Dykstras. Maybe they just rented for the summer."

"If I was born in September, then my mother and father slept together in January. That doesn't sound like a summer romance."

"Yeah, that occurred to me. But let's not say anything about him to Mrs. Dykstra. Talking about him yesterday got her pretty upset."

I turned onto Fountain St. and started up Heritage Hill. It really is a hill. Much of west Michigan is flat, thanks to the glaciers in the last Ice Age, but this bulge overlooks the Grand River and the downtown area. It includes 1300 houses, one of the largest historic districts in the country. The Dykstra house was a Queen Ann treasure (or monstrosity, depending on your taste in architecture). It rose three stories and sported at least four gables, just from the two sides I could see. It was painted several shades of green, highlighted by red and cream trim.

"*This* is the house?" Josh said in disbelief as we got out of the car and started up the sidewalk.

His strong reaction caught me off guard. These reunions can get very intense. I didn't want him to go into it already upset about something. "Yes, it is. Why do you find that so remarkable?"

"I've been in this house." He stopped and gazed at the house.

"What ... ?"

"For this drawing course I had in college, one of our assignments was to draw an old house. I spent a Saturday afternoon sketching *this* house. I worked on that sidewalk, under those two trees."

"That's an amazing coincidence." I touched his arm, a bit playfully. I wanted to keep the mood light, for my sake as well as his. "Do I hear the music from 'The Twilight Zone' in the background?"

"If you don't already, you will when I tell you the rest of the story. While I was working that day, a woman came out and talked to me. At first she just wanted to know what I was doing. Later she offered me a snack and let me use their bathroom."

"Are you telling me you've met your grandmother?"

"No. It was a younger woman. She said her name was Peggy."

I stared at him in disbelief. "You think she was your mother?"

"She must have been."

"What did she look like?"

"Something like that picture you showed me yesterday."

"That's why you did the double-take."

"Yeah. She wasn't made up that day, and she was wearing glasses. But she must have been my mother."

"Let's not rush to that conclusion."

24

"Why not? Peggy is a common nickname for Margaret."

"It's too uncanny. If a writer put that big a coincidence in a book, he'd never get away with it." I didn't want to crush what might be the only memory of his mother he would ever have, but I didn't want him to build false emotions either. "Do you still have the drawing?"

"No. I entered it in the senior art show and somebody bought it. I also made a sketch of her and gave it to her."

As we made our way up the walk, Josh seemed to sink into himself. I wanted him to be as outgoing as possible. In a sense, he was about to put on the performance of his life.

"Josh, it might be better not to say anything about the encounter with this woman yet." He nodded so slightly I wasn't sure I'd seen it.

Mrs. Dykstra herself met us at the door. From the size and age of the house I wouldn't have been surprised if a uniformed butler or a maid had invited us to step back into another century. Mrs. Dykstra was a short, chubby woman, who didn't look as old as she had admitted to being on the phone. But her head and hands trembled noticeably. She could not suppress her initial shock at seeing me. I've had people tell me, 'You didn't sound Asian on the phone.' Mrs. Dykstra's greeting was gracious, if restrained.

"Please, come in."

The front hall had a walnut wainscoting. The floor was parquet, but not the usual square pattern. The pieces of wood had been worked into diamonds, each with a star inside it. I had never seen anything so elaborate. The hall was dominated by an eight-foot-tall coatrack with a mirror and a seat and hooks on each side. Some day archaeologists might imagine it was a monarch's throne.

Mrs. Dykstra studied Josh unabashedly—the way old people and young children can stare at someone without worrying about embarrassing themselves—as she led us to what would have been called the front parlor in the nineteenth century, a place where she could serve coffee and chat. The parlor sat across the large entry from the living room, which—judging from the quick glance I got—had columns and the most ornate fireplace surround I've ever seen.

Mrs. Dykstra directed us to seats on a high-backed sofa while she sat in a wing chair opposite us.

"Forgive me if I move a bit slowly," she said. "I slipped on the ice and broke my hip two years ago. Blasted thing still isn't quite right."

I wished Josh would speak, but he seemed to have retreated inside himself, I suspected, reliving the encounter with his mother.

"I'm sorry to hear that," I said. "My grandmother broke her hip last year. It's quite an ordeal to get through."

"I shouldn't complain. At my age, though, complaining is one of the few pleasures left in life. May I offer you some coffee? Our cook made it before she left for the day." She gestured toward one corner, where an antique silver coffee service sat on a mahogany serving cart. "I'll ask you to pour. We have a woman who cooks for us, and a cleaning service, but there's no one here full-time any more."

"I'd love some," I said, and Josh nodded.

"The awkward part is," Mrs. Dykstra said, "I don't feel I can pour it, because of my Parkinson's. Would you mind, dear? That pot is difficult for me to handle. I'm afraid I'll have it in your lap."

She was looking at me, but Josh roused himself and did the honors. "Sugar, ladies? Cream?"

I took cream. Mrs. Dykstra took hers black. Josh put her cup and saucer on the table beside her chair. I enjoyed having the opportunity to study him while he was doing something other than sitting on a sofa across from me, although I was not nearly as overt in my ogling as Mrs. Dykstra was.

"I also ordered some *banket* from the bakery," Mrs. Dykstra said. "I know *banket* is usually for special occasions, but what more special occasion can there be than my grandson coming home? Would you mind slicing it, Josh?"

I groaned inwardly. *Banket*, a concoction of puff pastry and almond paste, is a favorite treat among the Dutch in west Michigan. My Asian tastebuds find it barely palatable. At least the piece Josh set in front of me was small. Maybe I could choke it down. Mrs. Dykstra waved him away when he offered her a plate.

"You did that very smoothly," she said.

"Dinner theater," Josh replied, taking a bite of the pastry. "I did a lot of dinner theater right after college, until a director told me I was a better waiter than an actor. Are you sure you won't have some *banket*, Mrs. Dykstra? It's really good."

"No, thank you, dear. I'm diabetic. No sweets for me."

"That's really a shame," I said.

"It's more of an inconvenience than anything. Because of the way my hands shake, I can't manage the insulin injections. My son practically faints at the sight of a needle, so my daughter-in-law, Katherine, helps me with that. If she's not here, my granddaughter can do it, although I hate to think where she learned about needles. But you're not here to talk about an old woman's miseries, are you?"

I couldn't help but smile and wish my own grandmother had been this feisty and outspoken. "Maybe what we've got to say can take your mind off other things."

"You say this young man is my grandson?" She leaned forward to examine Josh over her glasses.

"Yes, ma'am. He is."

"Thank you for seeing me, Mrs. Dykstra," Josh said. "I know it must seem strange to find yourself sitting down with someone you've never met and being told he's your grandson."

"I'd given up hope that this moment would ever come." Mrs. Dykstra smiled all the way up to her eyes. "Now that it's here, I'm not sure how I feel. Please don't take offense," she added quickly.

Josh shook his head. "Not at all. It's going to take some getting used to on both sides. I'm looking forward to meeting my uncle and aunt. Do they live here with you?" Josh asked.

Mrs. Dykstra nodded. "They do, with their daughter, Pamela." Her tone of voice suggested she wasn't happy with the arrangement. "She's sixteen and acts every bit of it."

"I thought there were two children," I said.

"That's right. The other one, Georgie, finished nursing school last spring and got married. They have an apartment out in Walker." She paused, as if thinking, then continued. "You might as well get to know your cousins. Georgie is, well, independent. Defiant might be a better word. She refuses to work in the family business. She paid her own way through school, then married a boy who's utterly beneath her—a security guard at a shopping mall, of all things."

I was finding it hard to establish any kind of 'pace' to this interview. The reunions I had arranged before had been between mothers and children. Things tended to happen pretty fast, with a lot of hugging and crying. I wanted to get into the more substantive part of our discussion, but I knew it was important to let Josh and his grandmother talk about what *they* wanted to talk about.

"Will any of your family be home soon?" I asked.

"Edmund is at the plant. Pamela will hang out with her hoodlum friends for a while after school. Katherine could be home at any time. She's the head of the company's accounting department. She tries to be home when school lets out."

I was opening my briefcase to get out the documents that verified Josh's identity when footsteps sounded in the hall.

"Speak of the devil," Mrs. Dykstra muttered.

A brown-haired woman appeared in the parlor door. If I hadn't known she had grown children, I might have put her in her mid-thirties. She must work out a lot, I guessed, to stay so slender and maintain that skin tone.

"I saw a car out front, Mother Dykstra," she said. "I didn't know you were expecting company." She seemed to be waiting for an explanation rather than apologizing for her intrusion.

"Katherine," Mrs. Dykstra began, "this is Miss DeGraaf, from the adoption agency. And this is Josh Adams ... Josh is Peggy's son. Your nephew."

Josh, who was closest to the door, stood and started to extend his hand. Katherine's jaw dropped.

"Who are you people?" she said, struggling to control her voice.

"I just told you," Mrs. Dykstra said.

"I don't believe a word of it."

"Katherine, it's time we faced our past. There are too many skeletons rattling around this old place. I want to lay this one to rest."

"So you welcome the first opportunist who comes to the door?"

"Mrs. Dykstra," I said, "I assure you that my agency has made a very thorough search to verify who Josh is." I pulled out his file. "You can look at the evidence yourself."

She waved her hand like someone accustomed to sending people away disappointed. "I won't waste my time. You've come in here with this preposterous story, trying to dupe a sentimental old woman. I won't let you get away with it. I want you to leave right now."

"Katherine!" The strength in Mrs. Dykstra's voice surprised us all. "Let me remind you that they are *my* guests and this is *my* house. Mr. Adams and Miss DeGraaf will stay as long as I want them to."

Katherine moved her jaw soundlessly, like an attack dog suddenly deprived of his teeth. She finally made what I could only describe as a growling noise. Then she turned and stomped out of the room. Somewhere in the back of the house a door slammed.

Chapter 5

"I'm sorry about that," Mrs. Dykstra said as Josh resumed his seat. "It's embarrassing that my family and I don't get along well."

"Would it be better if we left?" I leaned forward, genuinely concerned that Katherine might take out her anger on her mother-in-law. Reports of adults abusing their elderly parents are all too common. One of my coworkers at the agency recently had to intervene in a nasty situation of that sort. At least now people are reporting it.

Mrs. Dykstra waved me back. "No, no, dear. Keep your seat. Katherine and Edmund have always been particularly sensitive about any mention of Peggy. I imagine they'll demand all kinds of tests before they'll even consider believing you."

"I'd be happy to cooperate," Josh said. "DNA, IQ, EKG, MRI—you name it."

As Mrs. Dykstra laughed I put a hand on Josh's knee. He had no need to appear desperate or over-eager to cooperate. "That won't be necessary. The evidence we have leaves no doubt about who you are." I handed copies of the documents to Mrs. Dykstra.

"But it might be better to do some tests," Josh insisted, "just to remove any last trace of uncertainty. You know, babies switched at birth—that sort of thing."

"We can't do any of that this afternoon," Mrs. Dykstra said, "so why don't we just talk? I imagine you have questions for me."

Josh leaned forward. "I do. First, may I call you Grandmother?"

She beamed. "It would break my heart all over again if you called me anything else." She reached over and took his hand.

I try to maintain a professional demeanor in these situations, but I had trouble holding it. I hadn't seen such a gleam of delight in someone's eye since my five-year-old nephew's last birthday party.

"This is a little question, just for clarification," Josh said. "My mother's name was Margaret, but I've heard you call her Peggy ..."

"In the family we called her Peggy, or Peg. Once she got into her teens, though, she wanted to be Margaret. That's how people out-side the family knew her. I've come to accept it ."

"Okay. Then the big question I've always wanted to ask is what anyone in my position would ask, I guess." He glanced at me. "Why did my mother give me up?"

The rush of emotion seemed to make Mrs. Dykstra's head tremble even more. "Let me assure you it wasn't because she didn't love you. She would have kept you if the choice had been hers. Cornelius—your grandfather—and I have to take the blame. I'm guilty because I didn't stand up to him, and he's guilty because he was rigid and puritanical."

"But thirty years ago," Josh said, "people's moral views were changing. An unmarried woman could have kept her baby without the stigma of, say, the 1950s."

"That may have been true in some parts of the country. It was less true in west Michigan, and it was absolutely not true in this house. In this house it might as well have been the 1950s. We lived in a black-and-white world. Cornelius was a pillar of the church and keenly aware of his position in the community. An unmarried, preg-nant daughter was an embarrassment he would not endure."

"I suppose abortion was out of the question," I said.

"No one could have uttered that word in his presence."

"How did he hide what was happening?" Josh asked.

Mrs. Dykstra took a deep breath. "The timing worked out very well. Margaret got pregnant on New Year's Eve. She had planned the whole thing. She told us she and some of her friends were getting together. We had always thought we could trust her. I guess that's what she was counting on. Since she got pregnant in winter and was a chubby girl—which she got from me, I'm afraid—she didn't start show-ing until school was out. We own a cottage up north. Cornelius sent her up there with a nurse and a tutor. They were actually her jailers for the summer. A few days before her due date they brought her back here. Two days later, you were born, in this house. Cornelius had you taken immediately to the adoption agency. He wouldn't let your mother or me hold you." Her voice broke. "He didn't even want us to know whether the baby was a boy or a girl. The nurse—her name was Polly—at least had the humanity to tell us that."

I would never meet Cornelius Dykstra, but I was already develop-ing a hearty dislike for the petty tyrant. He sounded like an extreme example of the repressed Dutchman, a stereotype even the Dutch in west Michigan acknowledge holds some truth. I wondered how his daughter dealt with what amounted to severe psychological abuse.

"Two days after you were born Margaret was back in school. We were never allowed to say anything about you or take notice of your birthday. But, when Margaret turned eighteen, she started going out by herself on that day. She did that for many years afterwards."

"Where did she go?" Josh asked. "What did she do?"

"I never asked. I was just glad she found some way to get out from under her father's thumb. I hope you can forgive us, Josh. For thirty years I've regretted what we did. Or what we didn't do."

"That's all in the past, Grandmother. I've had a good life. My parents were wonderful people ..."

"Were?"

"Yes. They were killed two years ago when a gas heater in our cottage near South Haven blew up."

"Oh, my! I'm so sorry." She squeezed his hand.

"It has taken me a long time to deal with it. I thought it might help my healing process if I looked for my birth family."

"I am so delighted you've found us."

Josh glanced toward the door as though Katherine was still glaring at him. "Apparently not everyone here is."

"Oh, don't worry about Katherine and Edmund. They'll demand proof, but they'll accept the situation. I'll see to that."

"I don't want to cause conflict. I won't make a nuisance of myself."

"Don't be silly! We have too much lost time to make up for. And I don't have much time left to do it." She took a tissue from the box on the small table beside her chair. As she wiped her eyes Josh patted her shoulder.

"It's all right, Grandmother. That's all in the past."

"Yes. Thank God you've found us. It's funny, I said something to Edmund several months ago about looking for you. He said he'd see what he could do, but I'm afraid he isn't really interested, since he won't gain anything from it."

"I feel I've gained a lot already," Josh said. "Meeting you ..."

"Oh, dear boy, there's much more to it than that. But you wouldn't know about the trust fund, would you?"

Chapter 6

The grandfather clock in the hall bonged once for the half hour. The sound reverberated through the silence that fell over the parlor. "Trust fund?" Josh said. "I don't know anything about a trust fund."

I tried to read his face. He looked confused. Was it genuine, or just good acting? Once again, I didn't know what to make of Josh.

"Of course you don't," Mrs. Dykstra said. "How could you? No one in the family did until after Margaret's death. She started it when she was twenty-one and could keep it secret from us. She added to it over the years. She lived a spartan life. Everything she inherited from her father went into it. Bonuses from the company, royalties from her furniture designs, sales of her sculptures—all that went into the trust fund. It has over six million dollars in it."

Josh looked at me like an actor who's forgotten his next line. When I could trust myself to talk, I asked, "And it all goes to her son? Are there any conditions attached to it?"

"Just one. If her son isn't found by his thirtieth birthday, the money is to go to Margaret's favorite cause. But here you are, six months ahead of the deadline, so I guess The Art Place is out of luck."

"The Art Place?" Josh said.

"It's some hippy artists' group downtown," Mrs. Dykstra said.

"It's an artists' co-op and gallery, housed in an old factory," I added. "They pride themselves on being edgy, counter-culture."

"Sounds like something I'd like to see," Josh said.

"Margaret would be so pleased to hear you say that," his grandmother said. "She was a sculptor, you see. She rented a studio at The Art Place and displayed and sold some of her work there. They have one of her pieces on permanent display."

"I'd like to see that," Josh said, turning to me.

"We can go by there. It's not far from the office."

I wondered if Margaret Dykstra's work was anything like what I had seen recently when I attended a reception at The Art Place. The work of art being highlighted that evening consisted of hundreds of paper lunch bags meandering across the floor of the gallery, with a few chairs placed here and there.

"Mrs. Dykstra," I said, "would it be possible for Josh to see the instrument setting up the trust fund? I'd also like to know what information will be needed from my agency to verify his identity."

"Yes, of course, dear. We do have to get serious about this, don't we? In her will Margaret named me the executor of the fund, along with a lawyer who had never worked for the company or for her father. I'll call and set up an appointment for us. Is there a time that suits you two best?"

"For something this important," I said, "just let me know and I'll clear my calendar if I need to."

Josh nodded. "Same here. I freelance, so I work mostly from home. Any time would suit me."

We both gave her our business cards. I wrote my cell phone number on the back of mine. She studied Josh's card with great interest.

"You're a graphic designer? So you inherited some of your mother's artistic bent."

"I've never tried any sculpture, but I have always loved to draw and design things. In fact, by an amazing coincidence—"

A door slammed. We heard arguing voices of two teenage girls.

"Oh, my," Mrs. Dykstra sighed. "The demon spawn is home early with some friend of hers. I'm sorry, I shouldn't talk that way about my grandchild, but she is one of the most demanding, inconsiderate young people I've ever known. I wish I could blame it on her mother, but I'm afraid Edmund is largely responsible. He won't discipline her. He has no backbone. I wish someone would shove a broomstick up ..."

"We should be going," I said. Even after three years of doing this, I still found it difficult to gauge how long these reunion interviews should be allowed to run. The initial euphoria on both sides can start to drain quickly. An interruption can provide an ending that feels natural, not like one side is abandoning the other again.

"Must you?" Disappointment clouded Mrs. Dykstra's eyes and she grabbed Josh's hand. "This feels like thirty years ago. You're barely here and someone takes you away."

"I think it would be best," I said. "You've got a lot to talk over with your family. You have a lot of new information to think about."

I had only one new piece of information to think about, but it was a huge one. How did a six-million-dollar trust fund factor into this equation?

"I'll call you, Grandmother. I promise." Josh leaned down and gave her a peck on the cheek. "And you have my number. You can call me any time. That's different from thirty years ago."

* * * *

I didn't say anything in the car until we were out of sight of the Dykstra house, on the one-way part of College Avenue, heading down The Hill. Then I pulled over to the curb and turned to Josh.

"What's the matter"? he asked, drawing back. Maybe I looked like I was turning *on* him.

"I have one question for you, and I hope I can tell if your answer is honest."

"Thanks for the vote of confidence. I thought you were supposed to be on my side."

"This isn't about sides, Josh. Until this afternoon it was about reuniting someone with his family. Now I find out it's about a multi-million-dollar trust fund. Did you know about that fund?"

"No, Sarah. As God is my witness, I did not. You heard my grandmother. She didn't even know about it until my mother died. Nobody did, except the lawyer who helped set it up, I guess."

And as soon as I had that lawyer's name, I resolved, I was going to find out everything I could about him. If Josh had *any* connections with him—if he'd ever written an ad for him, hell, if he'd even waited on him at a dinner theater—I would ...

What would I do?

"What's going on, Sarah? Are you not sure I'm Margaret Dykstra's son? If you doubt me, tell me right now."

"No, I'm not doubting you." If anything, I was doubting myself. Had I let myself get suckered by those dark chocolate eyes? Should I have looked harder for that original file?

"Then what's the problem?"

"This whole thing has taken a very unexpected turn, Josh."

"Sarah, I'm no fortune-hunter. My parents left a substantial estate. I didn't ask you to find me a trust fund. All I wanted was your help in locating my biological family. I'll gladly do any kind of testing anybody wants to establish who my mother was. With samples from my grandmother, my uncle and me, a DNA test ought to be conclusive."

"Those are expensive."

"I'll pay for it. And I'll abide by the results, whatever they show."

"I have a feeling Edmund and Katherine are going to demand something like that, at the very least."

"Bring it on. I'm confident about the results because I trust you. I wish you felt the same way about me. Remember, I'm not the one who said I'm related to the Dykstras."

"You're right, Josh. I'm sorry. It's just that I've never stumbled over a pot of gold at the end of the reunion rainbow before."

Chapter 7

To get our minds off the trust fund, Josh and I decided to visit The Art Place to see why his mother was so interested in it. The Art Place is housed off Fulton Street, near the Heartside District, just a few blocks from Heritage Hill. The city put a lot of effort into revitalizing the area. Many of the buildings look almost new. But prostitutes and homeless people still comprise the majority of the people on the sidewalks in front of those charming refurbished buildings. Seeing them so close to my office makes me wonder if all the social workers and well-intentioned people in the world will ever make a difference.

Inside the front door of The Art Place sat a fish bowl on a stand with a sign in front of it saying that admission was free but suggesting a two-dollar donation. Josh dropped in a five-dollar bill. A young woman at the nearby reception desk said, "Thank you."

I hadn't noticed her until she spoke. She was almost hidden behind the desk and computer. I took a closer look at her. Her hair was black and shiny as shoe polish, and her lips an unearthly red. I noticed her most obvious feature—multiple piercings in ears, nose, lips and eyebrows—and I could hear my father say: 'Humph! Girl's got so much metal in her face she could set off airport security alarms from the parking lot.' What distressed me was that I was inclined to agree with him.

"Can I help you?" the girl asked. Her nametag identified her as Weslyn.

We must have looked ill at ease. I don't know what I was expecting to do. Just walk in and look around?

"I understand you have a sculpture by Margaret Dykstra on display here," I finally managed to get out. "We'd like to see it."

The young woman shook her head and light reflected off of her piercings like a disco ball. "I'm not sure. I've only been a volunteer here for, like, a few weeks. Let me see if somebody in the office can help you. Some of them have been here, like, forever."

She went through a door behind the desk. While we waited I noticed a rack of flyers and brochures on the wall beside her desk. I looked them over with no particular interest until I noticed the one on grants to west Michigan artists. Most the grants were small, perhaps a few hundred dollars for the purchase of materials. The new Margaret Dykstra Award, though, promised a 'substantial sum to a promising artist.' It was given at the discretion of the director of The Art Place and the chair of the Board of Trustees. That one I slipped into my bag.

The pierced girl returned a moment later accompanied by a grim-looking, short-haired woman in her late thirties who must have played softball in high school and college. She had the muscular legs and shoulders of a pitcher.

"I am Christine Grotenhuis," the woman said. "How may I help you?"

"Hi. I'm Sarah DeGraaf. This is Josh Adams. We were just visiting with Margaret Dykstra's mother up on The Hill, and she mentioned that you have one of her sculptures on display here."

"Yes, we do. It's back here, in the Margaret Dykstra Gallery." She pointed to her right, to an archway opening off the room where I had attended the reception. I now remembered seeing the plaque by the door as I mingled and noshed, but the name hadn't meant anything to me then.

"You have a whole gallery of her work?" Josh said.

"No. There's only one piece of hers in there. The room is named in her honor because her family raised the money and donated it as a memorial."

"I didn't realize my aunt and uncle were supporters of this place."

I cringed. It didn't strike me as a good idea to broadcast his claim before he was accepted by the family. News of an unknown relative of a prominent family could get around certain circles in Grand Rapids faster than a sexually transmitted disease on spring break. I could see its immediate effect on Ms. Grotenhuis. The corners of her mouth tensed and her eyes narrowed.

"I didn't realize the Dykstras had a nephew."

"I've been separated from the family for a while. I moved to Grand Rapids recently and I'm reconnecting with them. I have some arts background myself. I look forward to helping them support ventures like this."

"I see." The dollar signs in her eyes practically rolled up like one of those old cash registers in a cartoon. Ka-ching. "They've been involved with The Art Place since Margaret's death. Edmund volunteered to be on our board of directors. He'll become chair of the board next month. And Katherine took over Margaret's studio."

"Two sculptors in the same family?" Josh raised an eyebrow. "I didn't know Aunt Katherine had that kind of talent."

Ms. Grotenhuis hesitated. "She's ... working very hard to develop her own style. But she and Edmund have been quite successful in raising money for us."

"Did you know Margaret well?" I asked.

"Not at all. I started here four years ago. Now, let me show you her sculpture."

We followed her across the large gallery, where the lunch bags had been strewn the night I was there, to a smaller room. It was more finished—more like a regular museum—than the rest of the building, which retained the feel of an old factory, with high beamed ceilings and large open spaces in which the slightest sound echoed.

"This was just storage space until the Dykstras raised the money to remodel it. We keep Margaret's piece on permanent display. She left it to us in her will, with instructions that it not be sold. That's it, over there. The piece in the other corner is one of Katherine's."

Katherine's sculpture stood in a corner visible from the main gallery. Margaret's piece was diagonally across the room, as though it were a hidden treasure. Both sculptures were abstract, made of welded pieces of steel. But, even to my untrained eye, it was clear which was a well-crafted work of art and which an ungainly pile of scrap metal.

"That's certainly a powerful piece," I said, nodding toward Margaret's sculpture.

"That is our most popular exhibit. I've seen people stand in front of it and weep. Is there anything else I can help you with?" Ms. Grotenhuis asked.

"No," Josh said. "We appreciate your time."

As she left the gallery with one last glance over her shoulder I felt certain she was going to be on the phone to one or both of the Dykstras within minutes. I'd bet they were numbers One and Two on her speed dial.

"We probably ought to get out of here soon," I said.

We took a look at Katherine's sculpture, "Untitled #7."

Josh chuckled. "One of my professors used to say a work called 'Untitled' was an indictment of the so-called artist who allegedly created it."

We approached Margaret's sculpture almost as though it were a holy icon. Even before I looked at the title card on the wall beside it, I could sense pain and despair in the uplifted face and the outstretched arm of the crouching figure.

"Look at the title," Josh said.

The card read "Mother ... and Child?"

I put a hand on his arm. "Are you okay?"

"I'm not sure." He ran his hand over one of the statue's hands.

"She must have thought about you a lot," I said.

"Sarah, could I have a minute?"

"Sure." I squeezed his arm and stepped away. Nothing I could say now would be adequate or appropriate. Ever since he realized he'd met his mother in that house, I think he'd been reconnecting with her spiritually. Now even I could feel her reaching for him.

I spent a few minutes examining some of the pieces in the exhibit currently being featured in the gallery. None of them moved me, but they struck me as having more artistic merit than the lunch bags. If lunch bags are art, then why did I throw away all those creations I made from popsicle sticks in summer camp?

"Please don't touch the sculpture." From across the gallery Ms. Grotenhuis' voice sliced through the quiet.

Judging from the look in his eye as he turned to face her, I was afraid Josh was going to challenge her. He only pulled his hand back.

"I've just talked to Edmund Dykstra," Ms. Grotenhuis said. "He says he doesn't have a nephew. I don't know what you people are up to, but I'm going to ask you to leave."

That wasn't the first time today we'd heard that, I thought.

"Why?" Josh said. "This is a public place, isn't it? We made a donation as we came in." He folded his arms across his chest. "In fact, I'd like to join The Art Place."

"But ... you can't ..."

I was about to step in when my cell phone rang. In this situation I felt I had to answer it, to end the distraction.

"Ms. DeGraaf, this is Ella Dykstra, Josh's grandmother. I love saying that. 'Josh's grandmother'."

"Mrs. Dykstra, could you hold on a minute?"

She didn't seem to hear me. "I am calling to let you know I have set up an appointment with the trust lawyer, J. Spencer McKenzie, for Monday at nine o'clock. Here's the address—"

Fortunately the street address was easy to remember because I didn't have anything to write it down with. I was about to cut the conversation short when an inspiration hit. And where better to get an inspiration than in an art gallery?

"Mrs. Dykstra, do you know Christine Grotenhuis, at The Art Place?"

The old woman snorted. "I certainly do. She and her husband were up here for a reception two weeks ago. That woman puts away shrimp cocktail like a whale inhaling krill. I wrote her another check for that money pit she calls an art colony, just because it was cheaper than feeding her."

"Well, we're down here right now, talking with her. She's not clear on who Josh is."

"Let me talk to her, dear."

That was exactly what I was hoping she would say. I gave the phone to Ms. Grotenhuis and stepped over beside Josh, away from what I suspected was about to become ground zero.

Ms. Grotenhuis listened a lot more than she talked. "Well, I didn't know ... Certainly ... I didn't mean ... Yes. Yes, I will. Goodbye."

She handed me the phone and I punched it off and put it in my purse, hoping it wouldn't melt anything.

"There seems to be some misunderstanding," she said, touching her hair as if checking to see whether Hurricane Ella had left it in place. "Mr. Adams, you don't need to join The Art Place. Mrs. Dykstra says I'm to add you to her family's membership. Enjoy your tour of the galleries."

* * * *

On our way back to my office to pick up Josh's car I told him about the appointment with the trust lawyer.

"I'll be there. What about you?"

I nodded. "I can make it, but understand, I can't represent you in a legal capacity. You should consider consulting a lawyer of your own."

"I'll wait until I have a better understanding of the situation."

"All I can do is verify what I've learned about your identity."

"You can also give me the moral support I need."

He turned those big brown eyes on me, and I could sense what he was going to say next. I didn't want him to say it because I knew what my answer would have to be. I focused on his goatee to make it easier to turn him down.

"Would you like to have dinner with me tonight?" he asked.

"Josh, I can't. The agency has a strict policy about staff socializing with clients."

I pulled into the parking lot and stopped next to Josh's car. Like mine, his car was a '98 Honda Civic, four-door. The only difference between them was the color. Mine was red, his white. I was hoping he would just get out, but he didn't seem to be in any hurry.

"You make it sound like you'll be shot at dawn for fraternizing with the enemy," he said.

"Worse. I could lose my job."

"That seems a bit draconian, for having dinner with someone."

"There's a reason for it. It really confuses things when social workers or counselors see the people we're working with outside of the office."

"We could go someplace where no one would know us."

"Josh, I'm flattered by the invitation, but I have to say no."

He shrugged. "Okay, but it won't be the last time I ask."

As I watched him get in his car I found myself hoping the Dykstras would insist on DNA testing. It would be the only way to insure Josh was who I thought he was. Until this afternoon, in spite of slight misgivings—that missing file—I had had every confidence in what I'd found out, just as I do any time I reunite an adoptee and a biological family. In every case I have to be sure, but this time there were six million extra reasons to be absolutely positive.

* * * *

Another Friday night. Correction: another Friday night alone in my cookie-cutter apartment in my cookie-cutter complex off of 44th Street. That was bad enough, but as I was considering my options for supper I realized I hadn't run the dishwasher that morning. I had to reach up to the top shelf of the cabinet for a clean plate. The one I pulled down was one my boyfriend, Cal, left when he moved out. His Detroit Red Wings souvenir plate. I bought it for him for the one Christmas we were together.

Seeing Cal's plate after three months threw me into a total funk.

I thought about going to Rivertown Crossings Mall, maybe picking up something in the food court, and hanging out for a while. But that mall is big and noisy and seems to be geared to teenagers. Of course, it hadn't seemed that way when Cal and I used to eat there and ride the carousel.

For just an instant, I'm ashamed to say, I thought about 'accidentally' dropping Cal's plate, but I finally put it back up on the shelf. I'd have to call Cal and let him know it was here, if he even wanted it. I hoped I could get it to him without having to see him. Since the break-up we had talked three times on the phone—once about Margaret Dykstra's death, twice about missing articles of clothing—but I wasn't ready to face him. We were civil to one another; we weren't friends.

I found a plastic bowl and nuked a can of Spaghetti-o's. They would cost me extra time on the treadmill tomorrow morning, but, next to rice and kimchi, they were my favorite comfort food. And everybody knows, if you want comfort, you gotta pay for it.

Damn Cal anyway! Living with me was fine. But taking our relationship to the next level was more than he could handle. Since when did 'marriage' become a four-letter word? We were so good together, in every way a couple needs to be good together.

The wedge that widened the crack in our relationship was his badge. His real fear of commitment, he said, was connected to his fear of being killed and leaving a young widow with a family. He'd seen it happen to his first partner. 'A cop shouldn't get married,' he told me in one of our last conversations. 'He needs a woman who understands that.'

Or maybe my mother was right: Why should he buy the cow when he was getting the milk free? as she so delicately put it.

To distract myself I decided to work on Josh's case. Bad choice of words. But cops and social workers have cases. There's no getting around that.

First I Googled for the trust lawyer's name, J. Spencer McKenzie. Not likely to be many of those in the database. And there weren't. The three hits I got weren't very informative either.

Then I did a search for Joshua Adams and came up with over fifteen hundred hits, thanks to the genealogy buffs. It was a particularly popular name in the nineteenth century. Adding Josh's middle name, Lawrence, narrowed it down to no hits, so I went back to the first search and began skimming the list of sites.

Yeah, it was such a bad Friday night I was willing to skim a list of fifteen hundred web sites looking for information about one person.

I had gone through about two hundred sites when I hit a newspaper article about the accident that killed Josh's parents.

EXPLOSION KILLS BATTLE CREEK FAMILY

I clicked on the URL and read the article: "The explosion of a gas heater in their South Haven summer cottage killed a Battle Creek family yesterday. Matthew and Allison Adams and their son Joshua died in the blaze ..."

Chapter 8

My fingers shook as I punched in Cal's number. "Come on, pick up! Pick up! Oh, shit!" I said when I was transferred to his voice mail. "Cal, this is Sarah. I *really* need to talk to you. Call me. Please. Don't worry about the time."

If he was on duty I might not hear from him until tomorrow. What if he was dating? Could he have found someone else already? 'The kind of woman a police officer needs'?

Too nervous to sit still, I got on the treadmill and set it for twenty minutes, without increasing the incline. I wanted to work my brain more than my heart, and I needed to be moving while I tried to sort out this mess.

God! What had I done? How had I allowed Josh—or whoever the hell he was—to dupe me like this? I had to stop him before he did any serious damage. The Dykstras weren't the kind of people, I suspected, to take this lightly. And they had the influence to inflict a lot of payback. What if they sued the agency? What if they sued me? I carry $100,000 in personal liability insurance. It wasn't likely to be enough in this case. I could lose my job, maybe even my license.

And it would break Mrs. Dykstra's heart when I had to tell her the truth. She would have to lose her grandson all over again.

Where had I slipped up? I thought back over my role in this fiasco, the way Cal and I used to talk through cases that were proving tough for him. I could imagine what he would say as clearly as if he were here with me.

Josh called the agency and was referred to me because I'm the person who handles adoptee searches, I would point out.

So he didn't seek you out in particular, Cal would say.

No. And I followed all the procedures. I asked for his driver's license and Social Security number and ran a check on them.

If he got them from the real Josh Adams, they would all show up as valid.

44

The picture on the license was of this Josh.

Give me an hour and I could get my picture on that license. Or yours.

Let's take another angle. This scam is obviously all about the trust fund.

Right. So, who knew of its existence?

As far as I know, only McKenzie the trust lawyer, Grandmother Dykstra, and Edmund and Katherine. Surely Grandmother Dykstra isn't behind this scheme. I just can't see her cooking up something like this.

You mean you don't want to. She started treating Josh as her grandson from the outset. She expressed no doubts when you brought him to the house. She's added him to the family's membership at The Art Place.

You're right. She does have some deep resentment against her husband for the way he treated Margaret and her baby.

Could she be trying to get back at him in some way?

No, my instinct tells me she isn't capable of this kind of deception.

Oh, right. Your precious 'instinct'. But you wouldn't have thought 'Josh' was capable of it either. Not a nice guy like him.

Okay, I have a soft spot for stray cats and injured birds. Maybe that's why I do the work I do. Don't rub it in. I still can't see Josh as the initiator of whatever plan has been put into action. The brains behind it has to be someone who knew about the trust fund. That means one, or more, of the other three ...

Start with the lawyer—McKenzie.

Suppose he's no lover of art. Or he has big debts. He looks at that money and decides he needs it—or deserves it—more than The Art Place.

And it wouldn't be like stealing from real people? What does he need to get it?

A young man to play the part of Margaret Dykstra's long-lost son. Who better than someone with training as an actor? He probably saw Josh in a play.

A struggling young actor could be seduced by a couple of million bucks, maybe a lot less.

But wouldn't a lawyer anticipate that the Dykstras would insist on absolute proof before they accepted 'Josh' as their nephew? With DNA testing available today, how could he get around that?

Good point. Edmund and Katherine, on the other hand, wouldn't have to get around it.

Right! Suppose *they* were after the money. If they found someone to play the part of the nephew, they wouldn't have to insist on positive proof of his identity. After some initial huffiness, they could profess themselves satisfied with whatever proof the agency—*my* agency—provided. They wouldn't want anyone to look too closely. Just like they didn't want an autopsy performed on Margaret's body.

Then the 'nephew' gets his cut and probably decides to go live somewhere far away.

But why would Edmund and Katherine go to that trouble and take that big a risk? They're already rich beyond the dreams of most of us.

At least they appear to be. Are there cracks, some dry rot, behind that Heritage Hill façade? They wouldn't be the first well-to-do family to find themselves running on fumes.

Exactly. To see all of that money—money their sister inherited from their father, their family's money—going to The Art Place ...

And, speaking of The Art Place, what does Christine Grotenhuis know about this?

My phone rang. It was Cal.

"Sarah, what's the matter?"

The warmth and strength in his voice brought it all back. The first time we made love. The way he held me when I got the call that my father had had a heart attack. But he didn't want me. I had to remember that. He had left, not me.

I took a deep breath. "I was on the treadmill. Give me a minute."

"On the treadmill this time of night? What's up?"

"Cal, I think I've gotten into something that's way over my head. I need some help."

"That's all you have to say, hon. You know that."

Damn him! I didn't want to cry.

* * * *

Shortly before noon on Saturday I found a table in the food court at Rivertown Crossings Mall. I had a salad and a diet drink on my tray, but they were just for show. With my stomach in this big a knot, I'd never be able to eat anything. I took one more look at the papers in the folder by my tray. It contained the ammunition that was going to bring 'Josh' down.

Josh had agreed to meet me here at noon. At first he'd been puzzled that I was asking him to have lunch with me, after my little sermonette about agency policy. But I told him, quite truthfully, that this was agency business. I wanted to talk about our meeting with the lawyer on Monday.

I needed to center myself for what I expected would be a difficult conversation. Even before I took any meditation classes, I had my own technique of picking a point in the distance and focusing on it until everything else dropped away. Talking with other Asian women, I had learned that this ability must be inborn. One woman told me it had gotten her through childbirth without Lamaze or drugs.

Now, as I looked for a quiet spot to focus on amid the hustle of the food court, my gaze fell on a man sitting several tables away, slightly to my right. I wouldn't have paid any attention to him except that he seemed to be very interested in me. He had a drink and a newspaper open in front of him, but I could tell he wasn't reading it. I glanced away from him, but not before getting his face fixed in my mind. He had splotchy pale skin, almost albino-like. Under his baseball cap it looked like his head was shaved. He wore a goatee so bad I wondered for a minute if it was fake.

My cell phone rang. So much for meditation. "I'm here," Cal said. "To your left and slightly behind you. Don't look around. The guy you're meeting may already be here and watching you."

I stifled my urge to turn. "I wish you were where I could see you."

"No good. You'd be looking at me, not at the guy you're supposed to be talking to. Interesting place to meet, by the way."

"Don't read anything into it. It's public and it's near my apartment. That's all."

But it was also where Cal and I met. I was eating alone one evening and he asked if he could join me. My instinct said it would be okay. As simple as that. We rode the carousel that dominates the food court. The next day he called and told me to listen to the oldies radio station at noon. They played "On a Carousel" by the Hollies, dedicated to me.

"I wasn't hinting at anything," Cal said. "I'm going to hang up now. If your guy's as punctual as you say, he'll be here any minute. Signal whenever you want me to step in."

As I put my phone away the gaudy carousel started. It's full size, turquoise and yellow. The only thing I don't like about it is the way the name of the sponsoring supermarket is plastered all over it. And yet it still costs a dollar to ride. So what are they 'sponsoring'?

A young couple, holding hands, were riding where Cal and I used to. I would take the frog and Cal would ride the stag next to it. I used to kid him about kissing the frog and the whole enchanted prince thing. Then one night I explained the psycho-sexual meaning of that myth—by showing, not telling. He said he'd never be able to read the story to his niece again.

My instinct had told me Cal was the one. How could I be so wrong? Now I couldn't tell whether to trust Josh or not. Was I losing my touch? Had my instinct expired when I turned thirty? Or had tulips, wooden shoes and *banket*, made me lose contact with my Korean roots?

As the carousel came to a stop I saw Josh standing over my table. "Hi," I said. "Thanks for meeting me."

"No problem." He sat down with his burger and fries. "What do you want to talk about?"

There was no sense beating around the bush. My stomach couldn't take it. "About this." I pulled the print-out of the article about the Adamses' deaths out of my folder and slid it over to him.

He shook his head. "Oh, man! Not this again."

That wasn't the reaction I'd expected. "What do you mean?"

"I mean I spent a year correcting the mess this made of my life."

I thought I'd written the script for this scene. Josh was supposed to be on the defensive, not me. But he wasn't rattled at all. He took charge, like a director on a set. Or maybe like an gifted con man.

"Look, I can straighten this out. I've had to do it a dozen times."

So he had his lines well rehearsed.

"You see, my parents and I always went over to South Haven to open our cottage on the Saturday before Mother's Day. They needed somebody to help them because of their age. They were almost forty when they adopted me, so they were in their late sixties by this time. And my dad had had prostate cancer. He wasn't in great shape." His voice got a little quaky.

"Is there a point to all this?" At the risk of sounding callous, I wasn't going to let him distract me so I lost sight of which cup the pea was under.

"Yeah, sorry. It's just that whenever I start talking about this again, it gets to me."

Or he's able to tear up on cue, a useful skill for an actor.

"Anyway, they needed somebody with them to open the cottage. This time"—he pointed to the article—"I wasn't able to go. I had to finish a project for the agency I was working with. So my cousin Marion went with them. He was twenty-two, roughly my height and build. After the explosion, the police and the media came to the cottage and found three bodies, badly burned. One of our summer neighbors had seen my parents and somebody he assumed was me. The report got into the papers that I died in the explosion. It's amazing how fast that bit of misinformation got around. You should have seen the *In Memoriam* in my college alumni magazine."

"You mean this one?" I pulled another sheet out of my folder.

"You did a lot of reading." His eyebrows arched and he smiled.

"I scanned over a thousand hits, just to make sure I wasn't missing anything."

"It's too bad you didn't find where the paper printed a correction a few days later. Of course, it was a really small piece. Maybe your search engine missed it."

Or maybe it was in those last few hundred hits I didn't get to.

"Josh, you're asking me to believe an awful lot." The urge to turn and look at Cal was like an itch you can't scratch in public.

"If I'd known this was what you wanted to talk about, Sarah, I could have brought my file. I can show you my correspondence with credit card companies, Social Security, and all the rest. You don't know what an ordeal it is to convince people you're not dead. Once it gets into somebody's computer, it's worse than having it carved on a tombstone. Did you know that Jerry Mathers, the guy who played the Beaver, was rumored killed in Vietnam? Some people still believe he's dead, no matter how many times he's been on TV since then. I could show you a web site about that."

I took a sip of my drink. Was this what a victim of a con game felt like? His story made sense, but he was an actor. An actor who wrote ads. He had to be convincing. And if you didn't believe the words, how could you *not* believe those eyes?

"Josh, do you see my problem? How can I *prove*, beyond a shadow of doubt, that you're who you say you are? And, if I can't prove it, how can I support you on Monday when you go to see that lawyer? There's so much at stake here: my reputation—maybe my job—a family's integrity, not to mention six million dollars."

Josh clenched his fists in frustration. "I told you, I'll do anything, take any test. I know who I am, and I'm not afraid to do whatever it takes to prove it. I told you I would even pay for a DNA test."

"But it would take several weeks to get results from a DNA test, and the Dykstras would have to consent to being tested."

"I'm sure my grandmother would."

I'll bet she would, I thought. Especially if she's in this with you.

"Even if she agreed, I need something convincing before Monday."

"Just tell me what you want, and I'll do it."

The testiness in his voice scared me. I touched my left ear. That was Cal's signal.

When Cal came to our table, pulled out a chair and sat down next to me, Josh bristled. "Hey, buddy! This is a private conversation."

"It's okay," I said.

Cal extended his hand. "Josh. I'm Cal Timmer, a friend of Sarah's." Cal's tall but a bit on the thin side, so he doesn't feel overpowering. When I met him I guessed he was a teacher or an insurance salesman.

"It's *Detective* Timmer," I put in, "from the Grand Rapids Police Department."

Josh shook Cal's hand reluctantly. "So, who's the good cop, and who's the bad cop?"

Cal doesn't like cop jokes. Josh didn't know that, of course, but he'd find out if he made any more. With Cal you get only one freebie. "I'm off-duty," he said. "Sarah expressed her concerns to me, and I agreed to help her. While you and she were talking I've been on the phone with the Battle Creek police department. Guy there tells me the story of your death was erroneous. From the picture of you I sent him, he says you're the real Josh Adams."

"That's not surprising, since I *am* the real Josh Adams."

"But with so much at stake," Cal said, "it would be reassuring to have some indisputable proof. You say you're Josh Adams. A police officer, going by a cell phone picture, says you are, but we still don't have anything that would stand up in court."

Josh pushed away from the table. "What do I have to do to convince you people?"

Cal held out his hands in a calming gesture. "Have you ever been fingerprinted?"

"Yes," Josh snapped, "when I was arrested ten years ago."

Chapter 9

I didn't know whether to be angrier at Josh for not telling me he had been arrested or at myself for not doing a thorough enough background search. Where would the surprises end with this guy?

"Under what circumstances were you arrested?" Cal asked.

"A demonstration against a nuclear plant when I was in college."

"And they fingerprinted you for that?"

Josh looked at his uneaten lunch. "Things got a bit out of hand."

"Resisting arrest, assaulting a police officer?"

"Yeah."

I knew he was in trouble with Cal now.

"Well, if your prints are in the system, we can settle this question that's bothering Sarah in just an hour or so. Would you be willing to come downtown with me and be fingerprinted? This would be entirely voluntary on your part."

"Sure. No problem. Let's do it."

Cal drove his car and I rode with Josh, since he didn't know exactly where the police department was located. That meant somebody would have to take me back out to the mall to pick up my car. Josh probably wouldn't be speaking to me and I wasn't sure I was ready to be alone in a car with Cal yet.

"Josh, I hope you understand why I'm doing this." I twisted toward him as much as the seat belt would allow.

"Sure."

"I don't want you to be angry at me."

"I'm not."

So he was one of those men who clam up when they get mad, like my father. Cal was one of the other type, the ones who start yelling. That was the one thing I didn't like about him. He never raised a hand to me in anger, never got physical, just loud, the way he was at a hockey game. I found it hard to deal with, but this silent treatment wasn't much easier to take.

The main police station in Grand Rapids is in the Monroe Center, where Division and Fulton cross, right at the center of downtown, four blocks from my office. The building is fairly new and as pleasant as such a place can be. The current chief is working hard to establish better relations with the community, so there isn't even a metal detector at either of the doors.

"Sarah, why don't you wait in the lounge?" Cal said as he took Josh off to fingerprint him. "I'll talk to Tracey, or whoever's on duty, and see if we can do this off the books. I don't know how long it'll be."

I had read a couple of magazines and called for a cab to pick me up in half an hour when a tall, amazingly blond, amazingly statuesque woman paused in the doorway of the lounge. She made Xena look like a warrior prince. With her tight jeans and low-cut shirt, I thought she might be a hooker who had just been released and gotten lost on her way out. Then I saw the detective's badge clipped on her belt, where few men would look for it. "Are you waiting for someone?" she asked, stepping to the coffee maker.

"Yes. Detective Timmer."

"Oh, you know Cal?" She poured herself a cup of coffee.

"We're ... friends."

"Great! I'm Geri Murphy, Cal's partner." She extended her hand and I shook it. Or I let her pump my hand up and down a couple of times as I stared in shock.

"*You're* Cal's partner? You're Geri?" All this time I had thought it was Jerry, as in the guy's name, short for Gerald.

"I'm sensing Cal failed to mention a vital detail or two."

"He just said Derrick had asked for a transfer to Narcotics and that his new partner was Geri Murphy."

"And he didn't spell it or use personal pronouns?" She turned back to the coffee maker and added creamer and sugar to her cup.

"He hardly had time. We broke up a month after you two started working together."

"It's not what you're thinking," Geri said, stirring her coffee. "There's no cause-and-effect. Cal and I work together, that's all."

I guess we talked for a few minutes, but none of it registered. Her lack of a wedding ring was the only detail I noticed. I was too busy having an epiphany.

I think epiphanies are supposed to be accompanied by clouds parting and celestial trumpets blaring. Mine was humbler, but just as profound. I was waking up and smelling the coffee. Doing the math. A voice—too much like my mother's—was saying, Here's the picture, Sarah: Cal gets blond bombshell partner. One month later he leaves his girlfriend, who is not blond and is no bombshell.

"Speaking of my partner," Geri said as Cal entered the lounge. I guess she had been. I wasn't listening.

"Oh ... Geri." He obviously hadn't expected to run into her, any more than a deer expects to encounter a car while it's crossing the road. "What ... what are you doing here on a Saturday?"

"Trying to catch up on some paperwork. What about you?"

"Just needed a set of prints." He gestured at Josh, who stood outside the lounge, glaring at me. "Sarah, can we talk?"

He led Josh and me to his office. His desk and Geri's were placed to face one another. That wasn't how he and Derrick had them. How convenient this must make it for them to chat. With her leaning over her work, no doubt. I tried to stifle my resentment and listen to what he had to say.

"Okay, here's the deal," Cal said. "Josh's prints match those from his earlier arrest. The person who was Josh Adams ten years ago is the same one who is Josh Adams today."

"Like I told you," Josh said. There was no trace of good humor in his voice. "What do you want next, to dig up my cousin's body?"

"Josh," I said, "I'm truly sorry for the loss of your family, and I apologize for the inconvenience I've caused you. I hope you can understand that I had to be sure, with so much at stake. I will stand by you. If you still want me to."

"I'll see you Monday at nine," was all he said as he turned for the door. He didn't offer me a ride back to the mall.

Cal walked me to the street where my cab was waiting. As he opened the door I said, "I'm glad I got to meet your new partner. But she's not exactly new any more, is she?"

He wasn't going to let me embarrass him. "Yeah, Geri's a great cop. We work well together."

"Good. It's important to respect your partner, have a good working relationship. You know, not hold things back, or anything."

He finally broke. The veins in his neck began to bulge as he tried to keep his voice down. "Okay, Sarah! I should have told you Derrick had transferred and my new partner was a gorgeous woman. Christ! Why can't you just say what you mean?"

"All right, I will. Did you leave me because of Geri?"

He laughed—stood there and laughed in my face. "No, dear Sarah. Dear insecure Sarah. I left for the reasons I told you I left."

"So you're not having a relationship with that blond Xena?"

"Wouldn't that be every man's dream? Though Wonder Woman is more my fantasy. She bathes regularly. But—I'm sure you'll appreciate the irony—Geri would rather have a date with you than me."

Before I could do any more than gasp, he pushed me into the back seat of the cab and started to close the door.

"Oh, I almost forgot," I said before I told the driver where I wanted to go. "Your Red Wings plate is still in the apartment."

'The' apartment. No longer 'our' apartment, but I didn't want to shut him out by calling it 'my' apartment.

"So that's what happened to it. I was looking for it last week."

"Do you want to come by and get it?"

I couldn't remember ever seeing Cal Timmer flustered, not even when he told me he was moving out. He had been all business then, but right now his tongue was stumbling all over his teeth.

"Could you ... maybe bring it to your office? That ... that would be closer for me. Save me a trip ... all the way out to your place."

I tried to swallow my disappointment. I'd offered him a chance to rekindle the faintest spark of our relationship, and he doused it.

"Sure. I'll do that on Monday. Stop by and pick it up any time. If I'm not there my secretary will know where it is."

"That'll be great. Thanks, Sarah. It's been good to see you again."

"Yeah. You, too. Thanks for your help."

* * * *

When I got to the mall, I worked my way around the food court. I bought a corn dog, onion rings, one of those huge, ridiculously over-priced chocolate chip cookies, and the biggest Coke—not diet, the real thing—I could find. The perfect menu for a pity-party.

And I didn't get on the treadmill when I got home. That would be my usual punishment for pigging out. Today it didn't seem to matter.

I went straight to the kitchen, took Cal's Red Wings plate off the shelf, put it in a plastic bag, and dropped it on the floor. I didn't even look to see how many pieces it broke into. He could do that when he picked it up.

If he ever did.

Chapter 10

With my arms folded over my chest against a chilly breeze I was standing on my balcony looking out over the artificial pond the developer had put in behind my building. Even when I was in a good mood—like when Cal and I used to snuggle together in one lawn chair out here—I thought it was a pathetic attempt at beautifying the landscape. So was the row of pine trees lining the back of the property along the road.

My phone rang. Before my dad had a heart attack six months ago I could have ignored it if I wasn't in the mood to talk. Now I wanted to get it before the second ring. It rang three times before I could dig it out of my purse.

"Ms. DeGraaf?" an unfamiliar voice said.

"Who's calling, please?"

"This is Katherine Dykstra. I got this number off a business card you left with my mother-in-law."

"Yes?" My instinct—and the penetrating coldness in her voice— told me her mood hadn't improved since our run-in yesterday.

"My husband and I would like to talk with you. We'd like you to come to our house this afternoon."

I looked at the clock on the microwave. It was already after three. I didn't want to have to go out again, and I didn't want to confront the Dykstras on their turf. "It might be more appropriate to talk during business hours on Monday. Perhaps you could come to my office."

"Ms. DeGraaf, when you barge into our home, claiming to have found some long-lost relative and getting Mother Dykstra upset, you owe us an explanation. And we're not inclined to wait until Monday to get it. We'll expect you at four o'clock."

I don't like being ordered around. If this was something that affected just me, I would have told her to meet me in my office, take it or leave it. But I had a responsibility to Josh. If the family was going to be hostile, I ought to run interference. "All right, I'll be there. Should I bring Josh?"

"That won't be necessary. We'll deal with him later, if we have to."

I arrived at the house shortly before four and parked on the street. As I got out of my car, a beige Lexus turned in to the drive-way. A tall, slender man in his mid- or late forties with slicked-back dark hair graying at the temples, and a teenaged girl with similar build and features and brown hair streaked with blond got out and went in a back door. Retrieving my briefcase and locking my car, I reluctantly climbed the front steps and rang the bell.

When the door opened I found myself facing Katherine Dykstra. I had a feeling no one ever called her Kate or Kathy. She invited me in but didn't thank me for coming or offer any other social ameni-ties. As dry as my throat suddenly was, I wouldn't have minded hav-ing something to drink. But I knew not to ask.

"My husband just got home," Katherine said. "He'll meet us in the library."

This time I got a little farther into the house as I followed her across the front hall. The library was the next room beyond the parlor where Josh and I had talked with Mrs. Dykstra. Even more than in the rest of the house, here I felt I was stepping back into the nine-teenth century—mahogany paneling, floor-to-ceiling bookcases, a fire-place, two sofas, several lamps that probably weren't just 'Tiffany style', and, in the center of the room, a massive, old-fashioned desk covered with a piece of glass. Two chairs sat in front of it. Not a computer work station in sight. Their home office must be upstairs somewhere. This room was for impressing visitors, and it was working.

Katherine pointed to a chair in front of the desk. "Take a seat." It was a command, not an invitation.

I put my briefcase on the floor beside me as I sat down. "Will Mrs. Dykstra be joining us?" I wanted an ally.

"Mother Dykstra is resting. Your intrusion yesterday upset her so much that we had to give her something to help her sleep. I'm going to check on her now."

I didn't like the sound of that. I wondered if Mrs. Dykstra had told them about the appointment with the trust attorney on Mon-day. Could I check on her without Katherine and Edmund knowing? If she didn't show up on Monday, I would find a way.

I glanced around the library nervously until my eye fell on the picture above the fireplace. It was a pencil sketch—a gorgeous one—of the Dykstras' house. Could it be ... ?

I got up and studied the drawing more closely. In the lower right hand corner I spotted the initials JLA and a date.

"I'll be damned. She went to the art show and bought Josh's drawing. Her own son's drawing, and she didn't even know it."

Or did she? Had Margaret suspected or felt something that afternoon? I could feel a lump rising in my throat.

I turned away from the drawing. This was no time to let my emotions get the better of me. To distract myself I read the spines of some of the books surrounding me. Both of my parents are teachers, who instilled in me a love of books not only for their contents but for the works of art they can be. I wished I could bring them into this room. Most of the books—some of them leather-bound and gold-stamped—seemed to be contemporary with the building of the house, from the 1890s to the early 1900s. Names like Booth Tarkington and Mark Twain jumped out at me.

Only in one corner of the room, behind the door, did I find newer books. And 'newer' was just a relative term. I recognized some titles from the 1970s to the 1990s. On a bottom shelf I noticed several high school yearbooks from that era. I did some quick calculating and pulled out one I thought might be from Margaret's senior year.

Bingo! She appeared alongside three other Dykstras, nothing unusual in this community. On the facing page another girl, Mildred Driesenga, had written a touching message under her picture and signed it with her nickname, Mickey. The closing lines leaped out at me: 'all the fun we had and all the secrets we shared.'

I heard a noise in the hall, but it sounded still far away. I shifted the remaining books so that no gap remained and scurried to my assigned seat. The yearbook slipped neatly into my briefcase. Now if I could just get my heart to stop pounding.

Katherine Dykstra and the man I had seen getting out of the Lexus entered the room. He closed the heavy door behind them and took the plush leather chair behind the desk as she sat in the chair next to mine. I felt like I had been called into the office of the headmaster of an exclusive school. And I was not here to receive a commendation for my work.

I tried to size up Edmund Dykstra as he studied some papers on the desk. Even on a Saturday afternoon, his leisure clothes were impeccable, just like his wife's. Oh, those uptight Dutch. Their clothes were the only thing relaxed about them. They looked at one another like people joined by a secret, not by affection.

"How long have you worked for Oaktree Family Services?" Edmund started talking so abruptly, without looking at me, it was like someone had un-muted the TV and I had been thrown into the middle of a conversation.

"How long? Five years." I squelched the impulse to say 'sir'.

"And you work with adoptees who are looking for their biological families?"

"That's my main responsibility. I do more general types of counseling as well, especially with foster and adoptive families."

He looked at me for the first time. "Have you ever made a mistake before?"

"Before ... ? I'm sorry. I don't follow you."

He held up the papers he had been looking at, and I realized they were the copies of Josh's information I had given the elder Mrs. Dykstra. "Have you ever identified someone's birth family, only to have it turn out to be the wrong family?"

"No, sir." I couldn't squelch it in time.

"Are you sure?"

"Yes, I am. I'm very meticulous in my work."

"Well, in this case I'm sure you're wrong."

"With all due respect, Mr. Dykstra, I don't see how you can say that. The documents are all right there. Surely you're not denying your sister had a baby and that child was put up for adoption."

"No, I can't change that regrettable part of our family's past, as much as I'd like to. But I see nothing here to convince me that this Joshua Adams is my nephew."

I glanced at Josh's drawing of the house. Would that convince anyone, or was it just a huge coincidence? At the very least, it renewed my determination to stand up for Margaret and Josh.

"Mr. Dykstra, I've done these searches enough times to know that when you have the amended birth certificate, and you trace that back to the original birth certificate, you can't argue with the results. The state of Michigan is telling you Josh Adams is your sister's son, not me."

"And I'm telling you and the state of Michigan that we will not acknowledge him as such, no matter how many birth certificates you wave in our faces."

Damn! I knew I should have insisted Josh contact the family first by letters and phone calls. We should have followed agency procedures and done this whole process more slowly, let everybody gradually adjust to the new reality. What was it about Josh that had thrown all my best instincts out of kilter?

Edmund and Katherine exchanged a glance. I had the feeling they were a tag-team and Edmund had just told Katherine to step into the ring.

"How much do you want, Ms. DeGraaf?" Katherine asked.

"What do you mean?" I honestly didn't know what she was talking about.

"We know Mother Dykstra told you about the trust fund and how much is in it. You and your accomplice must have known something about it beforehand or you wouldn't be here."

"Wait a minute ... You have no right to talk to me like that."

"There is no way in hell we're going to let you and your boyfriend get your hands on that money," Edmund said. The words were forced out between his clenched teeth.

"What? My boyfriend? What are you talking about?" This was getting out of control. Both of them were in the ring now and there was no referee to stop them. I felt like I was being bounced back and forth between the two bad guys. Only this match wasn't rigged. I was getting dizzy as I whipsawed my head from one Dykstra to the other.

"Don't play naïve," Katherine said. "You don't do it very well."

Edmund leaned back in his chair. "We are business people, Ms. DeGraaf." All he needed was a big cigar to make him look like a gangster. "We're willing to offer you an inducement to drop this ridiculous claim and leave our family alone."

"You people don't have a clue," I said. "I don't want anything. I've done my job and helped Josh locate his birth family. How it plays out after this is no concern of mine. He's part of your family, and you'll have to come to terms with that fact. There is nothing for me to drop."

I stood up and picked up my briefcase, heavy with the weight of the purloined yearbook. Edmund stood behind his desk. I couldn't tell if he was just being a gentleman or if he would try to stop me from leaving.

"If you don't let go of this," he said, "you'll have to drop the rest of your life and prepare to spend a lot of time and money in court. Have you ever had to defend yourself against a lawsuit?"

"No, of course not."

"You'd be amazed how it can consume you. It can make Kafka's *The Trial* seem like a comic book."

"That's only one possibility," Katherine put in. "We're also considering calling in the police to investigate this fraud."

"These are not idle threats," Edmund said, moving around the desk.

"I assure you, Mr. Dykstra, I'm taking them very seriously."

"Then we understand one another?"

"I think I understand you very well." I turned and walked out.

Chapter 11

When I got home I locked my door and set the deadbolt before I took Margaret's yearbook out of my briefcase. As I held it in my trembling hands I thought, *I must have been crazy to take this thing.* If the Dykstras notice it missing, they'll be after me like Giants fans after a Barry Bonds home run ball.

Calm down. How often do people look at a thirty-year-old high school annual? I rationalized. *They probably don't even remember where it was.*

For supper I fixed a salad and a glass of water, to atone for my junk-food binge at lunch. While I ate I looked through the yearbook. Aside from clothes and hairstyles, which they all must regret now, Margaret and her classmates looked like pretty normal teenagers, as awful as that is to say about someone. Since this was a private, Christian high school, there weren't many rebels and malcontents in the crowd, judging from their pictures.

Each student's full name was revealed beside his/her picture. *What sadist came up with that idea?* I wondered. Margaret's middle name was Cornelia. Her father had to leave his imprint on everything, it seemed.

She could not be called pretty, even as tarted up as she was for her senior picture. Her face was too square, her hair not really Dutch blond, but not brown either. Her essential drabness showed through in a few other pictures showing school activities. Did she decide to have sex as a way of defying her father? Or was she looking for reassurance that she was desirable? I knew from my work and my own experience that teenaged girls can have long lists of reasons to have sex, from curing acne to thinking they're in love. Nothing I'd learned so far suggested she had been raped by this David character.

I found it hard to imagine how this sweet-looking, pudgy-faced girl endured having her baby snatched from her without going crazy. Nothing in her appearance suggested such strength of character. If I

61

hadn't seen her "Mother ... and Child?" sculpture at The Art Place, I might have concluded she didn't want the baby, that the pregnancy was just an accident and she was relieved to be free from the responsibility. But the sculpture and her mother's comments convinced me Margaret wanted to keep her baby.

How could she have continued to live at home then? To sit across the table from a father she knew was ashamed of her, even condemned her? And then to work for years with that man? Could anybody suppress all the rage she must have felt? It must have found an outlet somewhere. It had to, if she was to keep herself sane.

I've known clients in similar circumstances to resort to alcohol or bizarre behaviors. One of my clients was an avid hunter, and every animal he killed was his sexually abusive stepfather, he told me. The hunting wasn't bizarre in itself, but castrating every male animal he killed ... ? Maybe the pounding and hitting involved in Margaret's type of sculpture had been her release. Every piece of metal could have been her father's head. Or some other strategic part of his anatomy.

Next to each senior's picture was a list of clubs and extra-curricular activities. In her first two years of high school Margaret was a member of the pep band and several clubs. For her junior and senior years—after Josh's birth—the Art Club was the only activity listed. A number of her classmates had written notes as they signed her yearbook, but Mickey Driesenga's was the only one that suggested a close connection. Mickey was prettier than Margaret, but not in any absolute sense. Her face was a little too long and thin and her nose seemed to have been borrowed from someone else.

I got out the phone book and found a dozen Driesengas listed in Grand Rapids and the suburbs. There was no way around it. I started calling, pretending to be part of a committee doing the preliminary work for the thirtieth reunion of Mickey's high school class. It was my job, I told people, to compile a mailing list and locate people who might be married or otherwise be difficult to find. Cal had used this trick from time to time.

On my tenth try I got Mickey's brother, who told me she was now a Bolthuis, living in Walker, a suburb on Grand Rapids' northwest side. He obligingly gave me her address and phone number. Once again I was reminded that, by and large, people in west Michigan are still trusting souls.

I needed a different cover when I called Mickey. I was rather proud of what I came up with on my own. I told her I was writing an article on outstanding businesswomen in Grand Rapids' history. I understood she was a friend of Margaret Dykstra's and I would like to talk about Margaret.

She was hesitant at first. "I don't really know much about her as a businesswoman. We were friends in high school, but once we went to college we drifted apart and didn't reconnect until years later."

"That's all right. It would help me to have background on her if I could talk to someone who knew her when she was young. Those high school years can be so formative. Maybe she developed some characteristics then that made her successful later on."

We set up an appointment for two the next afternoon. I told her I was on a deadline. That was the only truthful thing I said to her.

* * * *

It was raining when I woke up Sunday morning. That fit my mood just fine. I rolled over and went back to sleep. When I did get up, the rain had stopped, but clouds hung heavy. It was going to be one of those gray days when the rain seemed to wash all the color out of the world. Four o'clock in the afternoon would look and feel the same as ten o'clock in the morning. Since I was feeling pretty glum anyway, I put the bag containing Cal's smashed up Red Wings plate in the car. I would drop it off in my office the next time I was there.

Walker is one of the most distant of Grand Rapids' bedroom communities and one of the last to experience gentrification. Beside modest older homes new subdivisions are springing up. The Bolthuises lived in a neighborhood east of Wilson, the main road through Walker. Some developer had carved out a maze of cul-de-sacs and filled them with houses that tried to look like something from the early 1900s, but the old painted ladies didn't have vinyl siding.

The woman who answered the door gave me the 'Oh, I never expected you to be Korean' look that I've gotten accustomed to. She was recognizable as Margaret's friend in the yearbook, in spite of a few more pounds, her glasses and her graying, shorter hair. The style fit her face better than her high-school do. If she would just fix that nose. She insisted I call her Mickey right from the start.

"Let's sit in the kitchen," she said.

She didn't have to point the way. I could follow the aroma of cookies just out of the oven and a fresh pot of coffee.

When I do a home study in connection with an adoption the first thing I notice about the family's kitchen is the pictures on the fridge. The Bolthuises had a lot of them. The one that stood out for me was of a girl, in her early teens, in a karate outfit and a brown belt.

Mickey caught me looking at it. "That's our younger daughter, Ashley. She started karate when she was seven. She's won several tournaments. I don't much like it, but I guess she'll always be safe on a date."

"I do tae kwon do, the Korean version of karate. I've never had to use it on a date, though I've been tempted."

"Please, have a seat," Mickey said, gesturing to the round oak table in a breakfast alcove with a bay window looking out over a yard that was a gardener's pride. Crocuses and daffodils were out. Even on a dreary day like this, the place gave promise of being a riot of color until October. I envy people who have the time and the skill for that. I can barely keep a window box on my balcony in bloom.

She poured us some coffee and put a plate of windmill cookies, another Dutch treat I've never acquired a taste for, on the table. I took a couple to be polite. As far as I'm concerned, once you've said chocolate chip, there isn't anything else to say about cookies.

"After you called," Mickey said, "I went up to the attic and dug out some stuff from high school." She pointed to two dusty boxes on the floor beside the table. "Is there something in particular you want to know about?"

"First, there's something I need to clear up. If you ask me to leave when I tell you this, I will. You see, I lied to you about my reasons for wanting to talk about Margaret. I work for the Oaktree Family Services Agency. I help adoptees and biological parents find one another."

"Oh, my God!" She put a hand on my arm. "Is Margaret's son looking for her?"

"So you did know."

"I was the first person she told. The only person outside her family, as far as I know."

"From what you wrote in her yearbook, I thought she must have confided in you."

"I should hope so. We'd been friends since fourth grade."

"How much did she tell you? Do you know who the child's father is?"

Pulling an envelope out of one of the boxes, she dumped the contents on the table. She rummaged through a pile of teenage souvenirs, stopping when she came upon a small black-and-white picture of a boy and a girl hamming it up in an automatic photo booth. She handed it to me. I suddenly saw where Josh got some of his features, especially those intense eyes.

"That's Margaret and David. David Burton."

"Nice looking young man. But that's a nasty looking scar." A short, jagged scar ran up Burton's left cheek close to his nose.

"He told us he got it in a knife fight. He claimed he stitched it up himself."

"And cleaned it out with testosterone, no doubt. Still, he is handsome."

"He was gorgeous, but he was also trouble, from the word go. The first time I met him I felt scared. I think Margaret was drawn to him for that very reason. You know, the sweet, innocent girl falls for James Dean. What's that old song, 'The Leader of the Pack'?"

"Did Margaret meet him at the candy store?"

"Close. It was at Kilwin's Ice Cream Shop. We hung out there a lot that summer. Margaret and I had turned sixteen and gotten our licenses. Her family has a place right on the water. They call it a cottage, but it's twice the size of this house."

"Did David live in Saugatuck?" I asked.

"For a while. He was from Chicago. His parents were divorced. He had gotten into all kinds of trouble. He was seventeen. I think his mother sent him and his sister to live with their father, to get him out of a bad environment. But he *was* the bad environment. His father had no control over him. Thanks to David, Margaret started drinking and generally acting kind of crazy."

"Weren't her parents aware of what was going on? I have the impression her father kept her on a short leash."

Mickey looked out the window and seemed to be weighing what she was about to say. "Margaret was always good at hiding things and pretending. I saw her tell lies to our teachers—just about little stuff, but they were lies—that nobody should have believed. It helped that she never got caught and so she had this reputation of being 'Little Miss Perfect'. Until she met David she almost was."

I chuckled. "It might amuse you to know her son's an actor and advertising man."

"That doesn't surprise me. And I don't mean to suggest Margaret was an evil, manipulative person. She was actually very sweet, but she could lie her way out of anything. And she did have a bit of a temper."

"Judging from the birthdate, she got pregnant in early January. Do you know if it was consensual? Had she been sleeping with David before that?"

"No. They didn't meet until mid-July. She didn't see much of him during the school year. At Christmas she told me she had set up a whole plan to lose her virginity with David on New Year's Eve. She wanted her first time to be something she would always remember. That's every girl's dream at sixteen, isn't it?"

I bit the vane off a windmill and blushed at the memory of a Fourth of July when I was seventeen with a boy whose pimply face I could no longer see clearly, although I could still remember my disappointment when the whole business was over.

"And she had the bad luck to get pregnant on her first try."

"I don't think Margaret had even considered the possibility of getting pregnant. That only happened to bad girls. When she told me, she was almost hysterical. For once she couldn't lie her way out of a mess. By then—it was early March, I think—David had turned eighteen, dropped out of school, and left Saugatuck. When Margaret tried to call him, his father said he didn't know where 'the worthless son of a bitch' was."

"What about the sister? Did Margaret try contacting her?"

"I don't think so. She was quite a bit older than David. That's all we knew about her. We never met her."

"Did Margaret consider having an abortion? It was legal by then."

"But the way our church preached against it, we all believed any woman who had one was going to the hottest, cruelest part of hell."

"Did she tell her parents, or did they just eventually realize what the situation was?"

"She managed to keep it hidden until the end of the school year. She was chubby." To underscore the point she pulled out a picture of herself and Margaret in swimsuits on a beach. "She just looked like she was gaining a little more weight. One morning in church, right after school was out, she told me she was going to tell them that afternoon. She knew in a few more weeks, she wouldn't fit into her clothes any more, so she didn't see any other option.

She gave me this picture to keep because she was afraid her father would make her get rid of anything associated with David."

"Her mother told me that her father went ballistic on her."

Mickey nodded. "She told me about it much later. Nobody saw her again until September. I called once and her mother told me Margaret was spending the summer at their place up north. Her father thought it would be a good experience for her to work up there. She wouldn't give me a phone number or an address. They didn't want her to be distracted, she said. When school started, Margaret still wasn't back."

"How did the Dykstras explain that?"

"What we heard was that Margaret wanted to try a boarding school out east. Then, one day in late September, she suddenly showed up in class again. The story was that she didn't like the boarding school."

"You knew what had happened. How did she seem to you?"

Mickey sipped her coffee and looked out the window. "Like a zombie. Likc her very soul had died."

"Did you talk with her about the baby?"

"I tried once. She told me that was over and done with and she never wanted to hear another word about it."

I don't like to do second-hand analysis, but I could see a personality type emerging. People who lie easily often can dissociate, convince themselves that some parts of their lives aren't really theirs. They can also repress emotions. But living like that for a long time can create as much stress as hard physical labor. Maybe Margaret really did have a heart attack the night she died.

"You said you lost contact with her."

"For a while. We drifted apart when we went to different colleges and became rather different people. Margaret was attracted to radical causes. She was angry at her father and took it out on the rest of the world. I think I've always been a soccer mom at heart, even before anybody knew what that was. We reconnected at our twentieth high school reunion, though, and talked a lot after that."

"Do you know if Margaret ever saw David Burton again?"

"Yes, she did. And she became very afraid of him."

Chapter 12

"Afraid of him? Was he threatening her?"

"Let me get another file." Mickey left the kitchen and returned in a couple of minutes with a thick folder and a disk. She laid them on the table but didn't offer them to me. "This is e-mail Margaret and I exchanged over the last few years before she died. My husband says I'm anal retentive. Maybe he's right, but I like to have records."

I almost gasped. Margaret in her own words, away from her family, talking to her closest friend since childhood! This could be a gold mine.

"The disk is a back-up," Mickey said. "You can take it with you."

"I appreciate that. Now, you said Margaret was back in touch with Burton. How did that happen? When?"

"It was about a year before she died. David actually contacted me first. He had called the alumni offices at some local colleges until he found the right one and got my address."

"What did he want?"

"He said he'd been going through a paternity suit. The child proved not to be his. He didn't have any children and was beginning to think he never would. That got him to thinking about Margaret and he wondered if, by any chance, she had gotten pregnant that night they spent together."

"Why didn't he just call Margaret?"

"He said he didn't know if she'd be willing to talk to him, since he ran out on her."

"So you told him Margaret had had a baby?"

"I thought he had the right to know he had a son somewhere," she said defensively. "I told him which adoption agency the baby had been taken to. That was all I knew. It was all Margaret knew."

"And then he called Margaret?"

"I gave him her private number at the plant. I shouldn't have, I know, but he's such a charmer, even over the phone."

Something he passed on to his son, I thought.

"Was Margaret angry at you for that?"

"A little at first. We talked and e-mailed. You'll see when you get into that disk. But she agreed to meet him for a drink. She told me she enjoyed being with him. He was the only man she'd ever slept with, the one person she could talk to about the most important moment in her life."

"But you said she was afraid of him."

"After they had met a couple of times he started unfolding his life story. He'd been in jail for a robbery, but he claimed he'd been in the car with a couple of guys and didn't know what they were planning until it was too late. He was having trouble getting on his feet because of his prison record. Margaret gave him a thousand dollars. He didn't want to take it, she said, but she insisted. A few weeks later he asked her for five thousand, so he could get an apartment and a car and hopefully a job. He said he wouldn't ask for any more."

I shook my head. "I can see this coming."

"Unfortunately, Margaret couldn't. She had a blind spot where this man was concerned, like she'd looked directly at the sun during an eclipse. I got an e-mail from her saying he wanted ten thousand. Here, this is the print-out." She turned to the back of her folder and pulled out the piece of paper.

Margaret's e-mail style was terse:

God, what an idiot I am! David wants 10K now. I told him no. He tried to sweet talk me. Said we made a baby together. We've got that bond. I told him the fact that we threw a few chromosomes together once doesn't entitle him to anything. The last thing he said to me was, "Just remember, I know where to find you." Mickey, what am I going to do?

The message was dated two weeks before Margaret's death.

"Did you hear from Burton after Margaret died?"

"No. That first phone call was my only contact with him."

"Do you have any idea where to find him?"

She shook her head. "There is an e-mail in here where Margaret forwarded me something he had said to her. She wanted me to see how nice he was." She pulled out the sheet. "It has his e-mail address on it. I don't know if that would be any help, after six years."

"I've searched for people with less information than this," I said to her. And usually been unsuccessful, I reminded myself.

"Is this going to cause Margaret's son any problems?" Mickey asked. "Would Burton have any kind of claim on him?"

"No, not since he's an adult. I'm not sure what all the legal ramifications might be. Burton never had a chance to waive his parental rights. But the statute of limitations on that ran out long ago. Still, he might make trouble for his son or for the Dykstras." Especially if he gets a whiff of a six-million-dollar trust fund.

"Have the Dykstras met the young man yet?"

"I took him to meet his grandmother on Friday. She was thrilled."

"That's great. I haven't seen her in years. I remember her as loving and a lot of fun. She was definitely *not* like my mother and the other Dutch women I knew. How about the rest of the family?"

"Let's just say the reception hasn't been as warm. In fact, if Edmund or Katherine happens to contact you, you probably shouldn't mention that you've talked to me."

She offered a refill on the coffee, which I accepted only to be polite. I just don't like hazelnut. "They always struck me," she said, "as a family that was going to blow up someday. I wouldn't have been surprised to see something awful about them in the paper. You know, one of those murder-suicide tragedies."

"I've gotten the sense that Mr. Dykstra—Margaret's father—was heavy-handed."

"He was a tyrant. Margaret used to call him Czar Cornelius the First."

I took a sip of my coffee and added a generous dollop of milk to kill the taste. "Was he physically abusive?"

"Not that I ever saw. He ruled by threats and intimidation. The first date Margaret or I had was in eighth grade. We arranged for one of the boys' fathers to pick us up at Margaret's house. I was going to spend the night there. When the poor guys came to the door, Mr. Dykstra made them come in, asked them all these questions about where we were going, told them he expected them to respect us and to have us home on time. Then he marched the four of us out to the car and talked with the father of Margaret's date. I was mortified, and he wasn't my father."

"Did that controlling tendency get worse after she had the baby?"

She nodded vigorously. "Definitely. I was surprised he didn't chain her in the basement after that."

"And yet he let her go to college at Wheaton, over in Illinois."

"They fought about that all through our junior year and into senior year. Her father wanted her to go to Calvin and live at home. Margaret told me she would run away if she had to stay here and go to college. She wanted to go to Berkeley or Columbia, someplace far away, in distance as well as outlook. I think her mother finally got Mr. Dykstra to compromise on Wheaton. It was—still is—Christian and very conservative."

All I knew about Wheaton College was that it had something to do with Billy Graham. Organized religion did not play a big part in my upbringing, although it flourished all around me as I was growing up. In my home town of Holland any corner that doesn't have a Reformed Church on it probably is occupied by a more conservative Christian Reformed Church. I had learned enough about the west Michigan varieties of Christianity to be able to speak the language with my clients, but I still felt out of place when people started talking about synods and the five points of Calvinism. I, for one, did not feel totally depraved. Well, maybe ... that first night I spent with Cal ...

I picked up the picture of the grinning, teenaged Margaret and David. "Could I take this picture?"

I could tell immediately that my request didn't sit well with Mickey. She reached out for the picture and I handed it to her.

"This was given to me as a kind of sacred trust," she said.

I was shameless. "I'm meeting with the Dykstras tomorrow morning. I'm sure it would mean a lot to them to see this."

"Let me scan it into the computer and print you off a couple of copies."

I followed her into a small office off the kitchen. While she scanned the picture and fiddled with the contrast and other features, I asked, "Did you and Margaret ever talk about how she felt about having her baby taken away from her?"

"The only time she ever opened up about that was when we were in college. Junior year, I think. We ran into one another over Christmas break and had lunch. There was a couple with a little boy at a table near ours, just about the age Margaret's son would have been. This little guy was adorable, and he was behaving perfectly. I could tell she was having a lot of trouble with it. That's when she told me her baby had been a boy and which agency he had been taken to. Then she said, 'My father took him away from me. Someday I'm going to take the thing he cherishes most away from him'."

"What do you think she meant by that?"

"His furniture company would be the thing he cherished most. But he intended for his children to have it, so I don't see how Margaret could have taken it away from him."

"She worked for the company, didn't she?" I asked.

"From the day she finished college till the day she died."

"Maybe she got over her bitterness somehow."

She looked at me over her shoulder. "You don't have any children, do you, Sarah?"

"No, I don't." As my mother constantly reminds me.

"If you did, you would know a woman could never get over something like that. It was tragic that Margaret was never reunited with her son."

I knew that wasn't entirely true, but explaining about the encounter between Margaret and Josh sounded like too much work. "Would you be willing to talk to him? I'm sure he would enjoy talking to someone who knew his mother as well as you did. And someone who had met his father."

"I'd love to. Give him my name and number."

"I will. His name is Josh Adams."

She turned around so fast she almost fell out of her chair. "*Josh Adams?*"

"That's right," I said, puzzling over her reaction. "Does that name mean something to you?"

"Only because it meant something to Margaret. She called me a couple of weeks before she died to say she'd gotten in touch with a young man who had drawn a picture of her house some years before. He was working at an ad agency in Kalamazoo and she had asked him to meet with her about doing some work for Dykstra Furniture. His name was Josh Adams."

Chapter 13

I left Mickey Bolthuis' house and drove a few blocks through the rabbit warren of cul-de-sacs. Once I was sure I remembered where the exit onto Wilson was, I pulled over to the curb. I wanted to make some notes of my conversation while it was still fresh in my mind. Another car passed me and turned left into the next cul-de-sac. I hadn't even been aware someone was behind me. I was still reeling from the mass of information Mickey had unloaded on me. And the questions it raised.

I opened the folder containing the picture of Margaret and David. What a huge piece of the puzzle of Josh's identity had just been handed to me! Tomorrow morning I would be able to show Josh his father. But not until he explained to me why he had neglected to mention that Margaret called him shortly before her death. How could he have sat there in my office, heard me tell him she was his mother, and not show some emotion? Was he playing me? I'm normally a calm, patient person, but if I find out somebody is jerking me around ...

And what should I do with the file of e-mails? Even if Josh could allay my new suspicions about him, I probably shouldn't turn them over to him without screening them first. There might be something else in them as disturbing in its own way as the message about Burton and the ten thousand dollars. Josh shouldn't learn who his father is and, at the same time, learn that he was threatening his mother.

All of this made me even more uneasy about the remaining piece of the puzzle—the original file on Josh's adoption. It had disappeared like that one piece of a jigsaw puzzle that falls on the floor and ends up under the sofa or in some other entirely unexpected place. Where was the blasted thing?

That question had been bothering me more than I wanted to admit. Michigan has no central location for adoption records. A file is kept in the Probate Court in the county where the adoption is finalized. A reliable agency—as I had always considered mine to be—is required to also have its own file. Maybe I had been slipshod in not keeping at it until I located the thing. I had never heard of anyone else at the agency missing a casefile.

What it came down to was this: if there had been a file on Josh Adams' adoption, it should still be there. If it wasn't, we were not only careless, we were in violation of state law. This was my case now, so that missing file felt like my responsibility.

I didn't want to face a long evening at home on such a gloomy day anyway, so I took a left on Wilson, got on I-196—also known as the Ford Freeway, for Gerald R., not Henry—and drove to the office. The parking lot, created by the demolition of an old building behind ours, was empty. Since it was starting to rain hard I parked in the RESERVED FOR DIRECTOR space, right next to the door. As I fumbled with the security lock I cursed the thing again.

When I started work here we had a simple, effective security system—a key and a lock. A couple of years ago somebody installed a state-of-the-art system. Now I had to punch a five-digit number into a keypad and wave a card over the side of the keypad. Problem is, I never have understood exactly which part of my card I'm supposed to wave over which part of the pad. I was on vacation when it was installed and got only a cursory explanation when I got back. I just keep waving the damn thing until the door clicks. Tonight, with my umbrella and the bag holding Cal's Red Wings plate in one hand, the whole business proved very cumbersome. After making sure the door locked behind me, I dropped Cal's plate in my office, picked a ring of keys off their hook under Joan's desk, and headed for our storage room.

We occupy the first two floors of a nice older building downtown. Some generous benefactor did the place up right when the agency moved in here eight years ago. Our main suite of offices and two conference rooms are on the first floor. The staff lounge, the storage room, our accounting department, and some more potential office space take up the second floor. There's an elevator between the two floors, but I rarely use it. Stairs are great exercise. And on a weekend, with no one else in the building, I didn't want to risk getting stuck in the elevator. I'm not claustrophobic. I just don't like the idea of being stuck somewhere—not even in my own apartment—for hours.

The storage room is about 15'x20', lined with shelves and four-drawer filing cabinets. In the center of the room sits a work table and several old-fashioned, heavy chairs. The place has an interesting smell, a combination of musty old paper and baby powder. The shelves are where we keep supplies for the babies we place with foster or adoptive parents. We have an endowed fund we can draw on for those supplies. That fund also allows us to keep a couple of pediatric nurses on call in case one of our babies needs extra care. One common reason for a birth mother to give up her baby for adoption is a medical problem the birth mother just doesn't feel she can cope with.

Josh's family's file should have been in one of the drawers in the cabinet with the other 'A' files. When Josh first contacted the agency, my secretary and I had plowed through all four drawers of that cabinet, looking in between and under files, making sure Josh's hadn't slipped down to the bottom of a drawer or gotten mixed in with another case. There were several other Adamses. As I looked at the fifteen remaining cabinets—my agency is sixty years old—I wondered if it was worth the effort to do that thorough a search of all sixty drawers. I unlocked a couple of drawers at random and skimmed the labels on the folders. Everything seemed to be in perfect order.

Could Josh's file be under another name? That didn't make sense. His family was named Adams when they adopted him. The birth certificate showed that. And they were still named Adams. They hadn't gone into the Witness Protection Program.

So, where the hell was that file?

All the file cabinets were kept locked, as state law required. The small keys on the ring from under Joan's desk were numbered to match the numbers on the cabinets. I walked around the room, opening a drawer here and there and looking through the files, as though the very one I was searching for would just pop up. Two of the cabinets sat on either side of a closet door. I'd never had occasion to look in that closet.

I tried the doorknob and found it locked. There were only half a dozen door-sized keys on the ring, so it didn't take me long to find the one that opened the closet door. Even as the key turned in the lock, my instinct was telling me not to open the door, just like you want to yell at a character in a movie, 'Don't open the door!'

But my instinct seemed to have been out of whack ever since Josh walked into my office, so why should I listen to it now? I opened the door, just like the people in the movies always do. They have to because it's in the script. I didn't have even that good a reason.

I found myself staring into the darkness of a decent-sized closet. The closets in my apartment should only be this large. I stepped into it and pulled the chain on the overhead light. Aside from a few cleaning supplies and an old, free-standing coat rack, the only thing in the closet was ... another locked file cabinet.

I wondered if one of the small keys on the ring I was holding would open this cabinet. A few of them did not have numbers, and this cabinet had no number. But would someone go to this much trouble to put the thing out of sight and then leave the key where anybody could pick it up? There was only one way to find out.

The fourth little key did the trick. My breathing quickened as I began thumbing through the files in the top drawer, just reading labels. I didn't want to be accused of prying into things that weren't any of my business. All I wanted was the file for the case I was working on. I had a right to that. The top drawer seemed to be financial records and correspondence of past directors of the agency. I deliberately did not look at any of it.

The second drawer seemed to hold a hodge-podge of files, some with family names on them, others with correspondence. And there, right in the middle, was the file for 'Adams, Matthew and Allison'. But it had been stapled all around the edges so it couldn't be opened. Across the front and back someone had written in large red letters: To Be Opened by Director Only.

This is the place in the movie where the villain—the creepy lord of some Gothic manor—suddenly appears behind me and, in his Bela Lugosi accent, says something like, 'Did you find what you were looking for, my dear?' He would be courteous, acting as though I was doing nothing wrong, snooping where I clearly had no business being. But the audience would know, from that moment on, I was doomed. I would soon be found hanging from a meat hook, or worse.

I took a deep breath and gave myself a little talking-to. *Any time you're in a place by yourself, you can feel spooked. That's all it is. No villain's going to creep up behind you.*

It didn't help. I couldn't shake the feeling somebody was watching me. That didn't stop me from taking Josh's file, though.

I locked the file cabinet and the closet door and started toward the stairs. They open onto the first floor near the back entrance to our offices, the door I had come in. Leading from the back door I could see several wet footprints on the concrete floor. Were they mine? Wouldn't my prints have dried by now? Had someone else come in?

"Hello!" I called. Silence.

I went to the back door and looked out through the glass panel. Mine was still the only car in the parking lot. I decided to assume these were my footprints. Maybe that would stop my heart from beating so fast.

Chapter 14

I returned the key ring to its place under Joan's desk. Then I went to my office, laid the file on my desk and sat there, looking at it, while I debated what I ought to do.

Open the file? In spite of an unmistakable warning that it not be opened? Once I popped those staples loose, there would be no way to disguise what I had done. And I couldn't say I didn't know I wasn't supposed to open it.

But I felt I had to know what was in the file and why someone didn't want it opened. One piece of paper in it had gotten caught in the staples at one end of the file. Lifting the edge of the file ever so gently, I could see it was an old piece of agency letterhead. What if that page and the rest of the file contained information relevant to our meeting with the trust fund lawyer tomorrow morning?

The only way I could legitimately get that information was to show the file to Connie and ask her to open it in her capacity as director. But she was on her way home from a trip and I wouldn't see her until late tomorrow morning, after the meeting with the lawyer.

I decided to call Cynthia. She had done adoptee searches before I took over the job. I was originally hired to do general counseling, but I started working with Cynthia whenever she had too many cases on her hands. When Cynthia was fired, two years ago—for reasons I never fully understood—I was moved into her job. We had talked a few times since she left, but not in several months.

Her husband answered and called her to the phone.

"Cynthia, I hope I'm not disturbing you."

"No, Sarah, not at all. What's wrong? You sound scared."

"'Uneasy' might be a better word. I'm working on an adoptee reunion. Nothing has felt entirely right about it from the first day."

"What do you mean?"

"Just let me walk you through what I've done. Tell me if you think I've botched anything."

"Okay."

"To begin with, I couldn't find the man's file."

"That should have raised a big red flag."

Great. Anybody with experience at this job should have been on high alert while I was sleeping at the switch.

"Did you go through the files in the storage room?"

"Yes. That turned up nothing."

"Did you check the Probate Court that finalized the adoption?"

"No, I didn't."

"That should have been your next step."

I cringed. Strike two. "I know, but the adoptee, Josh Adams, had found enough in his parents' papers for me to go on. I have a heavy case load right now, so I didn't take the time."

The long pause from Cynthia was more effective than any lecture. We follow procedures in this job. We don't take short cuts. This is what happens when we do take short cuts.

"What sort of information did he have?" she asked.

"Letters from our agency and his amended birth certificate."

"That should have led you to the original birth certificate."

"It did."

"And you checked to see if the birth mom had filed an FIA consent form in the Central Adoption Registry."

"I did. And she had."

"Good. Had Josh or his adoptive parents filed a form?"

"No. Josh said he'd never heard of the Registry."

"That's no surprise. The state never has publicized it enough. But it sounds like you've done everything you could, even without the original file. So, what are you uneasy about?"

"I found the file, just a few minutes ago."

"I thought you said ..."

"It was in a locked cabinet in a locked closet in the storage room."

"Oh yeah. 'Bluebeard's Closet'."

"Is that what it's called?"

"Just my personal joke. How did you get in there?"

"The keys are on the ring under Joan's desk."

She whistled softly. "I'm betting that's a mistake. That file contains stuff the Director doesn't want anybody messing with. It was in Connie's office until she got all her new designer furniture."

"That must have been before I was hired."

"Just a few months before, I think. Connie moved that file cabinet out because it didn't fit with her new décor." The sarcasm level in her tone began to rise. "She wanted a ficus in that corner. What else was in the file?"

"Mostly financial stuff and correspondence. There were just a couple of files with families' names on them. But none of them looked like this."

"What's different about this one?"

"It's stapled shut and has TO BE OPENED BY DIRECTOR ONLY across it in big red letters." I traced the letters with my index finger.

"Then I wouldn't open it."

"I'm not going to. I don't need to, really. I've found his mother."

"Don't tell me her name, since I'm not with the agency any more."

"I think I have to tell, so you can appreciate how important this is. Her name is Margaret Dykstra."

"My God!" Cynthia sounded almost panic-stricken. "Have you told anybody?"

"I took Josh to meet his grandmother on Friday."

"Oh, geez, Sarah! Tell me you're joking."

I tried to sound innocent. "Why? What's the matter?"

"Does Connie know about this?"

"No. She's at a conference and visiting orphanages in Hawaii. She gets back tonight."

"You might as well start cleaning out your desk."

I sat up straight. "Why?"

"Messing with the Dykstras was what got me fired."

I never had known the full story behind her departure. "What do you mean?"

"A few months before I was let go I got a call from a man asking about Margaret Dykstra's son."

I gasped. "Was his name David Burton?"

"Yes, it was. How did you know?"

"I talked to a friend of Margaret's this afternoon. She knew the whole story and had a picture of Burton. He's the biological father. Did he give you an address or a phone number?"

"No, but I used *69. He called from The Art Place."

"The Art Place?"

"It's an artists' co-op ..."

"I know the place. I was there Friday. I just don't understand why David Burton would call from there."

"He was using a pay phone in the building."

That didn't satisfy me. "How did that call get you fired?"

"I talked to Connie about it right after I got the call. She said I should forget I ever got it. Under no circumstances was I to pursue the inquiry."

I picked at staples on Josh's file. "Why would she tell you that?"

"Money, that's why. The Dykstras have been major contributors to the agency for years. For instance, when we moved into our nice new offices, we got nice new Dykstra furniture. We can get just about anything we want from them. All we have to do is ask. And Connie has asked for a lot during her time as director."

"So you think their generosity is a bribe?"

"Even better. A tax-deductible bribe. They want to make sure the agency isn't going to help Margaret's illegitimate son claim his place in their precious family. I don't really understand why it matters so much to them. Who cares about that kind of thing today?"

I knew the reason they didn't want Margaret's son to suddenly reappear had something to do with the trust fund, but I decided to keep that crucial bit of information to myself for the time being. If Josh didn't get it, it went to The Art Place, so I couldn't see what the Dykstras would gain by denying it to him. "You say they're big contributors. But I don't recall seeing them at fund-raising dinners or the golf outing."

"They keep a low profile. Whenever the family's name comes up in the agency, it's like there's some kind of force field surrounding them. Questions just bounce off. I asked Ellison in accounting if he could give me a rough estimate of how much they've contributed over the years. He said I didn't have any need to know that. Then he ratted to Connie. That was one more nail in my coffin."

"I didn't realize this was going to create such a mess. I thought I was just doing my job." A touch of desperation crept into my voice.

"You were. But it sounds like you've violated the prime directive in the process. You mentioned the grandmother. How far have you gone in connecting him to the family?"

"His grandmother's the only one he's met. I've talked with his uncle and aunt, or been talked to by them, to be more exact. They are not going to be as welcoming as the grandmother has been."

"Well, don't throw away the Help-wanted ads from today's paper. You'll be looking for a job soon, I'm afraid."

"Do you really think that phone call about Margaret Dykstra's child was what got you fired?"

"Telling Connie about it was what got me fired. She ordered me never to mention the name Dykstra again, and not to do any kind of search for Margaret's child."

"Did you search?"

"Let's just say I poked around enough to learn she had put a consent form in the Central Adoption Registry. Somehow Connie found out I'd done that. She started finding fault with my work. My next performance evaluation was lousy, and soon I was out of a job."

"How can she do that? She must know the law. An adult adoptee has the right to search for his birth parents. If a birth parent has filed a consent form, or if the parent is deceased, the adoptee is entitled to know identifying information."

I had to take my hand off of Josh's file to resist temptation. If I was going to lose my job anyway, I might as well open it. But if I had any chance of keeping my job, the last thing I wanted to do was open something that had been sealed like a pharaoh's tomb. All that was missing was the curse.

"Sarah, you're preaching to the choir. But this is bigger than the law. This is the Dykstra family's reputation. They'll do anything to protect themselves. And they're a lot better at it than we are."

I slumped in my chair. The words of a victim of the Dykstras' wrath scared me more than veiled threats from the Dykstras themselves. What had I gotten myself into? "You're probably right. Thanks for the heads-up."

"Glad to do it. I'm afraid you've stepped into the same pool of quicksand I did. I hope you can get out of it before it sucks you under, like it did me. Or maybe your guy Cal will come swinging in on a vine to rescue you, like in those old Tarzan movies."

"I'm afraid Cal has swung off to look for another Jane."

"Oh, Sarah, I'm sorry. When did that happen?"

"Three months ago."

"What ... ?"

"I'd rather not get into it right now, Cynthia. If you don't mind."

"Sure. Let's get together for lunch sometime and bash him around."

"Sounds like fun. I'll give you a call."

After we hung up I picked up Josh's file and turned it over in my hands. To get a better look I turned on my desk lamp. If I could get a really slender tool, like a nail file, and just straighten out the bent parts of the staples without removing the entire staples from their holes, I could reseal it by lining the staples up with the original holes and bending them back. I would only have to do one of the short ends to be able to slip the pages out. It would be tedious, but it might work. Maybe I'd better practice on a folder I stapled together myself, though. I would do that when I got home.

I wasn't ready to leave. Cynthia's comments about the Dykstras' financial support of the agency had piqued my curiosity about what else might be in that locked cabinet. Did this family of model citizens hold my agency as tightly in their clutches as they had The Art Place? Other files in that cabinet weren't sealed. No one would know if I looked at them. This would be my only chance to do it.

Listening for footsteps or any sign that someone else was in the building, I walked quickly to Joan's desk and retrieved the keys. An urge to forget all this nonsense and just go home swept over me. The gloom that had hung over the city all day was slowly deepening into evening and oozing into the building. The light shining in my office—the only light in our suite—suddenly stood out like a beacon. I went back and turned off my overhead light, leaving just the desk lamp on. I didn't bother to pick up my bag or Josh's file.

I had gotten to the stairs when I sensed more than heard what I thought was somebody else moving. I stopped and called out. "Hello? Is anyone there?"

That's really a stupid question. What if a voice said, 'No, there's no one here'?

I was letting my nerves get the better of me. *Don't spook yourself, girl.*

The footprints I had noticed earlier in the stairwell were barely visible now. I trotted up the stairs to the storage room. Opening the closet, I stepped into it and unlocked the file cabinet again. In the top drawer were several thick files relating to our endowed funds. As I pulled out the first file, the closet door closed behind me.

"What the ... ?"

Then I heard a thump. Something was pushed against the door.

Chapter 15

"Hey! What are you doing? Let me out of here!"

I pounded on the door and threw my shoulder against it. It wouldn't budge.

"Come on! This isn't funny!" I didn't think it was intended to be.

I glanced at the bottom of the door and saw the light in the storage room go off. Pressing my ear to the door, I couldn't detect any sound. Was I alone or was the person who locked me in here still lurking on the other side of the door?

I felt my anger giving way to panic. "Please open the door! Come on!"

I threw my shoulder against the door again. It didn't give, but my shoulder felt like it had. The door was old and solid, not a new hollow one.

I grabbed my shoulder in pain. "Okay. Stay calm. That's your top priority. Stay calm."

I took a few deep breaths and tried to center myself as I looked around the closet. My mother says that, even as a child, I had the ability to go into a calming kind of trance in difficult moments. No one taught me. I seemed to do it instinctively.

"Assess your situation," I told myself. "What's the worst that can happen? You're going to miss supper and have to spend the night in here. The custodians won't be in tonight since it's Sunday, but somebody will be here by eight in the morning. You'll get a lousy night's sleep and have to pee in the corner. You'll be uncomfortable and have a lot to explain in the morning, but you've got light, so you're going to make it."

But what if the person who locked you in here comes back? Maybe they've got something else in mind. I pounded on the door again, harder and louder.

"Can anybody hear me? I'm locked in the closet! Help!"

I slumped to the floor, my back against the file cabinet. At least the floor was carpeted.

Who would do this? Who knew I was here? Had somebody been following me? How did they get in the building after me? Was it somebody who had access to the building? Or was it somebody who was already in the building? Had I stumbled across somebody engaged in something underhanded?

I wanted to cry. But that would mean I was accepting the situation, and I wasn't going to let myself do that. I could at least make an effort to get out of here. I started looking for an escape route.

"Start at the top and work down." That's what my mother always told me when I was cleaning the house. I examined the closet ceiling. It looked solid. There was a third floor to the building, so there was no access to an attic. When the storage room and the rest of our space had been remodeled, a drop ceiling was installed, but not in this closet.

I picked up one of the brooms and poked at the ceiling anyway, just in case there was a hole or a weak spot concealed behind the plaster and lath. No luck. The walls of my little prison went all the way up to the original ceiling. There were no old vents. Everything was solid.

I began examining the walls of the closet. I tapped here and there, looking for a hollow space. Maybe something had been covered up when the building was remodeled. I had watched Cal locate wall studs when we were hanging some pictures. He could hear a difference of some kind just by tapping, like my dad could, but I couldn't pick it out. Even if I could find a hollow space, what would I do? Punch a hole in the wall with my fist? What good would that do? I had broken a board in a tae kwon do class once, but that exercise didn't seem to prepare me for this situation. And the board had taken me two tries.

"Okay, take a different approach. What have I got in here that I could use to get out?"

The brooms standing in the corner didn't give me any quick ideas beyond a flashback to 'The Sorcerer's Apprentice' in *Fantasia*. They might prove useful, though, if somebody decided to come in after me. And I did notice a bucket behind them. At least I wouldn't have to pee on the floor.

The old coat rack looked more promising. It was tall and solid. I put my arms around it and tried to heft it and point it at the door, like a knight's lance. If I could get some momentum behind it, I might bust the door open, but I couldn't even get it completely parallel to the floor. I had no room to maneuver the thing. The couple of puny taps I managed to give the heavy old door didn't even scratch it. And because of the file cabinet, I didn't have enough room to launch a kick that would have any punch behind it.

What if I could tip the file cabinet against the door? It was heavy enough that it might knock the door open. But it was also heavy enough that I couldn't move it. I couldn't get any of the drawers all the way out because the closet was too shallow and the drawers too long. If the door were open, I could take the drawers out. Can you spell Catch-22?

A few more minutes of pounding and yelling made it clear I was going to be here all night. Waiting for people to come to work tomorrow morning was looking more and more like my only option. By eight o'clock—fourteen hours by my watch—somebody would be coming up here to put lunches in the refrigerator in the staff lounge next door.

"Well, I came up here to look at some files. At least I'm not going to be disturbed."

I started with a few of the thinner files—correspondence between previous directors and some big-name donors, that sort of thing. Several of them mentioned they had been encouraged by one of the Dykstras to include the agency in their charitable giving.

"I hope you realize," one of them said, "what an untiring friend you have in Cornelius Dykstra."

I finally pulled out one of the thick files, labeled FOUNDLING FUND, the agency's biggest endowed funds. I regularly requisitioned money from it—line 1006—to help foster and adoptive parents buy supplies for their children.

The file contained mostly letters from donors to the fund and copies of letters to them. Not all of them mentioned the amount of the contributions, but, just counting the ones that said "enclosed please find my check in the amount of" or "thank you for your contribution of", there had to be a couple of million dollars in the fund. And the latest letter in this file was from five years ago. Connie must have the more recent ones in her office.

Then, at the back of the file, I hit paydirt. There was a letter from Cornelius Dykstra himself, dated three months after Josh's birth, and a copy of the instrument establishing the foundling fund. He had put up an initial five hundred thousand dollars and promised to urge his friends and business associates to add to that sum. But he didn't want his participation publicized. "As we discussed earlier, I prefer to remain inconspicuous in this matter, and I hope you and your agency understand how important it is that you respect my wishes."

If you were to look up 'veiled threat' in the dictionary, you might find that sentence as an example. But why was the old man doing this? Was Cynthia right? Was he just bribing the agency that helped him dispose of an unwanted grandson?

I try to be optimistic and attribute good motives to people. Cal used to kid me about being naïve. Maybe Cornelius Dykstra set up the fund out of guilt over the way he discarded his grandson. It could have been his way of trying to care for those babies the way he hoped Margaret's baby was cared for. Maybe there had been a beating heart under the stone exterior.

The instrument establishing the fund was short and to the point, as legal documents go. I actually understood most of it. The fund's primary purpose was to provide supplies for the babies in our care. Our foster parents can pick up supplies as needed, and adoptive parents can rely on the fund for the first six months after a child is placed. If the child has special needs, the adoptive parents can get supplies and counseling through the fund indefinitely.

That all looked above board. But then I noticed a clause right at the end of the description of the Fund. As long as the needs of the children were met, it said, the excess income from the fund could be used "for other purposes deemed appropriate by the Director of the agency".

Moment of epiphany. "I'll be damned. It's a giant slush fund."

I did some quick figuring. I could document a minimum of two and a half million dollars donated to the fund, as of five years ago. Some of it went back thirty years. How much interest had that earned? Assume another million in it by now. If it returned six percent a year, that would be over two hundred thousand dollars. I don't spend more than five thousand a year out of that. Factor in the other caseworkers handling adoptions, and we still wouldn't top twenty thousand in necessary expenses for the children in our care. That covered everything from diapers for the infants to counseling sessions for some of the older children in foster care.

And the rest of it? Connie could spend that any way she jolly well pleased, like on a two-week trip to attend a conference and visit orphanages in Hawaii

Chapter 16

A copier! A copier! My kingdom for a copier!

For the next few hours I had to make do with taking notes on the backs of whatever pages from the files seemed least important. I hadn't written this much by hand since I learned to type in eighth grade.

I was taking a break to get some circulation back into my hand when I heard a woman's voice call, "Hello? Ms. DeGraaf? Are you here? Hello!"

The sound was so faint I figured she was in the hallway and the door to the storage room was closed. I doubled up my fist and pounded for all I was worth.

"Help! I'm in here! In the storage room!"

I jumped up and down when I saw the light come on under the closet door.

"Over here! Please!"

I heard a scraping sound, followed by the glorious sensation of the door swinging open.

"Oh, thank God!" I grabbed the hand of a young woman in a nurse's uniform—white pants and top, a floral print tunic over them.

"Are you Ms. DeGraaf?"

"Yes. And I can't tell you how glad I am to see you ... But who are you?" I'd never seen her before. I wanted to reach behind me and grab one of the brooms for protection.

"I'm Ann Haveman. I'm the new pediatric nurse. I just started a few weeks ago, so we haven't met."

"Oh, yes. I saw your name in a memo." I breathed deeply and leaned against the door frame. "Sorry we have to meet under such odd circumstances."

She wrinkled her nose as if to say that 'odd' didn't begin to describe this situation. "How did you get in there? Why was the chair up against the door?"

"Those are questions I can't answer right now."

I hugged her because I needed the reassurance. Maybe she wasn't real. Maybe I was still in the closet and just hallucinating. But she felt solid enough. "You are truly a sight as welcome as any angel, Ann. But what are you doing here? Why were you calling my name?"

She gave me the 'duh' look. For people under twenty-five it's part of their native language. The rest of us can learn it, but never without an accent. "Because you called me and said some foster parents with a special needs baby wanted some help. You asked me to meet you here to talk with them."

"When did you get that call?"

"About six. You asked me to be here at eight."

"I didn't call you, Ann."

"Well, who did?"

"The same person who locked me in the closet, I'm sure."

"Why did somebody lock you in there? Shouldn't we call the police?" She pulled a cell phone out of her pocket.

I put my hand on hers. "No. It's all very complicated. Let's just say somebody is playing a practical joke."

"It's a pretty lame one, if you ask me."

"Well, they didn't try to hurt me. I think it would be better if you didn't say anything about this. I don't want to be known around the office as somebody who can't take a little teasing." I started gathering up the papers I had been making notes on and locked the filing cabinet and the closet door.

"You mean there's no foster parents bringing a baby in?"

"No, there's not."

The 'duh' look again. "But I'm supposed to get reimbursed for mileage and stuff whenever I come in." She put her hands on her hips in exasperation. Something about her in that pose struck me as vaguely familiar, but I had never met her before, so I must be kidding myself.

"Just send me your 1209. I'll approve it."

"Okay. Thanks." With that problem solved, she turned to leave.

"Hey, Ann," I called after her, "when you came in, did you see anything unusual? Was there anyone else around?"

"No. There was just one car in the parking lot."

"A red Honda?"

"An old one, yeah."

At least I wouldn't have to walk home. "Where did you go when you came inside?"

"I went to your office first. The door was open and your light was on."

"My light? You mean the desk lamp?"

"Yeah, that too, but your overhead light was on."

"Oh, shit! The folder."

"I didn't see a folder..."

She was talking to my back. "Thanks, Ann. Nice to meet you," I threw over my shoulder as I hurried down the stairs and back to my office. There sat my bag, with my wallet and cell phone still in it. The bag that served as a kind of urn for the remains of Cal's broken Red Wings plate was beside it, right where I had left it.

But Josh's folder was gone.

Chapter 17

All the way home I shook like I had a fever. I couldn't stop myself. Adrenalin and curiosity had kept me going while I was locked in the closet. Now I could feel myself imploding, like a building that's being demolished, with charges planted around it in strategic places. I hoped I got home before I collapsed completely. The rain started again, even heavier than it had been in the morning. I hate driving in the rain at night, especially when a car insisted on staying on my tail.

As soon as I got in my apartment I locked both doors, closed all the blinds and curtains, and turned on every light in the place. Then I curled up on the sofa and cried it out.

I wanted somebody to talk to. No, I wanted Cal to talk to. I got out my cell phone, then stopped myself. There was no way on earth I could call him now. He had made it abundantly clear he wasn't interested in resuming our relationship, and I wasn't going to keep playing damsel in distress to his white knight.

I could work this out on my own. Just think it through.

Whoever locked me in the closet took Josh's file. That was the first fundamental assumption I was sure of. And if I kept on pursuing this connection between Josh and the Dykstra family, I was asking for bigger trouble. That was the second assumption I had to work on. I was pretty sure of that one, too.

Locking me in the closet was a warning. They hadn't intended to hurt me. Not this time. That's why somebody had called Ann Haveman to let me out. They used my name and they knew Ann, even though she'd just started with us, so it had to be someone connected with the agency. Just knowing that would make going in to work tomorrow difficult. If Ann kept her word and didn't say anything to anyone, there would be only three of us in the office who knew about this incident—Ann, me and the person on the other side of that door.

But how could anybody have known I was in the office tonight? I hadn't planned the trip in advance. I hadn't said a word to anybody about going down there. Had somebody come in by coincidence and realized what I was doing? Or was somebody watching me? Are they after me?

"God, I sound like Mel Gibson in 'Conspiracy Theory'!" *But he was right. Somebody* was *after him.*

I looked again at the phone in my hand. My right index finger moved of its own accord to the first digit of Cal's number. Then it hit me—the person who took Josh's file must have called Ann Haveman at almost that same time. She said she got the call at six. Could that call have been made from my phone? Had I already ruined any fingerprints that might be on it?

Setting the phone down on the kitchen counter, I leaned over to put my ear next to it and pushed the redial button with my fingernail. As the phone rang I tried to think what I would say if Ann Haveman answered it. I should have planned this a little better.

"This is the DeGraaf residence," my father said.

"Oh, hi, Dad." I had called my parents yesterday evening.

"Hey, hon. This is a pleasant surprise. Or is something wrong? You sound a little shaky."

"No, I'm fine." I picked up the phone and forced myself to sound casual. "Actually, this is a little embarrassing. I ... hit the wrong button on my speed dial."

"Oh, so calling your old Mom and Dad is just a mistake, huh?" I could hear his smile as he said it.

"I don't mean it to sound like that, Dad."

"Don't worry about it. At least we're on your speed dial."

"What are you doing tonight?"

"We're playing bridge with Greg and Eden, so unless you've got something urgent on your mind, I'll 'bid' you a good evening."

"Good one, Dad. I'll talk to you soon. Love to Mom."

So, the call wasn't made from my cell phone. Tomorrow morning I would check my office phone. I was sure the person who made the call would want it to come from a phone connected with me, in case someone did check.

I poured myself a glass of white wine and wished for once that I kept harder stuff around. Maybe I had some cough syrup.

As the wine and some deep breathing helped me calm down, I

found myself standing over my phone, which was lying on the kitchen counter again. I couldn't call Cal, but maybe he had called me some time this afternoon. I picked up the phone and checked my messages. I had only one and it wasn't from Cal.

"Sarah," a woman's voice said, "this is Geri Murphy, Cal's partner. He gave me your number. I'd like to talk to you about something. It's not police business. If you could call me at home, I'd appreciate it. My number is 555-7171."

The call had come in about seven. I decided to go ahead and return it. If I was going to catch her at home, Sunday evening was the most likely time. I wanted to clear things up right away. Surely, if she and Cal talked about their personal lives at all, she knew that I wouldn't be interested.

But I needed to talk to somebody. Anybody.

Geri's low-key, almost sultry, greeting gave me an image of her draped over a bed or a cushion on a bearskin rug. "Hey, Sarah! Thanks for getting back to me so soon. When I thought about the message I left you, I was afraid you might take it the wrong way."

"'The wrong way'? What do you mean?"

"I figured Cal told you about me. He's talked a lot about you and how much he loves you."

"Then why did he leave me?"

"That's a longer conversation than we have time for now, girlfriend. Anyway, the reason I called is that guy Cal was fingerprinting yesterday." Now she sounded all business, like she was sitting at a desk, maybe with her computer in front of her.

"Do you know him?"

"No. After you left Cal mentioned he might be Margaret Dykstra's son. Boy, did that get my attention."

Damn Cal! The man always checked, last thing before he went out the door, to see that his fly was zipped. Why couldn't he do the same with his lip? Until we established Josh's link to the Dykstras beyond a doubt, I didn't want this story spread all over town. The Dykstras seemed to have connections everywhere. They were probably heavy contributors to the Police Benevolent Fund.

"What's your interest in this situation?" I asked Geri.

"First, I was one of the uniforms who responded to the call when Margaret's body was found."

She had me hooked. All she had to do was reel me in.

"Then, two years ago, just after I made detective, I was over at my mother's house in Zeeland when her book group was meeting there. One of the ladies, Denise van Putten, used to be Margaret's secretary. She said she hoped I could find out what actually did happen to Margaret."

"Is there reason to think it was anything other than a stroke or an accident?"

"I didn't see anything unusual that morning in her office. The custodian who found her hadn't disturbed the scene."

"What about the bruise on her head? Who decided that that resulted from hitting her desk when she fell?"

"The detectives and the M. E. on the scene."

"So there were no signs of a struggle?"

"No. I went back and read the file after Denise said what she did, and I read it again and looked at the photos of the scene yesterday to refresh my memory. I still don't see anything I would call suspicious, but it might be worthwhile to talk to Denise. Would you like to be there when I do?"

"Is that proper procedure? I don't want to get you in trouble." No sense spreading whatever plague I'd contracted to anyone else.

"This will be strictly off-duty. My mom invited Denise over for some dessert and coffee tomorrow evening. I thought we could chat."

* * * *

If I was going to talk to someone who knew Margaret, I decided, I should get better acquainted with her myself. Since I was too edgy to sleep, I got out the disk of Margaret's e-mail that Mickey Bolthuis gave me and proceeded to do some electronic eavesdropping.

Two hours later I had come to the conclusion that Margaret was a very cautious person. Even with her best friend since childhood she rarely let her guard down on a keyboard. From several references to phone conversations I gathered she was more open in that medium. I wondered if the anal-retentive Mickey kept tapes or transcripts of those calls.

On one occasion Margaret did apologize to Mickey for calling in the middle of the night when she'd been stopped for DUI and her car had been impounded:

I couldn't call home under those circumstances. I hope my lawyer can hush the thing up. Thanks again for coming to get me and for covering for me with my mother. I probably didn't sound very grateful at the time. I've been told I'm a mean drunk. I hope I didn't say anything you can't forgive.

The only message that shed any light on her attraction to David Burton was one from him that Margaret forwarded to Mickey with her comments:

I know you have doubts about David, even though you're the one who put us back in touch. I just wanted you to hear in his own words why he makes me so happy. Here's his latest note:

My darling Maggie,
It felt so good—no, so right—to be with you again last night. In all the years we've been apart I've never been happy when I was with someone else. From what you said, I don't think you have been either. Do you believe in Fate? Kismet? Destiny? By whatever name, I think it's what links us.

The man could dish out the treacle. It must have turned rancid in Margaret's mouth when he started hitting her up for money.

Chapter 18

I didn't sleep much better than if I had been curled up on the carpet in that damn closet, but at ten minutes before nine the next morning I was parking in front of the strip mall where attorney J. Spencer McKenzie's office was located. In my briefcase I carried the information I needed to verify Josh's relationship to Margaret Dykstra and the picture of Margaret and David Burton. I wished I knew whose briefcase Josh's file was in.

A week ago I would have said this was the end of my responsibilities in this case. Just introduce Josh to his new family and let them take it from there. Now I knew I would not be satisfied until I found out what happened to Margaret Dykstra. I also had to find Josh's file and the person who locked me in that closet. And I wasn't going to say anything about that to Mrs. Dykstra or to Josh until I understood his role in this whole business better.

At least the sun was shining. That and the cinnamon latté I was sipping made the beginning of the day bearable.

From the outside McKenzie's office didn't suggest walnut-lined conference rooms and leather chairs, the kinds of trappings I visualize when I hear the word 'lawyer'. The strip mall itself was located across the road from a Wal-Mart. Two names were stenciled on the law-office door: McKenzie's and S. K. Martin. On the whole it looked like the kind of place where you'd find an insurance salesman's office, and a not particularly successful one at that. I hoped McKenzie wasn't the legal profession's version of Willy Loman.

I didn't see a Mercedes or a Lexus in the parking lot. The only other vehicles in sight were an aging mini-van and several cars only slightly newer than mine. As I was taking the inventory, a car with tinted windows pulled in and parked at the other end of the lot. The driver stayed in the car, pulled out his cell phone, and made a call.

I was about to decide there was something familiar about the guy when Josh and his grandmother drove up and parked a few spaces down from me, blocking my view of the car with the tinted windows. It was exactly nine o'clock. That was late for Josh, but obviously he had picked up his grandmother. Give him some extra credit for that. I should have thought to do it. In my own defense, I had had a few distractions since the last time I saw Mrs. Dykstra.

I studied them as he opened her door and she put her arm through his for support. She was wearing a blue suit with a white blouse, a classic style but beginning to look a bit dated. Josh was wearing something I'd never seen on him—a tie, with a sport coat.

The pleasure and comfort Mrs. Dykstra derived from him couldn't be missed. I tried to detect—even imagine—any resemblance between them, but nothing stood out. Of course, the face of a thirty-year-old man and that of a woman in her late seventies probably wouldn't show any obvious similarities. Big noses or ears didn't seem to be Dykstra family traits. At least now I knew where he got those eyes. But what else did I *not* know about him?

I got out of my car to greet them.

"Good morning, Sarah," Mrs. Dykstra said. "Isn't it a lovely day?"

Josh just nodded. He handed Mrs. Dykstra her cane and tugged at his tie like a man waiting for the trap door to drop.

"Now, stop that," Mrs. Dykstra said. Then she turned to me. "When the dear boy came to pick me up this morning, he was wearing jeans and a plaid shirt and an old jacket. I told him that just wouldn't do for a meeting like this."

From the looks of the place, I thought it would do fine.

She went on, as lonely old women can do when they have someone to actually listen to them. "I couldn't think of any place that would be open this morning where we could get him a coat and tie in time. Then I saw all the cars at Wal-Mart and I asked Josh if they sold men's clothes. I've never been in one, you see."

"And I buy my clothes at consignment shops or the Goodwill Store," Josh put in.

"Let's not broadcast that," Mrs. Dykstra said. "Anyway, we went in—it's quite an amazing place—and we found him a decent sport coat, a shirt and a tie. I couldn't get him out of his jeans, though." She put her hand to her mouth and blushed. "Oh, my! That didn't come out the way I meant it."

"I'm sure you wouldn't be the first woman to try," I said. "You look nice, Josh."

"Thanks." He tugged at his tie again. "Sorry, I'm just not used to wearing one of these things."

"So, have you two been talking over the weekend?"

Mrs. Dykstra patted my arm. "Yes, we have, dear. I called Josh yesterday and we talked for quite a while. Are you sure the fingerprints satisfied you?"

I hung my head apologetically. "I hope you can understand, Mrs. Dykstra, that I had to make sure, to protect you and your family."

"And to protect yourself, too, I imagine," she said.

"In all honesty, yes. There's just too much at stake for everybody. I hope you aren't annoyed with me."

"Oh, I'm glad you did it. If Edmund and Katherine had found out about that newspaper article, they would have used it to raise all kinds of objections. But now we've defused that little bomb ahead of time."

She seemed not to know about my chat with her son and his wife. And she couldn't know about the other little bomb Mickey Bolthuis had placed in my hands.

Josh glanced at his watch. "Hadn't we better go in now?" Was he being compulsive about time or could he just not wait to get his hands on that six million?

"I'm not going in," I said, "until and unless I can get one more question answered."

"What would that be?" Mrs. Dykstra asked. Josh's eyes said, God, woman! What have you come up with now?

"When were you planning to tell us, Josh, that Margaret had called you and wanted you to do some advertising work for her?"

"Jesus Christ!" Josh snorted. "You're like some kind of robodetective. Where did you come up with that?"

"From a source I trust." He didn't say anything. "I'm waiting for your answer," I said.

"As am I," Mrs. Dykstra said, stepping back and turning to face him. Her knuckles whitened as she tightened her grip on her cane.

"There's really nothing to it," Josh said. "When I joined the agency in Kalamazoo there was an article in the paper. She saw it and gave me a call. We talked about that Saturday when I was drawing in front of her house. She told me how much she appreciated the sketch I made of her and asked if I would like to do some work for her company."

"Did you have an appointment to meet her?"

"Nothing definite. I was uncomfortable with the offer because I couldn't do freelance stuff while I was under contract to the agency. And she seemed to want me, not the agency. I told her I would have to get back to her."

"Did you?"

"No. A few days later I saw the article in the paper about her death."

I searched his eyes, wondering if there would ever be an end to my mistrust of him. "Did she say anything to make you believe she thought there was any connection between the two of you?"

"Hell, no. She was very nice. That was all."

I turned to Mrs. Dykstra. "Did Margaret ever mention anything to you about this?"

She shook her wobbling head. "No. But she didn't share much of anything with me the last few years of her life."

Silence fell around us until Josh said, "Are you satisfied? Can we go in now?"

"Sure, let's go in," I said.

We walked into a large room with a receptionist's desk in the middle of it. In one corner was a play area for children, with a few uncomfortable looking chairs for their parents. Behind the receptionist's desk were what must be workrooms and storage areas. I saw the flash of a copier light. Office doors opened off either end of the large room. With its scruffy brown carpet and worn furniture, the place had all the charm of a legal aid office. I wondered how Margaret had found a lawyer to handle her trust fund in such a low-rent district.

An attractive young Hispanic woman sitting at the receptionist's desk smiled at us. Her nameplate identified her as Juanita. "Good morning, Mrs. Dykstra. You can go on in." She gestured to the office door to her right. "Just have a seat at the conference table."

The office, which was unoccupied at the moment, was larger than I expected. In addition to McKenzie's desk and bookshelves, it held a nice conference table and several padded, swiveling chairs that seemed out of place. I suspected they were cast-offs from another firm. That was where we sat down. A couple of minutes later a woman in her late thirties entered, carrying a sheaf of papers. Reddish brown hair, cut short, framed her round face. She was starting to lose some skirmishes in her battles against age and weight. The buttons and zippers on her gray slacks and pearl blouse were straining.

"Sorry to keep you waiting," she said. "I was just making sure we had enough copies for everybody. Good morning, Ella. You're looking especially nice today."

"Why, thank you, Jennifer," Mrs. Dykstra said. "I'd like you to meet Sarah DeGraaf, from Oaktree Family Services."

I shook hands with J. Spencer McKenzie, but could think of nothing to say because 'You're a woman!' kept running through my head.

"And this," Mrs. Dykstra said, "is my grandson ..."

Jennifer actually looked at Josh for the first time and said, "Oh, my God! Eddie? Is that you?"

Chapter 19

As Josh shook Jennifer McKenzie's hand he said to me, "I know what you're thinking, but there is an explanation for this."

"With you, there's always an explanation," I said. "The problem is, there's always a need for one."

"I'm sorry," Jennifer said, looking from one of us to the other. "Have I hit a nerve here?"

"No, I can clear it up," Josh said. "I'm just glad you're here to help me out."

"It's been a while. I didn't recognize you. The goatee threw me."

On that point I could empathize with her. "How do you know him?" I asked.

"Do you want to tell the story?" Jennifer said.

Josh leaned back in his chair. "I'd rather you did. My credibility with Sarah is at an all-time low. She might even want you to show some ID. Maybe have you fingerprinted."

Jennifer looked puzzled as she turned to me.

"Inside joke," I said.

"Okay. It's really a funny story, the way Josh and I met. Josh knew my baby sister, Wendy, when they were in college. Josh and another guy and Wendy and another girl shared an apartment their junior year. Josh and Wendy dated a bit, but it wasn't anything serious, was it?"

"No," Josh said. "It was more like hanging out than dating."

"Wendy used to tell me about her two male roommates. The other guy was named Walter. Everybody called him Wally. Wendy said he was a lot like Wally on *Leave it to Beaver*. You know, a nice, wholesome kind of guy."

"And who was Wally's best friend?" Josh asked me.

"Eddie Haskell," I said.

"Right," Jennifer said brightly. "So that's what Wendy called Josh, as a joke. Although she did say you always seemed to have some kind of scheme up your sleeve."

"We all grow up," Josh said sourly as he saw me tense. I was working hard to remind myself that he hadn't lied to me yet. He just hadn't told the whole truth. I wished I could hook him up to a lie detector any time I talked to him.

"I met Josh," Jennifer said, "when Wendy brought him along on our family's ski trip one spring break. Sorry I couldn't remember your real name just now. The Wally and Eddie thing was such a hoot. That's how I've thought of you since then."

Josh squirmed, obviously eager to change the subject. "How's Wendy doing?"

"Really well. She's married. They live in Ohio. They've got a darling little girl."

Josh and I exchanged a glance across the table. There was a reasonable explanation, like he said, so why was I feeling so uncomfortable all of a sudden? Could it be aftershock from last night? Like someone who has lived through an earthquake—even been trapped under the rubble for a couple of hours—I panicked at the first hint of another tremor.

"And you're obviously married, too," Josh said to Jennifer. "Wendy's last name was Allen when I knew her."

"Right," Jennifer said. "But I'm divorced now. I kept the name because I've been using it since law school. One of my professors told me he would never be afraid to go up against a lawyer named Jennifer, so I started using the initial with my middle name and my married name."

"'What's in a name?'" Mrs. Dykstra said.

"A lot more than there should be," Jennifer said. "I believe I've won a few cases because opposing counsel were so discombobulated to find themselves facing a woman that they never got over the shock." She patted the stack of papers in front of her. "Well, we'd better end our little jaunt down memory lane and focus on business."

Passing out the copies she'd made, she put on her reading glasses and opened the folder in front of her. Before she could go any further, her receptionist put her head in the door.

"Jen, I'm sorry to interrupt. There's a man out here who insists on seeing you."

Jennifer tilted her head down to peer over her glasses. "He'll just have to wait."

"He says he's Edmund Dykstra's attorney."

* * * *

Edmund Dykstra's lawyer—pardon me, attorney—stepped into Jennifer's office with all the confidence a man could derive from being tall and athletic and wearing a three-thousand dollar suit and a watch that cost more than my car. For that matter, his after-shave probably cost more, per ounce, than my car. And my car didn't smell that good even when it was new.

"J. Spencer McKenzie?" he asked in a deep, mellifluous voice. If I'd been on a jury I would have given his client whatever he wanted.

"That's me." Jennifer stood up, and the other lawyer's face registered the surprise I hoped I had managed to keep off of mine.

"I'm Martin Vandervelde," he said, managing a nice recovery. "I represent Edmund Dykstra."

"Good morning, Marty," Mrs. Dykstra said in disgust. "What dirty little errand has Edmund sent you on now?"

"This is for your own good, Ella."

"Uh-oh," she said. "When they say that to an old lady, grab your purse and cross your legs."

He ignored her. I guessed she didn't sign his retainer checks. He opened his briefcase, took out a folded piece of paper, and handed it to Jennifer.

"This is an injunction prohibiting you, as executor of Margaret Dykstra's trust fund, from turning over those funds to any person claiming to be Ms. Dykstra's son, or to anyone representing such a person. As you can see, it was issued yesterday, so anything you've done here this morning is invalidated."

Jennifer pursed her lips as she glanced over the document. "Where did you find a judge to sign this on a Sunday?"

"They always have one or two in their pockets," Mrs. Dykstra said, "the way you or I carry an extra tissue."

The lawyer looked at Mrs. Dykstra with what I think was supposed to be sympathy, maybe pity. Then he turned on Josh and me.

"Mr. Dykstra was concerned that these two would be in a hurry to finish their confidence game while they still had his mother under their spell. I hadn't expected them to be quite so brazen, but I'm glad now that we took the precaution."

I opened my mouth to protest, but Vandervelde was reaching into his briefcase. He drew out two documents, which he handed to Josh and me.

"This is a restraining order which requires you, Mr. Adams, and you, Ms. DeGraaf, to stay at least one hundred feet away from any member of the Dykstra family and any property owned by the Dykstra family or by Dykstra Enterprises."

"Let me see that," Jennifer demanded, looking up from reading the first injunction. Josh handed her his copy and she skimmed it.

"You've wasted your time, Mr. Vandervelde. In the first place, I'm not going to turn over any money until I'm satisfied that Mr. Adams *is* Margaret Dykstra's son."

"And I can assure you, he is not," Vandervelde said.

"That remains to be seen. Secondly, Edmund Dykstra has no standing when it comes to his mother. He is not her guardian and does not have her power of attorney. She can associate with whomever she chooses."

Mrs. Dykstra stood and pointed a shaking hand at the lawyer. "And the house is mine, not Edmund's. Josh and Sarah are welcome there any time."

"But," Vandervelde intoned, "Mr. Dykstra can order these two to stay away from himself, his wife, and their children. And if even one member of the family is in the Heritage Hill house, which is their primary residence, then Mr. Adams and Ms. DeGraaf cannot come within a hundred feet of it. You'll also find attached to the injunctions a list of all the Dykstra properties, both personal and corporate." He turned back to Josh and me. "You will have to use a zig-zag path now when you go anywhere in Grand Rapids."

Mrs. Dykstra's face contorted in anger. "Marty, this is despicable, even for you and Edmund."

"Ella, it's necessary to protect the family from predators. Now, may I offer you a ride home?"

Mrs. Dykstra snorted. "The only way you could get me in a vehicle with you would be if it was a hearse and I was driving."

Chapter 20

We all stared at the door for a moment after Martin Vandervelde left, like people trying to comprehend what has just happened when a tornado tears through their town. Then Jennifer took Josh's restraining order and the injunction, spread them out on the table and studied them more closely.

"I don't feel very well," Mrs. Dykstra said. "A little woozy." She put her elbows on the table and cradled her head.

"I'll bet it's from that guy's after-shave," Josh said, putting a hand on her back.

I nodded, feeling a little giddy myself. Martin Vandervelde's after-shave, unlike Elvis, had not left the building.

Mrs. Dykstra raised her face, almost ashen now. "No, I think my blood sugar's too low. I didn't take the time to check it this morning. Do you have a donut or a candy bar around here?"

Jennifer jumped up and went to her office door. "Juanita, bring the donuts in here. Quickly, please."

The receptionist hurried in with a box of donuts and muffins. Josh started to pick out a bran muffin, but Mrs. Dykstra pointed to a donut with chocolate icing. Josh gave it to her on a napkin, and she took a bite.

"Thank goodness you're not all health nuts," she said.

"My partner says if God intended for us to eat fiber, she would have made it taste like frosting," Jennifer said. "As long as we're taking a break, why don't we have some coffee?" Josh and I accepted. He helped himself to a muffin.

"Are you going to be all right?" Jennifer asked Mrs. Dykstra as she poured coffee from a pot in one corner of her office.

"I'll be fine in a few minutes. Don't worry about me. We've got bigger problems. How can we get these injunctions lifted?"

"We can try," Jennifer said. "But Vandervelde is a street fighter. Susan and I do most of our work in Family Court. We handle child custody cases, deadbeat dads, domestic violence. This is a little out of our league."

"Then why did Margaret pick you to be the executor of the fund?" I asked. "And please forgive me if I'm being too blunt."

Jennifer met my eyes over her coffee mug. "In my job candor is refreshing." She took a sip. "And so is that first cup of coffee. I met Margaret down at The Art Place. I rented the studio next to hers for a while."

"Jennifer paints," Mrs. Dykstra said. "Still lifes. Wonderful stuff."

"I used to, when I could afford the supplies and had the time. Margaret encouraged me and gave me a lot of support during my divorce. The original executor for the trust fund decided to retire. I think she figured the retainer she paid me—and she set the amount, not me—would help keep this practice going for a while. We get a fixed sum out of the income from the fund each year. Susan and I would probably have gone under by now without it."

I wondered how they would survive once the fund was turned over, either to Margaret's son or to The Art Place. They might have a considerable interest in seeing that control of the money passed to someone over whom they had some influence.

For example, someone who always had a scheme up his sleeve.

I couldn't make any accusations against them yet, but the low-rent lawyer and the actor/adman were moving up on my chart of 'persons of interest'.

"Margaret must have thought you were capable of doing the job," I said. "She obviously considered this fund very important."

"I think she figured all I'd have to do would be to hand the money over to The Art Place when the time came."

"This may be none of my business, but I'm pretty deeply involved in this situation now." I was tempted to say something about the closet incident, then decided to stay with my original instinct. "Are there any conditions or restrictions on this trust fund?"

"None. If Margaret's son has been identified to the satisfaction of the executors—Ella and myself—then he gets six million dollars. Oh, and he also gets that sculpture of hers that's on display in The Art Place."

Josh loosened his tie and unbuttoned the collar of his shirt. "Did she ever say anything about trying to find her son?"

His grandmother leaned forward. "She went to the agency the

day after Cornelius' funeral. They told her they couldn't help her. The records were sealed." She looked at me as though that was my fault. Or maybe the glare was just her low blood sugar still talking.

"There isn't much an agency can do," I said, "unless the adoptee wants to be found."

"I looked into it for her," Jennifer said. "I did find out about the Central Adoption Registry. I almost had to threaten your agency with a lawsuit to get them to see if Josh had filed a form there. Since they couldn't find any male adoptees on file with the right birth date, there was nothing we could do except put Margaret's letter in the Registry and hope."

"Why does everything about adoption have to be so hush-hush?" Mrs. Dykstra said. "I thought things were changing, people were loosening up a bit. Heaven knows I have."

This was my area, and I sat up like I'd been called on to take charge of a meeting. "There's no one solution that works for every-body. Margaret wanted to be reunited with her son, and it's truly regrettable it never happened. But not everyone wants that."

Mrs. Dykstra looked incredulous. "How could somebody not want to be reunited with a parent or a child?"

"It happens," I said. "A few months ago I helped a young woman find her mother. The mother agreed to meet her. The next day the mother called me and said that meeting was the biggest mistake she'd ever made, even bigger than getting pregnant at age fourteen. She told me to tell my client she would not see her again. My client found out where she lived, though, and went to her house. Her mother yelled and screamed at her and told her never to contact her again, under any circumstances."

"Sounds like both of them will be in therapy for the rest of their lives," Josh said.

Jennifer nodded slowly, almost sadly. "We see cases here, more often than I want to think about, where the children are better off separated from the parents. It's crazy. You have to have a license to own a dog, but anybody with a set of gonads can become a parent."

"But my mother wanted to see me, didn't she?" Josh said.

"Yes, she did," his grandmother said, laying a hand on his arm. "Of that you can be absolutely sure."

"The two of you"—he motioned to his grandmother and Jenni-fer—"had a chance to talk to her about this. What did she say?"

His grandmother sighed. "She couldn't say anything around the house as long as Cornelius was alive. I'm sure she also felt I betrayed her by not standing up to him when you were born. Our relationship was never what it should have been after that. By the time Cornelius died, she was beginning to lose hope, I think, that she would ever find you."

"That was the tone I picked up from her, too," Jennifer said. "Despair, almost. She worked some of it out by pounding on those sculptures she made at The Art Place."

"She did keep a kind of diary," Mrs. Dykstra said. "She didn't write in it every day, just on your birthday or some special occasion—the day you would have started to school, things like that. I came in her room one day when she was writing in it. When she died, I looked all over for it, but I never did find it."

That's just what we need! I thought. Another missing document.

Chapter 21

"Are you feeling any better, Grandmother?" Josh asked.

Mrs. Dykstra nodded and sat up a little straighter. She checked her blood sugar and pronounced herself satisfied. "I'm going to be all right, dear. I brought some pictures." She reached into her purse and pulled out an envelope of photographs. "I was going to show these to Josh later, but this seems as good a time as any."

The dozen or so snapshots showed Margaret as a teenager, a cheerleader at her Christian high school, on the family's boat, and at her college graduation.

"Isn't the resemblance to Josh striking?" Mrs. Dykstra said. "Especially in the nose and the chin."

Jennifer nodded.

"Actually," I said, "he gets his eyes from his father." I felt like a magician pulling the rabbit out of the hat as I opened my bag and took out the enlarged picture of Margaret and David.

Mrs. Dykstra gasped. There were tears in Josh's eyes. "Where did you get this?" they both said.

I told them about my visit with Mickey Bolthuis.

"Oh, yes," Mrs. Dykstra said. "The Driesenga girl. She was a good friend of Margaret's. A quiet child, as I recall. With a big nose."

"It's fascinating to see the two parents together," Jennifer said, "and to have the child right in front of us. You're right about the eyes. Definitely from the father. But the nose and chin come from the mother."

I shook my head and studied Josh. "The nose I'll give you. The chin I can't see. Maybe it's the goatee."

Josh seemed to take that as a challenge. "I'd shave it right now if I had a razor."

"Juanita will give you one," Jennifer said. "We keep some disposables on hand. Sometimes we have to clean up our clients before we go to court."

Josh looked at me as if to say, Are you really going to make me do this?

"It'll grow back," I said. Given his lack of complete honesty with me, I didn't feel like cutting him *any* slack.

While Josh was depilating his chin, Jennifer, Mrs. Dykstra, and I huddled over the pictures of Margaret.

"No matter how much we think Josh looks like his mother," Jennifer said, "we need more than that to convince a court."

"Josh and I will be happy to do a DNA test," Mrs. Dykstra said. "We've agreed on that."

"That would clinch it," Jennifer said. "I know a lab that will expedite the work for us. We use them when we're trying to establish paternity in some of our cases. But it could take a while to get the results. There's so much demand for DNA testing these days the labs have a huge backlog."

"We have until Josh's thirtieth birthday," Mrs. Dykstra said. "That's six months away."

"It might take that long," Jennifer said. "I wonder if Edmund would give a sample. A third sample could make the results more certain. It would be gratifying to have him give evidence for our side."

A strange look spread over Mrs. Dykstra's face. I wondered if she was still having a problem with her blood sugar. "No," she said firmly. "Leave Edmund out of it. He hates needles and medical stuff."

"There's nothing to it," Jennifer assured her. "No needles. They just swab the inside of your cheek."

"I don't care. Leave Edmund out of it." Her fingers struck the table as she said the words.

* * * *

When I got back to my office a little before eleven the message light on my phone was blinking. I caught myself just before I picked it up. If I was going to use redial to see whether someone had called Ann Haveman from here last night, I had to do it before I checked my messages. But what about fingerprints? Would I ruin them? Could I ask Cal—or Geri—to come over and dust the phone? That would go over really well in the office. Maybe I could put the phone in a plastic bag and take it to the police station. No, that was ridiculous.

As I was sitting there, staring at the phone like I had some phobia about using it, Connie appeared at my door. She looked much browner and blonder than when she left.

"Good morning, Sarah. I wondered when you were coming in." Nice little oblique criticism of my apparent tardiness.

"I was with a client. How was your trip? Did you pick up any useful information about orphanages over there?"

"I'll have some recommendations in my report to the board."

Judging from her tan, one thing she learned was that in Hawaii they build their orphanages on the beach.

"Could I see you in my office, please?" She didn't wait for me to walk with her, so I had to follow her like a naughty child on her way to the principal's office. I closed the door as she seated herself at her large, uncluttered desk.

"Please, sit down." The voice was level, unemotional, but this was not going to be a pleasant chat. The ice in her eyes told me that.

"I've had a call from Edmund Dykstra. He says you're harassing his family, claiming to have found his sister's biological son."

"He *is* her son," I said. "What are the Dykstras so afraid of?" Rhetorical question, but I wanted to see her face when I asked it. Did she know anything about Margaret's trust fund?

"They're not afraid of anything," Connie said. "They are concerned about people taking advantage of them. One of the problems that comes along with wealth is fending off people who try to take it away from you." Her face didn't give away anything. I'd hate to play poker with her.

"But, Connie, I've gone through all the regular procedures, strictly by the book"—well, except for the missing file. "Josh Adams is Margaret Dykstra's son. I'm as sure of that as I have been of any adoptee reunion I've worked on."

She tented her fingers. "You've never worked on a case involving this family before. And you won't work on it any longer. If you pursue it, we could find ourselves facing a lawsuit. I won't have you dragging this agency into a legal mess."

I couldn't resist. "It's too bad we don't have extra money—some kind of slush fund—that we could dip into to pay legal fees."

That rattled her. Even under her tan I could see she was blushing. She snapped forward in her chair and shook her finger at me. "I'm going to review all of your work on this case. I'll need to see everything you've got—your notes, Mr. Adams' file, everything."

The way she looked at me when she mentioned the file seemed to offer a challenge. Go ahead, say you don't have the file. Say anything about the file. But maybe I was reading too much into it. It would be natural in any review to expect the caseworker to have an adoptee's file.

"All right, I'll get that stuff for you as soon as I can." Time to call the Probate Court in Battle Creek and see if I could get a copy of their file.

"I want it all before you go to lunch."

* * * *

I used my cell phone to call the Probate Court. One of the clerks there, a guy named Woody, had been helpful to me in the past. If he could find the file and fax it to me, everything would be all right. I was relieved when I caught him in his office, and I quickly explained what I needed.

"Adoption of Joshua Adams, eh? Let me search our adoption records." There was a short pause while he worked on his computer. "Sarah, I'm not finding anything."

Damn! How far could these people reach?

"Is the name spelled differently than I would expect? Two d's, maybe?" He started to sing, "'The house is a museum ...'"

"No, this is just plain old Joshua Adams."

"Let me do a general search of our files." A pause. "Here's a Joshua Adams. Son of Matthew and Allison?"

"That's him." I reached for a pen and paper in case I needed to take any notes.

"He shows up as the sole heir to their will when it was probated two years ago."

At least I didn't get another surprise about that. "You can't find anything in there about his adoption?"

"Nada. Zero. Zilch. Are you sure the adoption was finalized in Battle Creek?"

"Yes. I've seen the parents' copy of the court order and the amended birth certificate."

"Photocopies?"

"No. Originals, with the seals on them." I was wishing I'd kept the originals instead of copying them and returning them to Josh.

"Then I don't know what's going on." I heard him tapping a few more keys.

"Woody, could you have somebody look through your paper files? And I mean look thoroughly."

"What would be the point? If we ever did have a file on him, it would have been entered into the computer."

"I'm getting a little desperate here, Woody. As in, my job may be on the line."

"Desperate enough to have dinner with me the next time I'm in Grand Rapids?" The slime seemed to be oozing through the phone.

I'll be ashamed of myself as long as I live, but I said, "Yes. If you find that file for me, I'll have dinner with you." I'd never met Woody. Every time I talked to him, though, he joked about asking me for a date. He had seen my picture on the agency's web site. My survival instinct was kicking into overdrive, but I needed that file.

"And when do you need it?"

"By lunch today."

"Ouch! No can do, lovely lady. It'll be tomorrow morning before I can free somebody up to go over to storage and poke around."

Great. I'm going down in flames, and I have to wait until tomorrow before somebody can get 'freed up' to help me. "Well, whatever you can do for me, Woody, I'll appreciate it."

"I'm sure you will, lovely lady," he said slowly.

I wanted to slap a sexual harassment suit on his sorry ass, but I bit my tongue. At least he would have a strong incentive to search.

"Talk to you later, Sarah. We'll set up a time."

"*If* you find the file, Woody. *If* you find the file." I hung up.

Talk about mixed feelings. My job might hinge on him locating that damn file, but now I was hoping he wouldn't. I didn't relish the idea of an evening spent fighting off somebody who probably looked like Jabba the Hutt, lived in his parents' basement, and spent enough time watching old sitcoms that he could hum the themes.

But that was a problem for another day. At the moment—and it was now eleven-thirty—I had a more immediate issue to deal with. How could I give Connie a file I didn't have? I took the coward's way out. I copied everything I had and put the stuff in an envelope with a note explaining that I would have the original file by tomorrow. I put the envelope in Connie's mailbox, then ducked out to lunch.

* * * *

The sidewalks were crowded as I made my way to DeJong's Sandwich Shop. We get so little sunshine in west Michigan in March that, whenever we do get a reprieve from the cloudy gloom, people flock outside. It was nowhere near warm today, but people were eating

114

outside with their coats on, or just sitting and soaking up rays in some of the little parks and green spaces that try to beautify downtown Grand Rapids. They reminded me of lizards coming out to recharge themselves.

A poster in a travel agent's window caught my eye and I stopped. It showed some island off the coast of South Carolina. Maybe I should take a trip. That might help me get over Cal, maybe meet somebody new. But if I didn't have a job by the time I got back from lunch, how could I afford a trip?

As I studied the poster I became aware of a man's reflection in the window. I noticed him because everyone else in the reflection was moving, but he was standing off to my right, smoking a cigarette. He seemed to be watching me out of the corner of his eye. He didn't look like the man talking on his cell phone outside McKenzie's office earlier this morning or like the guy I saw at the mall on Saturday. This guy was wearing a knit cap and his hair stuck out from under it. And he had a Fu Manchu mustache.

I felt safe enough on a busy sidewalk in broad daylight, but I didn't like the feeling that I was being followed. How long had he been tailing me? I'd been too caught up in my problem with Connie and the file to pay any attention when I left the office.

The man pulled a cell phone from his pocket and punched in a number.

My phone rang.

Chapter 22

I looked at my bag like I'd just become aware it held a ticking bomb. How did he get my number? Why was he calling me?

Then, reflected in the window, I saw him talking on his phone. Mine was still ringing. It wasn't me he was calling. He ground his cigarette out with his shoe and walked off.

You are getting seriously paranoid, girl.

I took a breath and grabbed my phone. The call was from Geri.

"I'm calling to confirm the time for our meeting with Denise van Putten tonight," she said. "Would eight o'clock be okay for you?"

"That's fine."

"And you've got my parents' address?"

"Yes. 508 East Central in Zeeland. Listen, as long as I've got you, what would you think about bringing Josh along?"

"Frankly, I don't like the idea," Geri said. "It's going to be a big enough shock to Denise to learn that Margaret had a son. Let's give her time to adjust to the idea before she meets him in the flesh."

"But I'm looking at it from Josh's viewpoint," I said. "It might help him deal with the loss of his mother if he could talk to someone who knew her well, other than his grandmother. Edmund and Katherine obviously aren't going to be any help."

"All right." She sounded like she was agreeing against her better judgment. "But I take the lead asking questions. This is what I do."

"It's your call. Now, there's a favor I need to ask of you." I lowered my voice. "Would it be possible to have my phone dusted for fingerprints, without letting everyone in the office know about it?"

"Whoa! What's this all about?"

"I'd rather not talk about it in public."

"I could stop by this afternoon with a fingerprint kit in my bag. If you can close your office door, I can dust the phone discreetly."

"I have a client at two, but I'll be free at three. Could you make it then?"

She must have looked at her appointment book. "I'll be there."

"Great! When you come in, just tell Joan, the receptionist, you're my three o'clock."

I put my phone away and hurried to DeJong's, to beat the noon crowd. One part of my brain wanted to look over my shoulder to see if I was being followed, but another part wouldn't give in to the impulse.

DeJong's has the best croissants I've ever tasted. I have to make myself avoid them, but today I decided to indulge. Instead of turkey and low-fat cheese on whole wheat, I had chicken salad on a croissant. What's another thirty minutes on the treadmill? I had had a stressful day, and it was only half over.

I had barely finished my first bite when a man stopped by my booth. Before I could look up Cal's voice said, "I hoped I would find you here"

"Hi." That was brilliant, but it was all I could come up with.

"Joan told me you'd gone to lunch. I see this is still your first choice."

"It's close and quick."

He glanced at his watch. "I don't have time for lunch, but do you mind if I sit down for a minute?"

"No. Please. Sit." When did I regress to babbling monosyllables?

He slid onto the seat across from me and held the plastic bag containing his broken Red Wings plate in his lap.

"I stopped by your office to pick this up."

"I didn't know if you cared enough to bother." I looked at my sandwich with great interest.

"Sarah, don't be that way. It's an important symbol to me. Our first Christmas together, the B&B in Marshall—that's something I can't forget. Don't want to forget."

"It was our *only* Christmas together," I corrected him. "And that's not my fault."

"No, you're right. It's my fault, entirely."

"Cal, I am sorry about the plate. I'll get you another one."

"I don't want another plate. I want this one fixed."

* * * *

Connie wasn't in her office when I got back. The envelope I had put in her mailbox was gone. If we were to get up an office pool about where she was, I would bet on 'with Edmund Dykstra'.

Even though my mind was wandering, I got through my two o'clock appointment, a session with Carol, a high school senior who was pondering whether she wanted to find her biological parents. I hate it when I can't concentrate on what a client is telling me. Once in a while it's because they're really boring people and I just want to tell them to get a life. I've heard other therapists confess to having those moments.

But today it was my fault. I couldn't stop thinking about Josh, missing files, trust funds—his and ours—about Cal and whether a plate equaled a relationship, and about being locked in a closet. I shivered.

"Are you all right?" Carol asked.

"Yes. Sorry. It's a little chilly in here. Go ahead."

At three Joan called back to let me know that "a Ms. Murphy is here to see you. Are you expecting her?" She sounded like she was craning her neck to look up.

"Yes, she has an appointment."

"I don't see her on my master calendar. When you schedule an appointment, please let me know so I can put it on the master calendar. That is correct office procedure."

I wondered if this was the beginning of negative comments on my record that would eventually lead to my dismissal—'Doesn't list appointments on master calendar. Doesn't play well with the other children'. Could Connie have initiated the process so quickly?

"That gal's wound a little tight," Geri said as I closed my door. It felt odd to be looking up at another woman. There are some women I look up *to*, but at five-eight not many I look up *at*.

"Joan is very ... efficient," I said.

"Anal retentive and controlling would be my diagnosis," Geri said. "Probably resents being in a menial position and thinks she should be running the place. I'll bet she has slipcovers on every piece of furniture in her house. On her husband, too."

I was too stunned to do anything but laugh out loud. My own assessment of our receptionist could have been put in those very words, if I had anything like Geri's wit. "How did you ... ?"

"I have a Master's in psychology," Geri said. "But more to the point, do you want to tell me what this phone business is all about?"

As succinctly as I could, I told her how I had been locked in the closet and rescued the night before. "I think whoever did it might have called Ann Haveman from this phone, so it would look like I had made the call if anyone checked the records."

Geri shook her head in disbelief as I finished. "You've got some *cojones,* girl. I lock people up in cells, but if anybody ever shut the door on me, I would absolutely flip out. Do you think I ought to dust the storage room?"

"It would attract too much attention, and I don't think you'd learn anything. Everybody in this office has access to it."

"Well, 'Let's go to the phones', as they say on the talk radio shows."

Geri slipped on a pair of latex gloves and pulled the fingerprint kit out of her purse. She dusted the phone and lifted several prints off of it onto pieces of a special tape.

"Have you ever been fingerprinted?" she asked as she worked.

"Yes. The agency requires all employees and all our foster parents and adoptive parents to be printed, so we can do background checks. With all the problems that have come up lately about abuse in the child-care system, we're super-cautious."

"Good. That'll make it easy to identify your prints and anybody else in the office. Eliminate them and we can see who else has touched your phone."

I hoped it would be that easy. Nothing else about this case had been.

"I've got a couple of full prints, but mostly partials," Geri said. That's what you'd find on any phone because of the way we hold them when we use them. I don't want to give you any false hope. If somebody used your phone, they probably wore a rubber glove—even a sandwich bag would do—or they might have wiped it down with a tissue from your box."

"In which case there wouldn't be *any* prints, not even mine."

"Right. So, unless somebody was really careless, these are going to be your prints."

"I just thought it would be worth checking. Thanks for taking the time."

"Glad to do it."

"Now for the big test." I wiped the phone off, picked up the receiver and pressed redial. The phone rang several times before an answering machine clicked on. "It's Ann Haveman," I informed Geri as I hung up.

"And you're sure you wouldn't have had any reason to call her?"

"I didn't even know she existed until she opened that door last night."

"Have you noticed anybody following you?" Geri asked.

"I've seen a couple of guys the last few days who seemed interested in me, but guys have always stared at me."

"I can relate to that," Geri said, rolling her eyes. She took out a business card and wrote something on the back of it, then handed it to me. "If you're in a situation that makes you uncomfortable, call me. That's my cell number on the back. Don't hesitate, any time of the day or night. You could be in more danger than you think."

"I just feel like I'm getting paranoid."

"Remember what they say, 'Paranoids are just people with better information than the rest of us.'"

"Oh, that's encouraging."

"I'm not trying to scare you, Sarah. But it sounds like you ought to be particularly aware of people around you."

"Always be looking over my shoulder, you mean?"

"I'm afraid so."

"And while I'm doing that I'll probably run into something in front of me."

"Sometimes life is that way." She started to pack up her stuff.

"Oh, I almost forgot," I said, reaching for a piece of paper on my desk. "Since you're interested in what happened to Margaret Dykstra, you might like to see this. It's an e-mail that she sent to a friend of hers. She was forwarding a message from a guy named David Burton, who is Josh's father."

"You've identified the father? That could be huge."

"All I've got is a name. I don't know if you could trace anything from this e-mail address ..."

"A Social Security number would be better, but, hey, it's a start." She took the piece of paper, studied it, and put it in her purse.

"Thanks again for your help," I said.

"No problem." Geri put her hand on the doorknob, then paused, like someone who has been planning to say something all along but wanted it to appear to be an afterthought. "Listen, since we're going to my parents' tonight, would you like to meet somewhere for dinner beforehand? Dutch treat, of course."

"Sure. Sounds good."

She smiled as though she knew something I didn't. "Well. Congratulations."

"On what?"

"You just accepted a dinner invitation from a lesbian without the slightest hesitation."

I pushed the door closed again. "Could I say something, in all honesty?"

"That's the best way to say anything."

"I wish you would drop this attitude that you're on some kind of high moral ground or you're trying to shock me. I had a college roommate who was a lesbian. I have a cousin who is a lesbian. I'm not. I appreciate the help you're giving me and if you want to have dinner tonight, I would enjoy that. As far as the lesbian thing is concerned, it's old news."

She nodded slowly. "You do have *cojones*, girl. See you at six?"

* * * *

At four-thirty I was packing up to leave the office when my phone rang. Joan told me that Connie wanted to see me right away. So, this was it. No file probably meant no job.

Connie didn't say anything until I was seated in her office. "I've been informed that a restraining order has been issued against you on behalf of the Dykstra family and Dykstra Enterprises."

"Yes. I got it this morning."

"Did you read the list of properties owned by Dykstra Enterprises that was attached to the order?"

"Not yet."

She stood and looked out her window, then turned back to me. "If you had, you would know that you can't legally be in your office."

"What ... ?"

"This building is owned by Dykstra Enterprises. We lease it for a small sum. It's part of their contribution to the agency. But that means you're not allowed within a hundred feet of the building."

"But how can I come to work ... ?"

"That's just the point. You can't."

I took a deep breath, waiting for the axe to fall.

"You have a week's vacation with pay coming. Take it, starting tomorrow, and try to get this matter resolved. If it's not settled by next Monday, I'll have to place you on unpaid administrative leave."

"What about my clients?"

"They'll be rescheduled or moved to other caseworkers. Mr. Adams' case will be closed. You are not to contact him as a representative of this agency. Do you have any other questions?"

121

"As a matter of fact, I do. How am I supposed to resolve this business when I'm prohibited from having any contact with the Dykstras?" I stood up, my voice rising. "How can I talk to somebody when I can't get within a hundred feet of them?"

Connie leaned across her desk. "Watch your tone! You'll have to figure some way out of that dilemma by yourself. And maybe, in the process, you'll learn not to interfere in the affairs of a family who are accustomed to protecting themselves against fortune-hunters."

Chapter 23

So, I was to be fired in stages. This 'vacation' was just Step One.

I ran a few errands and then drove to the Italian restaurant on the west side of town where Geri and I had agreed to meet. From there it would be just a short drive over to Zeeland, one of the towns founded by Dutch settlers in the mid-nineteenth century. The countryside around Grand Rapids is dotted with place names like Overisel, Drenthe, and Holland, commemorating places from which these immigrants came. In recent years the area has seen an influx of Hispanics and Asians, including a number of Korean adoptees like me.

When I pulled into the parking lot I stayed in my car, just to see if anyone came in after me, someone who might be following me. There were only a few other cars in the lot, so I was able to park close to the door.

The next car to come in after me turned out to be Geri. She parked her almost new BMW on the empty edge of the lot, like people do when they don't want to get dinged by someone opening a door. I watched in my rearview mirror as she strode across the parking lot. She moved with the grace of an athlete or a dancer rather than a model or a beauty queen. She wore a pair of navy slacks and a light-weight, close-fitting white sweater that would keep all male eyes focused on her chest. If only they knew ...

As she drew up to my car I got out and greeted her.

"You look a little down," she said.

"If I just look a *little* down, I'm doing a pretty good job of holding things together." I quickly told her about my impending dismissal.

"That's tough. But today has been one of those days when I would almost welcome getting fired."

"Don't you like your job?"

"When Cal and I are working together, things are great. He's the best, most supportive partner I could ask for. But, in general, women are not well received in this police department. Maybe not in any police department. I had a run-in with my captain today that made me wonder how long I can stick it out."

"What else would you do?"

"I haven't gotten that far yet." She touched my elbow. "Look, why don't we declare jobs, misery and unhappiness to be off-limits tonight. Let's talk about something else and pick ourselves up."

"I'll second that."

"All in favor?"

We both shouted, "Aye!"

"Motion carried unanimously," Geri said. "Let's eat."

The restaurant wasn't particularly crowded, so we didn't have to wait to be seated and have our orders taken.

"Tell me something about yourself," I said. "Are you from Zeeland?"

"No, I grew up in Lansing and went to Michigan State. My dad worked for the state, a mid-level bureaucrat. When he retired, he and Mom moved here to her hometown."

"Is your mother Dutch?"

"Yes. She's a van Faasen."

"You've *got* to be kidding. My grandmother's a van Faasen. I can't believe how intertwined and connected families are up here."

"It's almost like the South, kind of incestuous sometimes."

"So how did you end up here?"

"I worked in Detroit for a while, but finally decided to come back closer to my folks."

I wouldn't have thought this part of the state is where you would be comfortable."

"Why? Because I'm part Irish?"

"Okay. *Touché*. I put that really badly."

"You're right, though. The religious conservatism around here isn't particularly receptive to people who identify themselves the way I do. I've heard the joke about the Dutch boy putting his finger in the dike enough to last me a lifetime. Fortunately, I can always run over to Saugatuck for the day and not feel like a freak."

The little town of Saugatuck and the village of Douglas, on opposite banks of the Kalamazoo River where it empties into Lake Michigan, have long been known as artists' colonies and retreats for gay/lesbian people from as far away as Detroit and Chicago. They boast some of the best restaurants and most exquisite shops in Michigan.

124

Geri raised her wine glass in a *salud*. "So here we are, the lesbian Dutch-Irish cop and the Korean girl with the Dutch name. To the misfits."

I laughed and clinked my glass to hers.

"Now," she said, leaning forward in anticipation, "you've obviously got an interesting story to tell. So tell me."

"I'm not sure how interesting it is. My father was an American soldier in Korea. I made a couple of inquiries about locating him, but without even a first name to go on, it would be impossible. I don't know anything about my mother. She—or somebody—left me in a church in Pusan when I was two. I spent a year in an orphanage, then my parents adopted me, and I grew up in Holland."

"And now you help adoptees find their biological families. Have you ever tried to find your mother?"

"No. It would be a monumentally difficult job in a culture I'm not familiar with."

"Have you been to Korea?"

"My parents took me when I was sixteen. I have studied the language and speak it reasonably well. I thought, if I ever should find my mother, I'd like to be able to talk with her."

"There are quite a few Koreans around here, aren't there?"

"Yes, both adoptees and natives who've moved to this area for various reasons. I go to a Korean church once in a while, just to work on my language."

The lesson in cultural diversity came to an end when the waiter brought our order, pasta primavera with shrimp for me and veal parmesan for Geri.

"You and Cal share a taste for seafood, I see," Geri said.

"Unfortunately, that's all we share these days."

"Sorry, I didn't mean to reopen that wound. I can understand why you feel the way you do about Cal. If I weren't otherwise inclined, I could be very interested. He's a sweetheart."

"Do you two talk a lot about personal stuff?"

"That we do." She shrugged. "With as much time as we spend together every day, police business and sports don't last long as topics of conversation."

"I know I shouldn't ask this, but I will. Has he said anything about me?"

Her face took on a pained expression. "That's a tough one,

125

Sarah. I'd like to tell you some things, but I don't want to violate my partner's confidence."

"That tells me something. It sounds like he has been talking about me."

She chuckled. "Some days he gossips like one of the girls. I think, because there's no possibility of any relationship between us, he relaxes and talks. Too much sometimes. I've tried to tell him he needs to be careful. It's not good for him professionally to be so loose-lipped."

"I can understand why he would loosen up. In a way, you're every man's dream—a beautiful woman who isn't likely to demand a commitment."

She drew back and looked at me quizzically. "I guess I'll take that as a compliment. I thought it might be because I have a Master's in psychology and know how to get people talking. But don't worry. Cal has been the perfect gentleman. He hasn't mentioned any private details."

"Has he told you why he left me?"

Geri cut some more of the restaurant's wonderful bread for us. "Okay, that one I am going to answer, because it's the core question for you two. He thinks he left because he's afraid of getting killed and leaving you behind."

"You don't believe him?"

"No. I think it's because he's afraid you'll leave him."

"Why would he think that?"

"Because his mother left his father and him when Cal was nine."

I would have been less stunned if she had leaned across the table and kissed me on the mouth. All I could manage to say was, "He told me his mother was dead."

"That's what he tells everybody. And she might as well be. He's seen her only twice since then. She came back when he was ten, stayed a couple of weeks, then left again. The last time he saw her was when she showed up at his high school graduation."

I slumped in my chair. "I had no idea he was hurting that badly."

"Neither does he. I've given him the name of a counselor who I think would be good for him. I don't know if he's made an appointment. I think he could get to the point where he can make a commitment, if he'll just talk to somebody about this thing with his mother abandoning him. He loves you, Sarah."

"Then why did he leave?"

"Anniversaries scare the hell out of him. He's never gotten past a first anniversary with a woman. Once you start counting years, he says, somebody is going to get restless."

"Like his mother did."

"That's his perennial fear. Give him a little time, would be my advice. But if you want a long-term commitment from him, hold firm. Don't give him any wiggle-room."

Chapter 24

Like all the small towns surrounding Grand Rapids, Zeeland has experienced growing pains in recent years. It now has two high schools. The athletic teams for the original school were called the Chix—from the chicken hatcheries that once abounded there—so the new school adopted Dux as its nickname. In spite of all the growth, the town has maintained the feel of a bygone era. Geri's family lived in a Dutch colonial house on the loveliest street in the historic district.

It was well after dark when we arrived. Josh was already parked in front of the house. After I introduced him to Geri she instructed him to stand behind us until she was ready to present him to Denise. Geri's mother had been briefed about the little drama that was going to unfold in her dining room and had promised not to alert Denise. We made quick introductions while we hung up our coats in the front hall. Josh stayed in the foyer as Geri and I entered the dining room and Mrs. Murphy headed for the kitchen.

One wall of the dining room was covered by an enormous mahogany breakfront, filled not just with china but with what appeared to be souvenirs of trips abroad. It was a piece of furniture that would work only in an old house like this, with its large rooms and high ceilings. The table and chairs were made of the same dark wood but were clearly not part of a matched set.

From an open drawer in the breakfront a woman I assumed was Denise van Putten was laying out silverware and napkins on the table. She was in her early sixties, medium height and still slender enough to arouse envy in younger women, even though she was wearing a 'World's Best Grandma' sweatshirt. She wore her gray hair cut short.

"Hello, Geri dear," she said. "So nice to see you. I understand you want to talk about Margaret Dykstra."

Geri gave the older woman a light hug and introduced me and mentioned my line of work.

"You work with adoptees?" She glanced from me to Geri and back again. Her voice fell to a whisper. "Is this about Margaret's boy? Do you know anything about him?"

I was beginning to wonder how well-kept this secret actually was. Geri's jaw dropped. "You knew she had a son?"

"Oh, dear. I wasn't supposed to say anything. I've kept it in for so long."

"It's all right," Geri said. She motioned for Josh to step into the room. "Denise, I know this is going to be a shock to you, but ..."

"My God! You're Margaret's boy, aren't you?" She hugged him like a long-lost relative.

Josh looked at me with an expression of triumph and satisfaction as he embraced Denise lightly. "How did you know?"

"Your chin, your nose. Why, there's no mistaking the resemblance." Denise stood back, still holding his hands, and gazed at him in wonder. "But your eyes are definitely your father's."

"Did you know Josh's father?" I asked.

"What? Oh ... no. I just meant, no, they're so different from Margaret's eyes. So dark. They must be like his father's."

I was going to have to look at those pictures more closely. I just couldn't see what everyone else was noticing. Maybe it was because they had actually seen Margaret and I hadn't.

"Who wants coffee and who wants tea?" Geri's mother chirped from the doorway into the kitchen.

Denise insisted that Josh sit next to her. She could hardly take her eyes off him. Mrs. Murphy excused herself, and Geri and I settled across the table from Josh and Denise.

Geri encouraged Denise to tell her story. "I'm sure we'll have a few questions as you go along, but tell us everything you remember. Even something that seems insignificant to you may prove to be important."

"Do you mind if I take notes?" I asked.

Denise shook her head and plunged into her story. "I was Margaret's secretary for several years before she became head of the company, and I stayed with her until the day she died, almost fifteen years altogether. She was very committed to her work. I used to worry about her because she never took vacations or let herself relax. The only time she did miss work was every year on September 24th. On that day she would disappear."

"That's my birthday," Josh said.

Denise nodded. "So I learned in time. If the 24th came during the week, she wouldn't come to work. It took me a few years to notice the pattern. She would call in that morning, tell me she wouldn't be in, with no other explanation. If I asked if she was sick, she would just say she wasn't coming in and wouldn't take calls. The next day she was always back, and she wouldn't answer any questions about why she had missed a day."

"Did she stay at home or go somewhere?" Geri asked.

"Her father asked me once where she was, so I guess she wasn't at home."

"How did he react to those absences?" I asked.

"He didn't say anything, but I could see he was really angry. For several days after that he wouldn't speak to her unless he had to."

"I'm surprised she worked with her father," I said, "considering how much she must have resented him. How did they get along?"

Denise sighed. "They argued a lot. Margaret didn't like dealing with the business side of things. After they argued, she would work on a new design or one of her sculptures. She was so pleased when that art studio place opened. It gave her an escape. An escape other than drinking."

"She drank a lot?" Geri asked.

"I'm afraid so. She kept a bottle in her desk drawer. Whenever she stayed to 'work late' she was actually just drinking. She tried to keep her mother from knowing, and she didn't go to bars."

"When did you find out she had a son?" Josh asked.

"Nine years ago she showed up for work on the 24th."

"That would have been my twenty-first birthday."

"That's right. Margaret didn't look so good, but she was there. I was surprised because I had come to expect she would be gone on that day. It was almost like an extra holiday. She told me to leave her alone for a while, and she didn't come out of her office most of the morning. Finally I had to take something in for her to sign. I could see at once she'd been crying. I closed the door and asked her what was wrong. She broke down and told me the whole story, about how her father took you away from her, how she couldn't say anything about you as long as he was alive. 'Today is his twenty-first birthday,' she said. 'He's grown up, and I've missed it all.' I just held her and let her cry it out. I even cried with her."

"Thank you for being there for her," Josh said.

Denise laid a hand over his. "She and I had grown close over the years. When I heard she was dead, I was devastated."

"A couple of years ago," Geri said, "you mentioned to me something about finding out what really happened to her. Do you think her death wasn't an accident? Do you know something about it, something you didn't tell the police?"

"I've never been sure whether this meant anything," Denise said, tightening her hold on Josh's hand. "I told the police, but they didn't seem interested. You see, Margaret kept a paperweight on her desk. It was the decorative finial off a bedpost, the very first piece of furniture her grandfather designed when he started the company. It was made of mahogany and looked like a pineapple, on a marble base. It was quite a heavy piece. It was on her desk the day before she died, but it wasn't there when I packed up her things."

"When did you do that?"

"About a week after she died. Mr. Dykstra told me we needed to move on and he needed to be able to use that office, since he was the new president of the company."

"When is the last time you can definitely say you saw that paperweight?" Geri's police instinct had obviously been aroused.

Denise stared at the mahogany breakfront while she thought. "It's so long ago, but I'm sure I don't recall seeing it after she died."

"Was anyone in her office after her death?"

"I was. Her brother was. We were trying to keep the company going. We needed things out of her files and her desk."

"Maybe Edmund picked up the paperweight." I looked up from my notes. "It was his grandfather, too."

"But he could have just gotten it when he took over the office," Geri said. "Why remove it by itself?"

"Who else could have taken it?"

"Someone who was in Margaret's office the night she died?"

I couldn't stop myself. My eyes locked on Josh.

Chapter 25

We spent another half hour listening to Denise reminisce about working with Margaret Dykstra. She had brought along a few pictures from company picnics and occasions of that sort. With his goatee disposed of, Josh did resemble his mother more than I had noticed before. I wondered when I should tell him about the file of e-mails Mickey Bolthuis had given me. My instinct was telling me the time wasn't right, but my instinct hadn't been right about anything in connection with Josh, so I just didn't know what to do.

When Denise showed us a picture of herself and Margaret on the porch of a lake-side cottage, Josh showed particular interest. "My grandmother and I drove around this afternoon and she showed me where my mother went to school and some other places that were favorites of hers. She said later this week we could go over to Saugatuck to see the cottage. She's pretty sure that's where I was conceived."

I cringed. "For some of us that's a tidbit that would be way too much information."

"My grandmother doesn't seem to have many inhibitions. She says she doesn't have enough time left to worry about what people think of her. She did that when she was younger. Now she's going to say and do whatever she wants."

"That's one advantage of getting older," Denise said. "About the only advantage, come to think of it."

Finally Geri gave me a signal with her eyes that could only mean she thought it was time to leave. It took a few minutes to pry Denise off of Josh's arm. He walked her to her car, then joined Geri and me beside my car.

"Are you doing okay?" I asked him. "You seem a little subdued."

"No, I'm good. Thanks for inviting me tonight. It means a lot to me to get these glimpses into my mother's life."

"It's a lot to take in, isn't it?"

"Yes, it is, especially the possibility my mother's death may not have been an accident or a stroke. And I wasn't in her office that night, by the way."

"Sorry," I said. "I hope you can understand ..."

He nodded. "I wonder if we should ask the police to re-open the investigation."

Geri raised a hand as though she was stopping traffic. "Let's not run too far in that direction yet."

"But the missing paperweight ... ?" Josh insisted.

"Speaking as a police officer *and* a psychologist, let me remind you that sometimes people become so used to seeing a familiar object in a certain place they don't realize when they're *not* seeing it."

"That's true, Josh," I added. "A lot of studies done on perception have proved it."

Geri seconded that with a nod. "The thing could have disappeared before Margaret's death and Denise just didn't notice. It would take more than that to re-open the investigation."

"It's something to think about, though," Josh said.

"Have you heard any more from Jennifer McKenzie about those injunctions your uncle slapped on us?" I asked, to get him off the subject.

"I'm not worried about them. My grandmother and I went to the lab Jennifer recommended and gave samples for the DNA test."

"I hope those results come back sooner than she indicated they might," I said. "Once we prove who you are, maybe I can get Edmund Dykstra off my case."

We said goodnight. As Josh walked to his car I opened the door of mine, but Geri put a hand on my arm.

"Are you aware you're being followed?" she asked.

"I've had a creepy sensation the last few days."

"You were followed from the restaurant tonight. I got his license number and called it in while I was driving over here."

"Who is it?"

"The car belongs to a private eye named Jake Folkert. He runs a security company. It's a pretty big operation, actually. He hires a lot of off-duty cops for parties, bodyguards."

"Why would a private eye be following me?"

"Well, duh, because somebody wants to know where you're going and who you're seeing."

"Should I be flattered because the head man is on my case?"

"It does seem odd for him to be doing a tail himself," Geri said. "Who would want to know ... Do you think it's Edmund Dykstra?"

"He's the odds-on favorite in my book."

"I wonder if this Folkert is the one who locked me in the closet last night."

"I don't know the guy personally, just by reputation. He was a cop for a couple of years but he was crooked and was kicked off the force. He's resented the police ever since. He doesn't cooperate with us and enjoys showing us up."

"Can you make him leave me alone?"

She shook her head. "There's no law against following somebody as long as you don't accost them or interfere with their activities. If you do, then it becomes stalking."

"So, I just have to wait until he does something to me?"

"We could talk to him. He's in the car down at the end of the block."

I closed my car door and started to turn in the direction Geri had indicated. She stepped in front of me.

"If we walk up to his car, he'll be gone. Here's what we'll do. The streets in this part of town are laid out on a nice rectangular grid. You go down two blocks and turn left. Folkert will follow you. Drive normally but make sure he doesn't lose you."

"Where are you going to be?"

"I'm going to turn left at this corner and then right two blocks over. We'll make a rectangle. I'll intersect with you and get behind Folkert. I'll call you on your cell once we're in our cars. Keep the line open. When I tell you to, you stop. I'll pull him over."

I nodded. I didn't like playing the part of the bait, but I wanted to know why this guy was following me.

"If we stand here much longer," Geri said, "he's going to get suspicious."

"Maybe you should kiss me. I bet he'd get a thrill out of that."

Geri's face told me at once that I'd stepped over the line.

"Sorry," I said. "My college roommate and I used to kid around like that."

"When we get to know one another better, maybe we can, too." Geri hugged me lightly, as gal pals do when they're saying goodbye. "Now, let's roll."

I did as Geri instructed me and turned left two blocks from her parents' house. Another car did start up as soon as my lights came on. I kept expecting my phone to ring. When it finally did, Geri apologized. "Sorry, I had trouble finding your number. Is he behind you?"

"Yes." I glanced in my rearview mirror.

"Good. I'm in position. I can see you coming. I'll get behind him."

With a sigh of relief I took note of her car pulling out as I passed the corner.

"Now, slow down, Sarah. Don't hit your brakes. Just take your foot off the gas."

I've always thought it trite when I heard people say it, but everything did seem to happen at once. Folkert's car drew much closer to mine and the blue light on Geri's dashboard started flashing in my rearview mirror. I expected Folkert to pull over, but he hit the gas instead. Without even thinking, I turned my steering wheel hard to the left. My car veered across the middle of the narrow street. All I could see was Folkert's headlights rushing toward me, filling up my entire window.

Chapter 26

I braced myself for the crash, for the side of my car to come crumpling in on me, for the airbag to burst in my face. Instead, I felt a gentle thump and heard a tinkling of broken glass. Then everything got quiet. At least I hadn't wet myself. I heard Geri's voice, in full command mode.

"Out of the car, slimeball! Right now!"

I knew she wasn't talking to me, but I tried to open my door and couldn't. Folkert's car was only inches from mine. I had to climb over the gear shift and get out through the passenger door. The pulsating blue emergency light on Geri's dashboard created an eerie strobe effect over everything. I stayed in front of my car, so I wouldn't get in Geri's way. Folkert's car was nudged up against mine, his right headlight broken. My car sported a new small dent over the left front wheel.

"Hands on the hood! Spread 'em!" Geri ordered.

"Okay, okay," Folkert said. "Geez! Take it easy. I haven't done anything."

"You didn't stop for a police officer who was telling you to pull over. That'll be the first charge."

I could see the man now, back-lit by Geri's headlights. It was the pasty-faced guy who had been watching me in the mall on Saturday, but his head was shaved and he didn't have a goatee. He must shave, I realized, to facilitate disguises. I wondered if he was also the guy I saw reflected in the travel agency's window. He leaned on the hood of his car as Geri frisked him. She was now wearing her badge and a gun and holster on her belt.

"Let me see some ID," she said. "Nice and easy."

The man drew his wallet out of his left rear pocket and handed it to her. "This is harassment," he said.

"This is figuring out why you're following a woman who's alone in her car at night."

136

"Come on! Two cars going in the same direction doesn't mean one's following the other one," Folkert said. He sounded like he was accustomed to talking to the police.

"I might believe that if you hadn't followed her all the way from Grand Rapids."

Folkert shook his head. "If you followed me from G. R., you're out of your jurisdiction. I don't have to put up with this crap."

"You know I can ask questions as part of an investigation anywhere in the state. If I need to arrest you, I can have a Zeeland cop here in five minutes. Do you want to make a production out of this, or do we just have a quick chat, then you go on your way?"

"Okay, okay. What do you want to talk about?"

Geri went through his wallet by the gleam of her headlights. "It's real simple. Why are you tailing Sarah?"

Folkert started to stand up straight, but Geri grabbed him by his shirt collar and pushed him forward. He had to slap his hands on the hood to keep his balance. He was not a big man, although he looked wiry.

"Keep 'em there, just like they were glued to it."

"All right. Watch the rough stuff. I've got a witness." He jerked his head in my direction.

"She looks more like the victim of a stalker to me," Geri said.

"Bullshit! I was hired to keep her under surveillance. That's all. There's nothing illegal about that as long as I don't invade her privacy or interfere with her activities."

"Locking me in a closet feels pretty invasive," I said. I knew I was supposed to stay out of it, but the idea that somebody had been shadowing my every move since Saturday, at least, wouldn't let me stay silent.

"What the hell are you talking about? I didn't lock you in any damn closet."

"Then who did?"

"When did this happen?" Folkert said.

"Sunday night, at the agency where I work, at Oaktree Family Services."

"So that's why you were in there so long."

"You were watching her then?" Geri asked.

"Yeah. I was sitting in my car, across the street from their parking lot. I saw her go in about five and come out about eight."

"Did you see anyone else come in or go out?" I asked.

"Yeah. Another car came in about six."

"Did you get a plate number? A description?" Geri asked.

Folkert shook his head. "Couldn't read the plate. It was dark and raining hard. It was a mid-sized car, tan or beige."

"That isn't much of a description from a guy who's supposed to be noticing details."

"I'm supposed to be following *her*." He nodded toward me.

"Did you get a look at the driver of this non-descript car?"

"Not a good one."

"Was it a man or a woman?" I asked.

"I couldn't be sure. He or she was wearing pants and a raincoat, walking under an umbrella."

"Was that the only person who went in or out of the building while you were watching?"

"Funny about that," Folkert said. "I kinda ... dozed off for a while. You know how it is on a long stake-out, Detective. Homeless guy woke me up, knocking on the window for a handout." He looked back toward me. "That was just a few minutes before you came out."

"Jake, Jake, Jake." Geri shook her head like a disappointed teacher. "Do people actually pay you for useless information like this?"

"Why don't you try hiring me and see what sort of information you get?"

I felt I had learned something important, but I kept it to myself for the moment. "Did you tell anyone—like the person who hired you—that I was in the building?"

Folkert shrugged and started to lift his hands.

"Hands on the hood!" Geri barked.

Folkert glared at her but smacked his hands back down on the hood. "What I tell my employer is between me and my employer. You ever hear of confidentiality?"

"Don't give me that bullshit, Jake," Geri said. "You're no priest or lawyer. P. I.s don't have confidentiality rights and you know it."

"So, what are you going to do? Beat the name out of me? That's the only way you'll get it."

"I can get it by making sure every police car in Grand Rapids is watching for you. We'll know everybody you talk to, everywhere you go. We'll be so close on your tail that when you fart we'll know exactly what you had for lunch."

Folkert smirked. "I love it when a babe talks dirty."

Geri put her hand on one of his and pressed it into the hood of the car. Folkert squealed like a girl and dropped to his knees. With his other hand he tried to dislodge Geri's, but the combination of her weight and leverage was too much for him. Tears welled up in his eyes.

"All right! All right! Here's what I'll do. Back off and I'll call my employer and quit the case." With his free hand he held up his cell phone, which he carried on his belt.

Geri eased the pressure on his hand. "Do it."

Folkert punched his speed dial. After what must have been three or four rings he said, "This is Folkert. Look, I'm going to have to withdraw from the DeGraaf case ... The police have spotted me. In fact, I'm having a chat with a very angry detective right now ... No, I haven't told them ... Now that they know me, I won't be able to keep the woman under surveillance ... You'll have my final report and my bill in the morning."

He hung up. "There. Does that satisfy you?"

"For about as long as you satisfied the last woman you were with." Geri grabbed for his cell phone. He jerked away from her and they fell to the pavement. As they struggled Folkert kept his arm outstretched, like a kid playing keep-away.

"Sarah, help me get his phone!"

I came around my car, but I didn't see how I could help. I couldn't risk a kick at Folkert for fear of hitting Geri. I felt like the schoolmarm in an old western watching the sheriff and the bad guy slug it out. Folkert had his arm and his phone under his car.

"Too late," he chuckled in Geri's face. He tossed the phone to her. "Knock yourself out. And I mean that literally."

Geri held the phone to her ear. "Damn! I wanted to push redial to find out who he just called," she told me.

"But I managed to hit another number on my speed dial."

"It's the answering machine in his office," Geri said, tossing the phone back to Folkert. They both got to their feet and straightened their clothes.

"Was it as good for you as it was for me?" Folkert smirked.

Geri's right hand balled into a fist and Folkert flinched. "Get the hell out of here, scumbag," she said. "And if you bother Sarah again, you'll find out just how miserable I can make your life."

139

I had to move my car out of the middle of the street. Then Folkert laid rubber all the way to the next corner. As we watched him roar off I said, "That was amazing. Thanks."

Geri took her holster off her belt and put it back in her glove compartment. "Don't thank me. We don't even know who he called. He could have been talking to his answering machine on the first call."

That deflated me pretty quickly. "Can't you check his phone records, like the police are always doing on TV?"

"That's TV. You know, TV ... real world." She pointed to two different spots. He's not a suspect, he's not involved in a case I'm investigating, and he's not a terrorist, so there's really nothing more I can do. Now, if somebody were to kill you ..."

I guess, even in the dark, she saw the look of panic on my face.

"I'm sorry, Sarah. That wasn't the least bit funny, was it?"

Chapter 27

Since I was 'on vacation' I had no reason to be up early on Tuesday morning, but I woke up at my usual 6:15 and couldn't get back to sleep, so I got up, exercised, and ate breakfast.

I had had trouble sleeping, thinking about that second car Jake Folkert claimed to have seen in the parking lot behind my building Sunday evening. I knew of three people in the office—Connie and two other caseworkers—who drove cars that could be described as mid-sized and tan or beige. The Dykstras owned a cream-colored Lexus. And Josh's white Honda might pass for tan on a rainy night.

My phone rang just as I was getting out of the shower. I wrapped a towel around me before I stepped out of the bathroom to pick it up. I'm no prude, but the possibility that somebody might be watching me was constantly on my mind now. Even if Geri had scared off Folkert, she had pointed out that he could assign someone else to follow me, someone I wouldn't recognize, or Folkert himself could put on another disguise. When I got home last night I closed all my blinds. Living on the second floor, that was something I never worried about before.

"Sarah," a vaguely familiar voice said when I picked up the phone, "this is Jennifer McKenzie, the lawyer."

"Yeah. Hi." Why on earth was she calling me at this hour?

"I have to make this quick. Josh just called me. He's been arrested."

"Arrested? Because of that stupid restraining order?"

"No. It doesn't have anything to do with that. He was involved in an accident on the interstate this morning."

"My God! Was he hurt?" My mood shifted from anger to worry. "Was it serious?"

"No, he says he's fine. He asked me to represent him. And he specifically asked me to bring you to the jail with me. Do you have time to do that?"

I almost laughed. "I think I can make room in my schedule. But I have to ask one thing up front. Does this involve the Dykstras in any way?"

"Not that I'm aware of."

"All right. Give me about half an hour."

As I dried my hair and got dressed I thought back over the six weeks that had elapsed since I met Josh Adams. Before he walked into my office, I was a busy, successful social worker, doing something I enjoyed, something that made a difference in the lives of my clients. Now I had a court order hanging over me and was teetering on the brink of unemployment. What had happened? Why had my instinct failed me so completely? Could I blame it all on Josh's chocolate eyes? Could I have done anything differently?

It was pointless to ask that. The only question that mattered was, Could I extricate myself from this mess?

A good step in that direction might be to cut Josh off and leave him to fend for himself. I had done everything I was morally and legally obligated to do for him. My boss had told me to have no further contact with him. I could go to Starbucks right now and enjoy a leisurely cinnamon latté while I read the paper. Probably the last latté—or paper—I'd be able to afford for a while. For that matter, I could just go back to bed. I hadn't made it up yet.

"Oh, hell," I muttered, "where are my car keys?"

* * * *

If downtown Grand Rapids is dying, as some people claim, I don't understand where all the traffic is going and why the streets are constantly littered with orange barrels. The local joke is that in Michigan there are two seasons: winter and road construction.

The Kent County Jail sits just north of I-196 at Fuller Street. It's an attractive new brick building and looks like an office complex or the downtown campus of a college except that the windows are narrow horizontal slits running in a band around each floor. Jennifer was waiting for me in the lobby. "I haven't had a chance to talk to anyone yet," she said.

We passed through the metal detector and she explained to an officer behind a desk whom we wanted to see. He made a call, gave us visitor's passes, and motioned us down a hallway to our right. We stopped in front of a door labeled Interrogation 3, where another uniformed officer was stationed.

142

"I represent Josh Adams," Jennifer explained. "May I see him?"

"He's in here." The officer opened the door and stepped aside.

"Let me speak to him for a minute," Jennifer said to me. She entered the interrogation room and the officer closed the door.

A jail is a busy place by eight o'clock in the morning, like a beach where all the detritus of the night before finally washes up. The police comb the beach, looking for ... Before I could finish that analogy, Jennifer reappeared. She hadn't even put her briefcase down.

"He wants you in there, too," she said to me.

"Okay." I glanced at the officer for guidance. "Is there a problem with that?"

"We don't have a policy against it," he said.

"The law does," Jennifer snapped. "The presence of a third party breaks attorney-client privilege. You could even be called to testify if this goes to court, Sarah."

Great, another complication. Was there anything about this man that didn't drag me farther and farther into some kind of mess?

"Have you explained that to Josh?"

"In no uncertain terms. He says he doesn't care. It's more important to him that you hear his story directly from him and that you not lose confidence in him."

"I don't want to hurt his legal standing or ... whatever."

"He says if you don't come in there he's not going to talk to me, so we don't have much choice."

Josh stood when we entered the room. I was surprised at how light and almost pleasant it was. It was not nearly as depressing as such places are portrayed on TV. No asylum-green paint peeling off the walls. No pipes showing or a single bare light bulb hanging down. The walls of this room were painted off-white. The table and chairs were new and almost comfortable. With a few decorative accessories, it could serve as an office.

Josh was wearing the sport coat his grandmother had bought him over a turtle-neck shirt and a pair of khakis. I was glad to see he wasn't handcuffed or chained to anything. I was disappointed to see that he was already re-growing his goatee.

"How are you doing?" I asked.

"Well, one advantage to getting arrested before breakfast is that my day can only get better." He tried to smile. "That's a little gallows humor."

We all sat down and Jennifer took out her legal pad. "I don't want to rush you," she said, "but we need to get to work. I have to be in court with another client at ten. Tell us what happened, Josh. Start from the very beginning. Don't leave out anything, no matter how unimportant you think it might be."

Josh folded his hands on the table. "I was on my way to have breakfast with a potential client when a car cut in front of me on I-196, near College Avenue, and braked suddenly."

" 'Potential client'? Was this somebody you had met or already had some contact with?"

"No. I got a call yesterday from a guy named John Beckwith. He wanted to talk to me about a free-lance project. I agreed to meet him for breakfast this morning."

"His suggestion or yours?"

"His."

"Did he suggest the place?"

"Yeah."

My instinct was yelling 'set-up', but I wasn't the lawyer and Jennifer didn't raise the issue, so I kept quiet. The fact that she had asked the questions made me think she suspected the possibility. I tried to peek at her legal pad, but her writing was illegible from my angle.

Jennifer made rapid notes. "Okay, a car cut in front of you and hit the brakes. Go on."

"I rear-ended him. There was nothing else I could do. He wasn't two feet away from me when he hit his brakes."

"Did someone in front of him slow down?" Jennifer asked.

"He claims an animal ran in front of his car. I didn't see it."

"When did this happen?"

"About ten till seven."

"So it was still pretty dark."

"Yeah."

"Isn't this some kind of insurance scam?" I asked. "They do this and then claim to have whiplash injuries. I saw it on an old episode of *Law and Order*." I suddenly felt silly bringing up a TV show to a lawyer. Like Geri said, 'TV ... reality.'

"That's a possibility," Jennifer said. "If that's what they're after, though, they usually pick nicer looking cars. No offense intended, Josh, but I've seen what you drive"

I tapped her on the arm. "Hey, watch it. Josh and I drive the same make and model."

"You and a hundred other people in this town. What was the other driver's name, Josh?"

"Carlos. I didn't get the last name. He was about five-eight, with a mustache, not as well dressed as me but not shabby looking."

"Did he appear to be hurt?"

"No. He was walking around just fine afterwards."

This wasn't making any sense to me. "So why are you in jail for a traffic accident? I know, when you rear-end somebody you're automatically considered at fault, but jail?"

Josh sighed, and I knew the scary part was coming and it was going to be really bad. If I was watching a video at home I would fast forward, but here I had to watch helplessly as it unfolded.

"When the police arrived," he said slowly, "this Carlos claimed to know me. He said he had ... bought drugs from me."

Chapter 28

I got up from my chair and stepped away from the able, looking at Josh with disgust, almost loathing. "Selling drugs! Christ, Josh! Every time I turn around, there's something else ..."

"And you're always ready to believe the worst," he snapped. "On the slightest suggestion or misunderstanding."

That stopped me before I could get into full rant. He was right. Every time some suspicion was raised about him, I immediately assumed it was true. As soon as I heard about the trust fund, I pegged him as a con man. After reading the erroneous article about his death, I had him fingerprinted. "I'm sorry, Josh, but I've literally put my job on the line for you."

"This isn't about you, Sarah. In case you haven't noticed, I'm the one in jail. And this time it's not true, any more than it has been any other time. I've never sold drugs to anybody, and I've never seen this guy Carlos before." He stood up and started around the table, but Jennifer held up a hand.

"All right! Calm down," she said. "We're being watched, you know." She pointed to a surveillance camera mounted on the ceiling in one corner of the room. "They can't hear us, but they can see us. Let's not turn this into performance art. Both of you, sit down."

We did as she told us. Even with my eyes fixed on the table right in front of me, I could see Josh trying to get me to look at him.

Jennifer wrote something on her notepad and resumed her questioning. "Had Carlos said anything to you before the police got there? Anything to suggest he knew you?"

"No." Josh didn't take his eyes off of me as he answered. "He was just mad about the damage to his car."

"Who called the police?"

"I did. On my cell."

"Did Carlos object when you made the call?"

"No."

146

"Did he try to say, 'let's just exchange insurance information', or anything like that?"

"No. The damage to both cars was bad. It wasn't a fender bender."

Jennifer turned to a new page. "What happened when the police got there?"

"I talked to them, told them my side of it. They talked to Carlos. He told them I had deliberately rear-ended him. Then they came over and asked me if they could search my car."

"Did you ask them why?"

"They said Carlos had identified me as someone he had bought drugs from. But it's not true. Absolutely not true."

"Is that what you told the police?"

"Yes. And I told them to search all they wanted to."

Jennifer shook her head. "The naiveté of the innocent. You should have made them get a search warrant."

"But wouldn't that make me look guilty?"

I saw a ray of hope. "Can't you get this thrown out because of an illegal search?" Once again I realized most of what I know about criminal law comes from legal shows on TV.

"They had probable cause," Jennifer said, "from the other driver's identification, and they had Josh's permission."

"I didn't think they were going to find anything."

"Why? Because you had it so well hidden?" I wasn't ready to let him off the hook entirely. He hadn't told me Margaret had contacted him. Other stuff might be incidental or accidental or coincidental, but that was deliberate.

"No, damn it! Because I thought there was nothing for them to find. I figured this guy had me mixed up with somebody else, or he was trying to shift the blame for the accident away from himself."

"But they found something?" Jennifer asked.

"Yeah ... ten ounces of cocaine and three thousand dollars."

I gasped and clutched at my stomach. "And you've got some glib explanation for this, just like you always do, I suppose. Do you understand why I'm leery of you?"

Josh reached across the table, but I wouldn't let him touch me. "Sarah, I swear to God I don't know anything about that stuff. I had never seen it before they pulled it out from under the back seat of my car. I have never sold drugs to anybody. I don't use drugs. You have to believe that. Both of you."

"And you have to keep calm," Jennifer said. "We're on your side, remember?"

"Yeah, but you'll be able to walk out of here in a few minutes. Not me. You ought to see the company I've got in that holding cell this morning. This lunatic named Vernon keeps getting in my face. And the rooms where the police interrogate people aren't nearly as nice as this one."

"We'll get you arraigned and post bail as quickly as possible," Jennifer assured him, "but you'll probably have to spend one night in there. You're lucky there wasn't more coke in your car or you could be facing a mandatory sentence."

"What do you mean, 'mandatory sentence'? I'm innocent."

"That's the assumption I'm working on. I'm just saying we at least have some room to maneuver. Now, let's finish your statement. What happened after the police found the drugs and the money?"

"I told them it wasn't mine."

"That explanation obviously didn't satisfy them."

"Carlos said he bought some cocaine from me at a bar Saturday night."

"Were you at that bar on Saturday night?"

"Yes, but I just had a couple of beers and played some pool."

"Do you remember seeing Carlos there?"

"No. There were dozens of people in and out." He ran his hands through his hair in frustration. "For Crissakes, it was a bar on Saturday night."

Jennifer slapped her pen down on the table. "Josh, don't get testy with me. I have to ask these questions. If this case goes to court, the D. A. will be asking them. I need to know the answers before he does. Now, did Carlos know your name?"

"He knew my first name."

"Had you told him your name after the accident?"

Josh closed his eyes, thinking hard. "I don't believe I did."

"Then how did he know your name?"

"I have no idea. If he was in the bar Saturday night, maybe he heard somebody talking to me."

"Isn't this all 'he said, he said'?" I asked. "This guy says you sold him drugs. You say you didn't. Unless they've got a witness, why would his word carry any more weight than yours?"

"Is there a witness?" Jennifer asked. From her worried look, I thought she was bracing herself for the next piece of evidence against her client, too.

"No," Josh said, and we both exhaled. "Not exactly a witness."

Oh, damn! I thought. Just like a Hitchcock movie, where you think you've gotten past the worst but you've only turned the corner to run into the real terror.

"What do you mean, 'not exactly a witness'?" Jennifer asked.

Josh sighed and leaned back. "Carlos told the police he paid me with a fifty dollar bill that had two X's on the back, on the left side of the Capitol dome, under the 'In God'. He had another fifty and a couple of twenties marked like that in his pocket."

"Did he explain why he had bills marked like that?"

"He said he likes to see how his money circulates. He wants businesses to see the buying power of the Latino community. The two X's are from 'Dos Equis', his favorite beer."

"Did he see the money before he said this?" Jennifer asked.

"No. The money was in bundles of one thousand dollars each, with rubber bands around them. He told the police to check the money and see if one of his bills was in there. One of the officers fanned through the bundles until he spotted it. Then they cuffed me and read me my rights."

"Let me get something straight," I said. "This guy causes an accident and admits he's using drugs, but he's not in jail?"

"He also didn't have a driver's license," Josh said.

"Geez! What *do* you have to do to get arrested around here?"

"Being found in possession of ten ounces of cocaine and three thousand dollars will do it every time," Jennifer said. "They need Carlos more as a witness against Josh. He's small fry compared to an apparent drug dealer."

"So, some drug addict's word is enough to put Josh in jail?"

Jennifer put a hand on my arm. "Sarah, this is the law you're dealing with, not logic or common sense. If they don't actually find drugs on somebody, they can't convict him of anything, no matter what he admits to having done. And in this case they don't want to. The more upstanding a citizen this Carlos appears to be, the better witness he'll make against Josh."

Josh slumped back in his chair. "Do you really think I'll have to go to trial?"

"There's enough evidence to indict you," Jennifer said. "Whether they can convict—I haven't seen the D. A.'s case or heard Carlos's testimony." She turned another page on her legal pad.

As Jennifer made a note I couldn't help wondering what kind of case the D. A. might have. Everything was so neat, so well-packaged. Too neat, too well-packaged. Could somebody be setting Josh up? What was it Katherine Dykstra said to me on Saturday? 'We'll deal with him later, if we have to.'

Jennifer's voice brought me back to the interrogation room. "One thing we have to be sure of is that there are no surprises the D. A. can spring on us in court. This is where you have to be totally, absolutely honest with me, Josh. And, for the sake of confidentiality, it really would be better if Sarah wasn't in here."

"No," Josh snapped. "I want her to hear everything I have to say. She has put her trust in me, and I want her to know it's not misplaced."

I folded my hands on the table. "So, say it. Lay everything right out here."

"All right. Here's the deal. Six years ago I attended a party in South Bend with a girl. She suggested we try a little coke, to enhance our sexual experience. Until that moment I hadn't known we were going to have sex. I'd been hoping ..."

"Some details we can do without," Jennifer said.

"Yeah, sorry. Anyway, what we didn't know was that two people at the party were undercover officers. I was young and stupid, and I bought a few grams of coke. It was all I could afford"

"Were the narcs selling?" Jennifer made a note.

"No. There wasn't any entrapment. But I didn't use the stuff. I was getting more and more uptight about the whole business and wondering if this girl was worth it. Some guy came up to me and wanted to buy my coke. I sold it to him."

"And he was a narc?" Jennifer asked.

"No, but one of the narcs saw the deal. I was arrested. The D. A. offered a plea bargain. My lawyer told me to take it. He wasn't sure we could win the trial and it could mean several years in jail if I was convicted. That possibility scared me enough to accept the deal. I got one year on probation for possession."

Jennifer drew a big box around several lines on her legal pad. I could read DA: South Bend Conviction. "We'd better go ahead and tell the prosecutor's office about that conviction," she said. "If they uncover it for themselves, it'll look like you're trying to hide it."

"Is it that big a deal?" I asked.

"I don't mean to discourage either of you, but with a charge like this, any other charges, however minor in themselves, add weight exponentially. The D. A. can make it look like you got off that time when you should have been convicted of dealing. Now, here you are, at it again on a larger scale. 'Ladies and gentlemen of the jury, don't let him get away this time.' That's how they'll present it, I think."

Josh rubbed his hands on his thighs and rolled his head back. "Sarah, please believe that I am innocent. I was in South Bend. I am now. Stupid, yes, but innocent."

"But can you understand how this looks? Every time I begin to feel some confidence in you, something undermines it. How can I trust you? Am I ever going to learn everything?"

Josh glowered at me. "Do we ever know the whole truth about anybody, Sarah? Would you want your life put under a microscope the way mine has been the last few days? Well, let's see, in case pornography becomes an issue, maybe I'd better tell you I had a subscription to *Penthouse* my first year in college. Everybody in my frat house did. Oh, and when I was nine I stole a candy bar from our local Minit-Mart."

"I'm trying to be serious, Josh."

"Believe me, I take this very seriously." He gestured at the locked door and the surveillance camera.

"Let's keep to the subject," Jennifer said. "Do you have any idea how the drugs and money got into your car?"

"Come on! Think about it. If I didn't put them there—and I didn't—then obviously somebody planted them. My apartment has a garage, and I use it. I have to. The lock on my right rear passenger door hasn't worked in months."

I wondered if Jake Folkert could have planted something, maybe even while we were talking to Denise van Putten. As a sleazy P. I. he probably had access to drugs, at least to people who knew how to get them. And his employer—if it was who I suspected—could put up three thousand dollars out of pocket change. "Josh," I said, "have you noticed anyone following you since Friday?"

"No."

"Where have you been the last few days?" Jennifer asked.

"Nowhere in particular. I went to the mall on Saturday. Oh, and to the police station. Something about fingerprints."

He looked at me and I blushed.

"I was at the bar for a while Saturday night. I was at your office yesterday morning, as you know. Then my grandmother and I went to the lab to give samples for the DNA testing. I was home right after lunch, worked on a project for a client. Then I went to Zeeland after supper. Sarah can vouch for that. So, now you know everywhere I've been since Friday."

There was a big gap, I noticed—a gap called 'all day Sunday'. In spite of my resolve to give Josh the benefit of the doubt, I couldn't help wondering where he might have been, about six o'clock Sunday evening, when somebody locked me in that closet. But what reason would he have had to do that? I'm trying to help him. And how would he have gotten into the building or known I was there?

Jennifer flipped her legal pad closed and put it back in her briefcase. "That'll have to do for now. I need to get ready for this other case at ten." She glanced at her watch. "I'll find out when you're going to be arraigned and be back in touch with you this afternoon."

"Can you let my grandmother know what's happened? We agreed we would talk every day, at least for a few minutes. She'll be expecting to hear from me."

Jennifer gave me a questioning glance.

"I don't think I could do it," I said. "Unless I was lucky enough to get Mrs. Dykstra herself, they would never let me talk to her or take a message from me."

"I'll call her. Can I give her your number, in case she wants to talk to somebody at greater length about this? As much as I appreciate the lady, I simply don't have time today for a lot of chit-chat."

I got out one of my cards, wrote my cell number on it, and gave it to Jennifer. "Tell her I won't be at the office number for a few days. I'm taking some time off." In response to her quizzical look I added, "Yes, because of the restraining order."

I don't know where that lump in my throat came from, but I fought it down. I wasn't going to cry in front of Josh, Jennifer, and whoever was manning the surveillance camera.

Jennifer laid a hand on my arm. "You have legal recourse if they fire you without cause. Here's my number." She handed me a business card.

152

Maybe I could sue them just for Connie's slush fund, I thought. I could retire on that.

"We have to go, Josh," Jennifer said, squeezing his hand. "Hang in there. You're going to be all right."

"That's easier to believe on your side of the table."

When we stood up an officer came in to escort Josh back to the holding cell. His shoulders slumped and his gaze stayed fixed on the floor, like he was being led away to his execution. He shuffled his feet to keep his shoes, without the laces, from flopping off.

Jennifer didn't seem to want to stop and talk outside the interrogation room. But a couple of things were worrying me. As I tried to match her pace down the hall, I said, "Does this feel like a set-up to you?"

She stopped by a soft drink machine and started pumping money in. "Set-up? Where do you get that? Another TV show?"

That rankled a bit. Just because I don't have Cal any more doesn't mean I watch too much TV. It's just that *Law and Order* is on every time you turn the set on. "No. Don't you think it's all a little too neat? The man Josh gets into an accident with just happens to be the man who claims to have bought drugs from him? And that marked money? Come on!"

Jennifer opened a Mountain Dew and took a swig. "Didn't have time for coffee this morning. Who do you think is setting Josh up?"

"The Dykstras. Who else?"

"Why would they do that?"

"Because of the trust fund."

"But putting Josh in jail doesn't affect his right to the trust fund. The trust instrument doesn't say he has to be an upstanding person, just that he has to be Margaret's son. The DNA tests will settle that, no matter what the Dykstras might do. They have no reason to do something like this, which could backfire on them, big time."

"But look what's happened since I introduced Josh to his grandmother. I'm being followed by a P. I. I've been locked in a closet, and I've had a restraining order slapped on me. Josh is in an accident, in jail, with a restraining order on him."

"The only thing in that whole list that you're *sure* was done by the Dykstras is the restraining orders. Those aren't illegal. Nor is it illegal to hire a private investigator to follow somebody. And, bottom line, where's the connection?"

Whose side was she on? "You know where the connection is. There are six million of them."

"Sarah, I know you're under a lot of stress right now, but I think you're seeing monsters under the bed. I'll defend Josh, but not by charging a prominent family with conspiracy. Maybe Josh pissed off somebody at that bar. We don't know. I think we can get him off, although that conviction in South Bend won't make it easier. As for the trust fund, all he has to do to claim that is to be alive on his thirtieth birthday."

Chapter 29

When I got back to my car I put the key in the ignition, then stopped myself. What was I going to do next? Where was I going? It would be a good idea to decide that before I drove out of here—to put my brain in gear before I put the car in gear.

What I really wanted to do was drive over to my parents' house in Holland, go up to my old room, get in bed and let this whole mess go away. When I got up, I would have some rice and kimchi and life would be good.

But reality impinged on that dream. Impinged on it? Hell, reality stomped all over it like a Klompen dancer's wooden shoes at Tulip Time. There were things I needed to do, people I needed to talk to. Ironically, my enforced vacation allowed me the time for that. I got out a notepad and started a list. I wanted to know more—a lot more—about Jake Folkert.

My phone rang. Damn! What must it have been like to live in the olden days, when you could actually get away from your phone?

"Sarah!" Mrs. Dykstra said. "Thank heaven I got you. I can't believe what I've just heard."

"About Josh being in jail?"

"Yes. It can't be true, can it? He wasn't selling drugs. He just couldn't be." There was no mistaking the anguish in her voice. After all those years of longing for this grandson, now to hear that she might lose him again if he had to spend a long time in jail ...

"I don't believe he's guilty," I said, "if that's any consolation."

"But how could this happen?"

"I think somebody planted the drugs and the money in his car."

"Who on earth would do such a thing?"

How could I answer that question? Tell her to talk to her own son? "Jennifer thinks it may have something to do with people Josh met at a bar Saturday night."

"She told me not to worry, but people always tell me that."

"It's good advice. Jennifer's going to take care of things."

"Sarah, she's not a criminal lawyer. She's a fine person, but I may hire some big guns to work on this. I'm not going to let my grandson go to jail for something he didn't do."

"Right now, it's important that you not get upset ..."

"Well, I am upset, damn it!"

Great. Now I had a sweet old grandmother cussing at me. How much lower could I sink?

"I'm—sorry, dear," Mrs. Dykstra said. "That was not called for."

"It's all right. I know how you must feel."

"I know I'm too upset to just sit here. Could you come over?"

"Maybe later today."

"Would you have lunch with me? My treat. How about Arnie's?"

"Sure. I love it."

"Could you meet me there at twelve-thirty? At the one on 28th Street?"

"Do you want me to pick you up?"

"That's not necessary. My granddaughter can run me over there."

"I thought she was in school."

"No, not Pamela. This is Edmund's older daughter, Ann. She stopped by for a visit."

"Ann? I thought you said her name was Georgia."

"Oh, that. Her name is Georgia Ann. Cornelius' middle name was George, you see. When Edmund and Katherine had a daughter instead of a son, Cornelius insisted that George be part of her name in some way. The man had to put his name on everything, like a dog marking his territory. We called her Georgie or George while she was growing up. But, as Margaret did with 'Peggy', she dropped the nickname and goes by Ann now, and she got married. I still slip and call her Georgie, but now she's Ann Haveman. She's a pediatric nurse."

* * * *

I put my phone down and stared out the front window of the car without really seeing anything. Ann Haveman was Edmund and Katherine Dykstra's daughter? Who could have seen *that* coming? It was just one more piece I had to put somewhere to make sense of a mess that was getting as complicated and improbable as the plot of a soap opera. There were missing documents—Josh's file and Margaret's diary—trust funds, a missing paperweight, somebody locked in a closet, drugs planted in a man's car, and a family that didn't want an autopsy performed when its most prominent member was found dead on the floor of her office. I felt like I had just dumped a 1500-piece jigsaw puzzle on the table and hadn't even begun to find the edge pieces yet.

Back to my notepad. Since junior high I have sorted things out on paper. Now I sorted things into lists and categories, hoping a pattern would emerge from everything I had gone through since Friday. But just trying to figure out what had happened on Sunday night alone was like one of those logic puzzles where Bob has red hair and his sister is two years older than twice the age of their cat in dog years, so which one drives a '65 Corvette? For all I could tell, the damn cat might be driving the 'Vette.

This was what I could reconstruct:

I went into the building after five.

Before six somebody else entered the building and locked me in the closet.

While I was in the closet, someone took Josh's file off my desk.

About eight o'clock Ann Haveman let me out of the closet.

Those were the only incontestable facts I had. When it came to questions, though, I had an overabundance, even a plethora—one of Cal's favorite words:

Who knew I had gone into the building? Jakc Folkert had the answer to that one.

Who entered the building at six? I was willing to bet Folkert knew the answer to that one, too. (Could he be as inept as he tried to appear to Geri and run a successful security company?)

Had the six-o'clock person gone out and someone else entered the building later?

Or had the six-o'clock person stayed and let me out?

In other words, was Ann Haveman the person who locked me in the closet?

Had she then called her own number from my office phone to give herself an alibi for being in the building?

Folkert claimed not to know who went in or out because he was asleep in his car for a while. Likely story.

As I looked over my notes I circled the name Folkert every time it occurred. If I'd had a red pen, the page would've looked like a measles epidemic. I had to know more about this guy.

My first stop was the nearest branch of the Kent County Library, where I showed my card and logged on to the internet. I Googled for Folkert's name and found the web site for 'Folkert Security and Investigations.' It appeared to be a good-sized firm, offering surveillance, installation of alarms, security for events, and 'all other security and investigative services.' A newspaper article from the Grand Rapids paper five years ago focused on the company's start-up. Before opening his own firm, Folkert worked for another security company, which provided services for Dykstra Furniture and several other downtown businesses.

It wasn't until after I'd read the article that I glanced back at the exact date. Two months after Margaret Dykstra's death. Somehow that felt significant. I printed off the article and circled the date.

Folkert appeared in a couple of other articles. One announced that Dykstra Enterprises, the parent company of Dykstra Furniture, had signed a contract with Folkert to provide security for all their properties, a contract worth over half a million dollars a year. That article was dated five months after Margaret's death. Edmund was quoted as saying, "We are familiar with Jake Folkert's work and are confident he can provide the type of services needed by our growing organization."

Pretty impressive for a recent start-up, I thought as I printed off the article and added it to my file. And again I had to ask myself, If this guy is running such a big operation, why is he tailing me himself? He must hire people to do that sort of grunt work.

While I was at the computer I decided to check out Dykstra Furniture's web site. In addition to an on-line catalog of their products, it had a page on the history of the company, with some nice pictures of various members of the family, from Our Beloved Founder down to Margaret and Edmund. Another page featured the company's 'Historic and Award-Winning Designs'. A disproportionate number of them were Margaret's work. There was a picture of the company's first design, the bed with the pineapple finial on the posts.

I couldn't make out much detail, given the size of the picture, but just seeing it reminded me of something I'd heard—probably on *Law and Order*—about the last person who sees a murder victim alive being the killer. What if I paraphrased that slightly: the last person who admits to seeing a missing object is the one who took it.

Denise van Putten was the last person to admit she had seen the pineapple paperweight in Margaret's office. It might be worth talking to her a little more about that. Geri didn't seem to think the matter merited police attention, but I didn't see why I couldn't ask a few follow-up questions.

I could have called her, but the work I do has taught me I can learn so much more talking to people face to face. Since my day had gotten off to such an early start with the visit to the jail, I figured I had time to see Denise before meeting Mrs. Dykstra for lunch. I got her address off the internet. Finding only one van Putten in Zeeland surprised me. The 'van' section of any phone book in the Grand Rapids area is as thick as 'Jones' or 'Smith' in most places.

* * * *

Denise lived on the same street as Geri's parents, but in a smaller house on the west end of Central Avenue, out of the historic district. It was a boxy little place from the 1950s, sided with white asbestos shingles accented by red shutters. The house and yard were both well-tended, even a bit prissy. A pile of yard trimmings sat on the curb. The arrival of spring in the small Dutch towns of west Michigan is marked by a two- or three-week period when residents can trim, rake, prune, and pile it all on the curb to be picked up.

No one answered the doorbell. A car was parked in front of the garage, so it seemed reasonable to assume somebody was home. It occurred to me that I didn't know if Denise was married. Could she be widowed? Maybe she was at home but in the bathroom.

I walked around to the back of the house. The large deck with the flowerboxes looked like a recent addition. The yard wasn't fenced, so I went to the back door and rang that bell. Still no answer. The back door opened onto an enclosed stoop, just a place to leave boots and coats. Through the glass I could see the kitchen door was open and the light on. Maybe the doorbell wasn't working.

I tried the doorknob. Growing up in a small town in west Michigan, I know many people here, especially long-time residents, still leave their back doors unlocked. Denise was one of them. I stepped into the stoop and poked my head through the open kitchen door.

"Mrs. van Putten!" I called. No answer. "Denise!"

Since I was already halfway in the door, I stepped into the kitchen. I wasn't breaking and entering, I argued with myself, just entering through an already open door. I wouldn't go any farther. Just check out the pictures on her refrigerator, which stood right by the door. Most of the pictures were on the front, of course, but a few were stuck to the side of the appliance, where they would be the last thing someone saw going out and the first thing coming in.

It looked as though Denise had two children, both of them married and producing grandchildren. But the picture that caught my eye was an old one on the side of the refrigerator. It was in one of those plastic holders with a magnet on the back, but it had faded a bit before it received that protection.

The picture showed a young Denise van Putten, probably around twenty, and a boy of nine or ten. Denise was seated on the bench of a picnic table at a park and the boy was standing beside her, leaning on her shoulder. The affection between them couldn't be missed. Neither could the small, jagged scar on the boy's left cheek.

I had seen that scar before. On David Burton's cheek in the picture of him and Margaret.

"What are you doing in here?" a voice said from the back door.

Chapter 30

Denise van Putten glared at me from her back stoop.

"Oh, Mrs. van Putten ... I'm sorry. I rang the bell ... and the door ... the door was open ... I just ..."

"My neighbors tell me I should be more careful about locking my door," she snapped. "I guess I should listen to them."

I was trying to talk to her while I was processing what I'd just seen in the picture on her refrigerator. Mickey Bolthuis said David Burton had a much older sister. It seemed reasonable to assume that sister—Josh's aunt—was standing in front of me.

"What are you doing in my house?" she asked. The anger in her voice had not entirely dissipated.

"I wanted to ask you a couple of questions about what you said last night. But I think this"—I pointed to the picture of her and David—"is what we really need to talk about."

She stepped over to the picture and ran her finger over the image of the boy, as she must have done countless times before. "He was such a beautiful little boy. If he'd only gotten half a chance in life, there's no telling what he might have made of himself."

I sensed she was letting down a defensive structure she had maintained for years. All she needed was an invitation to step out, not to surrender but to communicate with somebody for the first time.

"Would you like to tell me about him?"

She nodded and brushed a tear from the corner of one eye. "Where are my manners? Do you want some coffee?"

"Coffee would be great."

"I usually keep a pot made. I take some over to my neighbor, Gertie Nienhuis. She's eighty-seven and living alone. I check on her every day."

"I'm sure that means a lot to her, "I said as we sat down at a cheap maple table. I paused to put a little milk in my coffee, then looked at Denise and said, "You're David Burton's sister, aren't you?"

"Yes."

"That's why you mentioned Josh's eyes last night. You knew they looked like his father's."

"That's the strongest point of resemblance between them. David's eyes could bring you to your knees in fear or desire." She sighed heavily. "But I'd better start at the beginning."

"Good. That's how I like to hear stories."

"This is a rather depressing one, I'm afraid. The worst part of it is that our mother—mine and David's—died when he was born. She'd had a difficult time when I was born and I don't think she and my father planned to have any more children. I was eleven when David was born, and I became his surrogate mother. Our father remarried a year later, a woman named Joyce. He said we needed a mother. But I hated her and she didn't care about us."

I could already see some catastrophic dynamics developing in this family: the depressed father, the pubescent daughter who saw herself as wife and mother, the wicked stepmother. It must have been an emotional powder keg. "Do you think your father blamed David for your mother's death?"

"He said as much a few times when he was drinking." She mocked a man's drunken voice, "'If it hadn't been for you, I'd still have Donna.' What an awful thing to say to a seven- or eight-year-old child!"

"It must not have set very well with your stepmother either."

"No, but I didn't mind him hurting her. I wanted her to leave. I did everything I could to protect David from both of them. But, as time went on, they drank and fought more and more."

I took a sip of my coffee. It was bland, but it wasn't hazelnut. "Did one of them hit your brother and leave that scar?"

"Joyce." Denise spat out the name. "She slapped him, backhand, when he was seven. Her ring cut him. It was a bad cut, but Dad wouldn't take him to the hospital. We were so poor we didn't have any medical insurance. Dad said to put a bandage on it and it would be all right. I said I was going to take him to the emergency room. Joyce said if I did they would report us to Social Services for child abuse and they would take David away from us."

"That must have scared you."

"It was the worst threat she could make, and she knew it. So I got a needle and thread and told David he was going to have to hold on to his bedpost and let me sew it up."

I shuddered at the image. "Mickey Bolthuis said he told her and Margaret that he got the cut in a knife fight and sewed it up himself."

"That was the story he started telling in junior high. It enhanced his tough-guy image."

"How did you get from Chicago to here?"

"Dad had a sister in Saugatuck. We visited once in a while. He left Joyce and came over here a couple of times, but they always got back together. I promised myself I wouldn't get married or leave home until David was out of high school."

"You felt like he was your child, didn't you?"

"Well, wasn't he?" She got up, peeled the magnetic holder framing the two of them off the refrigerator, and sat back down with it on the table between us. "He spent more time on my lap than anybody else's. I taught him how to read and how to tie his shoes."

"I gathered from Mickey that your dad and stepmother eventually split up."

"They did. Dad came over here. I knew he was drinking worse than Joyce was, so I thought we would try to stay in Chicago until David finished high school. But we just couldn't stand to live with her. The guy who moved in with her started hitting on me, so we had to come over here. Things just got worse for David, though. He fell in with Margaret Dykstra and her crowd."

"The way I heard it, David was a bad influence on Margaret."

Denise dismissed that idea with a snort. "He was rough around the edges, but a sweet guy. Margaret and her friends gave him a taste for things he couldn't afford. She was driving a Mercedes when she was sixteen, for God's sake. What sixteen-year-old needs a Mercedes?"

She would get no argument from me on that point. "Did you know David had slept with Margaret?"

"Yes. She orchestrated the whole thing, he said. He wasn't really interested in her in that way, but she practically tied him down and jumped on him. He got tired of her calling him and chasing after him, so he left town as soon as he turned eighteen."

I wondered if his father's drinking and an overbearing older sister might also have figured into David's decision to bolt. Without talking to the man himself, who could know?

"You obviously don't like Margaret Dykstra. How did you end up working for her?"

"Once David left, I married the man I was dating and we moved to Grand Rapids. Dykstra Furniture had jobs for both of us. They pay well, and they're loyal to their workers. I also felt like they owed me something."

"In what way?"

"After being with Margaret, David decided he wanted to be rich. But he didn't have any skills and school never challenged him much. They just don't know what to do with a bright child."

Or an undisciplined trouble-maker, I thought.

"He fell in with a bad element back in Chicago. One night he was riding around with some guys he barely knew. When they stopped and went into a convenience store, he didn't think anything of it. He was just sitting in the back seat. Then he heard a couple of shots and the guys came running out. They had robbed the place."

"Was anybody hurt?"

"No, thank God. The clerk got the license number of the car and they were stopped ten minutes later. The clerk identified David as one of the men who came in the store, but he swore to me he wasn't."

Oh, Denise, I thought, how many ways can you spell DENIAL?

"How did you come to work so closely with Margaret, when you disliked her so much?"

"When she started working with the company, she wanted a secretary. I asked for the job because, in all honesty, I knew someday she would be a top executive and her secretary would be very well paid. She owed me that much for what she did to my brother's life."

"You didn't plan to get back at her in some way, undercut her?"

"Ms. DeGraaf, I'm not an evil person. I never intended to hurt Margaret. I just wanted to be in a position where I could know what she was doing, maybe gain some advantage for me and my brother from that. Over the years I actually came to like her. She had a mean streak in her, but she was very generous to me."

"Didn't she know who you were?"

"No. We never met when she was seeing David. And I never told her I had a brother. I didn't mention that to anyone at the plant. David spent a lot of those years in and out of jail. Once a man has a record, you know, it's hard for him to get back on his feet and easy for him to fall back in with the wrong crowd."

Especially if, as Mickey said, he *is* the wrong crowd. "Were you aware that Margaret had a child by your brother?"

"Not until that moment I told you about last night."

"It must have been a shock to you to realize the child she'd been grieving for all those years was your nephew."

"When I was holding her and letting her cry, I was crying almost as hard as she was. I guess she thought it was my sympathy for her."

"I know David got back in touch with Margaret a few months before her death. Did you have anything to do with that?"

"Yes, I did. David had been released from prison and came to stay with us. He always comes back to me." She said it proudly. "I told him about his son and about the trust fund."

"Then why did he call Mickey Bolthuis and act as though he didn't know about it?"

"I told him to. There had to be some way that he found out about it without it coming from me."

"So you made up the story about the paternity suit that he told Mickey."

"I was rather pleased with that," she said with a coy smile.

"And you advised Margaret to give him money the first time he asked for it."

"How did you know that?"

"Mickey Bolthuis saved a bunch of Margaret's e-mails. When I first read that one, I didn't think much about it. Now it has a whole new meaning. You found yourself in exactly the position you'd dreamed of. You could urge Margaret to give money to your brother without her suspecting where the advice was coming from."

She stood up, clutching the picture to her bosom. "Well, why shouldn't he have gotten some money from her? They had a child together. She was putting aside millions and was just going to throw it away on that art place if the boy wasn't found. David deserved something after she had set his life on such a bad course."

"But he came back and hit her up again."

"He was really trying to get his life straightened out and I didn't have the money to help him. I'm retired, on a fixed income."

That would explain her shiny polyester slacks and the generic sweatshirt, probably from a thrift shop. "Couldn't David get a job?"

"He got a job with Consolidated Security, on Margaret's recommendation. But he was fired after six weeks."

"For what?"

"David said the personnel director had pressured him to sleep with her." She must have caught my look of disbelief. "He's still a devilishly handsome man. He's kept himself in fine shape, working with weights."

In prisons, I wanted to tell her, guys who don't work with weights and keep themselves in top form become the victims. The guys who do the weight work see to that.

"Did David sleep with her?"

"He said he did a couple of times, but he didn't want to continue the relationship. So she fired him. I called the company and talked to the woman, told her we could sue for sexual harassment. She claimed David was fired because he was caught sleeping on a job."

"Sounds like you'd have a hard time proving David's case."

"He asked me not to pursue it. He said the woman was just an all-around bitch. I certainly found her combative. I can't believe she got the job she has now."

"What's that?"

"She's the director of The Art Place, Christine Grotenhuis."

Chapter 31

I made the drive from Zeeland to Arnie's on auto-pilot, trying to process everything Denise van Putten had told me. And wondering how much of it I could believe. She seemed to share Josh's penchant for telling only as much of the truth as she needed to at any particular time. She had sat there last night, gazing for the first time at her nephew, the son of her overly beloved brother/surrogate son, and she had kept her composure the whole time. She must have learned early on to mask her feelings in the hellish environment she grew up in.

And the brother. What a piece of work he seemed to be, thanks in large part to Denise doting on him and protecting him all his life, assuring him nothing was his fault. In my line of work we call that 'enabling'. It produces emotional cripples who always have to find somebody else to blame for their failures. If there's no one specific at hand, then 'the world' or 'society' will do.

David—and Denise—certainly had a lot going against them as children. Broken home, abusive stepmother, alcoholic father, poverty—any one of those factors alone could permanently damage a child. To David, Margaret must have looked like she had anything he could ever dream of wanting. But did envy of her wealth impel him into the life of a petty criminal? Did his attempt to extort money from her lead to an argument? A fight?

Did David kill Margaret?

I had asked Denise, point-blank, where David was the night Margaret died. She said he was at home with her and her husband. They had dinner and watched TV. Her husband died of cancer three years ago, so there was no way to verify or refute the story. I was inclined to believe her because I didn't think she would have raised the question of the paperweight if she thought there was any possibility her precious brother might have been involved in Margaret's death. She had not heard from David in almost a month. He was in either Chicago or Muskegon. She wasn't sure. She was sure he'd be back in touch soon.

I asked her to let me know if she heard from him. She said, with a sigh so painful I could feel it, that she almost hoped she didn't. Whenever he called now, it was to ask for money. He didn't seem to understand how little money she had. Or didn't care.

* * * *

I arrived at Arnie's at 12:25. Whenever I walk into the place I love to stand there for a minute and inhale the aroma of the breads and pastries, all baked on the spot. It's actually a good thing I live on the other side of town. I'm not sure I could put in enough hours on the treadmill to work off the calories I would consume here.

The lobby of the restaurant is large because it doubles as the bakery. Glass cases offer a mouth-watering selection of breads, cakes, pies, and other specialty items not for the weak of carb. A line of people were waiting to be seated. I spotted Mrs. Dykstra and Ann Haveman in a corner. Ann stood while Mrs. Dykstra was slumped dejectedly on a padded bench. The shaking of her head seemed more pronounced, and her face looked even more creased with worry. Before I could acknowledge them, Ann touched her grandmother's shoulder to keep her seated and walked over to me. She extended her hand, as though she were introducing herself.

"I haven't told Grandmother about you being locked in the closet," she said. "This is the first time I've seen her since then, and she's so upset over this Josh person being arrested that I didn't want to cause her any more alarm. Her heart isn't very strong."

"All right. I won't say anything about it."

I was glad now I hadn't mentioned the incident when we met in Jennifer McKenzie's office. I knew my reasons for keeping quiet about it. Why did Ann want it hushed up? What had she said when she let me out of the closet? She had seen the light on in my office, but she hadn't seen Josh's stapled file on my desk. Because she had already taken it? There was that principle again: the first person to claim something is missing is usually the person who took it. Could she be doing the legwork for her father and mother or for Folkert?

"Thank you," she said, leaning toward me like we were old chums. "Do you really think this man is my cousin?"

I decided to play things close to my chest with her. "All the evidence I have says he is. The DNA tests will tell us for sure."

"It's so strange. Until a few months ago I didn't even know

168

Aunt Margaret had had a baby. Nobody breathed a word of it around the house."

"How did you find out?"

"I overheard Grandmother arguing with my father one day. She was saying they ought to try to find Margaret's son before he turned thirty."

"What did your father say?"

"He said the past was past, and it was better left that way. I asked my mother what they were talking about, and she told me the whole story. She also said Aunt Margaret was more of a bitch than anybody in the family would admit."

Katherine would think that. Over Ann's shoulder I could see Mrs. Dykstra struggling to her feet. "I'd like to talk with you some more about this, but we'd better take care of your grandmother right now."

I worked my way through the people standing in line and took Mrs. Dykstra's elbow as she sat back down heavily.

"Are you all right?" I asked.

"Yes, dear. I'm just feeling weak. Ann wanted me to bring my cane, but I hate using that thing. It makes me feel so old."

Ann took her grandmother's wrist and started to check her pulse. Mrs. Dykstra jerked away. "Stop it! This isn't a doctor's office. Are you going to have me sitting on one of those tables in my underwear?"

"I just want to be sure you're all right, Grandmother."

"I'm fine. Sarah's here now, so you can go on about your business." She took my hand. "Oh, can you drop me off back at the house after we eat?"

"I'll be happy to," I assured her. Why not? I had no obligations. No job. Thanks to her son.

"All right," Ann said. "If you want to talk to me, Sarah, I'll be doing an information session for foster parents at the office on Thursday. Maybe we could get together then."

"I'm not going to be in the office for the rest of the week."

"Some vacation time?"

"No," Mrs. Dykstra said, just as angrily as I wished I could say it. "It's all because of your father and his damn restraining order. He's trying to get this poor girl fired."

Ann looked from her grandmother to me. She was obviously reconsidering whether she ought to leave the old woman in my care.

Or in my clutches.

"Are you sure you'll be all right, Grandmother?"

Mrs. Dykstra waved her hand toward the door. "I'm fine. You go on."

Ann turned reluctantly. "I'll call you later this afternoon"—no doubt to put me on notice that she was going to check to see if her grandmother got home safely—"and Roger and I will see you for dinner on Sunday."

She was barely out the door when the hostess called, "Dykstra. Party of three."

I assumed there were some other Dykstras in the line—an odds-on bet in this town—but Mrs. Dykstra took my arm and pulled herself up. "That's us."

"Who else is going to be eating with us?"

"Edmund. He should be here shortly."

"Oh, I didn't know ..."

"And he doesn't know you're here. Now, come on. I need to get something to eat before my blood sugar gets any lower."

* * * *

We sat across the table from one another, me with my back to the entry. Our server rushed our drinks and rolls out.

"Ann seems nice," I said.

"I never have understood the child," her grandmother replied. "She's almost a throwback to the '60s, determined to rebel at all costs. She refused to work in any of the family enterprises. She wouldn't let her parents pay for her college. Then she married a security guard."

"Who does her husband work for?"

"He used to work at Woodland Mall. Now he works for Jake Folkert's security company. Oh, here's Edmund. Brace yourself."

I wished I could have braced myself for the news that Roger Haveman worked for Folkert. That could skew everything I knew about who was following me or harassing Josh. Could he and Ann know about the trust fund? Could they think they might get hold of it if Josh were eliminated?

I barely had time to formulate those questions. Edmund was standing beside our booth before he recognized me. Slipping into the seat beside his mother, he said in a low voice, "What is *she* doing here?"

"I invited her," his mother said. "You two need to talk."

"First she needs to get at least a hundred feet away from me."

"Stop that nonsense."

"It's not nonsense, Mother. I've got a restraining order ..."

"Edmund, who owns the house you live in?"

The successful business executive's shoulders slumped. She must have played this card before. No matter how old we get, our parents can always turn us into children again. I was almost embarrassed for the man that he had to go through this in front of me. Almost.

"If you don't have that stupid restraining order lifted by the end of the day," his mother went on, "you'll find your suitcases packed and sitting on the sidewalk when you come home tonight."

"Mother, I do not have to listen to this. You invited me to have lunch with you. I didn't know you were setting me up ..."

"Like you set Josh up?" I said. It just popped out.

Edmund checked his mother's reaction, then glared at me. "I had nothing to do with that. Now, I have said all I'm going to say to you." He started to get up, but his mother grabbed his arm.

"I'm feeling faint, Edmund. I could pass out any minute now."

"Mother, don't ..."

"I know you dislike scenes in public places. You sit down and talk to Sarah or I'll create a scene that will keep people talking for days. Paramedics, an old lady wheeled out on a gurney. Considering who you are in town, it'll probably make the news on TV tonight."

Edmund balled his left hand—the one his mother wasn't holding—into a fist and pressed it to his mouth, probably where he would have liked to hit his mother at that moment. He took a deep breath and let it out slowly.

"All right, Mother. You win. Just like you always do."

"And the restraining order?"

"I'll call Martin as soon as we're finished here."

Our server came and took orders. Edmund didn't want anything. "Now, what do we have to talk about?" he asked.

I wanted to smack his smug, rich face, but I folded my hands on the table in front of me and said, "Let's start with the fact that I'm on the verge of losing my job because of you."

"Ms. DeGraaf, I am simply trying to protect my family." He shrugged in innocence. "You've brought in some charlatan, claiming he's my nephew, when all he's after is a trust fund he has no right to."

"With all due respect, sir, the DNA testing will determine whether he's your sister's son." I paused. I knew so much more about Josh and his father now, but I needed to keep a couple of trump cards up my own sleeve. "Why can't you wait for those results before taking the kind of drastic action you have against Josh and me?"

"Oh, I'm eager to get those results. So eager I went to the lab this morning and offered them a bonus to move that test to the top of their job list."

"How did you know about the test?" his mother asked.

"I make it my business to know things, Mother, so I keep in touch with people who can give me the information I need."

"You mean you have a spy in Jennifer's office."

Edmund made a disgusted face. "That's such an ugly word. I have business contacts in strategic places."

"How did you get them to move the test up?" I asked.

"I wrote them a check to buy some equipment they need. I even gave them a sample myself while I was there," he concluded proudly.

Mrs. Dykstra gasped and put her hand on her chest. "You did what?" I thought she really was going to pass out.

"I gave them a DNA sample. All they do is swab the inside of your cheek. Of course, you know that already."

"But ... but why did you do that?"

"To make the test more definitive. By the end of the week we'll know without a doubt who's related to whom, and who's not."

Our salads arrived. Edmund helped his mother put the dressing on hers and some butter on her bread. Her hands were shaking particularly badly today.

"If I'm going to get the restraining order lifted," he said, "and the DNA test results come in on Friday, is there anything else we need to talk about?" He sounded like a company president who wants to get out to the golf course as soon as the meeting is over. His underlings would know better than to raise any other issues.

"There is one thing I'm curious about," I said.

Edmund rolled his eyes. He would miss his tee time. "What?"

"Why is Jake Folkert following me?"

"He does security for us. I thought you represented a threat, so I asked him to keep an eye on you. That's what I pay him for."

"But why is he following me himself? He's the head of his company. Nobody would expect you to go into a factory and actually *make* a piece of furniture. Why is Folkert himself following me?"

Edmund suddenly seemed intensely interested in getting the edges of his placemat exactly parallel to the sides of the table. "I don't know. I don't tell him how to run his business. We have a contract with him to provide security for our family and our property. I told him to look into this. You'd have to ask him how he parcels out work assignments. Look, I'll tell him to stop following you. Will that satisfy you?"

"Thank you. Now, you knew Folkert before your sister died, didn't you?"

"What difference does that make? I said I would stop him from following you."

"I appreciate that, but after what you've put me through the last few days, Mr. Dykstra, I think I deserve some answers. Did you know Folkert before your sister died?"

He turned sideways, about to stand up. "Ms. DeGraaf, you're not a police officer or a lawyer. I don't have to answer your questions."

"You do," his mother said, "if you expect your family to have a place to sleep tonight."

Edmund turned back into the booth, his face screwed up like a ten-year-old who's been told he can't have dessert until he eats all of his broccoli. "All right. Yes, I've known Jake Folkert for about eight years. The fact that he worked for Consolidated, the company that used to provide our security, is a matter of public record. He started his own company and we signed on with him. What's your point?"

"Starting a business requires a lot of capital. Folkert went from rent-a-cop to owner of a fair-sized company in less than six months. How did he manage that?"

"He must have gotten a bank loan. Isn't that what people do to start a business?"

"I guess so, if they didn't inherit a ton of money." I couldn't resist the jab, and I could see him twitch from it. "The contract he signed with you must have been a godsend for him. Why did you switch from your old security company?"

"From what I knew of Folkert I thought he would be more cutting-edge than Consolidated. I was getting impatient with how slowly they were modernizing."

"Did Folkert have access to your sister's office?"

Edmund flinched before he said, "Yes. The same as everyone else who worked for Consolidated."

"Was there a security guard or guards on duty at your plant the night Margaret died?"

"There was a guard there every night."

"Was Folkert on duty that night?"

"You'd have to check with Consolidated to get that information." He looked at his watch. "I have to get back to the office. Why are you so obsessed with Jake Folkert?"

"A lot of strange things have happened to me in the last few days, Mr. Dykstra. I'm just trying to understand how they all fit together. Folkert seems to be the linchpin."

"Then you should be talking to him." He stood, dropped a fifty on the table, and strode out without saying goodbye to his mother.

* * * *

As I drove Mrs. Dykstra back to her house after lunch I could see my questions had troubled her. When we exited I-196 at College Avenue and turned south into Heritage Hill, she finally spoke up.

"Sarah, were you hinting that Margaret's death might not have been an accident?"

"Mrs. Dykstra, I'm not ..."

"Please, dear, call me Ella."

"All right. Ella, I'm not suggesting that." With no more information than I had, I didn't want to shatter any illusions she might cherish. To think that her daughter was murdered would open questions about why someone wanted to kill her. The answers to those questions could undermine every memory of Margaret she held dear. "I just don't understand Jake Folkert's role in all this. I thought, if I could figure out that little corner of the puzzle, some other things might start to make sense."

"He's so repulsive." Ella screwed up her face as though she could taste his vileness. "I don't know why Edmund works with him."

"You've met him?"

"He comes to the house now and then to talk with Edmund and Katherine."

"What do they talk about?"

"I'm not included in those conversations. Don't want to be. I just know Katherine is always upset after he leaves."

Chapter 32

Having the restraining order lifted would be a relief, but I almost regretted Edmund was going to do it so quickly. A couple of days off with pay would have been welcome. Now I needed to make the most of the few hours remaining in the afternoon.

When I had seen Ella safely in her front door I found myself funneled by the one-way streets in Heritage Hill toward downtown. Realizing I was only a couple of blocks from The Art Place, I decided to take another look at Margaret's sculpture, 'Mother ... and Child?' Aside from its sheer power, what was so special about it that she had willed it to her son?

The girl with all the piercings was behind the desk again. Today she had something dangling from one of the small rings in the upper part of her left ear, like a Christmas tree ornament. I started to put my two dollars in the fishbowl by the door when she said, "We're having a special membership drive right now. Would you be interested in joining? Members aren't expected to donate each time they come in."

"What's the offer?" I asked.

"Twenty-five dollars for a year's membership, instead of the usual thirty-five. If you come in just once a month, you've got your money back. Except for a dollar, of course."

Since my prospects for continued employment had improved over lunch, I got out my checkbook and signed up. The girl entered my data into the computer and printed me a membership card on the spot. For another dollar she even laminated it. Armed with my membership card, I proceeded into the gallery with the confidence to beard Ms. Grotenhuis in her den.

The Dykstra Gallery was deserted, so I could examine Margaret's sculpture more closely. The crouching figure stood about four feet high. Her right knee touched the floor. The other leg was bent, but with the foot on the floor. The left arm was extended, reaching for the child, I suppose, with the face upturned in the same direction. The right hand clutched at the figure's chest, touching the left breast. It was done in a rough style, with no effort made to conceal the welds. Both breasts had weld marks around them, like scars left from a bad boob job. When I tapped the figure in a couple of places, it sounded hollow.

I wanted my own record of this piece. A disposable camera had been riding around in my bag since Christmas. I hadn't finished it over the holidays at my parents' house, and I don't take pictures with any regularity. I had photographed the sculpture from every angle when Christine Grotenhuis' unmistakable voice said, "We don't allow cameras in the galleries."

"Sorry. There's no sign prohibiting them," I pointed out.

"Everyone knows a camera flash damages pieces of art work."

"I don't see how it can hurt a stainless steel sculpture," I said, slipping my camera into my bag before she could confiscate it.

She folded her arms over her chest. "Ms. DeGraaf, what are you doing here again?"

"I'm enjoying my membership in this fine organization."

"Membership? Since when?"

I whipped out my membership card and waved it in front of her face. "I'm a member of The Art Place, freshly laminated and in good standing."

She considered her options. "All right. I guess you can stay, since you have your membership."

"Could I, as a member, ask you a few questions?"

"What sort of questions?"

That one could lead to a philosophical seminar, but I wanted to stay on task. She wasn't likely to give me much of her time. "This building sits on a choice piece of real estate. How can a non-profit organization like this afford it?"

"We can't. The building is owned by Dykstra Enterprises."

"Really?" I guess she hadn't heard about the restraining order.

"It was their original warehouse. When they moved to their present location Margaret offered it to us. We started in an old house a few blocks from here. She paid for the renovations. We lease the property for a dollar a month."

That didn't strike me as a particularly smart business decision. This building was in a highly desirable location, just two blocks from an entrance to US 131, the major north-south freeway through Grand Rapids and western Michigan. The site, if not the building itself, must be worth quite a bit. If Dykstra Enterprises didn't need the building, they could sell it or rent it for a lot more than a dollar a month. But maybe there was some tax advantage to donating it to a non-profit group. Finance was not my strong suit, witness the balance in my 401(k).

"Is there anything else you want to know?"

I had to think quickly. I wish I could have made a list. I think so much better on paper. "The Board of Trustees. You said a few days ago that Edmund Dykstra will become chair of the board soon."

"At their next meeting."

"Are their meetings open to members?"

"That depends on the agenda. Some are closed."

"Doesn't Michigan have a Sunshine Law that requires them to conduct open meetings?"

"That applies only to public institutions. Now, if you'll excuse me, I have work to do."

"This won't take much longer, really. How long have you been director here?"

"I was hired four years ago."

"So you never met Margaret."

"No."

"And you said Edmund and Katherine got involved here only after Margaret's death."

"That's right. They said Margaret regarded this as her private space and didn't want other family members involved. But Mr. and Mrs. Dykstra have been active and generous supporters since she died. Katherine's not only a sculptor. She also keeps our books, *pro bono*."

I glanced at Katherine's sculpture in the opposite corner of the gallery. If a giraffe is an animal put together by a committee, her 'Untitled #7' looked like one of their early drafts. "I hope she's better at those kinds of figures than at this kind."

"She happens to be a CPA and chief financial officer for Dykstra Enterprises. Now, I do have work to do. Enjoy your visit and your membership."

"Just one more thing," I said, stepping between her and the entrance to the gallery.

"Ms. DeGraaf, you're trying my patience."

"I seem to have that effect on people lately. But I'm curious. What plans are you making for the six million dollars in Margaret's trust fund, and do you have a contingency plan if her son shows up to claim the money?"

"Trust fund? What are you talking about?"

"Didn't you know Margaret left a six-million-dollar trust fund? It goes to The Art Place if her son can't be found."

My question was meant as a direct challenge. From what I knew of David Burton, he struck me as a man who liked to impress the ladies. I was willing to entertain the possibility that he and Ms. Grotenhuis had slept together—even in her late forties she maintained an athletic figure—and I could imagine him mentioning the trust fund and his lost son. Could she then have gone after this job to put herself in position to administer that fund?

Or what if it was David Burton's idea for her to get this job? What if they were working together on some kind of scam? But would Burton go so far as to kill his son?

Ms. Grotenhuis put one hand on Katherine's sculpture to steady herself. "Six ... six million dollars?" If she was acting, it was a convincing performance. "I haven't heard a word about this. I had no idea she had a child. Has he been found?"

"You met him Friday. Josh Adams, the young man with me, the one you were so rude to. Oh, and Margaret left that sculpture to him, too."

"How do you know all of this?"

"I work for Oaktree Family Services. I reunite adoptees with their biological families."

"You're sure this man is Margaret's son?" She was seeing six million dollars disappear as suddenly as it had been dangled before her.

"I'm convinced. So is his grandmother. Edmund and Katherine Dykstra insist on DNA tests. Those results will be back on Friday."

"So the issue hasn't been settled." In other words, there was still a slim hope The Art Place might get the money.

"It's just a matter of time."

"Time. Well, I've given you all the time I can afford. Excuse me."

"Just one thing. Does the name David Burton mean anything to you?"

She brushed past me without answering.

Chapter 33

Leaving my car in The Art Place's parking lot, I walked the four blocks over to the Grand Rapids police department's main headquarters. The officer at the reception desk recognized me, signed me in, and gave me a visitor's nametag. She didn't have to give me directions to Cal's office.

Cal and Geri were both at work. It looked like they were devoting the day to catching up on reports. The Red Wings plate, glued back together, now hung over Cal's desk.

"Hi, Sarah," Geri said.

"What can we do for you?" Cal asked. He was looking at me, moony-eyed, like this boy in my tenth-grade English class used to.

"If you have a minute," I said, "I'd like to ask both of you about something."

"A police something?" Geri asked.

"Is this about your friend, that Adams guy who assaults cops?" Cal asked, drawing his eyebrows into a scowl. I wondered if he was ever going to let go of that business.

"He's not a friend. He's a client. But he's in trouble, and I think he's being set up." I described what had happened and my suspicions about the Dykstras. Cal's eyebrows did go up when he heard Katherine was a CPA and took care of the books for The Art Place.

"That certainly has some of the classic traits of a set-up," Cal said. "But what would the Dykstras gain from having Josh in jail? Is there any way I could see a copy of the trust instrument?"

"Jennifer let me keep a copy." I pulled the folder out of my bag. Cal skimmed the three pages.

"There's no morals clause," he pointed out, "no restrictions on where he lives or his marital status, anything like that. If the executors are satisfied he's the son, he inherits. Nothing else matters."

"There is one requirement," I said.

"Did I miss something?" Cal said, flipping through the document.

"He has to be alive."

"What do you mean? What motive would somebody have to kill him? According to this, if the son doesn't show up, The Art Place gets the money. Are you suggesting somebody there would have motive to kill Josh?"

I clenched a fist in frustration. "Doesn't it strike you as awfully convenient that Edmund Dykstra will become chairman of The Art Place's Board of Trustees next week and that Katherine Dykstra does their books?" Cal opened his mouth to protest. "*And*—I'm not finished—that the director of The Art Place doesn't know anything about the trust fund? Or at least claims she doesn't."

"But, Sarah," Geri said, "these are some of the richest people in town. Why would they resort to something like this?"

"That's what I haven't figured out yet."

"After you do get it figured out," Cal said, "maybe you could work on who fired the shots from the grassy knoll."

"Hey, I don't appreciate the sarcasm."

"I'm just trying to inject a note of realism. You don't have a shred of evidence ..."

"Evidence? Damn it, Cal! Somebody locked me in a closet. I've got a P. I. following me. I can't find documents I'm supposed to have. I've had a restraining order slapped on me. My client is in jail for something I know he didn't do."

I guess the stress had been building up more than I realized. Suddenly I was crying. I didn't want to be, especially in front of Cal and Geri, but I had my hands to my face and I was sobbing. Cal put his arms around me and didn't say anything for a couple of minutes. When I looked up he held out a box of tissues for me. Taking a wad of them, I turned to apologize to Geri, but she was gone and the door was closed.

"I'm sorry," Cal said. "I didn't realize how seriously you were taking all this."

"Don't you think somebody should take it seriously?"

"Tell you what. I'll call over to the jail and ask them to watch Josh closely."

"Could they put him in a separate cell?"

He screwed up his mouth. "I doubt it. Things are really crowded over there, but I'll do what I can."

"Thanks." I hugged him. When I stepped back he kept his hands on my waist. I let my right hand rest on his shoulder as I dabbed at my eyes with my left.

"I can't really help you with the other issues," he said. "The missing documents and stuff. But is there anything else I can do for you?"

"Actually, there is. As I've been looking over my notes I've noticed that phrases like 'two years ago' or 'a couple of years ago' come up a lot. For instance, Josh's parents and his cousin were killed in that explosion two years ago. All I know about it is what I read in a newspaper article. Could you call somebody in South Haven and see what information you can get about that?"

"Wasn't it ruled an accident?"

"Yes, but my instinct—I know, you don't like to hear about my instinct—but it tells me there's more to it than that."

"Okay, I'll see what I can come up with." He moved to his desk to make a note.

"Thanks. Again ... Well, I'd better get going." How could it feel so awkward to talk to a man I'd slept with for a year?

"Yeah. I've got some calls to make."

"Right." I took a step toward the door, then turned back to him. "Cal, about that plate ..." I gestured weakly toward the wall. "I'm really sorry I broke it. It was childish of me."

"It was exactly what you needed to do." I couldn't remember when I'd seen so much intensity in his eyes. "It's given me a lot to think about. That's why I've got it on the wall."

"Do you want to talk about what you're thinking?"

"Yes, I do. How about over dinner tomorrow night?"

Before I could do more than nod there was a knock on the door. Geri stuck her head in. "Sorry, guys, but I need a couple of things off my desk."

"That's okay," I said, "I'm on my way out. Sorry about that crying jag." Turning to Cal, I added, "Call me and we'll work out the details."

* * * *

I was back to my car and almost back down to earth when my phone rang. I chuckled as I dug it out of my bag. I hadn't expected Cal to call so quickly. But it was Jennifer McKenzie.

"Sarah, Josh's arraignment is set for 4:00 this afternoon."

"That seems quick. I thought it would be tomorrow morning."

"Apparently it's a slow day at the court house."

My call-waiting buzzed me. "Jennifer, I'm sorry, I've got another call. Give me just a minute." This would be Cal.

But it was Martin Vandervelde, informing me the restraining order against me had been lifted, contrary to his advice, he made sure to point out. I thanked him, cut him off, and reconnected to Jennifer.

"Okay, I'm back. And I'm free of that damn restraining order."

"Great! How did you manage that?"

"I had a little chat with Edmund Dykstra."

"I'm impressed."

"Don't be. His mother threatened to throw him out of the house if he didn't lift it. Should I get Ella and bring her down there?"

"You can, but most arraignments are done by closed-circuit TV now. It saves the time and expense of moving prisoners back and forth between the jail and the courthouse. Ella won't be able to see Josh or talk to him. You might ask her if she'll post bail for him."

"I'm sure she will. And even if she can't see him, I don't think she would forgive me if she wasn't there."

"I'm sure you're right. She's absolutely convinced Josh is her grandson. She called me this morning and told me to change her will. She wants to leave the house, the cottage in Saugatuck, and everything else that's in her name to him."

"She's jumping the gun, isn't she? Why can't she wait for the DNA test results?"

"That's what I told her. I even told her if Edmund got wind of this, he might use it to have her declared incompetent. But she is a strong-willed woman."

There seemed to be a few of those in this family. "Are you going to write her a new will?"

"Yes, but things are going to be *really* busy around here the next few days, if you get my drift. I won't have anything for her to sign before Friday. Gotta go. See you at four."

I called the Dykstras' house and was immensely relieved when Ella answered. When I explained the situation to her, she insisted on going to the courthouse. I assured her I would be there in a few minutes to pick her up.

When I pulled up in front of the Dykstras' house I noticed a couple of cars in the driveway. Katherine and Edmund must have gotten home by now. My worst fear was realized when Katherine opened the door. Over her shoulder I could see Ella pulling on a coat with her granddaughter's help.

Katherine didn't invite me in, just stood there blocking the door. "I hear you and my husband came to an understanding at lunch." Smirk.

"Of sorts. He agreed to call off his dogs until the DNA tests come back."

"I hope you won't be too disappointed when those tests prove that Mr. Adams is no relative of ours." A bigger smirk.

Suddenly I saw the significance of what Edmund had said at lunch. He had bought some new equipment for the lab. Would they show their appreciation by rigging the DNA test? "Why are you so sure he's not?"

"For one thing, he looks nothing like Margaret." A totally self-satisfied smirk.

"On that we agree. He looks more like his father."

The smirk disappeared. "How do you know that?"

Mrs. Dykstra elbowed her way past her daughter-in-law. "Let's go," she said. "We're going to be late."

Chapter 34

Like the Kent County Jail, the courthouse is new, clean and bright. From the outside it could be mistaken for a high-tech office building. Except for the massive metal detectors at the door, it feels more like an office building than a judicial facility where so much human misery is processed and people's lives are forever altered.

Ella had brought her cane. She leaned on me while it went through the detector along with our bags. She looked more tired than I had seen her in the few days I'd known her. But I think the cane and her gray hair got us a little more courteous attention. The officer at the information desk made sure we knew which courtroom we were going to.

Maybe I do watch too many episodes of *Law and Order*. I'm always disappointed when I see a real court proceeding, even a report of a trial on the six o'clock news. Real attorneys don't chew up the scenery like Jack McCoy; there's no sultry Assistant D. A. showing a lot of leg under the counsel table; and the courtrooms don't have that 1930s look to them, with the heavy dark wood, high ceilings, and ornate moldings.

This courtroom was furnished in a sleek, no-frills, modern style. The furnishings were made of a light-colored wood or faux-wood product, and the judge's bench was raised only about a foot off the floor. Ella insisted on sitting in the front row of seats behind the railing that separated the lawyers and the judge from the audience.

Everybody appeared to be just milling around, shuffling files. One of the two counsel tables in front of the judge's bench was occupied by what looked like a junior-high student but must have been the lowest ranking Assistant D. A. who got drafted for this duty. Whenever he spoke, I expected his voice to crack. As each case was called and dealt with, he moved a folder from one pile to another. When they were all in one pile, I presumed, he could go home and play video games.

Ella nudged me and pointed toward the prosecutor's table. "Do you see what I see, sitting right behind the prosecutor?"

It took me a second to recognize him from the side, but the man Ella was indicating was Martin Vandervelde. "What is he doing here?"

"I'll guarantee it's nothing good," Ella said.

The other counsel table was occupied briefly by a succession of defense lawyers, who used it primarily to drop their briefcases on. They hardly had time to get settled before a plea was entered and bail set. Jennifer McKenzie stood in a line of lawyers. The judge, the Honorable Bradley Stegenga, was a heavy-set man in his fifties who had gotten suckered into the goatee trap. He stared over his half-glasses at a TV screen with a small camera mounted on top of it.

"Docket 4091," the bailiff called out as we took our seats. "People vs. Joshua Adams." Jennifer stepped forward.

As Ella groaned softly I placed my hand on her arm. I felt responsible for contributing to her sadness. I had brought Josh into her life, raising her hopes of ending long years of grief. Now he was in jail, with an uncertain future ahead of him.

"Mr. Adams," the judge said into a microphone, "you're charged with possession of a controlled substance with intent to sell. Do you understand the charge against you?"

I couldn't hear Josh's reply, but it must have satisfied the judge. "Do you have an attorney?"

"I represent Mr. Adams, your honor," Jennifer said.

"Not your usual bailiwick, Ms. McKenzie," the judge said, looking at her over his reading glasses.

"This is ultimately about a family, your honor."

The judge looked puzzled. He scanned a page from the file in front of him. "I thought it was about possession of cocaine. How does your client plead to that charge?"

"Not guilty, your honor."

"All right, that plea is entered. Prosecution on bail?"

"Your honor, the prosecution asks for remand in this case."

Jennifer was clearly caught off-guard. "Your honor, may I ask what purpose would be served by keeping my client in jail?"

"It does strike me as unusual, Mr. Holwerda," the judge said, "in a case of this sort. We are talking about a minimum amount of cocaine in his possession, aren't we?"

"Yes, your honor, but the defendant is not steadily employed, only recently moved to Grand Rapids, and is under a restraining order to keep him from harassing one of the city's most prominent families."

Suddenly Ella stood up. I thought maybe she was just shifting to get more comfortable. But she put a hand on the railing to steady herself and spoke up. "Your honor, that is all a mistake. I've told my son he has to take care of it today."

Jennifer turned around, horrified.

The judge tilted his head down and peered over his glasses again. "Ma'am, with all due respect, this is just a hearing, to enter a plea. No testimony or questioning is involved."

"But you don't understand. Josh is a fine young man ..."

The judge rapped his gavel sharply. "Ma'am, you need to sit down and be quiet or I'll hold you in contempt of court. If you have anything relevant to say, you'll get your chance at the trial."

I pulled Ella down and Jennifer leaned over the railing. "This really isn't the time or place, Ella. This is just a formality. Please let me handle it. We don't need you in jail, too."

"Jail?"

"If the judge finds you in contempt, you could go to jail."

"Jennifer," I said, "doesn't the D. A. know the restraining order was lifted about an hour ago?"

"Yours was," she whispered. "They didn't lift the one against Josh. Vandervelde called me right after he talked to you. Edmund insisted on keeping the one against Josh in force."

We all glared at Vandervelde, who still refused to look in our direction.

"That son of a bitch!" Ella muttered. I wondered if she was talking about her son or his lawyer.

"Counselor, do you have anything to present against a remand order?" the judge asked Jennifer.

"Yes, your honor. It is ... entirely unreasonable. The restraining order is a result of a family misunderstanding which will be settled by the end of the week. The evidence against my client is all circumstantial ..."

"Your honor," A. D. A. Holwerda said, "Mr. Adams has prior convictions for possession and sale in Indiana and for assault on a police officer in this state. He has no ties to the community."

"Your honor," Jennifer parried, "my client, after a long separation, is in the process of being reunited with his family. His grand-mother, Ella Dykstra, is here today to show her support."

"Her enthusiasm has been noted," the judge said.

Vandervelde whispered something to A.D.A. Holwerda, who tried to remain standing and facing the judge while leaning over to listen. He nodded, referred to a note on his table, and said, "Your honor, the family connection to which Ms. McKenzie refers is merely alleged and has not been demonstrated to the satisfaction of any other member of the Dykstra family. Mr. Adams may face a fraud charge once his con game is exposed. We feel that possibility, on top of the felony charge in this case, makes him a flight risk."

Flight? How? I wondered. His car was totaled in the accident and was sitting in the police impound lot. And it looked like Edmund Dykstra's tentacles could reach anywhere Josh might try to go.

"I agree," the judge announced, "that we should err on the side of caution. The prisoner is remanded to custody in the County Jail until trial."

Chapter 35

After getting Ella calmed down and dropping her back at her house I headed for home. I deliberately chose a long route and made several unnecessary turns, checking all the while to see if anyone was following me. If Edmund had reneged on one promise, I figured he wouldn't hesitate to break another. But I couldn't spot anyone tailing me.

All my extra turns brought me up Ivanrest toward 44th Street. Meijer's—a home-grown precursor and rival to Wal-Mart—appeared on my left. It was originally called Meijer's Thrifty Acres; people of my parents' generation still talk about 'going to Thrifty's'. I decided to drop off my disposable camera and do some grocery shopping while the pictures were being developed.

I finished shopping in about forty-five minutes, so my pictures weren't quite ready. While I was waiting I called Connie to see if she knew the restraining order had been lifted and I could be back at work in the morning. Her response fell on my ears like a divine message.

"Why don't you go ahead and take a couple of days off? Your appointments have been rescheduled or canceled, so there wouldn't be much for you to do here tomorrow. I arranged to have the carpet in your office cleaned. It won't be dry tomorrow. I'll have Joan work on getting your appointments rebooked for Thursday."

"You're going to have my clients thoroughly confused."

"Isn't that why they're your clients to begin with?"

Connie was an administrator, with a business degree and no training as a counselor, but I had never heard her express such open disdain for what we were doing and the people we worked with.

"Is there anything else you need?" she asked.

"Actually, I do have one question." I had thought of this when I reached for my credit card and came up with the keycard that opened the outer door of our building. I never noticed before, but it had FSI lightly embossed on the bottom of it. The letters on mine were worn almost smooth. "When that new security system was installed in our building a couple of years ago, who did it?"

"Folkert Security. They handle that sort of work on all of Dykstras' properties."

Suspicion confirmed. And more questions raised. Folkert, or one of his employees, could get into our building any time he wanted. He, or Roger Haveman, could have locked me in the closet and made up the whole story about seeing someone else enter the building around six. But then who called Ann Haveman? It must have been a woman, because Ann thought it was me. Or did Ann call her own number from my phone, to give herself an alibi? But that didn't make any sense. What would she have been doing in the building to begin with?

* * * *

While I ate supper and played 'Twenty Questions' with myself I examined the pictures I had made of Margaret's sculpture. They turned out well Something about the way the figure's right hand clutched at her heart seemed to me to have more than casual meaning. I scanned a few of the pictures into my computer and was about to enlarge them when the phone rang. This time it was Cal.

"Hi," I said, feeling relief and excitement wash over me at the sound of his voice. "Is this business or pleasure?"

"Both. Which do you want to talk about first?"

"Umm, hard choice. Sometimes the pleasure is increased if you postpone it for a few minutes."

"Damn, Sarah, I forgot how sexy your voice sounds over the phone. Or did I get a 900-number by mistake?"

"Cal Timmer! If you were here, I would slap your face."

"Oh, I've been a bad boy. What else would you do to me?"

I was glad he couldn't see how red my face was—and I'm not old enough to be having a hot flash. "Okay, let's get off this topic. Right now. You said there was a business part to this call. Let's take care of that." As pleased as I was to feel that we were trying to reconnect, I wasn't in the mood for phone sex right now.

"Sorry. Okay, straight arrow time." He ruffled some pages. "The state police post at South Haven faxed me their file on the explosion that killed the Adamses."

That broke the playful mood quite effectively. "And ... ?"

"There's not much to go on. The cottage was built in the late '40s. The gas furnace was original equipment, from the old Holland Furnace Company. Did I ever tell you my grandfather worked for them?"

"No, you never mentioned that." And, I thought, you never told me your mother abandoned you, either. What other family history would you like to reveal while we're on the subject?

"Yeah, he was one of those left high and dry when the place went bankrupt in the late '50s. Anyway, the Adamses had their furnace cleaned and inspected every year, but that year's check-up hadn't been done before the explosion. There was so little left of the place that the fire marshal and the arson squad found no conclusive evidence it wasn't an accident."

"I thought technology was advanced enough now that they could detect just about any kind of explosive. A couple of molecules of this, trace residue of that."

"When you've got a gas line involved, the smallest device can cause a huge blast. If there was even a pinhole leak in the line and the place filled up with gas, then the spark from just switching on a light could cause the explosion. There was nothing left but the foundation of the house. Debris was scattered a hundred yards in any direction. To determine the cause of the explosion, you've got to be able to reconstruct the place to some extent. They had no reason to suspect foul play and they found nothing obvious to suggest it."

"Where was the cottage?"

"It was on Lake Michigan. Beach-front property."

"Beach-front on the big lake? That must have cost a pretty penny." Property fronting on even a small lake—of which Michigan has hundreds—is pricey. I've heard that property on Lake Michigan itself could cost thousands of dollars for each foot of lake frontage.

"I thought that too, so I checked with a realtor over there. I don't know what his parents paid for it, but Josh sold the lot by itself for two hundred thousand and change."

"What did his father do?" Funny, I'd never asked that question.

"He was a sales rep for a pharmaceutical company."

"Is that a particularly lucrative profession?"

"Not for an honest man. The people who make money selling drugs are the ones doing it on street corners. Or those who have cocaine and money stashed in their cars."

"That's a cheap shot, Cal. I believe Josh is innocent."

"Believing that and establishing it in court are very different things. You'd better hope the D.A.'s office doesn't get hold of the information in this file. It could raise questions."

"What kind of questions?"

"For instance, could this have been a drug-related hit? Maybe Josh—or his father—was horning in on someone else's territory. Drug dealers are absolutely ruthless, Sarah. They like to make examples of people who try to go behind their backs or undercut them."

"You're so far off the track right now, Cal." But he had sown a doubt in my mind. That's all the D. A. had to do in court. Plant a little seed of uncertainty about Josh's character in the jury's minds, water it with a reference to the arrest in South Bend, and let it grow.

"For your sake, Sarah, I hope I am wrong. Anyway, I've asked the guys over at the jail to keep a close eye on Josh."

"Thanks. That means a lot to me."

"Okay, I think that's the end of the business part of this call. Are you ready for the pleasure part?"

"By all means." I was trying to shift gears as fast as Cal. One of the hardest things to get used to was how quickly he could step from one mood to another, like going from one room in his mind to another and closing the door behind him. Because his work was so hard and he was so committed to it, he seemed to have learned at some point to compartmentalize. Or maybe he'd had to do that as a child, because of his mother. A woman who loves a cop has to know how to handle that.

"Dinner tomorrow night—how about Seoul Garden?"

I had to wonder at his choice. The superb Korean restaurant was where we went on our first real date after we met at the mall. Was he trying to recreate that mood? I could go along with him, if he was. "Yes, that sounds lovely."

"Can I pick you up at seven?"

"Sure, assuming some other disaster doesn't crop up by then."

I expected him to say something else or end the conversation, but he hesitated.

"Is there something else?" I asked.

"Could you wear that blue dress?"

"It's really not warm enough for that one yet."

"If you wear that dress, I'll be very warm."

Chapter 36

My phone rang at the very moment my alarm went off Wednesday morning. I knocked over the lamp on my bedside table as I fumbled with buttons.

"Sarah," Cal said when I got all my electronic equipment straightened out and stopped trying to answer my clock. "Sorry to call you this early. Are you awake enough to deal with some bad news?"

"I am now." I sat up on the edge of the bed and clutched the sheet for security.

"It's about Josh."

"Oh, God!"

"He's in the hospital. He was attacked in the holding cell."

"Is he badly hurt? What happened?"

"He was stabbed last night with a blade another inmate had hidden in the sole of his shoe. It's pretty serious, but he came through the surgery okay, I'm told. He's in critical but stable condition."

I pushed my hair out of my face. "I don't believe this! They take away Josh's shoelaces, but some guy manages to get in there with a knife. Don't they use a metal detector on prisoners?"

"The blade was hard plastic, and the false sole on the shoe was a professional job. No equipment we have could have found it."

"I thought you asked them to keep an eye on Josh."

"They can't watch one prisoner every minute." He sounded defensive. "They did the best they could. The guy who attacked him is a drunk and a psycho who's been in and out of jails and hospitals all his life. I guess the cops who checked him in just thought, 'It's old Vernon again.' He's never done anything really violent before. We think somebody put him up to it."

"Do you want my list of suspects? It's really short." It would start with Edmund Dykstra, but I had to remember that David Burton was no stranger to jails and the people who inhabit them. If he and Christine Grotenhuis hoped to get the trust fund through The

Art Place, Josh would have to be eliminated. But would Burton kill his own son?

I could tell Cal was yawning. "We're interrogating Vernon now, but he's not very coherent."

"At least Josh is still alive."

"Yes, thank God. Sarah, I'm truly sorry about this. And I'm sorry I didn't take your concerns seriously enough. It would have been inconvenient to isolate him, but we could have done it. Like I've told you before, one of the most frustrating things about being a cop is that we can't prevent bad stuff from happening. We just have to clean up afterwards. I've asked the captain to put a guard on Josh in the hospital."

"Thanks. Can I see him?"

"Not now. He's in intensive care at Grand Rapids General."

"Have you called Mrs. Dykstra?"

"I don't know if I should. We're supposed to notify next of kin. To the best of my knowledge, Josh's relationship to her hasn't been established."

"I'll call her. She'll want to know." If she was ready to leave her house to him, in her mind the relationship had been established.

I waited until I thought Ella would be up and maybe have had breakfast. I used to think elderly people get up very early, but in my experience as a counselor I've learned many of them take naps in the afternoon and then stay up as late at night as someone my age. I couldn't assume Ella was in a hurry to pop out of bed in the morning. With her weak heart and other health problems, I wasn't sure how much bad news she could stand before breakfast.

Pamela, the younger daughter, answered the phone. When I asked to speak to her grandmother, she asked who was calling, obviously working from her father's script. It was too early in the morning for me to come up with a convincing lie, so I just told her my name. I heard her call, "Dad!"

After a moment Edmund came on the line. "What do you want, Ms. DeGraaf?" The words were straightforward, but his tone of voice made it obvious that he was really asking, Why the hell are you still bothering us?

"I want to speak to your mother." After seeing him humiliated at lunch, I wasn't nearly as afraid of him as I was this time yesterday—though maybe I should be, if he was trying to have Josh killed.

"I'll take a message."

"No, it's important that I talk to her right now."

"About what?"

"Mr. Dykstra, you are not your mother's guardian. I don't think she'll appreciate your efforts to censor her calls, in her own home." I couldn't resist that.

I waited for a retort, but all I heard was Edmund's voice in the distance, calling, "Mother. Telephone. It's that DeGraaf woman."

I heard an extension phone being picked up. "I have it," Ella said. "Please hang up the other phone." She waited for the click. "Hello, Sarah. What a nice way to start the day."

I wished I could break the news to her gently.

"Sarah, you're awfully quiet. Is there something wrong?"

"I'm afraid there is. Just hear me out before ..."

"Something's happened to Josh." Her voice began to rise in panic.

"Take it easy, Ella. He's in the hospital, but he's doing okay." I guess being in 'stable' condition could be interpreted as doing okay. He apparently wasn't getting any worse.

Ella wasn't having much luck fighting back her tears. "Oh, God! What happened?"

I gave her the information I had.

"Are you going to the hospital?" she asked.

"I guess so." I hadn't thought about it. "Shall I pick you up?"

"Please. As soon as possible."

* * * *

Twenty minutes later, drive-through breakfast in hand, I pulled up in front of the Dykstras' house. Ella came out the door as I was getting out of the car. I met her on the sidewalk. She was shaking badly, but more with rage than from Parkinson's, I thought.

"I have put Edmund on notice," she said, lifting her cane and brandishing it back toward the house. "I told him, if anything else happens to Josh, I will disinherit him and Katherine and do everything I can to get the company's board of directors to throw them both out. And I told him I want him and his family out of the house by the time I get back. They can stay in the cottage in Saugatuck, but I will not have them under my roof right now."

"Aren't you being a little hasty, Ella? We don't have any proof Edmund is involved in any way." Did those words come out of my mouth?

"I'll guarantee you, he and that lawyer, Vandervelde, are right in the thick of it."

As we drove the few blocks to the hospital, she fumed and fussed about her son and Martin Vandervelde. Giving up ambulance chasing and dubious injury claims, Vandervelde had hitched his wagon to Edmund's rising star shortly after Margaret's death. "And I blame Jake Folkert for introducing Edmund to him."

"Folkert?" That name popped up for about the hundredth time in the last few days. "What's the connection between those two?"

"Marty is married to Folkert's sister."

* * * *

I let Ella out at the main entrance to the hospital. By the time I parked the car and trotted back to the lobby she was already deep in conversation with an admitting clerk. I walked over to the cubicle and stood behind her with my hand on her shoulder. She reached up and patted my hand.

"Sarah, maybe you can help me understand this. You've had more experience with forms and bureaucracies than I have."

"What's the problem?" I sat down in the chair beside her.

"Mr. Adams has no insurance," the clerk said. Her name tag identified her as Sabrina. Her broad face was polite, but she was clearly not enjoying a confrontation so early on her shift.

"That's not surprising," I said. "He's self-employed. Does that mean you're not going to treat him?"

Sabrina drew herself up, as though offended. "Of course not. We're already treating him. Surgery has been performed and he's in the ICU. There are limits as to what we can do for uninsured patients, but I assure you, he will receive adequate treatment."

"'Adequate'?" Mrs. Dykstra echoed. "That's not good enough for my grandson. Can I pay for his expenses?"

"Yes, ma'am, there is a form you can sign to assume responsibility for the cost of a patient's treatment. But, frankly, it can run into a lot of money." She glanced back at her computer screen. "The surgery last night and his care in ICU thus far come to $12,000."

Ella snorted. "Young lady, my husband paid for an entire floor of this hospital. I could hobble over to that cash machine"—she gestured at the ATM across the lobby—"and withdraw more money in five minutes than you'll make in your entire life." She caught herself short. I could see on her face that her basic decency had suddenly kicked in. "I'm sorry, dear. That was uncalled-for, but I'm a crotch-ety old woman and I don't have time for niceties. Please, give me that form."

With the financial business taken care of, we headed for the ICU. I didn't expect we would be able to see Josh, but with Ella on a rampage, there was no telling what we might accomplish.

Outside the doors of the ICU we found a nurses' station and a waiting area. The nursing supervisor was a tall, wiry woman who looked like she might prove a worthy adversary for Ella. Her nametag identified her as FRAN in large letters and Rietsema in smaller letters.

Ella charged right up to the desk. "I'm Ella Dykstra. I'd like to see my grandson, Josh Adams."

Nurse Fran punched up something on her computer. "Josh is still asleep, Mrs. Dykstra, from the anesthesia. I can let you go back for a few minutes, but he won't know you're there."

"That's all right. I just want to see him. Come on, Sarah."

"Miss, are you a relative?" Nurse Fran asked, frowning at me.

"No, I'm not."

"Sorry, relatives only in ICU. One at a time, for five minutes."

Ella was ready to huff and puff and blow another rule down, but I nudged her toward the door. "You go ahead. I'll wait here."

I stood at the doors and watched through the glass panel as Ella made her way back to Josh's bed. Then I realized something was missing. Cal had mentioned a guard.

"Excuse me," I said to Nurse Fran. "Don't the police have a guard on Josh?"

"Oh, that. Somebody was here when he came back from sur-gery. But the D. A. dropped the charges against him, so they took the guard off."

"Why?"

"If someone is here as a prisoner, we can bill the city or the county for their expenses. Once the charges are dropped, that's no longer possible."

"But he was stabbed in the county jail! Isn't it their responsibil-ity to take care of him?"

"Only until the charges are dropped. I know it sounds inhumane, but with all the budget cutbacks these days ..."

Thank God for Ella's deep pocketbook, I thought. "How is Josh?"

Nurse Fran glanced at her computer screen. "He's stable. The stab wound was severe, up under the rib cage. Somebody was going for his heart."

I shuddered. She had just confirmed all my fears. This was not a random attack by a crazed inmate.

"He was lucky to get help immediately," the nurse went on. "That's what made the difference. The doctor says his prognosis is good."

"Will he be safe here, without a police guard?"

"Who would try to hurt him here? This happened in a fight in a jail cell."

"There may be more to it than that. That's why there was sup-posed to be a policeman guarding him."

"Not even a policeman would be allowed to stay in the ICU. No one gets in there except family of patients and the medical staff."

She might have thought her house of rules was made of brick, but I was looking forward to seeing how quickly it collapsed with Ella at the door. "When will he be moved to another room?"

"In a couple of days, I expect. He's young and strong. I don't think you really have anything to worry about." She smiled and leaned toward me, as though we could share a secret. "Are you two in a relationship?"

"No. I've just been ... working with him recently."

A nurse brought Ella back to the desk. "I think he heard me talking to him," she said, smiling contentedly. "He definitely reacted when I patted his hand. He made this soft little sigh. When can I go back in?"

"You should let him sleep," Nurse Fran said. "His wound and the surgery were both very invasive. His body needs rest to recover from the trauma."

"Why don't we go get a muffin and some coffee?" I suggested. "We can check back here before we leave." I wanted her to under-stand that I couldn't stay all day. I had other things to do. To start with, to find out as much as I could about Jake Folkert and his con-nection to the Dykstras. I couldn't do that sitting around in a hospi-tal waiting room. But Ella stood firm when I took her elbow.

"I just want to make it clear to you," she said to Nurse Fran, "that my grandson is not a charity case. I signed the form to take care of all his medical expenses, so you give him whatever he needs."

"Of course," the nurse said, typing in a note on Josh's file.

"And I know you're busy," I put in, "but could somebody keep an eye on him at all times?"

Nurse Fran looked at me like I'd asked her to walk on water. "The nurses can't, not every minute. I suppose our security company could post a guard. It would cost you more, of course."

Ella and I exchanged a glance. Did she understand the full implication of what we would be doing? We were acting on our fear that Josh needed to be protected, perhaps, from her own son. She nodded at Nurse Fran. "Please do that, right now. An around-the-clock guard. Just put it on the bill. And I want the guard in there, sitting beside Josh's bed at all times. What do the young people say, 7/24?"

"Ma'am, that's against hospital policy." The nurse's flat tone made it clear she regarded 'hospital policy' as the ace of trumps, the end to any argument. She turned to her computer screen.

Ella reached over the counter and put her hand over the screen. "Someone tried to kill my grandson, Ms. Rietsema. If they try again and succeed, this hospital will be so deep in lawsuits ... How much personal liability insurance do you carry, by the way?"

Nurse Fran's eyes widened as the implications of Ella's threat sank in. "All right. I'll see what I can do."

She obviously didn't want the other nurses to see her cave in to an old lady with a cane. She turned to say something to another nurse, but Ella didn't move.

"Is there something else I can help you with?" Nurse Fran said, looking over her shoulder.

"I'm just waiting for you to call the security guard." Ella tapped her cane on the floor a couple of times for emphasis.

As I watched the exchange I realized that what I admired as feistiness in Ella was not so different from what I resented as imperiousness in her son. Having so much money for so long had convinced them both that they could get whatever they wanted, even if it meant running roughshod over people. How I reacted to it was all a matter of the spin I chose to put on it. My dad has this stupid saying, 'One man's poison is another man's *poisson*.' I was in high school before I learned that's the French word for 'fish.'

Once Ella could see Nurse Fran was actually talking to someone about getting a guard up to the ICU, she let me take her by the elbow and escort her to the elevator. When the elevator door opened, we found ourselves face-to-face with a blond Amazon. I introduced Geri to Ella.

"It's nice to meet you, Detective Murphy," Ella said, as Geri stepped off. "I'm afraid they won't let you in to see Josh. Family only in the ICU." She said it with a touch of pride.

"That's okay," Geri said. "I just came by to see how you two were doing." She shifted the black, zippered notebook she was carrying to her left hand and patted me on my shoulder.

"The doctors are optimistic," I said, holding her hand for a moment, "so we're relieved. We were just going to get some coffee. Do you have time to join us?"

"As long as you don't make any jokes about cops and donuts."

Chapter 37

We got to the cafeteria at the ideal time, in the lull between break-fast and coffee break. Ella checked her blood sugar and opted for a blueberry muffin. Geri and I hit the hard stuff. She had a cream-filled donut; I went for one with chocolate icing. The cafeteria was on the ground floor, and overlooked a patio and garden, heavy on evergreen plants. All that green probably made patients and families feel better. I usually like to sit with my back against a wall, facing the room, but I was glad I ended up looking out the window. I could feel myself calm-ing down as I stirred some creamer into my coffee.

"Cal really feels bad about what happened to Josh," Geri said as we settled at a corner table. "As a cop you don't often get a warning that something might happen to somebody. When you fail to pick up on it, you feel like you're not doing your best."

"At least they were able to keep him alive," I said. "And now the charges have been dropped."

"For what that's worth. I just hope he recovers quickly and fully."

"He'll get the best care money can provide," Ella said. "And, as soon as he's able, I'm going to move him into the house with me. Georgie can help me take care of him."

"Georgie?" Geri asked.

Ella explained about Georgia Ann's name and the curse of the 'Cornelius George' names and their feminine variants her husband had inflicted on the family. "Edmund's middle name is George and Pamela's is Cornelia, like Margaret's. It's almost as bad as the Kennedy's and their 'Fitzgerald' thing."

We sat quietly for a moment. The adrenaline rush that carried Ella and me to the hospital was wearing off and the caffeine hadn't kicked in yet. Finally Geri said, "I've been talking to some people at Consolidated Security, Folkert's old employer. That has raised some questions in my mind about the night Margaret died. Mrs. Dykstra, would it be too painful for you to talk about it?"

To judge from her body language, that question raised a spark of interest in Ella and something more—hope.

"Not at all," she said. "What's been painful is *not* talking about it. Any time I bring it up, Edmund tells me there's no need to revisit the past. It was regrettable, he says, but there's nothing to be gained by talking about it. Just let it go. For years nobody would let me talk about my grandson. Then I couldn't talk about my daughter's death ..." She took my hand and squeezed it as tears formed in her eyes. "I'd love to get everything out in the open."

Geri unzipped her notebook and opened it. Something about her gesture suggested we were about to take a momentous step. "I think you can be a big help to us, Mrs. Dykstra."

"How? I wasn't there. I didn't see anything."

"What I want to do is lay out what I know about that night and see if you can fill in any gaps or show me where I'm mistaken about anything. You knew Margaret so well. Maybe you can spot some inconsistency I can't see."

"I'll do whatever I can."

"Good. If you get tired or if this gets too intense, just let me know and we can come back to it at another time."

"Two things, dear. First, call me Ella. Second, I don't have enough time left to keep coming back to things. I want to know what happened to my daughter."

I looked at Geri expectantly. "Have you found out anything new?"

"I shouldn't get everybody's hopes up," she said. "I just want to talk through this whole thing. This is what Cal and I do when we're working a case. One of us plays hard-to-convince. That's going to be my role this morning."

This felt familiar. Cal and I used to talk about cases he found difficult. He said my instincts or my counseling insights were often helpful to him.

"I'm touched," Ella said, "that you take so much interest in an old case."

"Some of it's personal. I was one of the first uniforms on the scene."

Ella put her hand to her mouth. "My heavens! You were there? You saw ... ?"

"Yes, my partner and I responded to the call. He was a real macho type, though. He thought women on the police force were good for office work and making coffee. Jerk wouldn't even let me drive. He had me sealing off the scene and keeping people out that morning until the M. E. and the detectives arrived."

"What did you see?" I asked, adding a little more creamer to my coffee.

"Just what the case file says. Here, I copied the whole thing, except for the photos." She laid the file on the table and flipped it open. "Margaret was lying on her side, next to her desk. She was kind of curled up, the way somebody might be if they'd had chest pains or a heart attack."

"She had trouble with her heart and blood pressure for years," Ella said. "Her cardiologist tried to get her to lose weight, because of her father's history of heart trouble. Mine, too, for that matter. I had to have a stent in one of my arteries about four months before Margaret died."

"How much did she weigh?" I asked, thinking back to the pictures of the chubby high-school girl I'd seen.

"About 170," Ella said. "And she wasn't any taller than I am, or was when I could stand up straight."

She and I looked over the report filed by the investigating officers. It was short and to the point. Margaret appeared to have fallen and hit her head on the sharp corner of her desk. Everything in the office was in place. There was no sign of forced entry or a struggle and no other visible wounds or injuries.

"Could she have hit her head hard enough, just in falling, to cause a fatal injury?" Ella asked, pre-empting my next question.

Geri twisted her mouth. "That's hard to say. If she were pushed or thrown against the desk, sure. But there was no sign of a fight, no evidence that anyone else had been in the office. There was blood and hair on the corner of the desk and nowhere else in the room." She reached over and put her hand on Ella's. "I'm sorry if I'm being too graphic."

"There's no way around it, dear. It's all right."

"So," I said, "if she was just standing beside the desk and had a heart attack, you don't think she would have hit the corner hard enough to cause the injury she had?"

"I don't see how she could have. Now, if she tripped over something or stumbled, she might have hit it with enough force. I can imagine her running to answer the phone—maybe she'd stepped out of the office for a minute and it was ringing when she came back in—and she trips. The energy of her forward motion would be carried over into her fall. She would hit the desk pretty hard. I can also imagine if she had been drinking and lost her balance. I could smell alcohol in the office, and there was a bottle of Scotch in one of her desk drawers."

Ella's face darkened. "Are you suggesting my daughter had a drinking problem?"

"Several people who knew her well," I said, "have confirmed it."

"How ... ? I know she had a glass of wine or a cocktail now and then, but that's all."

"She made every effort to keep you from being aware of the problem," I said. "She may very well have been drunk that night and fallen against her desk."

Ella shook her head in confusion.

"An autopsy could have cleared things up," Geri said. "Why didn't Edmund let them do one?"

"He said he saw no reason to," Ella said, "if the police didn't suspect foul play. We all feared her heart would fail someday. And maybe he knew about her drinking. He didn't want the family's name dragged into the news any more than necessary, and he didn't want her violated that way. Edmund just can't stand knives and needles."

"He must have done some serious string-pulling to stop it, though."

Ella met Geri's eyes. "Detective, you have no idea how much influence my family has in this city. And I'm not saying that because I'm proud of it."

This wasn't the kind of revelation I had been hoping for when Geri unzipped her notebook. I wanted something that would nail Jake Folkert. "You said you talked to Consolidated Security. What did you learn from them?"

Geri pulled out a page of handwritten notes. "I found out that our favorite private eye was the security guard on duty at the plant that night."

"Folkert was in the plant that night?" I practically came out of my chair.

Geri held up a hand, signaling me to lower my voice. I looked around and noticed that people were beginning to drift in for their morning break.

"He was *in the plant*?" I said, leaning over the table.

"All night, by his own admission."

"Do you mean that son of a bitch killed my daughter?" Ella's trembling almost stopped, as if from the shock she had just received.

"That's a big leap to make," Geri cautioned us. "In my line of work we prefer to have some evidence. You know, fingerprints, a weapon, a motive. Folkert's prints were not found in the office, the desk makes an awfully clumsy weapon, and what's his motive?"

"I don't know about prints or weapon," I said, "but how's this for a motive? Margaret dies, Edmund becomes president of the company, and a few months later Folkert signs a big contract for his new company to do security work for the Dykstras."

Geri took a sip of coffee and eyed me steadily over the rim of her cup. "What do you think that proves?"

"That there's something going on between Folkert and Edmund."

"Yeah, something called business. That's not a crime."

"If Jake Folkert's involved," Ella said, "it probably is. But if Folkert was on duty that night, and you were the first police officer to the scene, didn't you see him? Question him?"

"He had already left," Geri said, taking a bite of her donut. "His shift ended at six, when he turned off the alarms and let the custodians in. It was half an hour later when they found Margaret. We sent somebody to take Folkert's statement later. There's a copy in the file. I read it before, but it's been several years. His name hadn't stuck with me."

I found Folkert's two-paragraph statement and skimmed it, with Ella reading over my shoulder. It added nothing to what we already knew. "But he was in the plant all night?" I asked.

"As you can see, he made no effort to deny it. He came on duty at eight. He was supposed to turn on the alarms and make rounds several times during the night."

"Where was he when he wasn't making rounds?"

"The security office," Ella said, "is located at the end of the plant next to the executive offices. It's just a little room with a desk, a coffee machine, and the monitors for the alarms. And a TV and a radio, I think. I haven't been in it since Margaret died."

Geri pointed to the statement. "Folkert says he made his first round about 8:30 and saw Margaret in her office. She was working late and he didn't disturb her. When he came around again at 10:00

her office door was locked and the lights were off. Going into offices wasn't in his job description. He was just supposed to make sure things were locked up."

"I wish we could go to the plant and walk through this," I said. "It would help me to visualize it if I could see the office ..."

"That wouldn't do any good," Ella said. "Edmund completely redid the president's office when he took over. As soon as the police told him it was okay, he had all the furniture taken out, the carpet ripped up. There's nothing in there now from Margaret's time. Even the arrangement of the room is entirely different."

"Doesn't that sort of haste arouse suspicion?" I asked.

Geri shrugged. "Not necessarily. Maybe he just wanted to get rid of unpleasant memories. There's a floor plan of the office in the file and a couple of pictures, back a few pages. While you look it over, I'll get us some more coffee."

I found the drawing and photos and Ella and I studied them a moment. The floor plan showed the entire suite—an outer office, a workroom, and Margaret's own office, with measurements. Coming through the outer door you would find the secretary's desk on your left and a bank of files on your right. Just beyond the file cabinets was a corridor that led to a workroom with a copier and storage for supplies. Going straight past the files and the secretary's desk, you came to the door of Margaret's office. Directly opposite the door, her desk sat in front of some windows, with a couple of chairs in front of it.

"She loved those big windows," Ella said. "She was drawn to light, like one of those plants that's always turning toward the sun."

How did she ever survive living in west Michigan? I wondered. For much of the year it's one of the cloudiest, gloomiest places in the country. Local weathermen keep track of what percentage of possible sunshine we get each month. The numbers we rack up wouldn't keep a TV show on the air past its first episode.

Entering Margaret's private office, the floor plan showed, you found a table and several chairs to your right, a sofa and an end table with a lamp to your left. In the far left corner was a bookcase. In the far right corner was the door to a private bathroom.

"'The presidential potty'," Ella said with a chuckle. "That's what she called it."

Beyond the bathroom, beside the big windows, was a door leading directly outside to the president's parking spot.

Geri returned with our refilled mugs. "Is that accurate?"

"It's very accurate," Ella said.

"Thank you," Geri said. "I drew it after ... the office was empty. Now, the official explanation of her death is that she locked the door between her office and the secretary's area, turned off the lights, and was probably headed for the private outside entrance when she fell."

"But why would she turn off the lights and then cross the room?" I asked. "Wouldn't she turn off the lights last thing, as she went out?"

Geri turned to Ella. "Is there a switch beside that outer door?"

"Yes. But this was July, remember. At that time of year it doesn't get dark around here until after 9:30. And the office faces west. She loved those big windows."

"And maybe she did turn off the light at the door," Geri said, making a note, "but realized she forgot something and went back. Or the phone rang. She's familiar with the office and there's enough light from outside, so she doesn't turn the lights back on."

"Wouldn't the door have been open?" I asked.

Geri sighed with impatience. "That would depend on the precise moment when she turned back and the precise order in which she did things. Was it: lights off, door open, turn back?" She stood and acted out opening a door and flicking a light switch, ignoring the stares of the people around us. "Or was it: door open, lights off, turn back? Or just: lights off, turn back? We have no way of reconstructing her movements with that kind of detail. There's no convincing evidence Margaret's death was anything other than what it appeared to be. She fell, for whatever reason—and I'm sorry to say her drinking looks like a big factor—and hit her head on the corner of the desk. Based on what we've got here, the D. A. would tell us to stop wasting our time and work on a case we might have a chance of solving."

"But what happened to her paperweight?" I asked.

Chapter 38

"Paperweight?" Ella said. "You mean that pineapple finial?"

"Yes," Geri said. "Denise van Putten told us it was always on Margaret's desk."

Ella nodded. "That's right. Her grandfather gave it to her when she was a little girl. It was a prototype. He carved it himself. She made the marble base for it. Big, heavy piece. She kept the thing on her desk at home all through high school. Any time I was in her office, it was on her desk."

"But Denise said it wasn't there the morning they found her, and I never saw it. There was a photo of her desk in the file, but I didn't copy it because if showed the blood on the corner. The picture shows the top of the desk, and the paperweight wasn't there. Do you know where it is, Ella?"

"No. I haven't seen it since she died. I thought Edmund boxed it up with the rest of her things, just to get any reminders of her out of his sight."

"I talked to Denise yesterday," I said. "I learned more about David Burton"—what an understatement, but I didn't want to get us off track—"but she couldn't tell me anything more about the paperweight. What happened to the stuff from Margaret's office?"

"It's in her closet at home. Four boxes. They're still sealed up. I've never had the courage to look through them."

"Why not?" Geri asked.

"Oh, you hear stories about what people find in their loved one's things after they die. I couldn't bear any more heartache over Margaret. Just sitting here, I've learned something I didn't want to know."

"I think it's important that you open those boxes," I said. "Finding the paperweight could be the key to understanding what happened to her."

"Would you help me?"

"Sure. We can do that when we leave here."

"Thank you. Maybe that will take my mind off Josh."

"And maybe we'll find evidence pointing to someone who might have wanted to hurt Margaret. Somebody like Folkert."

"Before you get a rope and lynch the guy," Geri said, "let me remind you that, from a police point of view, there is no evidence here to warrant re-opening this case."

"But he was there all night ... ," I said.

Geri held up her hand to stop me. "He had opportunity, you're right. But what about motive and means?" She turned to Ella. "Do you know of any argument or disagreement between Margaret and Jake Folkert?"

"I don't think she even knew the man existed. I never heard his name before she died."

"Do you think Folkert might have tried to seduce her or assault her?" Geri was shifting into her interrogation mood. "Or maybe *she* tried to come on to *him*. He rebuffed her, they got into a fight ..."

Ella shook her head vigorously. "No, that's preposterous. After the baby, she just shut down that part of her life. I don't think she ever looked at another man, or encouraged any to look at her."

Unless his name was David Burton, I thought.

"She never dressed up unless she had to," Ella went on. "She was happiest when she came home from work with sawdust in her hair or paint and varnish on her clothes. The people on the floor adored her because she would actually work with them."

"Do you know of anyone she had strong disagreements with?"

"You mean other than Edmund and Katherine?"

Geri and I both sat up. "What did they argue about?" I asked.

"Money. What else, with those two? The company had not been doing well for several years. Edmund was furious when Margaret leased company property to non-profit groups like The Art Place for a few dollars a year. Margaret was an artist, a designer. She didn't always look at the bottom line, the way Edmund does. Profits had been declining since she became president."

"For the furniture company, or for Dykstra Enterprises as a whole?"

Ella shook her head. "There was no Dykstra Enterprises then. Edmund reorganized everything when he took over."

"I know this may be hard to consider," I said, "but could Edmund have been angry enough at Margaret to ... to hurt her?"

The old woman snorted. "He wouldn't have the nerve to do that. His method would be to backstab her and undercut her until the board of directors had to get rid of her."

"Let me play devil's advocate," Geri said. "What we've established so far is that we don't know of anyone who had a motive to kill Margaret."

Should I say something? Did David Burton have a motive to kill her? But that didn't make sense if he hoped to get money from her. And he had an alibi.

Geri continued. "The only person who had the opportunity ..."

"That we know of," I intruded.

"Let me rephrase it. The only person who admits to being in the plant that night was Jake Folkert, but he had no motive."

"That we know of," I said, drawing a glare from Geri.

"Okay, granted. But if he killed her, could he have sat there calmly all night, knowing he was the only person in the plant? He made no effort to construct an alibi for himself. It seems to me that's how he would act if he *didn't* know anything had happened to her."

"Or if he wanted the police to think he didn't know," I said.

"Sarah, you're twisting this thing like a pretzel. Police officers soon learn that old Ockham had it right with that razor thing. The simplest explanation is the best and the most likely."

I hated that Geri was making sense. "Could anyone else have gotten into the plant?" I asked.

"Not without setting off the alarm," Geri said, pulling a yellowed brochure out of her notebook. "This is information about the alarm system Consolidated installed about 1980. No cameras. Just contact alarms on the exterior windows and doors. But if anyone had come in after the alarms were set, it would have registered in the plant's security room and at Consolidated's headquarters."

"What if Folkert turned off the alarms to let someone in?"

"That would have registered at Consolidated. There's no record of a break in service that evening." She pulled out a statement from Consolidated verifying that fact.

"Could somebody have been in the plant before Folkert turned on the alarms?" I asked.

"How would that person have gotten out? The alarms went off whenever a door or window was opened, regardless of whether somebody was going in or out."

"Not that back door out of Margaret's office," Ella said.

Geri and I stared at her. "What do you mean?" Geri asked.

"Margaret refused to let them put an alarm on her private office door, like Cornelius before her. They liked to come and go as they pleased. I'm surprised Consolidated didn't tell you about that. They argued hard against it. Said we might as well cut a hole in the wall."

"Wait a minute," I said, turning to face Ella. "Am I understanding this? Anyone could have come or gone through that door without setting off an alarm?" David Burton suddenly came to mind, demanding ten thousand dollars.

"Not anyone." Ella seemed almost defensive. "Margaret always kept it locked. No one could have gotten in if she didn't know them."

"Could she have kept somebody out if she didn't want them in?" I asked.

"What do you mean?"

"Is the lock on that door sturdy? A dead bolt?"

"No, it's not. You don't need a key to lock it. You just push the button."

"So it wouldn't take much more than a credit card to open it," Geri said. "And if someone got in, they could have locked it as they left. Do you have someone in mind?"

"Margaret had been back in touch with David Burton, Josh's father. He was trying to extort money from her."

Geri shot me an exasperated look, chiding me for withholding information. "And how do you know all of this?"

"From talking to Mickey Bolthuis and Denise van Putten."

"Denise ... ?" Ella said.

"She's David Burton's sister, Josh's aunt." I didn't know whether to be proud I'd discovered that fact or embarrassed that I hadn't already made it known.

Ella's eyes got big. "Josh's aunt? You can't be serious! And she worked with Margaret all those years?"

"She didn't know Margaret and David had had a child until Margaret told her. But she blames Margaret for being a bad influence on her brother."

Geri rubbed her forehead like I was giving her a headache. "Are you suggesting Burton as a suspect then?"

"He had better motivation than Folkert, I guess. But Denise says he was with her the evening Margaret died."

"Family members usually make pretty weak alibis," Geri said.

Ella tapped the table with a fingertip. "Maybe Denise is the one who needs an alibi. Margaret would certainly have let her into her office."

Geri held up both hands. "Now hold on. Ockham's razor, remember? Keep it simple. We haven't established that anyone, except Folkert, was in the building. And he claims—or admits—he was there all night."

"Is there any proof of that?" I asked.

"In his statement he said he watched the Tigers' game on TV. They were playing in Seattle that night, so it didn't start until 10:00. The officers who took his statement checked the schedule. There was a game on TV that night. He knew the score and the big plays, which he couldn't have read in the paper that morning because the game was so late."

"But he could have seen it on ESPN. And he could have come and gone all night through Margaret's door. Anybody could have done that."

Geri flipped through the file, stopping to read something quickly here and there. "Ella, do you know if the security company had a key to that door? Or if Margaret had given copies to anyone?"

"Margaret wouldn't give anybody a key to it. She was just like her father in that respect. And the master keys to the other doors wouldn't open that door."

Geri and I looked at one another across the table as we let this revelation sink in.

"I feel," I said, "like I've been reading one of those locked-room mysteries and all of a sudden I find out there's a secret panel in the bookcase. Who knows how many people came and went through Margaret's office that night?"

"Don't complicate," Geri said. "Folkert had a legitimate reason to be in the plant and we have no proof—not so much as a partial fingerprint—that he was ever in Margaret's office. If anybody killed Margaret, it's more likely to be somebody who was in the plant before the alarms were turned on or somebody she let in." She turned to Ella. "Can you think of anyone else Margaret might have let into her office that night?"

"Well, she would have let anyone in the company in, I'm sure. As I said, she was very well liked among her employees."

"But everyone was questioned and they all had solid alibis. They had all gone home at least a couple of hours before the time of Margaret's death."

"Why question people?" I asked. "Did the police suspect something?"

"No, it's just procedure. We didn't know how it would be ruled. As people came to work we questioned them and sent them home. It was a couple of days before the investigation was stopped and her death was officially declared an accident."

"What about Jennifer McKenzie?" I said. "Margaret would have let her in, I'm sure. And they must have had things to talk about. The trust fund was a secret between the two of them."

"But Jennifer is a fine person," Ella protested.

"When people share a secret, though," Geri said, "and that secret involves a lot of money, they can behave in unexpected ways. It might be worth asking Ms. McKenzie where she was that night, or if she knows about anyone Margaret might have been meeting."

We lapsed into silence, the way people do at a meeting when they've exhausted all the possibilities or when there's only one possibility left on the table, and it's the one nobody wants to talk about. Geri leafed through the papers in the file one more time, as though she might have missed some minor point.

"Ella, you may hate me for asking this," I finally said, "but ... where were Edmund and Katherine that night?"

Geri's face registered the surprise I expected to see on Ella's. But the old woman looked almost relieved. "Edmund was at home with me from about six o'clock on. He never left the house."

"What about Katherine?"

"We had an early dinner and she went to the mall to do some shopping for Pamela's birthday. It was coming up a week later."

"Was Pamela with her?"

"No, she went by herself."

Geri and I looked at each other, eyebrows raised.

"I know what you're thinking," Ella said. "But she had receipts for a couple of things she bought that night. I saw them in the bag she left on the kitchen table."

"What time did she get home?"

"About 9:30."

"How did she seem when she got in?" Geri asked. I decided to let her lead the way on this stretch of the interrogation as the terrain got more difficult.

Ella shrugged. "I don't know. I didn't see her. I was upstairs in my room. I just heard her talking to Edmund before they went into the library."

"What were they talking about?"

"I couldn't tell. As I said, I was upstairs. I just heard the murmur of their voices for a couple of minutes, then the library door closed."

"Did you notice anything different about their behavior the next morning?"

Ella glared at her as though she'd asked the dumbest question of all time. "We all behaved differently. We had barely gotten up when the police were at our door, telling us about Margaret."

"You didn't see Katherine before the police got there?"

"No. She hadn't come downstairs yet." Ella paused and lowered her head as though this was all too much to take in. "Surely you can't believe she killed Margaret. As little as I like her, I've never seen anything to suggest she'd be capable of something so awful."

Geri's cell phone rang. She answered it, looking at us apologetically, listened for a minute, and said, "I'll be right there ... Yeah, she is." Then she handed it to me. "It's Cal."

"Sorry to break up the coffee klatch," he said, his voice warm in my ear. "My partner and I have a call to a possible homicide."

"I hope you can solve it by dinner time."

"If you're going to wear that blue dress tonight, I'll find D. B. Cooper and figure out who Jack the Ripper was by then."

I could feel myself blushing. "I'll see you at seven-thirty."

Geri dropped her phone back in her purse. "To answer your last question, Ella, I'm not ready to accuse Katherine—or anyone else—of anything. Maybe, when all is said and done, the original conclusion was right: Margaret fell, or had a heart attack, and hit her head on the corner of her desk and died from the heart attack or from the injury. That's the simplest explanation, and stranger things have happened."

"But where's the paperweight?" I asked, thumping the table for emphasis.

"Sarah's right," Ella said. "If it wasn't on her desk the next morning, somebody took it. And they couldn't have taken it while she was alive."

"I agree," Geri said, "that the paperweight is the one reason I can't put this thing to rest. And I'm curious why Denise brought it up. She must be very confident she and David can provide solid alibis for one another. If you find it in those boxes of Margaret's stuff, then I'm ready to admit her death was an accident and we're wasting our time. If you don't find it, then we've got good reason to keep asking questions."

As we cleared off our table, one question began forming in my mind: What if Denise was trying to get rid of David? What if, after all these years, she was seeing him as he really was? Maybe he was becoming a drain on her meager resources, and she was just looking for a way to draw the police's attention to him. What did she know about the paperweight, and about that night, that we didn't know?

Chapter 39

Ella and I said goodbye to Geri at the elevator. When we got in, I pushed the button for the lobby, but Ella reached over with her cane and pushed 6, the floor the ICU was on.

"Those boxes have been there for five years," she said. "They can wait long enough for me to see my grandson one more time."

I don't know which bothered me more: having her impose her will on me—it wasn't nearly as much fun as watching her do it to other people—or being forced to wait to find out if the paperweight was in one of the boxes. The thought of that damn thing was starting to drive me crazy, like Moby Dick did Captain Ahab.

"Ella, there really isn't anything we can do for Josh right now. In a day or two, when he's awake and in his own room, there'll be time to hover over him."

"I want him to know we're caring for him," Ella said, and the set of her jaw let me know further argument was futile.

In my heart I couldn't entirely disagree with her. I know studies have shown that patients, even when they're asleep or in a coma, are aware of their surroundings and do hear what's being said. So she might actually be doing Josh some good. And Nurse Fran wouldn't let her stay for more than five minutes anyway.

Nurse Fran herself looked up from her computer as we got off the elevator. "Your security guard is on the way," she said, as if to forestall Ella's question. "Do you understand it will cost you thirty-five dollars an hour? If you want someone around the clock, that will be ..." She opened the calculator function on her computer.

"It will come to $840 a day," Ella said. "That's fine," she added, with no more concern than I would express when told the price of a quart of milk.

Ella turned toward the door to the ICU, but Nurse Fran said, "Josh's doctor is in there right now. Why don't you have a seat? I'm sure he'll update you when he comes out."

We had been waiting only a couple of minutes when a doctor emerged from the ICU. He was Indian, with a round face and smooth brown skin and dark hair, emphasized by his white lab coat. After talking with Nurse Fran he approached us.

"You are the family of Mr. Adams?" he asked in that staccato musical way most Indians speak English.

"I'm his grandmother," Ella said, remaining seated like a queen receiving an ambassador.

I wished we had definite proof of that relationship, I thought, as I stood and introduced myself.

"I am Dr. Bhandarkar. I'm a member of the surgical team that operated on Mr. Adams last night."

"Will he be all right?" Ella asked, gripping the head of her cane.

"He is doing well. Vital signs are improving. The next twenty-four hours will tell us how things are going to go. He should be awake by this evening, though he will be groggy and disoriented. I think we will move him to a private room by tomorrow, certainly no later than the next day."

"You don't have to rush him out," Ella said. "It's not some cost-cutting HMO that's paying his bill."

"Yes, I understand you have taken responsibility for his expenses. That is most generous."

"I just want to be sure he gets the best treatment possible."

Dr. Bhandarkar smiled, his teeth gleaming like he was in one of those whitener commercials. "He is getting precisely that, I assure you. Dr. Veenema, who did the surgery, has no equal. And we put only our top-notch nurses in the ICU."

"May I go in and see him?" Ella asked.

"For a few minutes, of course."

The good doctor excused himself and Ella scurried into the ICU. I checked my watch and settled back to wait. It was only 9:45. Somehow it felt a lot later. The tension of the morning began to win out over the caffeine. I propped my head on my hand, with my elbow on the arm of my chair. If I could just close my eyes for five minutes, I thought.

"Sarah, dear?"

I jerked as someone tapped me on the shoulder. It took me a second to recognize Ella and remember where I was, and why I had an awful crick in my neck.

"Sorry, Ella. I dozed off." I glanced at my watch. 10:00. I wondered whom she bribed or bulldozed to get those few extra minutes. "How is Josh?"

"He looks a little better. More color in his cheeks. And the security guard is here. She seems nice."

"What do you think of calling Denise van Putten and letting her know what's happened? Josh is her brother's child. I guess she has a right to see him."

Ella didn't hesitate. "That would be fine. Why don't you call her, and I'll let the guardian of the gate know another relative may be coming in."

I got Denise's answering machine and decided not to alarm her. I left my name and number and asked her to call me. "I need to talk to you about your nephew," I concluded.

Then I heard a click as someone picked up over the machine. "Hello?" a man's voice said, an older man, I thought. "Who is this?" I hung up.

Had I just heard David Burton's voice?

* * * *

"Pull into the driveway," Ella said, "so we can use the back door."

Behind the house the single-car drive widened into a parking space for about three cars. As long as none of them was an SUV. Through a glass panel in the garage door I could see the roof of a car, but the parking area was empty.

"Everybody's gone," Ella said. "Place looks like a Lexus dealership when Edmund, Katherine, and Pamela are all home. They each have their own car, and they bought me one. I think the dealer gives Edmund a discount for buying in bulk."

"Do you still drive?" I hoped she couldn't tell how much that possibility disturbed me.

"I haven't in almost a year. Sometimes one of my friends will drive my car when we go out. But I don't need the thing, any more than a sixteen-year-old needs her own Lexus."

My trusty old Honda sighed louder than I did as I killed the engine.

Ella was almost out of the car by the time I got around to her. I was starting to recognize that she didn't want to admit to needing help. I stood by in case my arm was needed, but I let her move under her own power.

Three steps led up to a short walkway and then two more steps up to the back porch. The glassed-in back porch was really just a mud room, a place to take off snowy boots and hang up bulky winter coats. It wasn't even heated, and the two of us made it feel crowded. Ella unlocked the door into the house and stepped inside.

"I've got ten seconds," she said.

As I wondered what she was talking about—until she wet her pants? had a heart attack?—she flipped up the cover on the security system just inside the door and punched in some code numbers. The DISARMED light came on and she lowered the cover.

"I'm so afraid I'm going to forget those numbers one of these days," she said. "I asked Edmund if we could write them down next to this box. Of course, that would defeat the purpose if somebody broke in. He finally agreed to write them backwards."

She motioned for me to look at the wall next to the security alarm. There was a sequence of five numbers. An intruder could see them easily, but when they didn't work in the order listed, he would not have time to try them again.

My face was right down on the security alarm. I noticed the letters FSI on a small sticker above the manufacturer's label.

"Jake Folkert did the alarms in your house too?"

"Yes, he does all of Edmund's security work."

"If I were you, I would call somebody and have this replaced right away. We may not know for sure if Folkert had anything to do with Margaret's death or what happened to Josh, but I would *not* want that man to have complete access to my house. And it is *your* house, not Edmund's, isn't it?"

Ella's face paled. "You're right. I'll call somebody this afternoon. I'll get it changed before I bring Josh here."

I closed the door and turned the deadbolt lock. Only then did I start to take notice of the kitchen we had entered. It was much larger than the typical kitchen in a Victorian house. In that era it was expected that servants, and not the mistress of the house, would work here. And who cared about the servants' comfort? The cabinets and fixtures in this room looked right for that period, but they were obviously new.

"Did you remodel this?" I asked.

"Cornelius and I did forty years ago. We got rid of a butler's pantry that was over there. Nobody has butled in this place since

World War II. Then Edmund and Katherine updated it when they moved in. They got all these antique-looking cabinets. Edmund made some kind of deal with the company that makes them, traded them some office furniture, I think. At heart he is *so* Dutch." She rolled her eyes.

"How long have they lived here?"

"Since Margaret died. They wanted me to move in with them, but I refused. And I won't go to a home until they have to carry me. So they moved in here to babysit the shaky old lady with the bad heart."

"Do you think they'll take your threat seriously and move to the cottage in Saugatuck?"

"They will if Edmund knows what's good for him. It'll just be for a few days. Once we've got the results of that DNA test and know for certain Josh is my grandson, they'll have to accept him and we can start to mend fences."

"Are you going to be all right by yourself for that long?"

"I'm by myself a good part of every day. It'll actually be a relief to have them out of here for a while. Those two have been tearing and clawing at one another since the day they moved in."

"You mean they fight a lot?"

"They don't just fight; they seem to live in a constant state of tension. I don't remember that they were like this before they started living with me. They seemed fond of one another and pleasant enough when we would get together. But, since they came here ... I know I'm not easy to live with, but I don't think I'm the whole problem."

I could imagine some of the stresses in Edmund and Katherine's lives: forced to move to a place where neither of them wanted to be. Edmund probably remembering his unpleasant childhood here, trying to run a company when everyone knew his father had passed him over as the successor. Katherine resentful of not having her own house. And caring for Ella—or for any aging, cantankerous parent—could be stressful enough by itself to destroy a marriage. I'd seen it happen to clients of mine, in spite of all I could do. That insight gave me a shred of sympathy for the dutiful son and daughter-in-law.

"Grab one of those knives, dear," Ella said, pointing to a large knife block standing beside the stove. "Better make it a serrated one. Edmund used a lot of tape on those boxes."

I found a serrated knife on my second try. "Are we going up here?" I asked, noticing a staircase leading off the kitchen.

"I'd rather use the stairs in the front hall," Ella said. "That's the old servants' stairs. They're too steep and narrow for me."

But who cared, in those days, if a servant girl stumbled on them as she came down before dawn to start breakfast for a family of rich folks? Take it easy, I said to myself. The Dykstras didn't build the house, and they didn't have servants. They just treat everybody else like servants.

"You haven't seen much of the house, have you?" Ella asked as I followed her through the dining room and living room into the front hall. The hardwood floors and twelve-foot high ceilings magnified the thump of her cane.

"Just the parlor and the library." Had it been only five days since Josh and I first set foot in this house? Surely it had been a lifetime.

"I would offer you a tour, but I think those boxes are the first order of business."

Except for our voices and Ella's cane the house was quiet.

"This is my favorite time of day," Ella said. "Edmund and Katherine are at work, and Pamela's in school."

With her Lexus in the parking lot, I thought.

But a house this old can never feel entirely empty or peaceful. It always gives off a kind of energy, like the constant buzzing in a beehive. As we walked into the front hall it was easy to imagine the anger and the silent anguish these walls had absorbed as this family struggled all those years. It seemed to fester behind the plaster, like some toxic mold that nobody can get rid of.

The Asian part of me felt a need to placate the guardian spirit of this place, lest it afflict me with some of the misery the Dykstra family had known, apparently as long as this had been their home. "It's such a beautiful house," I said a little louder than necessary. "You must get a lot of pleasure out of living here."

"I do, but the place is really impractical. I mean, who needs a living room that size? And that fireplace! We could roast an ox in the thing."

She was exaggerating, but not by much. Roasting a pig in the fireplace would be feasible. I took another quick glance at the surround and mantle. The tendrils and gargoyles looked like they had migrated from a Gothic cathedral.

"Must be a wonderful space for entertaining, though, like a great room in a modern house."

"Well, there is that. My widows' group enjoys coming over. We call ourselves 'The Last Wives' Club'. The name was my idea." She shuffled toward the main staircase and I stayed close behind her.

The main staircase started in the middle of the front hall and led up first to a small landing. That much I had seen on my earlier visits. This time, when I got to the small landing I turned to my right and looked up the next level of the stairs, which arrived at a larger landing. In the wall of that landing—the exterior wall of the house—was one of the simplest, yet most exquisite, stained glass windows I've ever seen. It wasn't especially large, and most of the glass was white and opaque. In the top third of the window, though, was a yellow tulip in a round medallion. Toward the bottom of the window were a few pieces of green glass, suggesting leaves. Against the dark wood of the stairs, the banisters and the wainscoting, the flower stood out almost like a neon sign.

The landing itself was large enough to have room for a slender table on which sat a couple of vases. To one side of the table stood an umbrella stand holding several canes.

"Do you collect these things?" I asked, teasing Ella just a bit.

"Since I'm here by myself for part of the day I keep them in strategic places around the house," she said with a weary chuckle. "Sometimes I'll start off without one, then realize I need it. Don't let anybody kid you, dear. Getting old is hell." She sighed and we continued our ascent.

The stairs curved to the left and up to the second floor. "This step always creaks," Ella said, "like me." As we put our weight on the third step up from the landing, it protested. Ella held on to the banister and seemed to be laboring. I started to take her elbow, but she drew away.

"I need to do this under my own steam," she said. "If the day comes when I can't get up and down the stairs, I won't be able to live here any more. Katherine hates this house. She's just waiting for any excuse to get me out of it so they can sell it for a B&B and go back to their posh suburbs. Won't they be surprised when they find out I'm leaving it to Josh?"

"If they don't want to live here, couldn't you hire a live-in companion? I'm sure my agency could provide you with a list of good people." Paying someone to do that job surely wouldn't be a problem.

"I'm just not comfortable with having a stranger in my house, dear. I don't think I could sleep. Edmund and Katherine will have to bear with me."

I felt a twinge of sympathy for Katherine.

The stairs led to an open hallway—a mezzanine, really—that ran around three sides of the second floor, like a block C. I saw four doors, one closed and three open.

"That's my bedroom," Ella said, pointing with her cane to the door nearest to us. "The next door is Edmund and Katherine's room. Pamela's is across the hall from them—with the door closed, of course—and Margaret's room is back here to our right."

We turned to our right and then right again along one arm of the C to the door of Margaret's room. Ella motioned for me to go in first. My initial impression was that the room was as big as both of my bedrooms together. The wallpaper, although still in good condition, looked like it must have been put up when Margaret was in high school. Something about it shouted, 'Teenager!' but also whispered, 'Teenager with good taste and a lot of money'. Ella confirmed my suspicion.

"I never could get her to redecorate," she said. "She didn't want to change anything from the way it was when she had her baby in here."

"As unhappy as she was with her father," I said, continuing my survey of the room, "I'm surprised she didn't move out."

"I wondered about that, too. At one time I thought she just wanted to be a daily reminder to him of how much she hated him. After her death, I realized she'd been saving every penny to put into her son's trust fund."

"Given the animosity between them, why did her father choose her to succeed him as president of the company?"

"He didn't really. She told the board of directors she wanted to be president, and she was the older child. Some of the members supported her only after Edmund assured them he wouldn't leave if he wasn't elected. I think he knew Margaret wouldn't be very good at the job and then the board would turn to him 'with shouts of acclamation' as the Bible says."

I stood in awe of Margaret's canopy bed and Victorian walnut dresser with its marble top and candle sconces. For my personal taste, they were heavy, dark—in a word, ugly—but I could imagine somebody on 'Antiques Roadshow' putting a value on them of, well, more than the total value of everything I own. The dressing table and the rocker in the corner didn't look as old. The wall to my right was taken up by a desk and file cabinets.

"You said you were reluctant to look through Margaret's boxes," I said. "What about her files and desk?"

"Edmund has gone into them for things connected with the business. I don't really believe we'll find anything awful, but I just can't bring myself ... It feels like a final admission that she's gone."

A picture hanging over the desk caught my eye. It was a framed pencil sketch of Margaret, about eight by eleven. I stepped over to it and made sure it was signed 'JLA' and dated. Ella noticed my interest.

"A young man made that sketch. Let's see, it was about ten years ago. He was drawing our house one afternoon and Margaret went out to talk with him. Even invited him in and gave him a snack."

"Ella ... that was Josh."

"What? Our Josh?" She put her hand on her heart, and from the expression on her face I was afraid she was going to be on the floor in a minute. "Josh was here? How ... ?"

"By some huge, amazing coincidence. That first day we came to visit you, as soon as he saw your house, Josh told me about that afternoon. Here are his initials." I took the picture down and held it so Ella could see what I was pointing to.

She looked at the corner of the picture, actually seeing for the first time something she had been looking at for years. "Oh, my God!"

She clutched the picture to her heart and began to cry. I held her until she settled down. Then I pulled out the desk chair and helped her sit down. Fetching the box of tissues from the nightstand, I put them on the desk close to her. She kept Josh's sketch in her lap, running her fingers over her daughter's face.

"That afternoon meant so much to Margaret," she said, dabbing at her eyes. "I wonder if, on some level, she sensed something. She said she hoped her son turned out to be as nice as that young man."

"What about you? How did you react to him?"

"I wasn't here that afternoon. I was out with 'The Last Wives' Club'. I believe we went to a new exhibit at Meijer Gardens and had lunch there. When I got home, Margaret just seemed so happy. She showed me this sketch and talked about this wonderful young man."

She tuned up to cry some more. "I got onto her for letting some-body in the house while she was here by herself. Just one more time, I guess, when I failed her as a mother."

I put a hand on her shoulder

When she calmed down again she said, "This isn't getting us anywhere, is it? The boxes are in that closet."

I was glad for the change in her tone. When clients cry a lot during a session I try to be patient, but at some point they've got to move beyond that stage. I opened the closet door. "It's unusual for a Victorian house to have closets, isn't it? Especially such big ones," I said.

Ella blew her nose. "Cornelius and I put in the bathrooms and closets in each bedroom. Originally there was only one bathroom in the whole house, down on the first floor. They must have still been using chamberpots when the house was built. We just shaved a few feet off of one end of each bedroom to put in a bathroom and closet."

Margaret's clothing still hung in the closet, all in plus sizes, and all of it frumpy. I pulled the four boxes out and set them in the middle of the floor. A couple of them felt heavy, the other two lighter than I expected. It didn't take long to open and rummage through them. They were packed carelessly, the way a man would do it.

"Just put the stuff on the bed as you pull it out," Ella said. "I'll sort through it this afternoon."

Soon the bed was cluttered with the detritus of Margaret's life: plaques and awards honoring her civic and charitable work, some sketches for sculptures she was planning, including 'Mother ... and Child?'

But the paperweight was nowhere to be found.

Chapter 40

I called Geri's cell number and got her voice mail. I didn't even identify myself. "The paperweight is not in Margaret's boxes," was all I said.

Turning to Ella, I asked, "Could it be in Edmund's office?"

She looked down again at the picture of her daughter which her grandson had drawn. "I don't recall seeing it there. Of course, I haven't been in the place in a couple of years and my memory isn't as sharp as it once was."

"You know, the only way to find out for sure," I said, sitting on the edge of the bed as if we were a couple of schoolgirls conniving on a plan to meet some boy, "is to go down there and see for ourselves."

"What reason could we have for showing up there?"

There's always a sensible one in these scenarios. "Oh, I don't know ... Tell him you wanted to ... show me around the plant."

"This would be an inauspicious day for a tour, considering that I threw him out of the house this morning. Maybe we should wait ..."

"You said you don't have time to put things off." I was manipulating her and I knew it.

"You're right. Let me see if he's in."

Ella went to the phone on the bedside table. "He has a direct line into his office," she said as she dialed. "Grace, good morning. This is Ella Dykstra. Is my son in?" She listened for a moment, then said, "Thank you, dear. No, there's no message."

"Well ... ?" I said as she hung up.

"He told his secretary he had to run over to Saugatuck. Something about opening up a cottage, she said."

* * * *

As she locked the back door I realized Ella hadn't set the security alarm. "Don't you want to turn the alarm on?" I asked.

"I usually don't during the day," she said. "It's just too much trouble. Nobody's going to break into a house up here, especially not during the day."

I wished I had her confidence. We got down to the driveway and I was reaching for my keys when Ella asked if I would mind driving her car.

"It needs to be taken out once in a while," she said, handing me the key. "Besides, it matches your eyes."

I felt like I did the first time my dad gave me the key to his car— excited and nervous as hell. I also remembered that I had an acci- dent—just a tiny ding on the rear fender when I backed into a post— on that first trip.

But I made it to the plant in the hunter-green Lexus without incident. I was just sorry the plant wasn't farther away, like maybe in Detroit. Edmund's private parking space, outside his private en- trance, was empty. We took one of the visitor's spaces closer to the front entrance.

I was halfway out of the car when my phone rang. I answered it with one hand while I watched over Ella getting out on her side. Denise van Putten was returning my call. I told her about Josh and invited her to visit him in the hospital if she wanted to, although he probably wouldn't be aware of her presence.

"I appreciate you letting me know about this," she said. "I will definitely stop by there."

I wondered if she would go alone, but I couldn't very well ask who was the guy that answered your phone. And I had no time for explanations if she offered one. Ella and I needed to get into Edmund's office while it was empty.

"It's smaller than I expected," I said to Ella as we approached the door of the plant. Could they have made all those millions from the small volume of furniture that could be produced in a building this size?

"This is our original plant," she explained. "Now we do high- end, custom furniture here. We have another plant in Kentwood that does office furniture and one in Walker where we make fur- nishings for schools and public buildings. At least that's how things were set up a few years ago. Edmund may have made changes he hasn't told me about."

The plant was a beautiful century-old structure, made of warm yellow, hand-molded bricks. The tops of the windows were arched, each with a granite keystone. I felt some disorientation when we stepped inside because the interior had been modernized. The reception area was small. Logically enough, since an operation like this wouldn't get much walk-in business. Executive offices opened off the central waiting room. The secretary was away from the desk, but a man in his late fifties, still fit and athletic looking, stepped out of the nearest office.

"Good morning, Mrs. Dykstra. We haven't seen you down here in a while."

He managed a smile, but it sounded to me like he wanted to add, And why are you spoiling a good thing today?

"Good morning, Boyd. We just dropped by to see Edmund."

"I don't believe he's in yet." The man turned his head as though he could see through walls and determine whether Edmund was in his office.

"That's all right." Ella lifted her cane in a wave and led me down a short hallway to the presidential suite. Beyond it I could see the door leading to the production part of the plant. EMPLOYEES ONLY one sign said. SAFETY GLASSES REQUIRED BEYOND THIS POINT another warned. The prosperous hum, whine, and buzz of wood-working machinery filtered through the door.

As we entered the outer office Edmund's secretary looked up from her computer and minimized whatever she was working on. A game of solitaire, probably. Ella introduced us.

"I just wanted to show Sarah around," Ella said. "Do you mind if we take a quick peek in Edmund's office?"

"Ah, no. I guess not. Go ahead." Grace didn't seem entirely comfortable with the idea, but she must have been aware of Ella's clout.

Edmund's door stood open. I stopped just inside it. The office looked so different from the diagram and the pictures I'd seen of it when Margaret was killed I couldn't even visualize it as the same room. Edmund's desk sat on the wall where the private restroom was. The center of the room was now occupied by a conference table and chairs. Edmund had even put vertical blinds over the big windows Margaret loved so much.

Ella and I did a fast sweep of the room. The paperweight was not on Edmund's desk or in the display case on the wall opposite the desk, featuring golf trophies and awards for his charitable work. I tried a couple of desk drawers, but they were locked.

"If it were here," I said, "wouldn't he have it out on display? He must take some pride in it. After all, it was *his* grandfather, too, who made it."

Ella looked uncertain for a moment, the way old ladies sometimes do. One of those senior moments? "Yes ... I suppose so. Edmund was quite young when old Mr. Dykstra died, though. He never got to know him the way Margaret did. I wonder if he might have it in his bathroom." She stepped into the bathroom to check.

I jumped as a key turned in the lock of the private entrance. The door swung open and Edmund and Katherine stepped into the room. Katherine gasped when she saw me. Edmund looked at me like he was encountering an extra-terrestrial.

"What ... what the hell are you doing here?"

Before I could reply Ella emerged from the bathroom. "Oh, Edmund, Katherine, there you are," she said. "I brought Sarah down to see the plant." That was our story and she was sticking to it.

"The plant's out there." He jerked his arm out toward the door. "This is my office. And I want you to leave right now, Mother, and take her with you."

"Edmund, you're being rude," Katherine said.

"I'm being rude?" He turned on her the way a person might do if he had broken off an argument with someone but now was eager to start it up again. "If she can throw me out of *her* house, I can throw her out of *my* office."

Katherine started to say something else, but Ella cut in. "We will go if you'll answer one question for me."

"I don't have to bargain with you." He clenched both fists, keeping his rage barely under the surface. "Just leave."

"Edmund, I have to know this." Ella took a step toward him, as if pleading. "Where is that paperweight—the pineapple finial—that Margaret kept on her desk?"

Her son shot a glance at his wife. I couldn't tell if he was gauging her reaction to the question or warning her not to say anything. "Wasn't it in those boxes of her stuff?"

"No, it wasn't."

"Then I have no idea what's become of it."

Margaret's best friend had told me Margaret could lie her way out of anything. I wondered if her brother inherited the same talent. What were his 'tells' when he was lying? I watched him closely. He missed a beat as he looked down and picked up the morning's mail on the corner of his desk.

"If there's nothing else," he said, slapping the mail into two piles, "I'll have to ask you to leave. We have work to catch up on, since we spent most of the morning in Saugatuck." His voice was heavy with sarcasm.

"All right, then," Ella said. She couldn't disguise her sadness.

"Mother Dykstra," Katherine called as we reached the door, "will you be all right by yourself?" Something about her face—the slight quiver around the corners of her mouth and the tightness of her eyes—gave me the impression she was trying with all her might to hold herself together until we got out the door.

"Yes. I think I can count on Sarah if I need anything."

I nodded as they all looked at me.

"How is that young man?" Katherine asked. "The one who was stabbed in the jail."

Ella hesitated, her eyes filling with emotion, so I stepped in.

"He's doing all right. The doctor says the next twenty-four hours are critical, but he's confident Josh will pull through."

"I'm glad to hear that," Katherine said with a nervous smile. "I really am. I know what you think of me, Mother Dykstra, but, as God is my witness, Edmund and I had nothing to do with anything that has happened to him."

"She's right," Edmund said. "We want to be sure we have indisputable proof of who he is. I think you'll agree that's only reasonable. But we wish him no harm, regardless of how things turn out. All I've been trying to do the last few days is protect the family and you, Mother."

My instinct was assuring me they were telling the truth about that. And I was equally sure they were lying about the paperweight.

Chapter 41

As we started back to Ella's house, she sank heavily into the Lexus' leather seat and closed her eyes. "All I want is to go home and take a nap."

"Do you think your blood sugar is low?"

"No, I'm just exhausted. It's been a very tense morning."

I glanced over at her. Her face seemed to be sagging and her whole body drooped. "I'm worried about you being by yourself. I could stay for a while, but I've got some things to do and ..."

"And you' must get ready for dinner with that man of yours."

I couldn't help but smile. "'That man of mine' may be overly optimistic, but at least we're going out."

"And I hope you charm the socks off him, and maybe some other articles of clothing as well."

I blushed.

She reached over and patted my knee. "Just because I'm old and falling apart, don't think I haven't felt a thrill or two in my time. And given a few, for that matter. Now, don't worry about me. I'll be fine."

"Well, I do worry. What if you fell or had a problem and couldn't get to a phone?"

"Somebody would find me in a day or two, I guess."

"Ella! Don't talk like that. Look, let's get you a cell phone."

"I've got phones all over my house. I've got one beside my bed."

"But you can keep a cell phone right with you. If you fall or feel ill, you wouldn't have to worry about getting to a phone."

She looked doubtful. "Can you show me how to use it?"

"Sure. Let's go to the place where I got mine. We'll get you set up and I'll program my number into your speed dial."

This errand required that we get on the interstate, so the Lexus really got to stretch its legs. There's one section of I-196 on the north side of town where the speed limit is 55 because of the congestion, but once you get past Lake Michigan Drive on the west side, it goes back up to 70. When I looked down at the speedometer I was doing 80. No wonder I was flying past everybody.

"You're quite the speed demon," Ella said. "Are you counting on Cal to fix your ticket?"

"He will if I wear that blue dress tonight."

"You wicked girl!" She slapped my arm playfully.

It didn't take long to get Ella fixed up with a phone. She just bought the 'all-the-minutes-you-want-at-any-time-you-damn-well-please' plan without worrying about what it cost or how it compared to other plans. I programmed my number for her, then stood on the other side of the store while she used her speed dial. On the way home she called all the members of her 'Last Wives' Club'.

By one o'clock I had her—and her car—safely back home. She checked her blood sugar and was satisfied. I was grateful I didn't have to help her with an insulin injection. On my way out I prevailed upon her to arm the security system, even if it was the middle of the day. She, in turn, insisted on giving me a key to the back door.

When I got home I sat down at my computer, fully intending to try to find out more about Jake Folkert and his connections. There would probably be other articles if he had signed other large contracts. But I was tired, and I wanted to be sparkly for dinner, so I decided to take a nap. Josh was safe for the moment, and Ella was all right. Maybe I could put all my responsibilities aside for a couple of hours and just crash.

My alarm went off at five. I treated myself to a long bath. Then I called the hospital and found out Josh's condition had been upgraded from 'Critical' to 'Serious.' Progress on that front, at least. Next I gave Ella a call on her new cell phone.

"I'm carrying it right here in the pocket of my robe," she said. "Like a good girl."

In spite of her joke she sounded depressed. "Is everything all right?" I asked.

Heavy sigh. "I'm going through the stuff in Margaret's boxes, and I'm looking through her desk drawers and files. It saddens me, but I should have done it several years ago."

"Have you found anything ... you didn't expect?"

"Nothing startling. You can look through it the next time you come over."

"I'd like to. I'll see you in the morning." I would have to check on her tomorrow morning. Since I bore some responsibility for her family not being with her, I felt I should keep an eye on her for a few days.

I put my hair up in a beautiful pair of combs Cal had given me, and then compared his favorite dress to the thermometer in my kitchen window. The mercury had dipped almost as low as the dress' neckline. Could I really wear this thing tonight? It showed a lot of cleavage and shoulder, and the fabric was lightweight. In west Michigan a dress like this wasn't comfortable until June. I remembered freezing in a strapless gown at my junior prom in May because my best friend and I were determined to be the girls everyone was looking at. My goosebumps that night were almost as prominent as my freezing nipples. For my senior prom I went with a high neck and sleeves.

But this was for Cal. Maybe I could wear my nice white cardigan over it.

About 6:30 the phone rang.

"Hi, Sarah," Cal said, and I knew there was going to be some sort of delay or emergency. "Look, I can't make it in time to pick you up and still get to the restaurant for our reservations. Could you meet me there?"

"Sure." Any woman who has a relationship with a cop, I reminded myself, has to expect this sort of thing. "Reservations are for 7:30?"

"Right. I'll be there by then, without fail."

Putting the phone down, I hung the blue dress back in the closet and pulled out a gray wool number with a high neckline and long sleeves. Cal had once compared it to a suit of armor. He might not be warm tonight, but I would.

* * * *

My parents did everything they could to keep me aware of my Korean heritage, even when I just wanted to be a teenager and fit in with everybody around me. It helped that they liked Oriental food and that Grand Rapids has one of the finest Korean restaurants in the Midwest. The Seoul Garden is located near Woodland Mall on the city's southeast side.

The people at the Seoul Garden are very courteous to me— maybe because they know I speak the language—but I always get the feeling I get whenever I'm around Korean people that I'm some sort of half-breed and a cast-off to boot. Koreans are extremely conscious of family lineage. That's why few Koreans will adopt, even Korean children. I've been told that, if a couple does adopt, the wife pretends to be pregnant—putting a pillow under her dress and going to 'visit a cousin' for the last couple of months—and they pass the child (always a boy) off as their own. But no Korean family would adopt a child like me. If it hadn't been for my adoptive parents I would have grown up in the orphanage and gone to work in my early teens, probably making sweatshirts or athletic shoes for some American company.

But I couldn't dwell on stuff like that. I was going to have a fabulous dinner with the man I still loved, in spite of the last three months.

I pulled into the parking lot after 7:20 and waited in my car. Cal arrived at 7:25, driving fast. I could see his disappointment at my dress when I got out of the car, but he didn't say anything except, "Sure has gotten chilly this evening, hasn't it?"

We started with a couple of appetizers. Bin dai duk is traditional yellow bean pancakes with diced pork, onions and carrots. My favorite, though, is Mandoo, a fried dumpling stuffed with ground beef and vegetables. For my entrée I got Hae Mool Jun Kol, a spicy seafood casserole. Cal likes seafood, but nothing really hot, so he got his usual shrimp with peapods, what I call 'wimp shrimp'.

As we sipped hot tea and I ate kimchi, he wanted me to catch him up on the situation with Josh and the Dykstras. After telling him about my day, I asked if he had any more information about the man who stabbed Josh.

"Not really. We interrogated him a couple of times today, but he just rambles incoherently most of the time."

"Are you going to charge him with anything?" Nice romantic conversation.

"Yeah, attempted murder. He'll end up in a state hospital until the next round of budget cuts. Then he'll be back on the street." One of Cal's biggest frustrations about his job was the feeling that he couldn't pull criminals off the street as fast as the system turned them back out. I guess a lot of cops feel that way.

"Has anybody showed up to post bail or to defend him?"

"No. He has a public defender. Who do you think would help old Vernon?"

"I just thought, if somebody hired him to kill Josh, that person might want him silenced, or at least out of police custody."

"Do you still suspect the Dykstras?"

I thought back to the confrontation in Edmund's office and Katherine's protestation of their innocence. "Not directly. But Jake Folkert ... Now there's another story."

"But that would be a little too obvious, wouldn't it? If Folkert showed up to post bail, or sent somebody who's connected with him to do it?"

I had to agree with Cal. I couldn't imagine Martin Vandervelde showing up to post bail for a psychotic drunk who would probably try to steal his Rolex or drool on his Armani suit. But David Burton ... Or what if Folkert was using Edmund's son-in-law Roger Haveman as a front?

The waitress brought our entrees and some more kimchi. It felt like a good time to change the subject, but Cal beat me to it.

"How are your folks doing?" he asked. He had met my parents several times and spent one weekend at their house, not even chafing at my father's rule that, no matter what you do elsewhere, if you want to sleep with his daughter under his roof, you have to marry her.

"They're fine, thanks. How's your dad?" Cal's father and step-mother live in Florida, so I had yet to meet them.

"Doing well. I talked to him last night."

"What about your mother?"

"Elaine's doing all right. She won some kind of amateur golf tournament last week."

"Not your step-mother. Your *mother*."

"Sarah, why would you ask that? You know my mother's ..." He looked down at his food and then back up at me. "Geri told you?"

"Yes."

"Damn! I thought I could trust her not to tell anybody."

"And I thought I could trust you to be honest with me. Why did you think you couldn't tell me? You know my history. If anybody's going to understand what it would be like to be abandoned by their mother, it's me."

"On some level I know that, Sarah, and I wanted to tell you the truth. But for years I've been telling everybody that she was dead. I figured if I told you something different, eventually it would come out, and ..."

"Oh, so you think Geri can keep a secret but I can't. Well, surprise!"

I didn't care if I sounded accusatory, even gloating a bit. That's exactly how I felt.

"No, it's not that ..."

"Cal, I'm in a profession where I *have* to keep people's secrets. If I didn't, I would lose my license."

"I know, I know." He leaned back so far I was afraid he was going to get up and leave. "I didn't plan to tell Geri. It just kind of ... slipped out. Sometimes our conversations are more like therapy sessions."

"That's not very professional of either one of you. If you need to talk to a therapist, you should go to one."

"Yeah, I know. Geri gave me a couple of names, and I've made an appointment."

"Good. I hope it'll help you resolve some things."

"The main thing I want to work on is how I managed to mess up my relationship with you. Nothing has ever been more important to me than being with you. Even on the day I left I was thinking to myself, 'Why in the hell am I doing this?'"

"That question crossed my mind, too."

He reached across the table and took my hand. "I love you, Sarah. Is there any chance we can repair the damage I've done?"

"I love you, too, Cal. But we need time to work through a few things. We can't just magically go back to the place where we were three months ago."

"I figured that was the message you were sending with your 'suit-of-armor'."

"Well, here's another message: Be patient. This isn't the only dress I own."

We passed the rest of the meal in small talk, almost as though we were getting to know one another on a first date. When we were done I was glad we had come in separate cars. We wouldn't have to face that awkward moment when Cal dropped me at my place and I didn't know whether to invite him up. Deciding how passionately to kiss him in the parking lot was awkward enough, especially when I felt the hunger in his kiss and the weakness in my knees.

I stayed up for a while when I got home. I was afraid if I went to bed too soon I would have what I call The Dream again. Whenever I'm around Koreans, or any Asian people, for a length of time, I find myself dreaming that I'm running through the streets of Seoul looking for my mother. Maybe if I stayed up late enough to really tire myself out, I would sleep without any disturbance.

About twelve-thirty I was putting on my pajamas when my phone rang. I thought it would be Cal saying good-night (or begging to come over), but a woman's frightened voice whispered, "Sarah, somebody's in my house!"

Chapter 42

"Ella? Is that you? I can hardly hear you."

"I don't want him to hear me."

"Him? Who?"

"There's someone in my house. I can hear him bumping around."

"Are you sure it isn't somebody in your family?"

"None of their cars are in the driveway. I can see that from my window."

"You're in your bedroom?" I was trying to recall the layout of the second floor.

"In my bathroom."

"Are your doors locked? Bedroom and bathroom?"

"Yes."

"Have you called the police?"

"I thought it would be quicker to call you. I had the cell phone in the pocket of my robe."

I was flattered by her trust, but frustrated she hadn't called 911 first. "Okay, here's what we do. First, don't hang up, no matter what."

"No, I won't."

"You need to go back into your bedroom and call the police on your regular phone."

"Sarah, I'm afraid to go out there." The quaver in her voice convinced me she wasn't lying.

"Okay, put me on hold and call them on the cell phone."

"How do I put you on hold?"

The image of her punching buttons at random was enough to panic me. "Never mind. You might cut me off. I'll put you on hold and call 911. Don't do anything. I'll be right back."

No doubt, this would be a wasted call. Car in the driveway or not, I was willing to bet the 'intruder' was somebody in her family sneaking in for something they'd forgotten. Or sixteen-year-old Pamela and a boyfriend looking for some privacy.

Just in case, though, I decided to call Cal instead of 911. He could cut through the crap and I could get back to Ella right away.

"Hey," a groggy Cal said, "I was just dreaming you called me."

I quickly disabused him of any romantic intentions behind my call and told him what was happening at Ella's house. As I described the situation, my instinct began raising flags. I threw on some sweats, grabbed my bag, and headed for my car.

"I'm on my way," Cal said. "I'll call for backup and tell them to get there ASAP." He paused. "Sarah, did I hear a car starting?"

"I'm going to Ella's house."

"No! Don't do anything stupid. Let us handle this."

"I've got to help her if I can, Cal. Whatever is going on, she's terrified. I've got to get her back on the line, and talk her through this."

Before he could say anything else sensible I cut him off and re-connected with Ella.

"He's coming up the stairs!" she whimpered. "I heard that one step creak." Her breathing was becoming labored. How was her heart holding up? I wondered.

"I'm on my way, and the police are coming, too. If you keep quiet, you'll be all right. This guy probably doesn't even know you're there. If your door is locked, he'll go to another room. These punks are always looking for the path of least resistance."

"How soon will you be here?" She was on the verge of crying.

"I'm on 196, flying low. It'll just be a few minutes. The police will be there before I am."

I exited at College Avenue and barely slowed down at the top of the ramp. With my tires squealing I turned right and headed south. I caught a green light at Michigan and ran a red at Fountain Street. I slowed down as I approached Ella's house, expecting to see a couple of police cars out front with their lights flashing. But the street was dark. I parked and got out of my car.

"Ella, are you still okay?"

"Oh, Sarah! He's trying to pick the lock on my door!"

"It's all right. I'm here. Just stay where you are."

I looked up and down the street. Where were the damn cops? I ran around to the back door. I used the key Ella had given me and reached for the security box as I stepped into the kitchen. The DIS-ARMED light was already on.

"Oh, God!" Ella squealed in my ear. "He got the door open! He's in my room!"

Now I had no choice. I turned on the kitchen lights and bolted up the servants' stairs two at a time. I hoped noise and light would scare the intruder off, but I wasn't optimistic. Cal had told me most B&E guys will run at the first sign of somebody on the premises. But this guy had sought out the one occupied room in the house. That scared me.

I yelled as loud as I could when I reached the second floor. He popped out of Ella's room. Not a very big guy, wearing a ski mask, a sweatshirt and jeans. Because I didn't know if he was armed I didn't rush him. I braced myself for him to charge at me. Instead, he started down the main stairs.

"Stay where you are, Ella!" I shouted, forgetting I had her on the phone. "Everything's okay."

In the distance I heard a siren. The guy in the ski mask heard it too. He wasn't going to waste time fighting me. But if I didn't delay him, he would fade into the darkness by the time the cops got here. He would go out the way he got in, I thought, so I ran down the servants' stairs and was standing in the middle of the kitchen when he charged in.

"Get out of my way, bitch!" he growled.

"This is your way out," I said as I assumed the position to start a bout. My sneakers would hamper my movement a bit, but they would also add some extra wallop to any kick I landed.

He laughed. "Ooh, karate shit. I'm scared."

"It's tae kwon do," I said. "It's Korean. And I'm good at it." Actually I was good at sparring competitions where I knew what my opponent knew and we both followed the rules. Confronting a desperate attacker was something I'd never done before. And I'd never felt this sort of adrenalin rush before.

He reached under his sweatshirt and pulled a small revolver out of his belt. "Well, this is a Smith and Wesson. It's American, and I don't have to be any good with it to kill you."

Facing this worst-case scenario, I stepped aside just enough to give him room to sidle past me. He was trying to keep an eye on me and find the doorknob. His ski mask partly blocked his lateral vision.

My first kick knocked the revolver out of his hand. The room seemed to explode as the gun went off. I heard the bullet hit something with a thunk, but I kept my eyes on my opponent. The gun clattered across the tile floor. He turned his head to follow it and my second kick caught him on the jaw. He dropped to the floor. I stood back from him, bouncing on the balls of my feet, confident now that I could see flashing blue and red lights outside the house.

The intruder got up to his hands and knees.

"Stay down and I won't kick you again."

But he wouldn't listen. As he pulled himself up he picked up one of Ella's canes hanging on a drawer handle. He gripped it tightly as though he was going to swing at me with it.

"I don't want to hurt you," I said. As I aimed a kick at his midsection he proved quicker than I'd anticipated. He dropped into a crouch and hooked the foot I had planted on the floor. In one motion he drew back to avoid my kick and yanked my foot out from under me. I tried to roll, to absorb the force of my fall, but my head hit the ceramic tiles hard.

* * * *

There was something cold on my head and I was lying on something hard and cool. This wasn't The Dream. It wasn't like any dream I'd ever had. I gradually became aware of activity, of people talking, moving around, hovering over me. Was I going to see a tunnel with a light at the end?

"Looks like she's coming around," an unfamiliar voice said. That sounded like good news. "Better get Detective Timmer." I liked the sound of that even better.

"Sarah?" Cal said, kneeling over me.

I opened my eyes. "What happened?" An ice pack slid off my head onto the floor as I started to get up.

"Stay still," Cal said, putting a strong hand on my shoulder and replacing the ice pack. "The EMT's want to see if you have any head or neck injuries. You took quite a spill."

"Yeah. He pulled my foot out from under me. Did you catch him?"

"We've got him. And Mrs. Dykstra is fine. A little over-excited, but no real harm done. We asked her to lie down on the sofa in the parlor, to keep her out of the way. I thought she was going to take her cane to this punk. Now, let Cameron check you out."

I lay back and a guy with the gentlest hands I'd ever felt on my body removed the ice pack and probed around my neck and shoulders as he asked me a series of questions. I knew my name, the date—actually he got me on that one because I forgot it was after midnight—where I lived, who the president was, and so on.

"I don't think she's got a concussion," Cameron told Cal, like I wasn't even there. "And I don't see any evidence of a neck injury. I recommend we take her to the hospital and do some x-rays, though, just to be sure."

"Do I have the right to refuse treatment?" I asked from the floor.

"Sure," Cal said. "But shouldn't you play it safe?"

"I feel fine, except for the bruise."

"You're going to have quite a lump there," Cameron said. "Keep some ice on it for the next twenty-four hours." He handed me the ice pack and I applied it to the side of my head. How could I keep it there? At least the bruise wouldn't show much under my hair.

Once I had signed a form acknowledging that I declined further treatment Cameron and Cal allowed me to sit up. After I proved I could master that, they let me stand up. I had to lean against a kitchen counter to keep from falling right back down, but after a couple of minutes I began to feel like I might actually live. My right shoulder hurt almost as much as my head.

"I think that took most of the force of the fall," I told Cal. He started to rub it, but that hurt more than the injury itself. I moved his hand away. Regretfully.

"Why don't you come in here and sit down," he said, leading me into the dining room.

"What took you guys so long to get here?" I asked.

"There's a big disturbance at a night club on South Division. We had to pull a car away from there to get anybody over here."

As I took a seat at the dining room table I could see through the archway into the living room. Two uniformed officers were standing on either side of the intruder, now unmasked and seated in a straight-back chair, the most uncomfortable-looking piece of furniture in the room. His eyes looked old and burnt out, but he was young and drug-addict slender, with three or four days' growth of beard and a purpling bruise on his left jaw. That was my work, and I was damn proud of it.

"Who is he?" I asked Cal.

"Micah Freeman. Two-bit hood with a long record of burglaries and drug possession. Probably even longer if we could unseal his juvie record."

"Why was he after Ella?"

"He claims he wasn't. Says all he was doing was looking for something to steal."

"Bullshit. He walked past all kinds of silver and antiques and went straight for her room. And he was carrying a gun."

"That's one thing we need to clear up," Cal said. "He claims it isn't his gun. Says you pulled it on him. The serial number's been filed off. We couldn't get prints off of it. He's wearing gloves, of course."

"It most certainly is his gun," I said. "He pulled it out of his belt and pointed it at me."

"Did he fire it?"

"It went off when I kicked it out of his hand."

Cal took a few steps over to where the kid was sitting. "You see, Micah, we have a witness who says you were carrying the gun. Are you aware that carrying a gun while committing a felony automatically adds several years to your time in jail?"

Micah jerked his hand toward me in a kind of 'gangsta' motion, with a couple of fingers out at odd angles. White guys look so ridiculous doing that. "Hey, it's her word against mine."

"You want to bet on who a jury will believe?" Cal asked.

The young punk sneered. "If you could pin anything on me, you'd have arrested me by now."

"You haven't arrested him?" I said.

Cal came back over to me, leaned over, and said softly, "It's a technicality. If we arrest him, we have to Mirandize him and let him call a lawyer. If he were under arrest, you couldn't be here. Right now, we're just talking to him as 'a person of interest', and I wanted you to be in on it."

"He's the 'alleged' intruder? I saw him in Ella's bedroom."

"'Allegedly' in her bedroom," Micah said.

Cal rolled his eyes at one more reminder of the restrictions and technicalities of his job.

"Hey, could I get some ice for my jaw?" Micah called. "I think that bitch broke it."

"Then ice won't do you any good," Cal said over his shoulder.

"Police brutality!" Micah whined.

"Steve, would you get him some ice, please?" Cal asked one of the officers.

"My lawyer's gonna file an assault charge against her," Micah snarled.

I sucked in my breath. I had heard of crazy cases where criminals filed suits against their victims. What was even crazier was that sometimes they won.

Cal laughed. "If you file that charge, you'll have to explain what you were doing in somebody else's house in the middle of the night. So why don't you go ahead and explain it to us, just for practice."

"I already told you, man, I was looking for stuff I could sell. I've got ... needs."

"You mean a drug habit," Cal said. Micah just shrugged.

"Why did you pick this house?"

"It was dark. No cars in the driveway. Looked like nobody home."

"How did you get past the security system?" Cal asked.

"Didn't have to. It was turned off."

"That's not what Mrs. Dykstra says. She says she armed it earlier today and checked it before she went to bed."

"I saw her turn it on this afternoon," I said.

Micah made another 'gangsta' move, with both hands this time. "Old bat like her, she don't know if she was turnin' it on or off, man."

I couldn't dismiss the possibility that Ella might have gotten confused and turned the system off later, thinking she was arming it. I wasn't going to volunteer that information, though. Micah could have found the numbers written beside the alarm box. But he couldn't have known they were written backwards unless somebody told him. Somebody like Edmund Dykstra. The only other way he could have disarmed the system was if somebody—namely Jake Folkert—had given him the code number.

"Micah," Cal said, "you're not convincing me. Every B&E guy I've ever known was a devout coward. The slightest noise, they're out of there. But you were trying to pick a lock to get in an old lady's bedroom."

"I didn't know it was no old lady's bedroom, and you can't prove I did. She didn't say nothin'. No light on. I just figured, if the door was locked, you know, there might be some good stuff in there."

"So you walked past thousands of dollars worth of silverware and candlesticks, just in the dining room buffet alone, and looked around for a locked door because there might be something more valuable in that room."

"Yeah." Micah hitched his shoulders up.

"Cal," I said, "could I ask a question?"

He considered for a moment, then said, "Tell me what it is and let me ask it, just to keep everything on the level."

"Okay. Ask him what connection he has to Jake Folkert."

As Cal repeated my question Micah put his elbows on the arms of his chair and laced his fingers in his lap. His knuckles turned white as he pressed his fingers together hard. His head was beginning to twitch ever so slightly. From my counseling experience I thought I saw signs that he was beginning need his next fix.

"I don't know Jake Folkert," he said, his eyes darting from side to side. "I've heard of him. Some kinda rent-a-cop, ain't he? But I don't know him, man."

Cal's cell phone rang. He talked to someone for a couple of minutes, then turned to Micah. "They found your car a few blocks from here. They're getting a search warrant. What do you think they're going to find?"

"They can have all the dried-up french fries under the seat."

"Apparently you're a messy boy, Micah. On top of the dashboard, in plain view from outside the car, is a bunch of papers. The officers saw them when they were checking for the VIN number. Sarah must be psychic, because one of them is a pay stub from Folkert Security. Now, do you want to reconsider your answer to my last question?"

The punk's feet began to tap dance. "Okay. Yeah. I've worked part-time for Folkert, you know, doin' security at clubs. Shit like that. But I ain't done nothin' for him since Christmas."

"Not even trying to scare an old lady to death?" I asked.

Chapter 43

Before long Micah was arrested, Mirandized, and escorted to the Kent County Jail. Cal promised that a patrol car would stay in the area for the rest of the night. Edmund and Katherine would be notified of the break-in first thing in the morning. Ella didn't want them dragged out of bed in the middle of the night and wanted to get to sleep herself. I volunteered to spend the rest of the night with her, and the offer was accepted. As soon as everyone else was out of the house, Ella got out the manual for the security system, and I changed the code numbers.

"Are you going to be able to get back to sleep?" I asked her.

"Katherine has some sleeping pills. I think I'll take one."

"Taking someone else's medications isn't a good idea, Ella."

"I'll just take half of one then."

I wished I felt only half as concerned, but I wasn't her mother. "Where would you like for me to sleep?"

"In Margaret's room," she said, "if you're comfortable with that."

"Sure. It won't bother you to have somebody in there?" It looked to me like the room had been preserved as some sort of shrine.

"No. I think Margaret would be pleased to have the person who brought her son back to us staying in the room where he was born."

We went upstairs and she showed me where towels and bath supplies were kept. I didn't even have a toothbrush, but there were new ones and some soap and shampoo in a closet in the hall.

"I'll fix breakfast about 6:30," I said. "Is there anything you especially like?"

"Scrambled eggs and toast suits me. I like the basics."

"Good. Basics I do pretty well."

She hugged me. "You're a remarkable young woman. I'm pleased to have had a chance to get to know you."

"Well, you're quite a piece of work yourself, Mrs. Dykstra."

In no time Ella was snoring loudly. I closed the door to Margaret's room and sat down at her desk. As keyed up as I was, I didn't think I would get to sleep any time soon. I was also more worried about the bump on my head than I admitted to Cal and the soft-handed EMT. When I was in high school I got a concussion in a tae kwon do tournament. This felt similar, but I wasn't entirely sure. I know people with concussions are supposed to stay awake. To keep myself up, I decided I'd spend some time going through Margaret's desk. First I got another towel to wrap around my ice pack so it wouldn't drip on the stuff I was looking at.

Ella had put the best of her daughter's things from the boxes on top of the desk. The rest she had packed carefully into two of the boxes. I had no interest in the plaques and awards. They were part of Margaret's public persona. The inner Margaret was who I wanted to know. Fortunately Ella had left the sketches out. I looked at the 'Mother ... and Child?' sketch for a few minutes. The most intriguing feature of the piece, for me, was still the way the right hand was clutched to the chest, touching the left breast. Maybe tomorrow I could go down to The Art Place and compare this pencil drawing to the sculpture itself. Putting it aside, I turned my attention to the desk.

It was made of solid maple, not veneers, high quality, like everything in this house. I started with the middle drawer and then went through the four regular drawers, three on the left side and one on top on the right. They held office and art supplies and junk. Margaret must have cleaned up like I do. As long as there's nothing on the surface, the room is clean. I promise myself I'll go through those drawers one of these days. The next time there's some cosmic conjunction of rain on Saturday and *Sleepless in Seattle* on TV.

Finally I was ready to delve into the file drawer. At least Margaret kept her files in good order. Unusual for an artistic type. I pulled out the first ten or twelve and stacked them on the desk in front of me. Each person she corresponded with had his or her own folder, with the last name on the tab. They seemed to be arranged in order of importance to her, not alphabetically. I glanced at the thick file of correspondence with Mickey Bolthuis but didn't see anything I hadn't seen from Mickey's end.

I looked through a few of the files carefully, but the letters—and then e-mails—revealed nothing about the aspects of Margaret's life I was interested in. I was anxious for any glimmer of an insight into this woman's personality. Who she was, I felt, was an important factor in what happened in her office that night.

She did keep up with some college classmates for a long time, it seemed, though not with any from high school, except Mickey. They took part in an on-line book group, exchanged accounts of vacations, and kept one another up on their kids' doings. That must have been especially hard for Margaret.

I skimmed the rest of that stack, moved them aside, and pulled out another dozen or so. Halfway through that second stack I began to run into collections of articles Margaret had cut out of newspapers and magazines, articles about mothers and their children who were separated and reunited years later.

I wondered if my Korean mother had anything like this.

Margaret even tried to write a story about a reunion between a mother and son who had been separated for years. Judging from the rough draft, she made a wise choice to concentrate on sculpture as her artistic outlet.

Toward the middle of the pack of files I noticed one with the name 'Nathan' on the tab. That struck me as unusual. All the other correspondence files had a person's last name on them. I pulled the file out and read the first letter, dated six months before her death.

My darling Nathan,

Well, I've finished it. I call it 'Mother ... and Child?' How I wish you could see it. But, of course, if you could see it, I wouldn't need to make it, would I? You would be here and I would actually have some reason to care about my life. Not a waking hour has gone by in the past 25 years when I haven't thought of you. I wonder where you are, what you're doing. I pray—and it's the only thing I pray for—that you're safe.

Obviously 'Nathan' was the name she would have given the man I knew as Josh. There were only a few of these letters, written in the last year of Margaret's life. Ella said Margaret kept a diary of some sort about her son. Had she done something with that— put it in a safe deposit box, maybe—and then taken to writing these letters? They were the only letters written in longhand. Everything else was typed.

I decided I would leave them for Josh to read. I didn't feel like I should intrude ...

Oh, who was I kidding? I didn't read them because I knew I would break down and cry all over them, thinking about Margaret and Josh and about my own mother in Korea. Margaret had no choice about giving up her baby. My mother did. Did she ever regret her decision? Did it cause her the kind of pain Margaret experienced? Did she love me—ache for me—the way Margaret loved Josh?

I started crying anyway. Relief of tension, I told myself.

Josh and I were both fortunate to end up with loving parents, but I think most adoptees feel a sense of incompleteness they can never entirely overcome. It's that lack of a bond with the woman who bore you that leaves you feeling lost. Josh would have a grand-mother and other family members now, but not his mother. Even if he made contact with his father, David Burton didn't sound like he had much potential to fill the void left by Margaret's absence.

My parents had offered to help me look for my mother, if I ever decided I wanted to. We made a trip to Korea when I was sixteen, just to visit, not to search. Sitting at this desk, looking at the picture of his mother that Josh had unwittingly drawn, I wondered how big a job that search would be. The skills and connections I had culti-vated in my job wouldn't be much use in such an alien environment.

I pulled out the next dozen or so files. That was when I saw one file lying on the bottom of the drawer, under all the others. It was perpendicular to the upright files, so I didn't think it had just slipped down and gotten lost, as I've had a file do now and then. I pulled it out. The folder was newer than the rest in the drawer, and it had no name on the tab. I laid it on the desk and opened it.

The first thing I saw was an old piece of my agency's letterhead stationery with a row of staple holes across the top.

I stopped breathing. This was Josh's original file!

I flipped through the pages quickly. Everything was there that should be there—his original and amended birth certificates, copies of correspondence with his parents, the application they had filled out, home study reports—everything.

How the hell did this file end up in this drawer?

With every fiber of my being I wanted to think Jake Folkert had planted it here. But that immediately raised all sorts of questions. Little ones like, Why? And big ones like, How would he get in here to do it? Did he think somebody would find it, that it would incrimi-nate the Dykstras in some way?

Maybe the simplest explanation was the best, like Geri said. In this case the simplest explanation was that one of the Dykstras took the file out of my office. Their daughter, Ann Haveman, was in the building that night and admitted she had gone into my office. She claimed not to have seen the file.

But how would Ann have known what was in the file? What reason would she have had for taking it? The original file just said 'Adams, Matthew and Allison' on the tab. If Ann was the one, then the explanation got more complicated. Someone had to tell her what to be looking for. She said it was a woman who called her and told her to come to the agency that night. Was that some employee of Folkert's? And if Folkert had someone take the file, how did it end up here?

The simplest explanation was that the woman who called Ann Haveman from my office was the person who picked up the file off my desk and the person who tried to hide it in this drawer. Starting from this end of the puzzle, what woman had access to this desk? Ella obviously wasn't the right answer. She wouldn't have invited me to look through the desk if she had hidden this in it, and she couldn't get from one place to another without someone to drive her. Her granddaughter, Pamela, could come in here at any time, but what could she know about all this? Ann said they didn't even know, until a couple of months ago, that Margaret had had a child.

That left Katherine Dykstra.

And that 'simple' explanation raised more questions than I wanted to deal with alone.

* * * *

I set my clock for six so I could be dressed and have breakfast before Edmund and Katherine got to the house. Even after a shower I looked a wreck, on three hours sleep with the lump on the side of my head and no clothes to put on except the sweats I had worn last night. I did look in Margaret's closet, but the short, dumpy Dutch-American had nothing that would fit a tall, slender Korean-American. Talk about role reversal!

Cal called shortly after seven. "I just left the Dykstras' cottage in Saugatuck."

"How did they take the news?"

"They were genuinely horrified, I think. They'll be at the house in record time."

"When will you get here?"

"Am I needed? I told them all I could about last night and assured them Mrs. Dykstra was all right and that you were there."

I explained about finding Josh's file in Margaret's desk drawer. "We've got to confront them about this."

"You're right. That changes everything. I'll be there as quick as I can. Don't say anything to them without me."

Chapter 44

Ella and I were having a second cup of coffee when we heard a car pull into the driveway. The heavy tread of a man in a hurry hit the back steps and the back porch. Before I could get up a key turned in the lock and Edmund loomed in the doorway.

"Uh-oh," I said as he reached for the security alarm. I guess it was a habit for him to check it each time he came in. When he saw it was turned on—because I'd forgotten to turn it off—he punched in what he thought were the code numbers. His brow furrowed when the DISARMED light didn't come on. Then, as Katherine stepped in the door, all hell broke loose. The alarm was as loud as any police or fire siren I'd ever heard.

"What the ... ?" he said.

I scooted over to the alarm and punched in the new numbers. "I changed the code last night, after the break-in."

"Well, entering it now doesn't do any good." He didn't say 'you stupid cow', but he might as well have.

The phone rang. Oh great, I thought. What next? A barking dog?

"That's the security company," Edmund said as he picked up the phone. He identified himself and gave them a confirmation number. Within seconds the alarm fell silent.

It took us all another few seconds to readjust to the quiet. Katherine still stood by the back door, as if uncertain of her welcome. Edmund went to his mother, knelt down by her chair like a suppliant before a queen, and said, "Mother, are you all right?"

Ella patted his arm. "Yes, dear, I'm fine. Thanks to Sarah."

Edmund stood. Talking to me while he was still on his knees would be too humbling, I guess. He kept a hand on Ella's shoulder. "Detective Timmer told us about last night, about what you did to protect my mother. I'm very grateful."

"I am too," Katherine said. "It was very brave of you." She seemed to have put down roots by the back door.

"I just did what I could. Ella was a real trooper. She did some quick thinking."

"Is there anything we can do to show our appreciation?" Katherine asked.

"No, I don't want anything ..." The one thing I did want was to stay out of debt to these people. If they gave me anything, there would be a hook hidden in it, I was sure.

"Oh, everybody stop being so damn polite," Ella said. "Edmund, hand me that folder on the counter." She had brought it out of the office next to the kitchen earlier.

Edmund's head jerked when he picked up the folder. "Mother, these are the car titles."

"I know that. Find the one for my car."

"Why ... ?"

"Just do it."

Edmund pulled out the appropriate title.

"Now, sign it over to Sarah," Ella said.

I gasped along with Edmund and Katherine. "Ella, no ..."

"Mother, you can't be serious ..."

"Hush!" Ella snapped. "Not another word from any of you. Do as I say. This young lady literally risked her life for me last night. Put your finger in that bullet hole in the cabinet door if you need to be reminded. I can't drive that car any more. And besides," she winked at me, "it matches Sarah's eyes."

Edmund, his face darkening, turned the title over and signed it. As I took it from his hand he held it tightly for one last second and made me tug it away from him. Ella pulled the keys to the car from the pocket of her robe and slid them across the table to me.

"I don't know what to say," I said, "except thank you."

"Well," Katherine said, finally stepping further into the room, "now that that's settled, we can get back to normal."

I knew nothing was going to be normal in her life once I showed Cal the folder from Margaret's desk, but I couldn't do that until he arrived. I didn't want to screw up any potential legal proceedings with inappropriate questions. "Have you had breakfast?" I asked.

"I figured you'd be coming here, so I scrambled enough eggs for everybody."

"And they're not all dry," Ella said, handing her plate to Katherine for her to refill it. Katherine's face reddened.

"I don't feel like eating just now," Edmund said.

"All right," Katherine said. "Let's go on down to the plant."

"No!" Edmund snapped. "I want to talk to the police. I told you in the car, when my mother becomes a target, we must do something."

"But, darling, this incident is over." Although Katherine managed to keep her voice even as she heaped eggs on Ella's plate, she could not hide the uneasiness in her eyes. "That nice detective gave us all the details, and now you've talked to Mother. She's all right ... I think things are settled."

I got up and put the title and keys to my new car in my bag. Not just my new car—my new Lexus. It was going to take a while for that to sound real. My hand was on Josh's file when the front doorbell rang. If Edmund wanted to talk to the police, he was about to get his chance.

Cal had brought Geri with him. Edmund escorted the two of them into the kitchen and introduced Geri to Katherine, who shook hands with her and offered everyone coffee. She seemed even more rigid than usual, but having a police officer come to your door will do that to people. I was too excited about my new car to pay close attention to anyone else. One part of me wanted to show Geri the title and take her for a ride; another part just wanted to know how I was going to pay the insurance.

"It's fortuitous that you're here, Detective," Edmund said. "There is something my wife and I would like to talk about."

"Actually," Cal said, "several things need to be cleared up. Why don't we all sit down somewhere comfortable?"

"Let's go into the library," Edmund suggested.

He helped his mother up and we all followed them. I picked up my bag so I would have the folder I'd found with me. And I guess I wanted to keep my new car close at hand, too.

Geri fell into step beside me. "This is starting to look like the final scene from one of those old British mystery novels," she said softly. "The detective gathers everybody in the library and explains how Lord Faversham was killed. But I don't see any butlers around."

"And I don't think we know how anybody was killed. Or have you figured out something since we talked in the hospital?"

"No. I've been working on a couple of other cases, but Cal knows how interested I am in this one, so he called me. I hear you played Bruce Lee last night."

I gave an 'aw-shucks' shrug. "I had to do something. The guy was going to get away."

"It was brave of you. Brave, but stupid, going up against some guy with no idea whether he was armed. Once you scared him out of Ella's bedroom, you should have stayed out of his way and let us catch him. That's our job."

"I know. I got away with it once. I wouldn't do it again."

As the others filed into the library she put her hand on my head and turned it to get better light. "Doesn't look like you got away with it entirely."

When we entered the library Cal was already leaning against Edmund's desk. Geri positioned herself off to his left. Edmund and his mother took seats on the sofa. That left the two chairs in front of the desk for Katherine and me. We pulled them away from the desk to make a rough circle.

"We're glad you're here," Edmund said to Cal. "As I said, my wife and I would like to talk about something with you." He looked a lot more eager to talk than Katherine did.

"Before we get to that," Cal said, making me wonder what it was going to be like having two alpha males in this discussion, "I'd like to talk about something Sarah has found."

I took his gesture toward me as an invitation and pulled the file out of my bag.

"These are the materials from Josh's original file," I said. "Until Sunday they were in a different folder in a file cabinet in my agency's office. That file was taken off my desk Sunday evening. I found this last night hidden in a drawer in Margaret's desk upstairs. I'd like to know how it got there."

Katherine gave a short gasp.

"You had no right to be looking through my sister's desk!" Edmund said, starting up from the sofa. Cal and Geri both tensed.

Ella pulled on her son's arm. "I told her she could. It's my house and I told her she could look at anything she wanted to."

"Mr. Dykstra, Mrs. Dykstra," Cal said, "can you explain how this file got from Sarah's office to your house?"

"We want a lawyer," was all Edmund would say.

Cal folded his arms across his chest. "That's your right."

"Did one of you ... ?" I started to ask.

Cal held up his hand. "Sarah, once he's requested a lawyer, we shouldn't ask any more questions until the lawyer gets here, just to be sure we aren't violating any civil rights."

"You're not going to call that scumbag Vandervelde, are you?" Ella said in disgust.

"I certainly don't want one of our corporate lawyers trying to handle this, or even knowing about it. Who else can I get?"

"Jennifer McKenzie lives just a few blocks from here," I said. "She has an apartment in one of these old houses." I found her card in my bag and handed it to him. He looked at it as though it were written in ancient Sumerian.

Ella patted his knee. "Ms. McKenzie's a good person, son. Your sister trusted her."

I was surprised Edmund didn't ask us to leave the room while he made the call. He seemed oblivious to all of us, even his wife, as numb as a man who's seen his whole life's work suddenly wiped out by some disaster. He apologized to Jennifer for calling her at home and so early, explained that he needed some legal advice, and asked if she could come to his house right away.

"She'll be here in about twenty minutes," he said as he hung up, "in spite of some misgivings about conflict of interest. Do you mind waiting that long?"

"Waiting is a big part of our job," Cal said.

"Sarah fixed some scrumptious eggs and toast," Ella said. "If you haven't had breakfast, why don't you get some? There's coffee and juice, too."

"If you'll excuse us," Edmund said, "Katherine and I need to talk in private. We'll be upstairs. Please, help yourselves to anything you need in the kitchen."

"Yes, please do," Ella said. "I'll join you in a few minutes." She waved off any assistance and shuffled off in the direction of the first-floor bathroom.

"I've got to make a call," Cal said, with a glance at Geri. "I'll stay in here."

Geri and I made our way to the kitchen. When she got her coffee and juice and sat down at the table, her shoulders slumped.

"Are you not a morning person?" I asked.

"A cop has to be a twenty-four-hour-a-day person," she said. "I'm just wondering if I ought to be a cop at all."

"Whoa! Where's this coming from?"

"It's been building up for a while. I've had a couple of run-ins with our captain. Yesterday he made the joke about the Dutch boy putting his finger in the dike. Again."

"Geri, that's blatant harassment! Why don't you file a grievance against him?"

"Cops who do that get a reputation. Being who I am to begin with, I don't need the extra baggage."

"Have you said anything to Cal?"

"Yeah, that's why he's on the phone. He's going to try to help me resolve it informally. If we can't, I may just quit."

"You mean, go somewhere else?" I'd known her only a few days, but I knew I would feel a keen loss if she left.

"No. I want to stay in this area because of my parents. I might consider some other career options. Maybe do something with my counseling degree."

Cal's entrance into the kitchen cut off any further conversation.

"We've got a meeting at eleven today," he said to Geri, "about that ... matter."

"I told Sarah," she said.

"Oh, yeah, I forgot. No secrets between you two. Any eggs left?"

* * * *

Jennifer McKenzie arrived in less than fifteen minutes, looking like one of those fortunate people who's never fazed by an invitation to a 'come-as-you-are' party. She spent another fifteen minutes in the library with her new clients, then invited the rest of us back in.

"I have advised Mr. and Mrs. Dykstra to be completely forthright," she said, "and to answer all your questions. Ella, this is going to be difficult for you. Are you sure you want to be here?"

"Nothing is as difficult as not knowing," Ella said.

Judas Priest! I thought. I just wanted to know how the file got here. What were they so upset about? Why did they need a lawyer?

Edmund and Katherine now sat together on the sofa, under Josh's drawing of their house. Katherine took Edmund's hand and he patted her knee with his other hand, the first show of any connection or affection I'd seen between them. Jennifer pulled the chair out from behind the desk so she could sit close to them. Geri moved a wing chair out of one corner and placed it so Ella sat facing her son and daughter-in-law. Geri and I sat in the chairs in front of the desk, like pupils waiting for Professor Cal to enlighten us. Cal even looked the part as he leaned against the desk in his sport coat with the patches on the elbows.

"Thank you, Ms. McKenzie," Cal said, "for getting here on such short notice. I do want to make it clear that no one is under arrest. We would just like to know how a particular file from Sarah's agency came to be in a drawer of Margaret Dykstra's desk. Can we start with that question?"

"That's only one small part of a much larger issue," Edmund said.

"Then where do you want to start?"

Katherine turned her face upward, as though she were praying. "I killed Margaret!" she cried. "God help me, I killed her."

Chapter 45

My first reaction to Katherine's wail of guilt was to see how Ella was taking it. She leaned forward in her chair, her jaw clenching and her knuckles turning white on the head of her cane. I thought for a minute she was going to use it to beat Katherine. Maybe not such a bad idea. A little vigilante justice, some closure. The lawyer spoke up.

"I hasten to point out," Jennifer said, "that the situation may not be as clear-cut as Mrs. Dykstra thinks. I hope you'll all reserve judgment until you've heard the whole story."

"Are you going to be able to tell us what happened, Mrs. Dykstra?" Cal asked in that gentle good-cop voice that I considered one of the sexiest things about him.

Katherine nodded quickly. "I'm sorry. I've been living with this for what feels like my whole life. Mother Dykstra, I am *so* sorry. I would give anything if I could undo what happened that night."

Ella's mouth trembled, but she couldn't seem to find words to accuse or forgive. What must she be feeling, I wondered, knowing now that the person who killed her daughter had been living under her roof for five years?

"Please tell us what did happen," Cal said. "Start at the beginning and don't leave anything out."

Katherine shuddered with a deep sigh. "I had been the company's chief accountant for about six months."

"Margaret never did want you in that job," Ella growled.

The comment seemed to galvanize Katherine. She straightened her shoulders and her eyes sparked as she shot back, "No, she didn't. And do you know why? Because the man who had the job before me was a crony of hers who could barely balance his checkbook, let alone keep track of the finances of a multi-million-dollar company. It took me four months to figure out how much money was missing and to see that Margaret was making decisions which were ultimately going to ruin the company."

"Are you saying she was doing this deliberately?" Ella asked. I remembered Mickey Bolthuis' comment that Margaret said she wanted to take away what her father valued most, to pay him back for taking her baby away. What did Cornelius Dykstra value more than his company?

"I couldn't prove it from the spreadsheets alone," Katherine said, "but it looked like a bigger problem than just inept management. I thought Margaret was embezzling money."

Edmund groaned. "I've told her again and again, if she'd just said something to me. We could have gone to the board of directors ..."

"I wasn't sure what your reaction would be," Katherine replied. "You're always talking about how important your family is to you. I thought you might be protective of Margaret. And if I made an unfounded charge, we would have looked foolish. Margaret probably would have had the board sack both of us."

"Did you go to Margaret's office the night of July 9?" Cal asked before the two Dykstras could completely dissolve into bickering.

"Yes. I was on my way back from the mall. I had run across some particularly troubling figures that afternoon, and I knew I would have to talk to her before long. She was spending a lot of time at the office then."

"Mother was just out of the hospital," Edmund put in, "after some heart surgery, and she wasn't doing well. We were staying at the house to help out. I guess it was all too much for Margaret. She was 'working late' a lot of nights."

"Did she let you in through that private door of hers?" Geri asked.

"Yes," Katherine said.

"How would you describe her mood?"

"She was surly, bitter ... Drunk."

"Margaret did not get drunk!" Ella protested. "Sure, she drank a little more than I liked, but I never saw her drunk."

"She was very careful about that, Mother," Edmund said. "She didn't want to spoil your image of her. She drank heavily, and she was a very unpleasant drunk."

Ella sank into her chair as though Edmund was beating her with something more substantial than words. She might have dismissed the second-hand reports I'd given her, but she had to believe her own son.

"How did you approach her that night, Mrs. Dykstra?" Cal asked.

"I told her I had seen some things in the company's financial records that worried me, and I wanted to talk to her about them."

"What was her reaction?"

"That I was wasting my time. 'Once Mother dies,' she said, 'I'm going to see to it that this goddamn company goes belly-up. It shouldn't take more than six months. You and Edmund, don't get too comfortable up there on the Hill. I'm going to sell that house right out from under you.'"

Ella took some tissues out of her pocket and dabbed at her eyes. I scooted my chair closer to hers to be ready to comfort her. It looked like she was going to lose the vision she cherished of her daughter even as she finally found out how she had died.

"What did you say next?" Cal prodded.

"I told her she had no right to ruin what three generations of her family had built up. The company and the house were as much Edmund's as they were hers. They were the future for my children."

"That probably upset her," Geri said, looking up from her notes.

"Yes, I never should have mentioned children. I knew how the subject infuriated her. But it just slipped out. 'Don't throw your children in my face!' she said. 'Nobody took your baby away from you and gave him to some stranger.' I pleaded with her to be reasonable. Edmund and I had nothing to do with that. Why did she want to punish our family for something that happened so long ago? What would we do if she ruined us?"

"How did she react to that?"

"She just sneered. 'Your brats can flip burgers, like real teenagers,' she said. 'And you can do tax returns for H&R Block, for all I care.' I tried to appeal to her sense of responsibility to her workers. 'They trust you and look up to you,' I said. 'You'll be destroying their lives.' She just waved her arm and said, 'Let 'em go work for Wal-Mart. That's where we're all gonna end up anyway.'"

Ella thumped her cane on the floor. "That's enough! Margaret would never have said anything like that. She was a loving person. All we're hearing is your self-serving version of what happened. You can vilify Margaret all you like and she can't defend herself."

"Mrs. Dykstra does have a point," Cal said. "We're certainly interested in what you have to say, but we will have to consider if there's any way to verify it."

"There weren't any tape recorders or security cameras in the office," Edmund said dourly.

"We'll worry about that later," Cal said. "For now, let's just hear the rest of your wife's story."

"Well," Katherine said, "I tried to leave, but Margaret blocked the door. 'You're not going to tell Edmund,' she said. I told her I had to. He's my husband. I couldn't let her destroy everything for him. That's when the argument turned into a shouting and shoving match. Margaret was heavier than me and, as drunk as she was, she was difficult to stop. She picked up the paperweight and took a swing at me. I did the only thing I could. I yanked the paperweight away from her. When she came at me again, I swung it at her."

"Did you mean to kill her?" Cal asked.

"God, no! I didn't mean to do anything but protect myself. I just wanted to get out of there."

Cal nodded, as though absorbing what she was saying. "What happened next?"

"Margaret fell to the floor, with a bloody spot on the side of her head. I didn't know what to do."

"Was she moving? Did she make a sound?"

"No."

"Did you check to see if she was dead?"

"Before I could do anything Jake Folkert appeared in the office door. He was making his rounds."

"What did he do or say?"

"He said, 'Is there a problem here?' I asked him to call an ambulance, but he knelt beside Margaret and felt for a pulse. He told me she was dead."

Jennifer McKenzie leaned forward from her chair. "Please note that there is no way of knowing if Margaret actually was dead at that point. Jake Folkert has no medical training that we're aware of. He could not determine for certain whether she was dead or alive. And, as my clients will tell you, he had his own motives for wanting Katherine to believe Margaret was dead."

Katherine looked at her, her face as vacant in amazement as if she'd just seen a heavenly vision. "Do you mean I may not have killed her?"

"Without an autopsy it could never be established in a court of law that the blow you struck actually caused Margaret's death."

"Is that true?" Katherine asked Cal.

He shrugged. "I'm not a judge, Mrs. Dykstra. My job is to take your statement, gather evidence, and turn it all over to the District Attorney. He'll decide whether the case is worth prosecuting."

"All I was trying to do was defend myself. That's all I was trying to do." Her voice was rising.

Jennifer McKenzie held up a hand to calm Katherine. "You don't have to convince him," she said.

Cal nodded. "Your attorney is correct. All you have to do now is tell us what happened. After Folkert told you Margaret was dead, what did you do?"

"I told him it was an accident. He said it didn't look like one. That was when I realized I was still holding the paperweight. I told him I was sure the police would understand that I would never hurt Margaret deliberately. He said, 'You never know what the police will think. It would be a lot simpler if nobody knew you were here in the first place.'"

"How did you respond to that?" Cal asked.

"I asked him what he meant. Then he took a pair of latex gloves out of his pocket and told me to give him the paperweight."

Geri snorted. "He just happened to have a pair of latex gloves in his pocket?"

"He carried them all the time," Edmund said. "He told us later that he used to go through people's desks and files. He was stealing some of our designs and selling them to our competitors."

"He knew where everything was," Katherine said. "He even knew which drawer Margaret kept some plastic bags in. He got one out and put the paperweight in it and said he would get rid of it. I told him somebody would notice it was missing because Margaret always had it on her desk. We needed to clean it up and put it back."

"It would be virtually impossible to get all the blood off," Cal said. "We've had tests for some time now that can find blood, no matter what someone has done to get rid of it."

"That's what he told me. He said if even one speck was left, it would show up. And with my fingerprints all over the paperweight, the case against me would be airtight."

"Do you know where the paperweight is now?"

"Folkert still has it," Edmund said.

"And he's been blackmailing you for five years?"

"Yes."

"But there was blood on the corner of her desk," Geri said. "I saw it that morning, and the M. E. on the scene said Margaret died when her head hit the desk."

Katherine turned pale. "I don't know how I can tell you the rest of this with Mother Dykstra in here. It sickened me at the time. Just thinking about it now almost nauseates me again."

Chapter 46

We all looked at Ella.

"You'll have to drag me out," she said. "I have a right to know what happened to my daughter, no matter how awful."

"Just remember," Katherine said sadly, "I did try to warn you."

I put my hand on Ella's arm as Katherine got ready to resume her gruesome story.

"Folkert said the office didn't look like there had been a fight. One of us had kicked the trash can over, but nothing else was out of place. The main thing we needed to do was to make it look like Margaret fell and hit her head on something sharp. And we had to do it quickly, before the blood congealed."

"Did you make any suggestions?" Cal asked. "Or give him any encouragement in this plan?"

"No, I swear it. I was in such a state of shock, all I could do was follow his lead. He told me to help him pick Margaret up. I had no idea what he was going to do. I grabbed her around the waist and lifted her up. He grabbed her hair and—oh, God! I can barely bring myself to say it—smashed her head ... hard against the corner of the desk, right on the spot where I had ... hit her with the paperweight."

As Katherine dissolved into tears Edmund put his arm around her shoulder. I felt Ella's arm tighten under my hand. "God have mercy," she whispered. "God have mercy." I wondered if she was praying for her daughter or her daughter-in-law.

"Do you want to take a break?" Cal asked softly.

"No. I need to finish this." With obvious effort Katherine pulled herself together. "I told Folkert I was going to be sick. He told me not to throw up on the carpet. We would never get it out. I made it into Margaret's private bathroom. I was on my knees, hanging onto the bowl, when he came in."

"Is that why you had new tile put in the bathroom, Edmund?" Ella asked.

Her son nodded but couldn't look at her. "I couldn't take a chance that there might be some trace of ... material left for the police to find somewhere down the line. I know that probably makes me guilty in some way, but I had to protect my wife." Katherine looked at him in teary gratitude.

"We'll sort those details out later," Cal said. "What did Folkert do, Mrs. Dykstra, after you got sick?"

"I said, 'Sorry, I guess this is one more mess for you to clean up.' He grabbed a fistful of paper towels, got them wet, and threw them at me. 'This part you're going to do,' he said. I just looked at him, dumbfounded. He grabbed my hair and shoved my face up against the bowl. I'll never forget how awful he sounded when he whispered in my ear, 'Listen, rich bitch, if you don't like cleaning toilets, you're going to hate being in prison. Have you ever cleaned a toilet with your tongue?' That made me throw up some more."

"Did he assault you or harm you in any way?" Geri asked.

"No. When we finished cleaning up, he told me to go home and not say anything to anyone. He would take care of everything else."

"Is that what you did? Go home?" Cal asked.

"Not right away. I was hysterical. I drove a few blocks, then pulled over and sat there until I could stop crying and shaking. I knew I would probably see Ella and my girls when I got to the house, and I couldn't face them in the shape I was in."

Edmund squeezed her shoulder. "I was in the kitchen when she got home. I could see immediately that something was wrong. Fortunately, Mother was upstairs and Georgie and Pamela were watching television. I brought Katherine in here and she told me the same story she's just told you."

"What was your reaction?" Cal asked.

"I told her we should call the police and go back down to the plant."

Ella leaned over to me. "At least one of them had some sense."

Cal glanced at her to silence her, then turned back to Edmund. "How did your wife respond to that suggestion?"

"In panic. She said it was too late for that. Even if she wasn't charged with murder, there could be charges for what she and Folkert did to cover up the incident."

"Tampering with a crime scene comes to mind," Geri said. "And accessory after the fact."

"Exactly," Edmund said. "Katherine convinced me that doing anything at all would just make an awful situation worse. She was so terrified at the prospect of going to jail I decided I had to do things her way."

I hoped it didn't occur to Ella that Margaret could actually have been alive when Katherine left the office. If she and Edmund had called for help, they might have saved her.

"When did the blackmail start?" Cal asked.

"The day after Margaret's funeral. Folkert came to the house and demanded five thousand dollars in cash. He expected the same each week thereafter."

"So you've been paying him five thousand a week for five years?" Geri asked. "That's well over a million dollars already."

"Yes, and that's in addition to the contracts for his company and hiring his ambulance-chasing brother-in-law and recommending them to friends and business associates of mine."

"That must be putting a strain on you financially," Geri said, without any sympathy in her voice.

"We've been able to absorb it thus far," Edmund replied, "but we were starting to look for some way to get him off our backs. Margaret's trust fund for her son was our secret at that point."

"You hadn't told The Art Place they would be getting the money?" Cal asked.

"No. I didn't think they deserved to have it. Some of it was money Margaret embezzled from the company—from us. But I didn't want to go to court to break the trust."

"Bad publicity," Cal said.

"Exactly. With both of us involved in running The Art Place, we thought we could funnel that money to our own use and offer Folkert a lump sum buy-out."

"I'm guessing you offered him less than the full amount of the fund," Cal said.

"Two million. But the catch was that we couldn't be sure where the boy was. If he showed up in time to claim the money, we were doomed."

Ella shook her cane at him. "Did you send that monster after my grandson?"

"No, Mother. All we did was ask him to locate the boy and keep an eye on him, so there wouldn't be any last minute surprises. We never, either directly or implicitly, suggested he should harm anyone. He took it on himself to bribe the director at Ms. DeGraaf's agency to get the information and got her to let him know if anyone started asking questions about Margaret's son."

"Then he came to us two years ago," Katherine said, "with that newspaper article about the Adamses being killed in an explosion. He said he could guarantee Margaret's son wouldn't get in our way, and if we had any idea of going to the police, he would implicate us up to our eyeballs."

"That's why you were so surprised when I brought Josh here," I said.

"Exactly. We thought he was dead."

"If you weren't involved," Cal said, "how could Folkert implicate you?"

"We couldn't even imagine," Edmund said. "But after dealing with him for several years, we knew he was capable of anything. We couldn't undo what he had done, so it seemed best just to keep quiet."

"We've gotten good at that," Katherine said.

Edmund's voice broke. "I can't tell you what a relief it is to finally tell someone about this, no matter what the consequences. You'll never understand what our lives have been like since that night."

"Every morning," Katherine said, "we wake up thinking about Margaret and knowing we're indirectly responsible for the murders of Josh's family. We can hardly bear to look at one another. And yet we have to go on with our lives as though nothing were wrong."

Tears were actually running down Edmund's face. "Then my sister's child walks into my house, after all these years, and I can't welcome him, give him a hug. I have to make threats against him, have a sleazy lawyer slap a restraining order on him. I've become the monster you think I am, Ms. DeGraaf."

I wasn't going to let him off the hook so easily. Tears are just salt water, as my mother says. "Did you set Josh up for that accident and then have somebody attack him in jail?"

"We had no knowledge of any of that until we heard about it from Mother. I'm sure it was all Folkert's doing."

We all fell silent. Ella shook her head slowly. Edmund and Katherine looked at each other. I don't think they dared look at anyone else.

"What happens now?" Katherine asked. "Are you going to arrest us?"

Cal shook his head and glanced at Geri. "I'm sure we and others will want to talk further with you. We'll ask you to come downtown with us and give a formal statement. The D. A. will have to decide whether to press charges or accept your self-defense explanation, Mrs. Dykstra. I suspect there will be a request to exhume Margaret's body."

"What purpose would that serve?" Edmund asked.

"An autopsy should tell us how she died."

"It could tell us that she died from a blow to the head," Jennifer put in, "but which blow? From what my client described, Folkert's action probably destroyed, or seriously compromised, any evidence of the original injury."

"I don't want her violated," Edmund insisted.

"We won't be able to answer all our questions without an autopsy," Cal said. "We can get a court order if the D. A. decides to press charges against your wife. And I don't think you'll be able to pull enough strings to block it this time."

"I still haven't gotten an answer to my question," I reminded them. "Who took this file from my office and who locked me in that closet?"

Katherine reddened. "Folkert locked you in the closet. Then he called me and told me to come down to your office. He had me call Georgia Ann."

"Didn't she recognize your voice?"

"He put a device on the phone that made me sound different."

"What was the purpose of all this?"

"To scare you away from asking questions about Margaret's son. When I got there he told me he was going to tamper with your car so you'd have an accident on your way home. I told him he'd never get another dime from us if he did."

So, I was supposed to be grateful? "Was it Folkert's idea to take the file?"

"No, it was mine. I don't believe he even realized what it was. It was under your bag. But I saw the name on the label and thought I would keep it hidden, until we learned how things played out."

"I'm going to insist on returning it to the agency," I said. "State law requires us to keep all these files."

"Of course," Edmund said. "And all we can do is offer our most abject apologies for the way you and Mr. Adams have been treated. We really aren't the kind of people you've seen these past few days."

Cal rubbed his hands together. "I think that wraps things up for now. We'll put out an APB on Folkert. We'll start with murder and obstruction of justice charges. The blackmail is a federal crime. Mr. and Mrs. Dykstra, you do need to come with Detective Murphy and me."

Edmund was about to say something when the phone on his desk rang. He answered it, listened for a minute, then said to us, "It's the lab with the results of the DNA test."

Chapter 47

"Shall I put it on the speaker?" Everyone nodded and Edmund punched a button. "Go ahead," he said.

"The results are in a little early," the lab person said. "Joshua Adams is definitely a member of the family of Ella Dykstra and is related to you. If you want to come in and go over the results in more detail, we'll be happy to sit down with you."

I sighed and hugged Ella, who was crying again.

Edmund thanked the lab person, hung up, and said, "We'll need to get to the hospital as soon as Josh is able to have visitors. We've got a lot to apologize for."

"It might be a good idea to let Sarah go with you," Cal suggested.

"You're right," Edmund said. "We could use an intermediary, after all the damage we've done."

"I owe him a few apologies myself," I said. "I've been suspicious of him at several points in this process."

"Well," Cal said, "Detective Murphy and I will take you downtown now. We have to go to a meeting, so you may have a bit of a wait before we can take your formal statements."

"That's all right," Katherine said. "To get this settled will be worth any inconvenience."

"I know you're feeling better now that you've admitted the truth," Cal said, "but there are still a number of legal issues to sort out."

"And some personal ones, too," Geri said, nodding toward Ella, who had heaved herself up and was walking out of the library without so much as a word to her son or daughter-in-law.

"I'll stay with her," I said.

I followed Ella to the kitchen, where she was pouring herself the last of the morning's coffee. "Do I need to make some more?" I asked.

"No, I don't really want this. I just had to get out that room." She switched off the coffee maker. "Can we go somewhere? I don't think I can stand to be in this house right now."

"You're going to have to talk with them at some point."

"But this isn't that point. For five years I've felt angry at the world about Margaret's death. Now I find out she wasn't the person I thought. And I don't seem to know my son either. I've never thought I was a great mother, but I can't believe the mess I've made of my family."

My training as a counselor kicked in, even though I regarded Ella as a friend and not a client. "I don't see anybody dumping blame on you, so don't make yourself the scapegoat. Everybody involved here was an adult, making their own choices and their own mistakes. If you want to get away for a little while, we could go see Josh. Maybe he'll be awake by now and we can tell him the good news." I pulled the keys to my faithful old Honda out of my bag.

"Aren't you going to drive your new car?" She sounded hurt.

"I don't have it on my insurance yet. And I have to get the title switched over." And I was scared to death to take responsibility for that nice a car.

"It'll still be covered on my policy. Don't worry about it. Let's just go."

Although the sun was out, it was a frosty morning and the car— *my* car—had been sitting in the garage, so the leather seat was still chilly. As I pulled out of the driveway I couldn't stop worrying about driving an expensive car that was now my responsibility. This might be ordinary for people like Edmund and Kathcrine, but I was already seeing it as a mixed blessing. *You could have refused to accept it*, I told myself.

Then Ella turned on the seat warmer. "I call it the bun warmer," she said. *This is going to feel so good in December and January,* I thought as the glow radiated up my back and down my legs. *End of ambivalence.*

Ella looked out the window for a minute, then said, "I just can't believe this."

I hoped she would be able to focus on Josh, but she had taken a very hard blow this morning. "It's going to take some time for all this to sink in."

"How can I make sense of it? Especially about Margaret. I know she hated her father, but how could she have planned to ruin the business and leave the rest of us with nothing?" She turned pleading eyes on me. "Did I not know my daughter at all?"

"She was working hard to keep you from knowing her."

Ella looked back out the window as she said, "I guess we all have things we don't want to blab to everybody."

I didn't have to be a trained counselor to pick up on that invitation. "Is there something else you'd like to talk about?"

"I'd like to see you in a professional capacity, so I can be sure things will be kept confidential."

I was mildly offended. "Ella, I guarantee I won't tell anyone what we talk about. It doesn't matter where the conversation takes place."

"I know, dear, and it's not that I don't trust you, after all we've been through the last few days. But there are some things ... I wish you had your own office, so I could see you without going through Oaktree and having other people know I'm seeing you."

"If you need to talk about something, I will promise you absolute confidentiality, no matter where we talk."

She sighed heavily. "All right. Here goes. I've never been ... absolutely certain Edmund was Cornelius' son."

I pulled over to the curb as quickly as I could and turned to face her. "Sorry, but I can't drive an unfamiliar car and talk about this. Do you mean you had a relationship with another man?" I felt like my own grandmother had just confessed an infidelity. It's hard enough to imagine your grandparents having sex with one another, but with somebody else ... ? Ick!

"Yes, dear. I had an affair one summer with the man who did our yard work. I guess I can understand Margaret's attraction to a 'bad boy'. When I told him I was pregnant, he did the manly thing and left town. I've never been sure who the father was. In some ways Edmund is unlike Cornelius, but he has his business sense and his absolute lack of a sense of humor."

"This is why you were so upset when Edmund told you he'd given a DNA sample."

"Yes, I was afraid the tests would reveal that there's somebody else's DNA in the mix. Based on what I heard this morning, I still don't know for sure."

"Do you want to go to the lab and get more details? I'll be happy to take you." With this car to drive, I'd take her anywhere.

"No, I don't think I want anybody looking into it any further. I just hope Edmund is satisfied with what he knows to this point. He and Josh are related. The exact degree of relationship ... well, maybe we don't have to pursue that."

* * * *

I dropped Ella at the front door of the hospital and found as isolated a parking spot as I could for my new car. Owning it would have one unexpected benefit, it seemed—the additional exercise I would get walking from distant parking places.

I walked briskly back to the hospital. Even though the sun had come out, the weather was still chilly enough and the wind still strong enough that briskly was the only way to walk. The bun warmer in my car had already started spoiling me.

As I approached the front door I passed a row of reserved spaces. Most were for handicapped parking, but two were marked SECURITY VEHICLES ONLY. One of those spaces was occupied by an ominously familiar car. I stepped around to the front of it and saw the broken headlight.

It was Jake Folkert's car.

Oh, shit! I thought. Folkert does security for the hospital. Why didn't it occur to me to ask about that? We put Josh right in his hands.

As I rushed into the lobby I called Cal on my cell but got his voice mail. He and Geri must be in their meeting. I left a message explaining the situation. Then I called Geri and left the same message. I didn't know which of them would check messages first after the meeting.

"What's the matter?" Ella asked when I got off the phone.

"Folkert's company does the hospital's security, and Folkert himself is here now. I just saw his car."

"Then we've got to get to Josh."

In spite of her cane Ella kept up with me as I hurried to the bank of elevators. If there hadn't been one waiting, I would have panicked. The ride to the sixth floor seemed to take most of the morning.

"He'll be okay as long as he's in the ICU, won't he?" Ella asked. "The nurses are around all the time. Surely Folkert won't try anything in there."

"I suppose you're right. I'll just feel better when we can see him and know he's safe."

Nurse Fran was at her post and greeted us when we got off the elevator.

"I need to see my grandson," Ella said.

"I'm afraid you're too late," nurse Fran said.

Chapter 48

"What?" Ella slumped heavily against me. "Oh, dear God!"

"What happened?" I demanded.

"No, no, I'm sorry," nurse Fran said. "I just meant you're too late to see him here. He's doing much better, so we're moving him to a private room." She glanced at her computer. "Room 408."

"Is the security guard here?" I asked.

"He went to get something to eat while we're moving Josh."

"Is he a bald, pasty-faced guy?"

"Yes, that's him." Her revulsion showed in her face and her voice.

"It's Folkert," I said to Ella. "We've got to get to Josh's room." I pushed the call button, but the elevator had already left.

"Take the stairs," Ella said. "I'll catch up as soon as the elevator gets here."

"Call 911. Remind them there's an APB out on Folkert."

I bolted down the stairs to the fourth floor. When I got to room 408 a nurse was checking Josh's IV and other tubes to make sure everything was hooked up properly. Or was she one of Folkert's accomplices? She was young, blond, and pretty in the way that nurses are in men's fantasies about naughty nurses. From the door I watched her every move, trying to stay under a ten on the paranoia scale.

"I'll be out of your way in a minute," she said. "Are you ... family?" In other words, Josh didn't look Korean.

"I'm ... adopted," I said. That was true, just not into this family.

"Well, he's still in and out. He's got a lot of Demerol in him."

I moved to the opposite side of the bed from her and touched Josh's hand in a sisterly sort of way.

"All set," the naughty nurse said. "Just push that button if you need anything." She smoothed the covers one more time and left.

In high school I was a candy-striper, and I spent a lot of time in a hospital room the couple of months before my grandmother died. From what I knew of such equipment, everything here seemed to be functioning normally and assuring me that Josh was alive. His breathing was shallow but regular. I did check his pulse, then allowed myself to draw a deep breath and look around.

The room was large enough to hold two beds, and it had the curtain divider hospital rooms always have. The window looked out over the front entrance and the parking lot. I could see Folkert's car from the window. I would probably need a telescope to spot mine. There were three chairs in the room, which could be pulled out to provide a place to sleep if a family member wanted to stay overnight. Maybe we should make Edmund and Katherine spend the night here, as the first step in their penance. But, realistically, I knew if anyone was going to do that, I would be the most likely to be sleeping on one of those torture racks tonight. Somebody had to be here to keep Folkert at bay. After barely three hours' sleep the previous night, that was not a prospect I looked forward to.

"Is he all right?" Ella said as she hobbled into the room.

"Yes, the nurse just left."

Ella stood by the head of Josh's bed, drew a deep sigh, and beamed. "Isn't he beautiful?" She sounded like she was gushing over a newborn. "I wish I'd had the chance to enjoy him when he was born."

"That must have been a traumatic night."

"It was hellacious. The baby crying, Margaret crying, and me crying. Cornelius barking orders at us and at the nurse. And it ruined so many things for me. I couldn't appreciate my friends' grandchildren. When Georgia Ann was born, I had to act like she was my first grandchild, knowing all the while she wasn't. I think that's one reason I've never had a good relationship with those girls."

I pulled one of those awful chairs over so she could sit down beside the bed. "Your family's going to need some time to heal, after what you've learned about Margaret's death."

"Do you think it was really an accident? Was Katherine telling the truth?" She looked up at me, asking me to give her hope.

"My instinct says yes. What reason could she have had for going to the office intending to kill Margaret? She didn't carry a weapon with her. Would somebody have gone to the office planning to use the paperweight? What she told us this morning seems reasonable. An argument escalated into a tragedy. I hope you can forgive her."

"I'm sure I will. I also need to ask their forgiveness."

"For what?"

"I never have opened my heart to Edmund the way I did to Margaret. I felt such guilt over my affair and I was so afraid he would grow up looking like another man's son."

"I know some counselors who could help you get connected with your family."

"We may need to do that. But right now I need to use the bath-room. Do you think they'd throw me out if I used this one?"

She pointed to the bathroom door. The sign said FOR PATIENT USE ONLY.

"Josh has a catheter in him," I said. "He won't be using it, and you're paying for the room. I'd say, help yourself."

I gave her an arm to get across the room, then stood looking out the window. The world looked so nice with the sun shining, but that was just a deception since it was still so chilly outside. Probably a moral there, I was thinking, when a man's voice behind me growled, "What are you doing here?"

I turned to find myself facing Jake Folkert in all his pasty-faced repulsiveness. He was wearing dark corduroy slacks and a lined jacket with an FSI logo on it. The right side of the jacket hung a little lower than the left. My instinct warned me that he was probably carrying a gun in that pocket.

"I'm making sure you don't do anything else to Josh," I said. I put my hand on Josh's arm, as if that would really protect him from anything.

Folkert gave me a puzzled smile, all innocence and smarm. "What are you talking about? My company's been hired to protect him."

"Cut the crap. Edmund and Katherine confessed everything to the police this morning."

"Confessed everything? What do you mean?"

"Just what I said. We heard it all. How you hit Margaret's head against the desk. The paperweight, the blackmail. Killing Josh's family. Even stealing designs to sell to other companies. Everything."

"There's not a shred of proof." He cocked his head to one side, like the smart-ass kid in high school who knows the principal can't pin anything on him.

"Maybe not, but there's an APB out for you already." I hoped Cal had gotten that call in by now.

The toilet flushed and Ella opened the bathroom door. Folkert couldn't stop himself from gasping when he saw her. "You here too?"

"Yeah," I said. "Your guy, Micah, didn't get the job done."

"What are you talking about? Micah who?"

"Micah with your pay stubs in his car."

"Damn that little crack-head!" Folkert's eyes told me he was starting to weigh options. I wondered if killing everybody in the room was one of them. But surely he wasn't that desperate. "Yeah. Okay, Micah's worked for me in the past, but you've got nothing to connect me with whatever he did last night."

"Did I say it was last night?"

Folkert pursed his lips in disgust and put his hand in his jacket pocket, the side that was hanging lower. The outline of a gun barrel became unmistakable. Maybe that option had become more viable.

I had to keep him talking. That's what they do on TV—keep the killer talking until he confesses or the police show up. "He was supposed to make it look like she fell down the stairs, wasn't he? Just one more accident, like the explosion that killed Josh's family."

"You're the one writing this story. I'm not saying anything."

Ella edged toward me for protection. I wished she would move farther away from me, so Folkert would have to divert his attention to cover both of us. Pinned between her and the chair and bedside table, I couldn't move. If I had room to maneuver, I might be able to take Folkert down, but I would have to be sure I had a clear shot at him. I couldn't risk something that would endanger Ella and Josh.

"Did my son or daughter-in-law tell you to kill me?" Ella asked.

Folkert laughed. "That pair of lame-asses? They don't tell me to do anything."

"So you decided on your own to kill Josh's parents?"

"Like I said, you're writing that story."

Damn! The killer was supposed to admit everything once he was cornered. I've really got to stop watching so many lawyer/cop shows.

"I'm going to change my will," Ella said. "I'm supposed to sign the new one tomorrow. I'll bet he knew about that. He thought he had to make sure I didn't live long enough to do it."

The slight curl in Folkert's lip told me that Ella was right. "How did you know about that?" I asked.

"I have a source in Jennifer McKenzie's office." There it was, the first crack. An admission to something.

"She was just leaving the house to Josh. She wasn't changing anything else."

Folkert shrugged. "All I knew was that she was changing her will. I couldn't take any chances."

"With five thousand a week in unreported income, you should be able to buy better information than that."

"How did you know ... ?"

"I told you. Edmund and Katherine spilled everything to the police this morning."

"Oh, let's quit gabbing and call the police," Ella said.

"I thought you already called them," I said in dismay.

"I couldn't get a tower or something when I was in the elevator. You'll have to show me again how to use it. All I know how to do is get you on the speed dial." She reached for the phone in her bag.

"Ella, don't." I took her arm to stop her. "He's got a gun. Just stay calm and still."

"That's good advice," Folkert said.

I'm not sure what he would have done next, but the naughty nurse stepped into the room and stopped when she saw us standing around the bed. We must have looked like a concerned family, not a killer and his next victims. "I'm sorry," she said. "I can come back in a few minutes."

Folkert moved his right arm slightly, just as a reminder.

"Thank you," I said. "We'll be done shortly." Done or dead.

"It would be better if you kept your visit short," the nurse said. "Just leave the door open when you're ready for me." She took a quick look at the read-out on the IV pump and left, closing the door.

Assured of some privacy, Folkert pulled his hand out of his pocket and waved the gun at us. "Both of you, get away from the bed. Back up against that wall, away from the window, and don't move."

"I have Parkinson's," Ella said. "Some part of me always moves."

Folkert pointed the gun at her head. "Maybe I should just put you out of your misery then."

"Take it easy," I said, stepping toward Ella. "If nobody can pin anything on you, why start killing people right here? You'd never beat these charges."

"Shut up! I need to think." He lowered the gun from Ella's head and pointed it at me. "Sit down!"

I dropped into one of the torture-rack chairs. Folkert reached into his left jacket pocket and pulled out several of those plastic cable-ties that police often use now instead of handcuffs. Shifting the gun to his left hand, he pinned one of my arms to each arm of the chair and one of my feet to a leg of the chair, being careful not to get in a position where I could kick him in the groin, which was exactly what I intended to do if he got careless. Then he felt around in his pockets.

"Damn! I thought I had a couple more. This'll have to do. You won't be going anywhere."

"You won't be going anywhere but jail," I said.

"They'll have to catch me first." He rifled through the drawer of the bedside table and found gauze and a roll of tape. He stuffed some gauze in my mouth and wound the tape around my mouth and neck a couple of times. "You're right. I can't kill you. I'll have to settle for this." Then he hit me hard on my right jaw with his fist. The punch snapped my neck back and left me seeing stars. Ella's quick scream added to the unearthly quality of the experience. Folkert pointed his gun at her to quiet her, then turned back to me.

"That's for being such a pain in the ass lately," he said. "Things have fallen apart since you stuck your nose in. I was going to get two million, then you showed up with *him*." He pointed the gun at Josh. I gave a muffled squeal. That got me another blow. This time he caught me from the other direction with the back of his hand across my face.

Ella lunged at him and whacked him across the shoulder with her cane. "Stop it!" she cried. She wasn't strong enough to do any real damage. Folkert grabbed her wrist and pushed her against the wall.

"One more stupid move like that and I will kill all three of you. And you'll be last, so you'll get to see these two blown away."

He stuck the gun back in his pocket and straightened his jacket. "Now, you old biddy, we're going to walk out of here cool and calm. Just like I'm escorting you to your car. You're going to be my guarantee that nobody bothers me."

"I don't drive," Ella said. "I came with Sarah."

"Then get her keys."

Ella fumbled in my bag. The keys to the Lexus were in the pocket of my sweatshirt. I wondered what she was doing until she drew out the keys to my old Honda.

"Gimme those!" Folkert stuffed the keys in his pocket and jerked Ella's arm. "Let's go."

Ella looked over her shoulder at me. I tried to nod my head confidently. Folkert closed the door as they went out.

Chapter 49

I took a deep, centering breath and could feel some blood trickling from my nose. The urge to wipe it was like an alcoholic's need for a drink. I quickly assessed my situation. With the door closed, the nurse wasn't likely to come back for a while. Sitting here and waiting for her wasn't an option. I couldn't reach the call button on Josh's bed and he was too out from the drugs to do it for me. I had to do something to get that nurse in here STAT, as they say in hospitals.

Still uncertain just what I was going to do, I began to work my way to the other side of Josh's bed. That was where all the equipment was, and that equipment would provide my only means of getting a nurse's attention.

By jerking myself to one side and using my free leg to push I was able to scoot the chair a few inches at a time. The fold-out bed made the damn thing weigh a ton, but I could slide it thanks to the tile floors and the plastic tips on the legs and my own good physical condition. I was working my way around the end of Josh's bed and negotiating the straight between the bed and the partially open bathroom door when I noticed a cord hanging from the wall in the bathroom. The sign over it said, NURSE'S CALL. Hallelujah! The quickest and safest way to summon help.

But as I tried to maneuver the chair past the door and turn so I could go in the bathroom, I bumped the door. It swung shut with a privacy-guaranteeing thud.

"Shit!" I shouted into my gag. The handle was one you pull down, but I couldn't even reach it, let alone pull it, with my hands restrained the way they were. Folkert had cinched the cable-ties so tight I didn't have much circulation left in my hands.

By the time I finally scooted and bounced myself around Josh's bed and next to the IV stand I was breathing hard. I kicked the stand, hoping I could knock it over or jar the pump enough that the alarm would go off at the nurses' station. But I couldn't get a solid shot at it.

Since it was on wheels, when I tried to wrap my foot around it and tip it over, it just rolled. And what would it do to Josh if I did knock the stand over and suddenly ripped the IV out of his hand?

If I couldn't dislodge the pump, was there any other way I could make the nurses' alarm go off? That seemed to be my only hope. I looked the pump and the stand over carefully, trying to find some vulnerable spot. Then I noticed the plug. Pull that and it should alert somebody. But how?

The only free appendage I had was my left foot. With a lot more effort than I would have imagined it would take, I wriggled out of my sneaker, clamped the toe of my sock under my right foot, and pulled my left foot free. I scooted my chair closer to the IV stand. The electrical outlet wasn't down close to the baseboard but about waist-high on the wall. The cord did drag down, though. I grabbed it between my big toe and the next one and pulled.

The cord came out, but the monitor never blinked. Then I remembered from my grandmother's time in the hospital—battery back-up!

Okay, what else could I do?

I took a closer look at how Josh's IV was inserted. It ran from the pump, through the railing of the bed, into his left hand. My best option seemed to be to yank the tube out and hope a nurse would get there before he bled too much. When the IV bag started draining too fast, that should set off the alarm. But how could I dislodge the thing?

Even though the nurse lowered the bed when she finished tending to Josh, it was still high for someone sitting beside it in a low chair, trying to reach up. After three tries, my leg cramping and my hamstring crying that it wasn't meant to stretch this way, I managed to grasp the IV tube with my toes—and couldn't get leverage. And the thing was so slippery ... This was useless. I didn't have time to waste like this.

Think! Think! What causes the alarm on the IV pump to go off? When the flow is stopped. What stops the flow? A kink in the tube could do it.

I was figuring how I could get my chair in position to kink the tube when I heard a timid knock on the door. I tried to call out, but Folkert's gag was very effective. Then a woman's voice, still on the other side of the door, said, "May we come in?"

It was Denise van Putten.

I gave a muffled cry and bounced my chair. The door opened a bit and I could tell she had stuck her head in. "Hello? May we come in?" Then I heard the expected "Oh, my God! Oh, my God!"

A man's voice said something I didn't catch, then the two of them came rushing into the room.

"What happened?" Denise asked.

"She can't tell us until we get her loose," the man said.

I looked up and couldn't miss the ugly scar on David Burton's left cheek.

He pulled out an impressive pocket knife and began cutting me loose. "What the hell happened?" he asked as he removed the gag.

I spat out gauze. "There's no time to explain. Just get a nurse in here to take care of Josh and call the police. Tell them there's a killer in this hospital. And he's got a hostage."

"Shouldn't somebody call security?" Burton asked.

"Security *is* the killer," I said. "I'm going after him."

"Are you sure you're all right?" Denise said. "Your nose is bleeding."

"I'm fine." I slipped my sneaker back on, *sans* sock, and bolted out the door, wiping my nose on my sleeve as I went.

I felt like I did have a little time to catch up with Folkert. This wasn't like a movie where the bomb was going to go off in two minutes. Ella couldn't move very fast, and Folkert couldn't be seen hurrying her along without blowing his cover. I was sure she would move as slowly as she could get away with. She didn't even know exactly where my car was parked. And if Folkert was looking for a Honda, he would never get out of the parking lot.

But what if he took out his frustration on Ella? I couldn't leave her in his hands any longer than absolutely necessary. And how long could I leave Josh with his father and aunt?

I trotted down the stairs and walked quickly through the lobby. I didn't want to attract the attention of any security guards who worked for Folkert and might be loyal to him. Once I was out of the building, a glance assured me Folkert's car was still in its parking place. The parking lot extended to my right, then wrapped around the building. I scanned it and saw the two heads I was looking for, the gray-haired one and the bald one, about fifty yards away, bobbing toward my Lexus. Ella must have spotted it. Folkert glanced back every few seconds.

I used a couple of pillars and some shrubbery to cover me as I set off after them. Once I got to where cars were parked I could conceal myself between them and time my advance against Folkert's check of his rear. But I had parked so far from anyone else; the last ten yards or so I would have to cover in the open. Against a man with a gun and a hostage.

Where was a cop when you needed one?

By the time I got to the last car I could hide behind, Folkert had realized the keys in his hand weren't going to open the door of the car in front of him.

"Stupid old bat!" He slung Ella against the car. "Where's her car?"

"I must have picked up the wrong keys," Ella said. "I get confused, you know."

"All right, we'll just have to go back to my car. Come on!"

I crouched down. They would pass right by the car I was hiding behind, and Folkert was the one nearest to me. If I just had something to rattle him ... I patted my pockets and felt the keys to the Lexus. One of its electronic gizmos was a panic button. As Folkert stomped past my hiding place I pushed it. The Lexus' horn started blaring and its lights started flashing.

"What the ... ?" Folkert jerked around. He left himself wide open to a kick and I landed one in his stomach. He doubled over, gasping.

"Get away from him, Ella!"

But she couldn't react quickly enough. Folkert grabbed her coat with his left hand. She brought her cane up into his crotch. With a moan Folkert went down on one knee. Ella hadn't hit him hard enough to completely disable him. He kept his grip on his gun. One of those 'out of my cold dead hand' guys.

My next kick disarmed him and sent the gun sliding under a car. He was turning to scramble after it as another kick caught him high on his chest, around his shirt pocket. It wasn't where I was aiming; he moved just as I started the kick. He grabbed his chest and looked up at me with an odd expression. As he crumbled to the pavement, Ella hobbled over and cracked him once on the head with her cane.

"That's for what you did to my daughter, you bastard!" Folkert didn't flinch.

I grabbed her arm as she drew back for another shot. "Ella, don't! He's down. Let's tie him up and let the police deal with him."

I reached under the car, found Folkert's gun and gave it to Ella. "Keep it right on him," I told her, although I wasn't sure she could aim that well. Then I rolled Folkert over far enough to unbuckle his belt and pull it out. I couldn't tie his hands as tightly as he had tied mine, but I didn't think he would go anywhere before the police got there. I took the gun from Ella.

Folkert lay strangely quiet, face down on the blacktop. I expected him to berate us or try to bribe us. "Not feeling so high and mighty now, Jake?" I asked him. He just shuddered and let out a moan.

I looked around for a police car. "Do you have your phone, Ella? Let's try calling Cal directly. He and Geri must be out of their meeting by now."

As Ella fished her phone out of her bag she said, "Are you sure he's all right? He looks funny to me."

"He's probably hoping I'll get close enough so he can do something to me."

"How can he? His hands are tied. You've got his gun. Check on him, please."

To placate her I knelt beside Folkert, on the alert for the slightest movement, and touched his shoulder. He didn't respond. "Come on, Jake. I don't care what kind of act you put on. I'm not going to untie you." Still nothing. I rolled him over and raised one of his eyelids.

"I think there's really something wrong," Ella said in alarm, bending over me.

I felt his neck for a pulse. "Oh, my God—he's dead!"

Chapter 50

"Dead?" Ella cried. "My God! What did you do?"

It was more a matter of what I was going to do, I thought. I took a CPR course five years ago and a refresher course last year. This was the first time I'd ever had to use it. Still expecting Folkert to spring up and grab me, I untied his hands and laid him flat on his back. When I pulled his jacket back and opened his shirt, some pens and stuff fell out of his pockets. The man's thin chest was as pasty and hairless as his head. He even shaved his armpits. I didn't want to think about where else his razor might roam.

Even as I was getting ready to do CPR, all kinds of thoughts were elbowing one another in their race through my head. This guy was a killer, the worst kind of cold-blooded killer. He blew up Josh's family. He hired people to try to kill Josh and Ella. Now he was dead. Why not leave well enough alone?

Who made you God? a voice seemed to ask. *The rest of the world missed that memo.*

I checked to make sure his air passage was clear and began the fifteen pumps on his scrawny chest. He had a small bloody spot just to the left of his sternum, like he'd scratched a mosquito bite. I dearly wished I had some latex gloves and a mouth shield.

Fighting my own gag reflex, I pinched his nose and blew into his mouth. I tried not to think about what I might be picking up from him. I had repeated the process three times when I heard sirens.

"Wave them over here," I told Ella. "Once I start, I can't stop."

Cal and Geri rode in one car. The other carried two uniformed officers. Cal dashed over to me while Geri checked on Ella. The uniforms started securing the area.

"What's the ... ?" Cal started to ask.

"He collapsed or had a stroke or something. I can't get a pulse."

"Get a doctor out here!" he yelled to the uniforms. "Get me a microshield and a couple of pairs of gloves."

One of the officers brought him two pairs of latex gloves and the CPR mouthpiece. He handed me the shield and took my place over Folkert's inert body. "I'll pump. You blow."

We worked on him for several minutes with no success. The uniforms brought a doctor from the E. R. He examined Folkert and pronounced him dead.

"I'm sorry," he said. "Was he a friend of yours?"

"There's no need for condolences," I said. "Believe me."

The doctor looked at me funny and called for a gurney to transport Folkert into the hospital. The flashing lights and commotion were starting to draw a crowd. Cal had me sit in his car. Geri brought Ella over to join us.

"What did you do to him?" Cal asked, a little too much like a police officer.

"She kicked his butt," Ella cackled.

"Not literally," I said. "I did kick him a couple of times, but just in the ribs and stomach. Nothing that would have killed him." But what if, I wondered, that last kick—the one in his chest—had stopped his heart? I knew stuff like that could happen. A guy on my dad's softball team died when he got hit in the chest with a line drive.

The E. R. doctor examined the areas where my kicks had landed and came over to the car. "There's a puncture wound in his chest, right over his heart. It's fresh."

"That bloody spot? I saw that. I didn't stick him with anything. Ask Ella."

Ella shook her head vigorously. "No, she didn't. She kicked him a couple of times and I conked him with my cane."

"All I know," the doctor said, "is that there's a puncture wound."

"What could have caused it?" Cal asked.

"This would be my guess." The doctor held up a hypodermic syringe with the needle sticking through the protective plastic cap. "It was in his shirt pocket."

"That's where I kicked him the last time. He was falling over."

"Can you tell what was in it?" Cal asked the doctor.

Before the doctor could answer, Ella said, "It's potassium something. That's what Folkert said."

The doctor sniffed the tip of the syringe. "She's right. Potassium chloride."

"Good Lord!" Cal muttered.

"What is that?" I asked.

"Potassium chloride is a lethal toxin," the doctor said. "It's used in executions in some states. It short-circuits the heart's electrical impulses, causing cardiac arrest. This is a three-cc syringe. That much would be fatal in a couple of minutes, if injected directly in the heart."

I shuddered."Can you inject things directly into the heart?"

"Under certain circumstances," the doctor said. "We sometimes have to with digitalis if a patient has a heart attack and we don't have time to start an IV. Was he leaning over when you kicked him?"

"He was on one knee and doubled over. And he started to turn just as I kicked."

"But what was Folkert doing with a syringe full of that stuff in his pocket?" Cal asked.

"He intended to kill Josh," Ella said. "He griped about how his perfect plan was ruined. He said he was going to inject it into the IV."

"That would be easy," the doctor said. "It might look like the patient died from after-effects of surgery, reaction to medication..."

"He must have known he was going to die," I said, "as soon as he felt the jab of the needle. That look on his face ..."

I took Cal's hand. Unprofessional, his look told me, but he didn't pull away. "Am I going to be charged with anything?" I asked.

"I'll have to file a report. Whatever results from that, you know I'll stand by you."

"You cannot be serious," Ella sputtered. "That piece of trash kills three or four people, blackmails my son for years, and Sarah could end up in jail?" I thought she was going to get out of the car and whack Folkert's lifeless corpse one last time as the gurney rattled by.

"I don't believe anything like that will happen," Cal said. "But we'll need a statement from you. Then I have to write a report and the doctor has to sign a death certificate."

"Did you intend to kill him when you kicked him?" the doctor asked.

"No, of course not."

"So the fact that you hit him on that spot was an accident?"

"Absolutely."

"Then the cause of death will be death by misadventure."

"And my report will stress that Folkert had a gun and was threatening a hostage," Cal said.

"Case closed," Geri said.

Chapter 51

In the two weeks that passed after my confrontation with Jake Folkert—what Ella called the 'Kick-out at the O. K. Corral'—I was kept busy arranging and chaperoning Josh's visits with his new families. All sides felt the need for a mediator.

I didn't mind, though. I needed to be busy. Whenever my attention wasn't focused on something, I kept coming back to the fact that I had killed a man. No matter how many times Cal reminded me that it was accidental, that Folkert had killed several people, that he would have killed me and Ella, it didn't change the reality: I had killed a man. Cal could offer all the sympathy in the world, but ultimately he couldn't know what that meant to me because he had never done it.

So I kept busy.

Edmund and Katherine's first visit with Josh was touching but awkward. They apologized profusely for their part in what had befallen him, either directly through their actions or indirectly through what Folkert had done on his own initiative. I think Katherine would have crawled from the parking lot to Josh's bed if we had asked her to. They accepted their responsibility for hiring Folkert and Josh said he understood they were under duress.

Edmund set out to avenge as many wrongs as he could. He fired Martin Vandervelde as his personal attorney and urged his friends to do likewise. He informed Vandervelde he was going to try to get him disbarred. He then hired Jennifer McKenzie as his new personal attorney. He did insist she fire her receptionist, Juanita, Jake Folkert's mole.

After conferring with the Dykstras and their new attorney, the D. A. decided not to charge Katherine with anything. The reasoning, Cal told me that night—the first night he'd spent at my place in over three months—was that if Katherine's story was true, she acted in self-defense, without premeditation. If Folkert's was the blow that killed Margaret, then there was no case against Katherine. She could have been charged as an accessory after the fact, but the D. A. saw nothing to be gained from pursuing that.

"What it really boils down to," he concluded, "is that the Dykstras are rich and the D. A. is running for state Senate this year."

"Are you saying Katherine should be charged?" I wondered if we would always be having such macabre pillow-talk.

"I wish we could get independent verification of what happened."

"Do you want some independent verification of how Jake Folkert died? Ella's not a very impressive witness, after all."

"No, hon. Those are two entirely separate situations. There's no comparison."

He tried to take me in his arms, but I pulled away. "I see one big similarity: somebody ended up dead and somebody else can't get rid of the guilt for causing it, even though they didn't mean to cause it."

"Sarah, you will get over this." He stroked my hair and I let him. "It's a trauma that takes time to heal. You know, when a policeman shoots somebody—even if it's not a fatal shooting—they're taken off active duty for a while and given a chance to talk to a psychologist. That's what you should do."

"I *am* a psychologist."

"Does that mean you're immune to what any normal person would feel after something like this?"

"What would it look like if I went to psychologist? I know these people. They know me."

"I'm seeing one that Geri recommended in Muskegon. You could try him, or look around in Holland or Kalamazoo."

"I'll think about it," I said.

As soon as Josh was able to sit up in bed and Jennifer McKenzie was satisfied that he knew what he was doing, she had him sign the paperwork to get his trust fund. The next day, David Burton tried to hit his son up for some money.

* * * *

The day before he was to be discharged from the hospital Ella and I stopped by to see Josh. Jennifer was there and Josh was signing some papers. "You're just in time," Jennifer said. "You can witness these and I won't have to call a nurse in here."

"What are they?" I asked as I dropped my bag in a chair, probably the same chair Folkert had tied me in. Before I killed him.

"I'm setting up trust funds for my father and my aunt Denise," Josh said. "Five hundred thousand each."

"That much?" Ella said. "What have they done to deserve that?"

I searched his face to see if the sudden wealth was already corrupting him. One of the least endearing qualities I had observed in the Dykstras was their tendency to throw money at situations—and people—to make them behave or go away.

Josh scribbled his name in the appropriate places. "It's a small price to pay to keep those people away from me."

From their first visit I had sensed that Denise and David did not inspire any familial feelings in Josh. The conversation consisted mostly of Denise gushing about how much they had to catch up on. David Burton didn't seem to know what to say to the son with whom he had never had any connection. Or maybe he was just wondering how soon he could ask him for money. And how much.

The scene made me wonder what my biological father would say to me if we were reunited. As far as I knew, he had no idea I was alive. Would we have anything to talk about? How much did I resent him for running out on my mother?

"But, Josh," I said, poised to sign where Jennifer showed me, "that's a million dollars. Are you sure you want to give away that much?"

"Five million? Six million? I can't comprehend having either amount," Josh said. "Could you?"

"Not really, but I think about it when I spend two dollars for lottery tickets every week."

Josh chuckled, then groaned and clutched at his wound. "In the long run having a million less will make a difference, I know, but not being bothered by those people will be worth every penny."

I hoped I could persuade him to meet with his father a time or two, just to establish some boundaries, but this didn't seem a good time to put that possibility on the table. After I signed in several places I took a file folder out of my bag and handed it to Josh.

"These are letters your mother wrote to you in the last year or so of her life. I thought you might want to take a look at them before you move into that house and start settling into the family. I glanced at the first one before I knew what it was, but I haven't read any of the rest. As far as I know, nobody but your mother has seen them."

He seemed almost reluctant to take the letters. "What sort of person do you think I am, Sarah?"

"What do you mean?"

"Thanks to you, I've discovered my biological roots, only to find out my father is a money-grubbing bum and my mother was a vengeful alcoholic who was set on destroying her family to get back at her dead father. Coming from stock like that, what sort of person am I?"

Before I could reply Ella burst out, "You're not being fair! Not to yourself and not to your mother. Margaret was a loving, generous woman. She helped people who worked for her when their insurance wouldn't cover something. Helped them out of her own pocket. Her only flaw was that she loved you so much. I wish you could have read her diary, the one that I couldn't find after she died. You'd see her best side. I only got to read a few pages that one time I stumbled onto it, but the real Margaret came through."

"You have no idea what happened to it?" Josh asked.

Ella shook her head. "None whatsoever."

* * * *

I didn't see Josh again for almost a week. In that time I tried to focus on my job, but my heart wasn't in it. The office was in turmoil. Edmund the Avenger asked friends of his on the agency's board of trustees to request an accounting of the director's slush fund and examine how it was administered. Word around the office was that Connie's job was on the line. I was uncertain whether I could stay at the agency. Even if Connie was removed as director, I no longer felt comfortable there. I'd had a painful lesson in how much influence a few wealthy people can have over an organization, even one with the worthiest of goals. I wondered if I would ever be able to work for another agency or company.

What if I went out on my own? Most of the agency counselors I know have thought about setting up their own practice. Our work lends itself to flexible hours, and all we need is a couple of rooms in an office building or a house. But I would be working without a net. How would I attract clients? How would I survive until I had built up a client base? And I wouldn't have any health insurance.

I could sell the Lexus and live comfortably for a year, I told myself, but myself dismissed the idea. After driving that car for two weeks, I'd be more likely to give up my apartment and live in the Lexus.

Those were the kinds of thoughts jumbling through my head on a Thursday afternoon when Josh called.

"So, how are things with you and the family?" I asked.

"We're slowly getting accustomed to one another."

"Are you living at the house?"

"I haven't given up my apartment yet. I've spent a couple of nights here, but I'm waiting for Edmund and Katherine to move out before I settle in. They'll stay in the cottage in Saugatuck while they build a place."

"It's a big house. Isn't there room for everybody for a while?"

"Katherine hates this house. She thinks it's dark and gloomy. And she and Grandmother aren't going to be comfortable around each other for a long time, I'm afraid. It's best for all of us if they're living somewhere else."

"Well, I hope you can get past that awkwardness soon. Hey, I've got a client in a few minutes. Is there anything I can do for you?"

"I'd like to invite you and Cal to The Art Place—Saturday morning, ten o'clock."

"What's going on?"

"I'll let you know when I figure it out. There'll be brunch. I know that much. If you'll give me Geri Murphy's number, I'd like to invite her, too. Oh, and Mickey Bolthuis."

"Will your dad be there?"

"Not if I can help it."

* * * *

The Art Place normally didn't open until noon on Saturdays, but Ella and Josh had made arrangements for a private gathering in the Dykstra Gallery at ten. In addition to the guest list I already knew, Edmund, Katherine, and Jennifer McKenzie had been invited, as well as the Dykstra daughters and Ann's husband, Roger. Geri was the last to arrive. She and Cal huddled in a corner and talked seriously for a few minutes while the rest of us enjoyed eggs, French toast, fresh fruit, and juice and coffee. I was glad Mickey had a lot to say to Edmund and Katherine because I didn't. Jennifer stayed at her new client's elbow.

Folding chairs had been arranged in a semi-circle in front of Margaret's 'Mother ... and Child?' sculpture. I took one that allowed me to see Geri and Cal by glancing over my shoulder without being *too* obvious. Finally they embraced and moved to join the rest of us. While Cal filled a plate, Geri just got a cup of coffee and sat down beside me.

"Hey, girlfriend," she said. "It's been a while."

"It has been. Aren't you hungry this morning?"

"I can't eat right now. Not until my stomach gets unknotted."

"What's the matter?"

"I just quit," she said.

"Quit? You mean the police force?"

"Yep. Turned in my letter twenty minutes ago. I was going to do it yesterday afternoon, but Cal asked me to sleep on it one more night, as a favor to him."

"So what are you going to do now?"

"I think I'm going to see if there's room for another counselor in this area."

"You're going to set up your own practice?" She was daring to do what I didn't have the courage for, just jumping out of the security of the nest and seeing if she could flap hard enough to remain airborn.

"You know," she said, "there could be a lot of advantages to a two-person practice. Would you be willing to consider a partnership?"

Before I could answer Ella and Josh entered the gallery. Josh was wearing the sport coat his grandmother had bought him at Wal-Mart. It didn't look like he was going to throw his money away on clothes. He carried a leather notebook in one hand and supported Ella's elbow with the other. Ella looked stronger. I hadn't seen her since we had lunch on Tuesday. She was still hurt and angry about Katherine's role in Margaret's death. I was glad to see her speak to Edmund and Katherine, even if her greeting couldn't be effusive. I hoped she had enough time left to restore some kind of relationship with them.

Josh invited everyone to sit down. He stood in front of his mother's sculpture, still bent over slightly from the stitches in his wound.

"I want to thank all of you for coming here this morning," he said. "I may be making too much of this, but I wanted certain people to be present when we unlock what I hope will be the Dykstra family's last secret. And God knows we've had more than our share.

"While I've been convalescing I've read some letters my mother wrote to me. Well, to her son, not knowing it was me ... You all know what I mean. In one of those letters she described this sculpture and a feature of it that no one has suspected. There is a secret compartment in the piece, in its heart."

Damn! I thought. I knew there was something fishy about that hand clutched to the breast. I just never had gotten back to my pictures of it or to Margaret's sketch.

"The question, though," Josh continued, "was how to open that compartment without damaging the sculpture or whatever is inside. In another letter my mother reminisced about the day a certain young art student sat sketching on the sidewalk outside her house. She loved the pencil drawing he did of her so much, she said, that she was going to entrust the secret of her sculpture to him."

We all looked at one another now, wondering what Josh had found.

"It took me a while to realize what she was saying," he continued. "Obviously she hadn't entrusted anything to me personally. Then I realized she must have been talking about the sketch I made of her. It was framed and hanging over the desk in her room. When I examined it, I couldn't see any alterations or anything written on the drawing. The frame was deep, though, and the back covered with paper. I cut that off and discovered this taped inside."

He reached into his leather folder and drew out a crudely fashioned key. "I've examined the sculpture and I believe I know how this works. But I haven't actually tried to open the compartment, so I hope I haven't asked you all here to watch me embarrass myself. At least you have had a good breakfast. So, now, the moment of truth."

Josh turned to the sculpture and inserted the key up inside the curled fingers of its right hand. We all leaned forward as he jiggled it until it seemed to slip into place. When he turned it, it sounded like a small bolt slid. He pulled on the hand and the lower part of the arm swiveled at the elbow. The hand pulled away from the chest, taking the left breast with it.

"Everyone, please, gather around," Josh said.

Katherine took Ella's elbow as we stood around Josh, craning to see into the hole in the sculpture's chest. Josh reached in and pulled out a plastic bag containing an old notebook.

"It's her diary," Ella said. "That's your mother's diary."

Meet the author:

Albert Bell's published works include: historical fiction and myster, *All Roads Lead to Murder*, *Kill Her Again* and *Daughter of Lazarus*; children's mystery, *The Case of the Lonely Grave* and nonfiction, *Resources in Ancient Philosophy* (co-authored with James B. Allis) and *Exploring the New Testament World*. His articles and stories have appeared in magazines and newspapers from *Jack and Jill* and *True Experience* to the *Detroit Free Press* and *Christian Century*.

Dr. Bell has taught at Hope College in Holland, Michigan since 1978 and, since 1994, as Professor of History and chair of the department. He holds a PhD from UNC-Chapel Hill. He is married to psychologist Bettye Jo Barnes Bell; they have four children.

Bell discovered his love for writing in high school with his first publication in 1972. Although he considers himself a "shy person," he believes he is a storyteller more than a literary artist. He says, "When I read a book I'm more interested in one with a plot that keeps moving rather than long descriptive passages or philosophical reflection." He writes books he would enjoy reading himself.

ALL ROADS LEAD TO MURDER
by *Albert A. Bell, Jr.*

ISBN: 097130453X
Illustrations: 30 line drawings by
William Martin Johnson from the first
edition of Ben Hur by Lew Wallace, and
supplemented with a glossary of terms.
hardcover, pp: 248, $21.95
**High Country Publishers/ Ingalls
Publishing Group, Inc.**

All Roads Lead to Murder is a wonderful historical mystery set in the
Roman Empire during the early
Church and St. Luke's time frames
...The author, a classicist, helps the
reader experience what it was like to
live during Roman times. The book
provides us an education through the
author's superb use of setting and
characterizations. Historical figures
come alive in his expert hands. – Bob
Spear, *Heartland Reviews*: Rating: ♥♥♥♥♥

All Roads Lead To Murder is a superbly crafted, wonderfully written
murder mystery that treats the reader to a thrilling detective story meticu-
lously backgrounded with accurate historical detail. – *Midwest Book
Reviews*

Colorful characters, both fictional and historical, are well blended to reveal
the sordid web of money, greed and ruthlessness hidden behind the facade of
civilization. One hopes to see Albert Bell's Pliny again in the future. – Suzanne
Crane, *The Historical Novels Review*

All roads lead to a masterful blend of history and mystery. Albert Bell has
written a wonderful book. with splendid characters, vivid history and a
fair and puzzling mystery. I heartily recommend it.– Barbara D'Amato,
award-winning author of three mystery series, Past President of Mystery Writers
Internationals and Sisters in Crime International

Find ***ALL ROADS LEAD TO MURDER*** and other books
by Albert A. Bell, Jr. at bookstores and on-line retailers.

Watch us grow!

Claystone Books is the latest addition to the family of **Ingalls Publishing Group**. Beginning with fine titles authored by Albert A. Bell, Jr., the imprint will evolve into a line of quality mysteries and historicals by authors whose work meets our high standards, but whose settings are beyond the scope of our regional focus.

By fall, 2006, other of Albert Bell's novels will be available though **Claystone/Ingalls.** Before that time, find these books at online retailers.

Kill Her Again

by Albert A. Bell, Jr.

Corie Foster, a travel writer, and professor Michael Herrington meet while staying in a small town in Italy and observing an archaeological excavation. But someone is following Cone, who seems to bear a striking resemblance to the late wife of a wealthy Italian senator. When two women on the excavation team are murdered, Michael and Cone are certain that Cone is the real target.

As their investigation unfolds, it seems to hinge on what they can find out about the senator's wife. As they work together, Michael and Cone are drawn closer. But does Cone have her own reasons for coming to Italy? Is she who she appears to be?

Case of the Lonely Grave
by Albert A. Bell, Jr.

When flowers appear for the first time on an old grave near their homes, Steve Patterson and Kendra Jordan try to find out who put them there and why. Their investigation leads them to uncover secrets about the grave and its history that they never suspected. Their search takes them all way the back to the Civil War and the Underground Railroad.

Daughter of Lazarus
by Albert A. Bell, Jr.

Lorcis, slave of decadent Roman aristocrats, unknowingly holds a clue to her past. Aided by a fellow slave and a kindly nobleman, she undertakes a journey that leads from the ashes of Vesuvius and the bloody horrors of the Colosseum to the emperor Domitian's palace and the secret meetings of the Christians.